THE SECOND SON

THE
SECOND
SON

JONATHAN
RABB

SARAH CRICHTON BOOKS

FARRAR, STRAUS AND GIROUX   NEW YORK

SARAH CRICHTON BOOKS
Farrar, Straus and Giroux
18 West 18th Street, New York 10011

Library of Congress Cataloging-in-Publication Data
Rabb, Jonathan.
    The second son / Jonathan Rabb. — 1st ed.
        p.   cm.
    ISBN 978-0-374-29913-2 (alk. paper)
    1. Fathers and sons—Fiction.   2. Police—Fiction.   3. Germans—Spain—Fiction.
4. Missing persons—Fiction.   5. Spain—History—1939–1975—Fiction.   I. Title.

PS3568.A215 S43 2011
813'.54—dc22

                                                            2010023556

Designed by Abby Kagan

www.fsgbooks.com

1   3   5   7   9   10   8   6   4   2

For Andra,

again and always

SPAIN, ca. 1937

Bay of Biscay

FRANCE

SPAIN

Zaragoza   Osera de Ebro   Barcelona

Bujaraloz

Madrid   Cuenca   Teruel

Coria   Toledo   Tarancón

Villar del Rey

PORTUGAL

Badajoz

Seville

Cádiz   Málaga

MEDITERRANEAN SEA

Strait of Gibraltar

Tangier

ATLANTIC OCEAN   Tetuán

ALGERIA

Rabat

Casablanca   MOROCCO

0 Miles   100   200

0 Kilometers   200

© 2010 Jeffrey L. Ward

THE
SECOND
SON

1

BARCELONA

There was nothing but heat and sun. And, from time to time, the young man forced himself to arch his neck just to feel the lines of sweat dripping down his back.

What had he expected, a German in Spain? It was his job to sweat and look sickly doing it. His cheeks had gone a nice pasty red, even through a three-day growth of beard. He wasn't smelling all that good either, but then neither were any of the others in the row, staring across the plaza, cameras at the ready, cigarettes hanging limply from parched lips.

The young man had thought about keeping the beard, but he knew his wife would tell him to shave it off the moment he got back to Berlin. It would probably scare the boy anyway—"Where's my papi! Where's my papi!" ringing down the hall, screams and tears before all the presents came tumbling out of the suitcase. Presents were always good with a boy of four, even from a father he didn't quite recognize.

It hadn't been that long, he thought. Not this time—had it?

The young man kept his right arm on the crank of the movie camera, his eye at the viewfinder, as, with his left hand, he tried to grope for the can of water he had set down somewhere on the cobbled pavement.

He must have looked ridiculous doing it because a voice down the line blurted out, "You do juggling tricks as well, Hoffner, or is it just the balanc-ing act?"

The words were Spanish, but it was a thick Eastern European accent that muddied the sound.

Georg Hoffner pulled himself back from the camera. He brought his long body upright, blinked the sweat from his eye, and stared down at a fat Bulgarian with a hand-held Leica strung across his chest. The camera looked twenty years old, cutting-edge for a Bulgarian.

"Why?" said Hoffner. "You have some balls that need juggling?"

There were a few laughs, those dry uncomfortable laughs that come with heat and sweat, but almost at once the line fell silent. Across the plaza, the doors to a vast building opened. Hoffner quickly repositioned himself behind the camera and peered through the viewfinder. He focused on the banner hanging above, hastily painted but still impressive:

PEOPLE'S OLYMPICS, 19–26 JULY, 1936, BARCELONA FOR THE PEOPLE,
FOR THE WORKERS

A line of young men and women began to pour out the doors, all dressed as workers, with red neckerchiefs and berets to signify their exalted station in life. To be a worker in Barcelona these days, a member of the proletariat—that was the stuff of dreams. To be a worker athlete—well, that was pure legend.

The fat Bulgarian snapped his shots as he tried to squeeze past the line of Guardia Civil: patent leather hats, patent leather boots—patent leather men with patent leather souls. How these soldiers were managing to stay upright in the heat was anybody's guess. Still, Bulgarians were never much good at maneuvering through large Spaniards with cudgels. The Bulgar-ian pushed once too often and his camera went crashing to the pavement.

Hoffner heard the moans from down the line, but it wasn't enough to draw his attention from the smart set of Germans striding across his lens. Hoffner cranked as they walked, his arm remarkably steady as he followed them along the plaza. There was something almost Soviet to the way these boys moved, triumphant and bedraggled all at once, their nobility protruding from the angle of their heads and the broadness of their chests. He recognized them from this morning's press conference outside the Olympic Stadium. It had been a hell of a time getting the cameras into the funicular and up the mountain, where the smells of wheat and cow manure and maybe beets—he hadn't been able to place that one—followed the tram all the way up.

It had been the German contingent on the podium this morning. The place of honor. After all, they were the ones protesting their own Olympic games—Hitler's chance to show the world the best of Nazi Germany. Hitler, however, would have to wait another ten days before parading his Aryan ideals in Berlin. Until then, it was the worker athletes here in Barcelona—Germans, Swedes, Russians, English, on and on—who would remind the world that sport was pure and not meant to be used as a tool of politics. Hoffner suspected it was a logic only the Left could follow.

Truth be known, most of these boys hadn't seen Germany in years. They were Jews and Communists and socialists—exiles living in France or England—but still they had come to compete as Germans. Proletariat Germans. Protesting Germans. Take that, you fascist bastards.

The boys reached the buses parked at the edge of the plaza. They turned and waved to no one in particular and then got on. Hoffner stopped the crank and stood upright. The Bulgarian was still yelling at the Guardia. The buses began to move and the Guardia, no less bored, headed off in various directions, leaving the Bulgarian to shout into the emptying plaza.

"Come and have a drink," Hoffner said, as he began to fold up the legs on his camera. "We'll let Pathé Gazette pay for it—what do you say?—and maybe we'll find you a camera lying around somewhere."

The Bulgarian stopped squawking. He picked up the cracked pieces of his Leica and headed over. His smell preceded him by a good ten meters.

The bar was down in the Raval section of town, near the water and the docks, a good place for pimps and drunks and journalists. At two in the morning there was little chance of telling them apart; now, at four in the afternoon, it was primarily journalists. And one or two whores. They were big girls, with big chests, dark black hair like dripping tar, and tight skirts that hugged the thighs like two thick columns of flesh. The skirts were a kind of protective measure for men too eager to get a passing hand up and inside.

"The games are a joke," the Bulgarian said to Hoffner. Two others were sitting with them, all four drinking what passed for whiskey. "You'd think if they're going to protest your Nazis, they'd have someone outside of Spain who actually cares that they're protesting."

Hoffner was reading through one of the letters he had gotten from his wife. He liked reading them over and over, especially when he was sitting with Bulgarians and Poles and—he couldn't remember what the dozing fourth one was, Russian or Czech. What did it matter? These types all got drunk the same way, spoke the same kind of broken Spanish, and tried to get the girls for cheap. But they all liked that Pathé Gazette picked up the bill for the first few rounds. Hoffner liked it as well. He would have to remember to put in for it.

The Bulgarian said, "You think Hitler cares that a few Communists decide to run the long jump? Or a socialist can throw a hammer?" The Bulgarian was fat and small, a winning combination. "I interviewed one of them. He's here for the chess. Can you imagine it? Chess as Olympic sport? This one was terribly impressive after he cleaned his glasses and patted down his bald head. Now that's an athlete."

Hoffner continued to scan the letter. "My son's been reading the front page of the *Tageblatt* all by himself," he said. "Every word."

The Pole was pouring out his third glass. "He likes the news?"

"Let's hope not."

"How long has he been reading?"

"The last few months. He's four and a bit."

"I've been reading much longer than that. Are you impressed?"

"Only if you read better than you write."

The Pole smiled and drank.

The Bulgarian was leaning back over his chair and staring at one of the girls at the bar. She was staring back with just the right kind of indifference. The Bulgarian turned his head to the table. "She wouldn't go for less than ten pesetas, you think?"

"She wouldn't go for it when you asked her last night," said the Pole. "Or the night before. But don't let that stop you from asking again."

The Bulgarian peered over at Hoffner. "Must be nice to have a wife who writes letters. And a little boy."

"Must be," Hoffner said distractedly.

"I have one somewhere. A wife. Not the writing type." He leaned forward. "So tell me, why is it that Pathé Gazette has a German working for them? It's English newsreel. Shouldn't you be with Ufa-Tonwoche or Phoebus? One of the German studios?"

Hoffner folded the letter and placed it in his pocket. "Phoebus never did newsreels."

"So why not Ufa?"

Hoffner took hold of the bottle. "Not too many Jews working out at Ufa these days." He poured himself a glass. "I'd say none, but then there's always one or two who've managed to slip through the cracks. Too good at what they do for some government statute to force them out. I wasn't that good in the first place." He drank.

"I'm a Jew," said the Pole.

Hoffner poured himself another. "Good for you."

The Bulgarian said, "And Pathé Gazette just happened to have an office in Berlin? How nice. I'm thinking they haven't had time to set one up in Sofia just yet."

"Don't sound so bitter," Hoffner said with a smile. "The girl'll think you don't really want her."

The Bulgarian shot a glance back at the bar. The girl was chatting up the barman.

The Pole pushed back his chair. "I have an interview with the Swedish fencing team," he said. "We're very keen on fencing in Warsaw." He stood. "Anyone interested?"

"Are there women on the team?" said the Bulgarian.

"I imagine so."

"My God. Swedish women in those outfits. And socialists to boot." The Bulgarian was on his feet. He piped his voice toward the girl at the bar. "No more negotiating, capitalist. I'm off to the Revolution."

The girl glanced over. She smiled and winked and went back to her barman.

"And yet she knows I'm a capitalist at heart. How it kills me." The Bulgarian picked up his rucksack from the floor. It was holding a new Zeiss Ikon, courtesy of the English Pathé Gazette Company. The Bulgarian had promised to get the camera back in one piece. Hoffner wasn't holding his breath.

"Fifteen pesetas for an hour," said the Bulgarian, as he hoisted the strap over his shoulder. "It's a crime."

"Enjoy the Swedes," said Hoffner. He picked up his own bag.

The dozing Czech or Russian opened his eyes. Hoffner stood. He left a few coins on the table and headed for the door.

His room smelled of wood polish and garlic and stared out at the expanse that was the Plaza Catalonia. His hotel, the Colón, stretched the length of one side of the square and seemed to be perpetually in direct sunlight. Eight in the morning, nine at night, there was no escaping the glare. Hoffner thought it must have been some sort of architectural coup, but all it did was make the room unbearably steamy.

He had worked his way through descriptions of the square, the view of Barcelona, the taste of the food—a letter each day required topics to fill it. Lotte had written back with things far more compelling: their four-year-old Mendy had remembered to flush the toilet twice in the last three days; Elena, their cook and nanny, had experimented with Spanish rice (a gesture of solidarity for an absent father—not a success); Sascha, his brother, had inexplicably come calling—it was three years since they had last spoken. Lotte reminded Georg that she had never been fond of his brother. And finally Nikolai, Hoffner's father, had insulted the gardener. Something to do with the placement of a ladder. Lotte hadn't been terribly clear on the details but, save for the appearance of his brother, Hoffner was glad to hear that things were moving along at their usual pace. He would be home soon enough. Until then, he would continue to live for her letters. He started to write.

My love,

Have I mentioned it's hot? Very hot, and they seem to think that water makes you less of a man. I wouldn't mind it so much, but I get thirsty from time to time and they offer wine or whiskey, and I find myself no less thirsty. Can you imagine it? (I hope you're laughing. I need to know I'm still wonderfully funny and charming to you.)

I smell awful. There's no reason to bathe (see water reference above). And yet, among the other journalists, I'm one of the few I can actually bear the smell of. There's a nice Frenchman who I think has an unlimited stash of women's perfume, and I'm coming close to asking him for some, but several Czechs have asked him to dance, so I think I'll hold off for as long as I can.

I ate bull's tail yesterday. Thick brown sauce. A little like brisket but stringier. And then apples, I think, in the same sauce. Not quite as effective. The whiskey was a help there.

I miss you—terribly. I'm amazed I've waited this long to say it. And Mendy. I try not to think about that. I suppose he's still trying to be very brave, but I do hope there have been some tears. Selfish of me, I know, but at least that way I can think I'm not forgotten (yes, there are always a few lines of self-pity in here, so you'll just have to bear with me—you always do).

Still, I am finding it fascinating here. All these idealists pretending to be athletes. I suppose it makes some sort of point. They're all very kind to me when they find out I'm a German. "Brave, German," they say. "That'll show Hitler." Of course I don't tell them I work for an English company. I think it would deflate me a little in their estimation, and you always get a better reel of film and an interview when they think more of you than they should.

As for being a Jew, no one cares here. It's almost as if I'd forgotten what that was like. You say you're a Jew, and they say *Oh* and move on as if you've asked for the salt. There are the few who realize I'm a German, and the pieces start to click together, but for the most part there's nothing more to it.

Can you remember what life was like when that was true? Can you imagine raising a son without having to explain that? They manage it here quite wonderfully, even with their aversion to water. Excuses aside, your father and I will have to sit down and have that talk when I get back. It can't go on. Is he still thinking the racial laws will be recalled? Is he still trying to stay as quiet as he can? Does he still shake at night?

I'm sorry. I don't mean to be so shrill about your father, but you and I both know the time has come.

Did I mention it's hot? And that I miss you—desperately? It is desperation. I love you beyond all measure. I'm a fool to go away as often as I do. So let's all go away.

I've been told I'm trying *suquet* tonight. No idea what it is. Maybe fish and potatoes. Think of me when you eat.

Your Georgi

He folded the letter and placed a wrapped piece of chocolate inside for Mendy. He would post it on his way up to the park. He checked his watch. He had time for a nap.

The sun was low across the horizon as Hoffner set the camera on a narrow shelf of stone and tile. He had borrowed a car to make his way up to this particular park—Park Güell—Antonio Gaudí's homage to sweeping curves and staggering colors and a mind unburdened by things of this world. It was like walking through a child's gingerbread fantasy, except here all the garden walls seemed to be sprouting from trees or dripping from their branches. Hoffner tried to find a straight line somewhere among them, but it was pointless.

The city below looked equally untamed, pale stone and arching roofs, sudden openings here and there where a column or spire might rise from the disarray. The strangest and tallest was Gaudí's Sagrada Família, his unfinished cathedral, whose towers looked to be made of sand, as if a spider were caught belly-up and struggling to right itself. Farther on stood the hills and Montjuïc, with its ancient fortress and the new Olympic Stadium. To the left, the sea.

Somehow, staring out, Hoffner felt a sudden rush of calm. It might have been the air of a Mediterranean night or the silence all around him. Or maybe it was just the genius of Gaudí. Whatever it was, Hoffner let himself take it in.

A couple stopped next to him. They stared out for a few moments and then moved on. Somewhere, a lute began to play.

The sun spread across the few clouds, and Hoffner bent over and began to film. It would make a nice opening shot, Montjuïc in the distance, the sky the rust of early sunset, and the first lights beginning to shimmer inside the buildings. Hoffner panned slowly across the city until he heard footsteps on the gravel behind him. They stopped. He heard the flare of a cigarette lighter, then the snap of the top as it clicked shut.

"Hello, Georg."

Hoffner stopped the crank and slowly stood upright. He turned.

A tall man with a shock of white hair stood staring at him. The man let out a long spear of smoke and offered Hoffner a cigarette.

"Thanks, no," said Hoffner.

The man nodded once. The hair might have been white, but he was no more than fifty, and his arms in shirtsleeves showed lithe, taut muscle.

His name was Karl Vollman, and he was an Olympic chess player. A German. The two had shared a bottle of whiskey a few nights back. Vollman slid the pack into his shirt pocket and took another long pull.

"It's a beautiful view," Vollman said.

"Yes."

"Just right for your sort of thing." Vollman deepened his voice. "City of lights, city of dreams—Olimpiada Popular, and Pathé Gazette is there." He smiled to himself and took another pull.

"No chess tonight?"

"There's chess every night. Later. Down in the Raval. Seedy and smoky. Just right."

"I met a Bulgarian who finds it rather silly—chess as sport."

"I find Bulgarians rather silly, so I suspect we're even."

Vollman had spent the better part of the past ten years in Moscow, teaching something, playing chess. He said he liked the cold.

"You just happened to find yourself in Park Güell tonight?" Hoffner said.

"They say you can't leave the city without seeing it. Here I am. Seeing it." Vollman looked past Hoffner to Barcelona. "Peaceful, isn't it? Sad how we both know it won't be that way much longer."

Hoffner measured the stare. Whatever else Vollman had been doing in Moscow, he had learned to show nothing in his face.

Hoffner said, "I'm sure they'll have a wild time of it when the Olimpiada starts up."

Vollman's stare gave way to a half smile. "Oh, is that what I was talking about? The Olimpiada." He finished his cigarette, dropped it to the ground, and watched his foot crush it out. Thinking out loud, he said, "I suppose it's what you're here to film, what I'm here to do. Much simpler seeing it that way."

Hoffner had felt a mild unease with Vollman the other night. This was something more.

Vollman said, "I don't imagine either of us will be in Barcelona much longer, do you?" He looked directly at Hoffner. "All those fascist rumblings in the south—Seville, Morocco. Only a matter of time."

Again, Hoffner said nothing.

Vollman pulled out the pack and tapped out a second cigarette. He lit it and spat a piece of tobacco to the ground.

"Fascist rumblings?" Hoffner said blandly. "I hadn't heard."

Vollman's smile returned. "Really? A German, working for the English, in socialist Spain just at the moment the fascists are thinking of turning the world on its head, and he hasn't heard. How remarkable." He gave Hoffner no time to answer. "What are you, Georg, twenty-nine, thirty?"

Hoffner was twenty-five, but why give Vollman more ammunition?

"Something like that," Hoffner said.

"Then you're still young enough to take some advice." Vollman spat again. "We both know why you're in Barcelona. Which means the Spanish know why you're here. And if the Spanish know—well, wouldn't you think the Nazis would know as well?"

Hoffner didn't like the shift in tone. "And do the Nazis know why *you're* here?"

Despite himself, Vollman liked the answer. Again he smiled.

"English, Russians," he said, "Italians, Germans. Aren't we all just waiting for the Spaniards to figure it out for themselves? And when they do"—Vollman shook his head with as much pathos as a man like him could muster—"that's when we take sides. And that's when the real games begin." He took a last pull. He was oddly quick with a cigarette.

Hoffner said, "You mean when they start killing each other."

Vollman hesitated even as he showed nothing. He tossed his cigarette to the ground and then bobbed a nod out at the city. "You keep on getting whatever it was you were getting. When you need more, you know where to find me."

Vollman started off.

"It's Paris," Hoffner said.

Vollman stopped. He turned.

"The city of lights," Hoffner said. "Not good to be confusing Paris and Barcelona these days."

Vollman waited. There was no telling what he was thinking. He said nothing and moved off. Hoffner watched as Vollman stopped for a few moments by the lute player, dropped a coin in the man's hat, and headed for the stairs.

Back at his room, Hoffner was finishing his third glass of whiskey when he placed an empty sheet of paper on the desk. His head was spinning—from Vollman, from the booze—but there was always one place he could go to clear his mind.

He began to write.

A ladder?

Brilliant, Papi. Make sure the gardener doesn't take a shovel to your head the next time.

It's past eleven. They're all heading off for dinner, so you're the best I can do for company. Don't pat yourself on the back. I've had a few, and we both know what that does to my letters to Lotte. You won't tell her.

I can't promise coherence. Then again, there isn't a lot about Spain these days that inspires it, so I think I won't worry. Oh, and there's nothing else to tell about the police, except that their hats are ludicrous. I'd try to draw you one, but it would come off looking like a dying bat or a headless peacock. Wonderfully appropriate but not terribly accurate.

So that leaves the politics. Yes, the politics. At last. Just for you. I can hear you laughing. I had a strangely unnerving conversation tonight—the place seems to thrive on strangely unnerving conversations—but there's no point in going into that. Still, it put me in the frame of mind.

You'd feel right at home. It's like Berlin after the Kaiser, except here the Lefties manage it without a dinner jacket or soap. They take the worker thing very seriously. Lots of shirtsleeves and bandanas. It's Mediterranean Marxism, which has a kind of primitive feel to it— everyone sweating and opening shirt buttons and going without shoes. They have rallies all the time and write large, imposing posters with lots of dates on them. Women wear trousers a great deal, which seems to go counter to the whole heat-inspired politics of the Left. Wouldn't a dress be cooler? It makes you wonder how much the cold had to do with paving the way for Hitler, but that's for another time. (If the line above is blacked out by the censor, I probably deserved it, so don't worry.)

I've met anarchists and socialists. I've eaten with Communists and anarcho-syndicalists and Marxist-nihilists, and something simply referred to as a non-Stalinist Soviet. I thought the person introducing me was talking about a kind of napkin until a very earnest young woman began to spew in a much-too-quick Spanish for me to follow. Best recourse is just to nod.

The bizarre thing is that they all seem to think they're the ones running the show. Not together, of course. That would be asking too much. (At least Weimar got that right for a while.) The socialists hate the anarchists. The anarchists hate the Communists. And the Communists have no power whatsoever and seem to hate even themselves.

I think there's a central government somewhere, but Barcelona doesn't like to admit that. The Lefties they elected in February—socialists calling themselves a Popular Front, which is bizarre when no one really likes them and they're well behind the curve at every turn—are a kind of mythological beast that shouts at everyone from Madrid and tells them how to be proper Lefties—who to adore, who to hate. This week, I think it's the anarcho-syndicalists—I still have no idea what that means—whom we're all supposed to be burning in effigy. And that's just the boys who are in their own camp.

It gets much easier when they turn to the Right. There it's basically two groups that the Lefties scream at—hard-line monarchists and hard-line fascists, and both of them marching with crosses. Very big crosses. Vast crosses. Epic crosses. There's a scent of the Crusades in all this.

The first call themselves Carlists. They want the king back. Very Catholic. Lots of pedigree. Spanish arrogance drunk on holy water.

The second are the Falangists, a version of Mussolini's Fascisti, although I suspect they find Hitler just as inspiring. They're relatively new. I think they invented themselves around the same time the Reichstag burned. Catholic (as long as the priests tell the people to follow them). Militarists. And hell-bent on rooting out anyone who even recognizes the name Marx.

Unlike the Left, the boys on the Right actually talk to each other. That makes them far more dangerous.

It's only a matter of time before it all blows up. So it's going to be news, and that means you'll have to bear with me. You'll also have to make sure Lotte can bear it as well. I need you for that. I'm asking you for that. Not for too long, I hope. But then there are always those unnerving conversations.

Anyway, I'm losing my train of thought. And I'm tired. That seems to be a constant.

I imagine most of this letter is blacked out. I know. My apologies.

Watch the papers. It won't be long. And Pathé Gazette will be there.

Cock-a-doodle-doo,

Georg

He was right, of course. The opening ceremonies of the Olimpiada Popular, slotted for the nineteenth of July, never happened. Instead, two days earlier, all hell had broken loose.

The first reports started arriving on the afternoon of the eighteenth. They were of no help, wires and rumors coming in from Morocco and the south: ten dead, then fifty. Something had happened in Melilla on the northern coast of Morocco; a colonel had arrested a general. The question was, was the colonel on the Left or the Right? More than that, whose soldiers were dying, and what were they dying for? By the time Georg made it to the consulate for confirmation, the number was at two hundred. A fascist group of officers—calling themselves rebel Nationalists—had secured all of Morocco, and another group on the mainland was heading for Seville.

Georg read the wire from the prime minister in Madrid—THEY'RE RIS-ING? VERY WELL. I SHALL GO AND LIE DOWN—and knew the Lefties had no idea what they were in for. By 9 p.m., word had come through that Queipo de Llano—one of the more vicious generals in the uprising—had marched into Seville with four thousand rebel fascist soldiers and taken her in a matter of hours. Queipo was clever: he simply arrested and shot anyone who wouldn't join him.

Hoffner took his camera and headed for the Rambla. Everyone was out. News never waited long in Barcelona.

There were already loudspeakers up on the trees, music for the most part—for some reason Rossini was getting the majority of the playing time—but every so often an announcement would come through:

"These are isolated incidents."

"The government has put down the failed military rebellion."

"Do not take matters into your own hands."

"Anyone arming himself will be arrested."

The anarchists were not so convinced. Georg latched onto a small group who were more than eager to have a foreigner film their fight to save Spain.

Down at the harbor, while waiting for more men to arrive, Georg found a sheet of paper and began to write to his father:

11 p.m. The place is madness. They've already started putting up barricades, waiting for God knows what out of the barracks. An hour ago I saw thirty men armed with knives, bats, and guns that hadn't been used for over twenty years. They broke into a police armory. The commanding officer handed out every last weapon before joining them.

These are anarchists. They know what happens if the army finds no resistance. Women are armed as well. I suspect I'll be seeing children. They speak about the fascists as if they were an army of foreign conquerors—not Spaniards, not brothers. They have no shared history. They are the enemy.

We're down at the docks. The smell of fish is overwhelming, nets abandoned, the heat suffocating. Food will be crucial soon enough, but it's guns they need now. We're crouching behind a pair of trucks. I've heard the crack of rifle fire from time to time, but everything is strangely calm. My group is after the ships. There's a shipment of dynamite on one of them. No organization. They simply wait for critical mass and then run at what they need. They've told me where they want me to stand as I film. They want it filmed.

Fifteen more arrive. They don't look like revolutionaries. They wear trousers, leather shoes, well-shaved. Each has the red and black bandana around his neck. They, too, are glad I'm here.

We're not the rebels, one of them tells me. We defend what is ours. The fascists are the enemy of Spain.

They ask me to film them as they crouch behind the trucks. They run and I film.

They're on the ships now. Either they'll come back or they won't. I'll give them another ten minutes, and then I have to get back up the Rambla. We'll see where I sleep.

Throughout the night, the workers found guns and rifles and grenades and fitted trucks and cars with armor plate. And they waited. Georg stole two hours of sleep at a café, Tranquilidad, on the edge of the Raval. It was an anarchist stronghold. News kept pouring in until the first real shots came just after dawn.

10 a.m. I'm in a building across from one of the big fountains, I can't remember which one. We've been on our feet, running from barricade to barricade for the last three hours. The smell of horse manure and blood comes up at you everywhere you go. Someone handed me a pistol. I haven't had to use it yet.

The entire country is in it now. Madrid sends orders that aren't orders. The Republican government—anarchists, socialists, Communists (imagine those meetings)—are letting everyone run free. The prime minister is gone. His replacement, Barrio or Barria (no one speaks clearly enough for me to catch the name), lasted for all of about two hours. The fascist generals are claiming control of a third of the country—it's inconceivable how easy it was for them—and we're focusing on taking the telephone exchange.

We've heard of churches pillaged, priests beaten (or worse). I saw something I couldn't understand. A man next to me explained. Nuns, he said. Mummified corpses of nuns dragged out onto the streets. You could see the ripped cloth around the bodies, the bones. They were thrown across the steps to the church. I wanted to look away, but there's no doing that through the viewfinder. My hand cranks and it all happens. I'll burn the film.

We've just heard there's a battalion of Falangist rebels getting ready to take the Diagonal (they'll cut the city in half if they do). There's also an artillery regiment of fascist rebels marching from the Sant Andreu barracks—90,000 rifles inside. Whoever gets the Diagonal takes Barcelona. My hotel is under rebel control. I suppose I won't have time for a nap.

While Georg found another safe nook, a General Goded was arriving by seaplane from Majorca. He had been told to take the city for the rebels. He wasn't counting on the Guardia Civil joining the workers, a column of four thousand men, eight hundred of whom were climbing the Via Lai-etana toward the Commission of Public Order. The crowds roared, rifles and fists reached to the skies, and the Republican fighters—with some crack sniper fire—retook the Ritz and the Colón, while the anarchists overran the telephone exchange. And all this by 2 p.m. It was now just a matter of time before the fascists were done for.

4 p.m. Only a few pockets left. Hard to think I would have been up in the stadium right now, seeing flowers and doves and hearing anthems for the games. It's unimaginable.

I'm in the Avenida Icaria, down near the water. They've turned huge rolls of newsprint into barricades. It's keeping the fascist regiment from the Sant Andreu barracks back. The other rebel soldiers are cut off.

There was a moment of remarkable bravery a few minutes ago. A rebel machine gun was wreaking havoc. Two workers stepped out from behind the barricade and, raising their rifles over their heads, began to walk toward it. It was startling to watch from the barricade. It must have been even more so at the machine gun, because the firing stopped. The two workers shouted to the rebels that they were firing on their brothers.

"Your officers have tricked you!" one of them shouted. "You must fight *for* Spain, not against her."

They continued walking, rifles over their heads. A minute later, the rebel soldiers turned their machine gun around and began to fire on the fascists. It was—I don't know what it was. The rebels surrendered a minute later.

It gives me hope.

Two hours later, General Goded admitted defeat on the radio and was promptly shipped off to face court-martial. So ended the first full day of civil war in Barcelona. Six hundred lay dead, four thousand wounded.

As for the People's Games, Spain was well beyond games.

After that, there were no more letters from Georg. There was nothing more from Georg. Nothing.

And his silence headed east.

2

BERLIN

"You're a Jew, then?"

Pimm was dead. It was six months since they had pulled the body from the water, a single shot to the back of the head. Several of his boys had been posted to the usual spots where things tended to float up—down by the grain mills, or along the little inlet just beyond the Oberbaum Bridge—but it had taken almost a week before one of them had spotted him.

Not that it should have come as a shock. Run with the syndicates, swim in the Spree. That was the old line, and even bosses weren't immune. Tach and Wetzmann had been idiots back in 1916, trying to horn in on Pimm's hold on the Turkish sugar market. What had they expected? Both had ended up bobbing against the rocks. Still, the Spree was usually reserved for ratchet-and-pick men or a sloppy garrote. Bosses usually got better.

Things had changed, though. They had changed, and the world had watched and applauded or turned away, or whatever the world does when these things happen. The new boys wanted things cleaned up—they were very keen on cleaning—and criminals were an easy target.

"Herr Hoffner?"

Kriminal-Oberkommissar Nikolai Hoffner looked back across the desk. He was finding his mind wandering these days—to Pimm, to Martha, even to Sascha—especially when the windows were so tall and the sky beyond such a nice clean gray. The office was a throwback to the Kaiser's Berlin, a vast hall with two-story drapes held tightly among the rococo swirls of gold inlay that followed the moldings up and around. Above, someone's idea of an Arcadian romp filled the ceiling and spilled down onto the upper reaches of the walls, although even the little cherubs seemed smart enough not to stray too far down. A portrait of Hitler hung behind the desk: best to remain out of the Führer's gaze.

Hoffner refused to look at the file on the desk. Not that he was much on reading things upside down, but he knew it was the expected response. Why give this Herr Steckler the pleasure?

Hoffner corrected him. "It's Chief Inspector Hoffner."

Steckler continued to scan the pages. "Yes." He looked up. "So you're a Jew?"

It was impressive how Steckler had waited this long to ask, the small spectacled face doing its best at indifference, though mocking it all the same. These days it was where things always began or ended: Jew, the calling card of bureaucracy. This one, however, was shaking things up, slipping the question in at the middle.

"Technically," said Hoffner. "Yes."

Steckler returned to the pages. "It's a world of technicalities now, isn't it?"

Hoffner said nothing.

"And to have it go unnoticed for over three years," Steckler added. "Remarkable."

The Nazis had passed the *Berufsbeamtengesetz* in April of 1933, the Law for the Restoration of the Professional Civil Service—a clever little piece of legislation to weed out the Jews and the Communists.

Steckler continued to read. "Your mother. She was a Jewess. Ukrainian."

"She converted," said Hoffner. "To Lutheranism." It might have been Methodism—Hoffner had never known which—but why burden Steckler with the details.

"But not before you were born," said Steckler.

"No." Hoffner was no less offhand.

"And then she converted back. In 1924. She became a Jew again."

"She was very persistent."

Steckler looked up. Moments of uncertainty always brought a tight smile with men like this. He went back to the file. "Probably why there was the confusion."

"Probably."

"She died in 1929?"

"She did."

Steckler turned the page. "You could retire now, you know." He seemed to be warming a bit. "Take your pension."

"Not my full pension," said Hoffner. It was going to be a morning of corrections.

Steckler glanced down to the bottom of the page and then closed the file. He looked up. "I'm sure we could work something out." A chummi-ness seemed to be struggling to find its way through. "Only a few years left, Herr Chief Inspector. What are you—fifty-five, fifty-six?"

"Sixty-two," said Hoffner.

"Really? Even better." Steckler had no reason to push too hard on this one; time was on his side. "It's a new generation, Herr Chief Inspector. New direction. New methods. Alexanderplatz isn't the place you once knew."

"No," said Hoffner. "It isn't."

"And you've had such a very nice career. Impressive, even. Why muddy it now?"

It was uncanny how the Nazis always tossed everything onto everyone else's lap: Hoffner was the one now muddying things.

"It's been a good career, yes," he said.

He wondered if Pimm had sat in a chair like this, commended for his estimable career marks—the takeover of the five territories, the boy and heroin trade north of the Hallesches Gate, his work in rooting out "un-desirables" during the Red scare. Probably not. And probably no mention of his help in the Luxemburg and Ufa episodes, not that those were some-thing to crow about these days. In the end, it had come down to Pimm the Jew. Pimm the crime-boss Jew. A bullet to the skull had been more than sufficient.

Hoffner reached into his jacket pocket. "But if you think we can work something out," he said, pulling out a pack of cigarettes and matches, "I'd be happy to leave the murder and mayhem to you and your new generation, Herr Steckler."

Steckler's smile returned. "Undersecretary Steckler," he corrected.

Hoffner nodded, lit up, and said, "Now—about my son."

Berlin had never looked so red.

Hoffner gazed through the tram window and doubted whether the Nazis recognized the irony. Little Rosa Luxemburg had been dead almost twenty years and yet the streets bled—red with black, of course (who could miss the black at the center), but it was the red that flapped in the air: flags, pennants, flowers. The scarves that hung around the children's necks were particularly fetching, as if even their little throats were soaked in it. It might have been the rain—this had been a particularly wet, cold July—but why reduce it to weather?

Irony, though, was for those on the outside, those with something still to gain, although surely this bunch had been on the fringes long enough to appreciate it just a bit. Wasn't there an irony in their having been elected at all, in their claims to victimization by the Bolsheviks, Versailles, the Jews? Fascinating to see earnestness wash away even the most stubborn traces of the truth.

The tram stopped, and Hoffner stepped off to a nice dowsing of his trousers from a passing truck. The lettering on its side had it heading west to Döberitz. Everything was heading west these days—food, horses, prostitutes—all of it to keep the Olympic athletes happy. Most were already settled in; the last few stragglers would be setting up digs in the next day or so, with their sauna and chefs and shooting ranges and private showers. Hoffner tried to picture the genius who had seen fit to call such lush accommodations a village.

But for those who had invaded to cheer the athletes on, Berlin was determined to quell any lingering doubts. Thoughts of Olympic boycotts might be long forgotten: everyone who had threatened not to come was already here. Even so, the Jew-baiting signs that had so troubled the French and the English and, of course, the Americans (would they be bringing their Negroes?) had been pulled from shop windows, stripped from the

Litfassäulen, and replaced with odes to sport and camaraderie and international friendship. Not that the Greeks had been much on mutual friendships or protecting their weak—mountainsides and babies came to mind—but they had come up with the ideal, and wasn't that what the new Germany was all about?

It was a cloud of gentle denial—ataraxia for the modern world—that had brought this cleansing rain, and Hoffner wondered if he was the only one to feel the damp in his legs.

He turned onto Alexanderplatz and saw the giant swastika draped across the front of police headquarters. It billowed momentarily. He imagined it was waving to him, a gesture of farewell, good luck, "It was swell, Isabel, swell." The telephone call from the ministry had no doubt preceded him. The paperwork would follow, but he was out. There was no need for the flag to be anything but gracious in victory.

The look on the sergeant's face at the security desk confirmed it. The usual nod of deference was now an officious bob of courtesy.

"Ah, Herr Kriminal-Oberkommissar," he said. At least the man continued to refer to him by his title. Hoffner had been one of the very few to insist on his old rank after the SS had absorbed the Kripo and the Gestapo into what was now known as the Sipo. He had never considered himself a major or a captain, or whatever rank they had tried to foist on him. Inside the Alex, "detective" would have suited him just fine, but even the Kripo had its standards. So "chief inspector" it remained, if only for a few more days.

"Herr Scharführer," Hoffner answered.

"Will you be needing help with any more boxes, Herr Kriminal-Oberkommissar?"

Hoffner had anticipated the ministry's response. He knew the letter he had sent them a few weeks back would bring his file into play. He knew it would mark the beginning of the end—of everything. The rest was academic. Most of his office was already packed up and gone, thirty-five years neatly stacked in boxes across town in his rooms on Droysenstrasse.

"I think I can manage it, Herr Scharführer," Hoffner said. He nodded, then pushed through the oak doors and stepped out into the Alex's vast glassed-over courtyard. The smell of ammonia, with a nice lingering of mildew, pricked at his nose as he headed for the far corner.

The rote quality of the walk to his office had taken on an unwelcome nostalgia in the last weeks: Why should he care that the once-familiar cobblestones now lay buried beneath a smooth flooring of cement? Had he really spent that much time in the subbasement morgue to mourn its dismantling? Was there anything truly lost by riding an elevator up to the third floor rather than taking the stairs? There was a sentimentality here that troubled him, and Hoffner wondered if it would be this way from now on, even beyond the Alex? Was it possible to be disgusted by a self not yet inhabited?

At least he could still take one last stroll past the offices on the floor, stop into the kitchen for a cup of bad coffee, or hear the general incompetence spilling from the desks and telephone conversations. There had been a distinct drop in the quality of police work since the politics of crime had superseded the crimes themselves. The newest officers were hacks and morons, and their brand of policing was growing ever more contagious. Why make the effort when dismissals and convictions rested on political affiliations, even for the most despicable of rapists, murderers, and thieves? At least Hoffner was on his way out. For those with five or ten years left, the Alex had become a cesspool filled with nouveau petty posturing or, worse, old-guard yearning for invisibility until their pensions came due. Either way it was an abyss.

"Nikolai."

The voice came from the largest office on the floor. Hoffner had long given up trying to figure out how Kriminaldirektor Edmund Präger knew when someone was walking past. There was nothing for it but to pop his head through the doorway.

"Herr Gruppenführer," Hoffner said. Präger had been given no choice but to take on the new rank.

"Have a seat, Nikolai."

Präger was pulling two glasses and a bottle from his desk drawer. Over the last few months it appeared as if the desk had been moving ever closer to the window, as if Präger might be planning a jump, albeit a gradual one.

Präger said, "I just got the call." He poured two glasses while Hoffner sat. "So it's finally done. I can't say I'll miss you."

"Can't or won't?"

Präger allowed himself a half smile. "The Kripo might be filled with thugs and idiots now, but at least they do what they're told. It's a different sort of babysitting with them, and for another four months I can manage that." He raised his glass and they both drank.

"And then?" said Hoffner.

"We've a place outside Braunschweig. My wife's family. We'll go there and wait for this nonsense to pass while they pay me my pension."

Präger poured out two more and Hoffner said, "Sounds very nice." He took his glass. "So—how many Gypsies do you have locked up out in Marzahn now? Four hundred? Five?"

Präger had the whiskey to his lips. He held it there another moment before bringing the glass down. "Just once, Nikolai, I'd like to have a drink, a chat, and then see you go. Wouldn't that be nice?"

"You still think it's nonsense?"

Präger drank and Hoffner asked again, "How many?"

Präger thought a moment, shook his head, and said, "What difference does it make?" He set the glass on the desk. "There's something wrong with having just one of them out at that camp, isn't there?"

Hoffner appreciated Präger's decency, even if it always surfaced despite itself. Hoffner took a sip. "Good for you," he said, and tossed back the rest.

"Yah," said Präger. "Good for me." He thought about pouring out two more but instead put the bottle away. "The camp can house up to a thousand," he said. "It's around eight hundred now. Until the games are over. Then we'll set the Gypsies free. Happy?"

"Not that you're keeping count."

"You know what it's like with these people. The SS likes its papers in triplicate. I've no choice." Präger lapped at the last bit of booze in his glass and then placed it back in the drawer. "You'll stay in Berlin, of course. Can't imagine you anywhere else."

"I hear there's some nice farmland outside Braunschweig."

"My relatives know how to use an ax, Nikolai. I'll tell them you're coming."

"It's been guns and rifles for a while, now."

"Has it?"

Präger sat back. In twenty years peering across a desk at the man, Hoffner had never seen him strike so casual a pose.

"You and I are too old to be concerned with any of this," Präger said. "Take your pension, join a bird or card club, learn how to make a few friends, and wait to die. I think even you can manage that."

Hoffner pushed his glass across the desk for a refill. "But not outside Braunschweig."

Reluctantly, Präger opened the drawer and pulled out the bottle. "It's the walking dead in Braunschweig, Nikolai," he said, as he poured Hoffner a half-glass and returned the bottle to the drawer. "How would you learn to make a friend?"

Hoffner smiled and then drank. "I've managed this long." He set the glass down and stood.

"You should take in some of the games," said Präger, retrieving the glass and filing it. "You like sport."

"I prefer my chest-thumping in private."

"Then you won't be disappointed." Präger closed the drawer. "It's no uniforms at the stadium. The memo just came down. Supposedly they had a rough go of it last winter for the skiing. All those foreigners outside Munich thinking they were in a police state. Imagine that? Even the SS will be in mufti."

Hoffner took a momentary pleasure in picturing the discomfort that would cause. "So how much of it are they having you attend?"

"It's not all that bad," said Präger. "The opening thing tomorrow and then some of the running events. I'm in a box next to Nebe, who's in a box next to Heydrich. And next week I've been invited to give an address to a contingent of Dutch, French, and American policemen. 'The City and the Law.' Very exciting."

"I'll be sorry to miss it."

"Yes, I'm sure you will. I'll pass on your regrets to the Obergruppenführer."

At the door, Hoffner fought back the urge at sentimentality. Even so he heard himself say, "Be well, Edmund."

The gesture caught Präger by surprise. He nodded uncomfortably, pulled a file from his stack, and began to read. For some reason, Hoffner nodded as well before heading off.

His office was unbearably neat. There were scuff marks along the walls where books and jars and shelves—now gone—had rested for too many years without the least disturbance. The bare desktop was an odd assortment of stained coffee rings and divots, the grain of the wood showing a neat progression from healthy brown—where the blotter had sat—to a tarlike black at the edges: it made Hoffner wonder what his lungs might be looking like. And along the floor, imprints from file books—either thrown away or shipped off to central archives—created a jigsawlike collection of misaligned rectangles. Someone would have a nice job of scrubbing those away.

There was nothing else except for a single empty crate that sat in the corner under the coatrack. It had the word "desk" scrawled on it in black ink.

Hoffner stepped over, tossed his hat onto the rack, and set the crate on his chair. He had left the drawers for last. He imagined there was some reason for it, but why bother plumbing any of that now. He pulled the keys from his pocket and unlocked the desk. Tipping over the middle drawer onto the desktop—a few dozen business cards, along with a string of pencils, spilled out to the edges—he then did the same with the side drawers, the last of them leaving several pads of paper on top. He placed the cards, pencils, and pads inside the crate and began to sift through the rest.

Most of it was completely foreign to him. There were various scrawled notes—some dating as far back as twenty years—which had somehow eluded filing and now lay crumpled in balls to be opened and tossed away: a list of streets—Münz, Oranienburger, Bülowplatz—several telephone exchanges underneath the word "Oldenburg"; the beginning of a letter to a Herr Engl, where the ink had run out; and endless names he had long forgotten. The usual assortment of Gern clips and pencil shavings fell to the desk with each new handful of paper, but it was the smell of tobacco-laced formaldehyde that was most annoying.

The only thing worthy of any real attention was the neatly rubber-banded stack of folded maps. There was no point in opening any of them:

Hoffner knew exactly what each would show: a pristine view of Berlin, although probably no more recent than 1925 or 1926. He had stopped using them around then.

For twenty-five years, though, maps like these had been a mainstay in the Hoffner Approach to Detective Work. They had made him famous, albeit in rather limited circles. Young Kriminal-Assistents—now far higher up on the rungs than he—would stand at the doorway and watch as he traced his fingers along the streets and parks and canals in search of the variations. That was always the trick with Berlin. She was a city of deviation, not patterning, each district with its own temper and personality. It was always just a matter of keeping an eye out for what didn't belong and allowing those idiosyncrasies to guide him.

These days, however, she was too sharply drawn, too meticulous, and too exquisitely certain of herself to make the subtleties of genuine crime appear in bas-relief. Those idiosyncrasies were no longer the results of human error: a miscalculation in the timing of a bread delivery truck, or the unfamiliarity with the newspapers most likely to be left on a bench after four in the afternoon (years ago, Hoffner had caught two very clever second-story men on just such slipups). Instead, the deviations were now self-constructed, printed in laws inspired by Munich and Nuremberg. They left Berlin no room for shading and made her no more impenetrable than the most insignificant little town on the distant fringes of the Reich. Why seek out differences when impurity was the only crime that mattered? Flossenbürg, Berlin—to Hoffner's way of thinking, the two might just as well have been the same place.

He tossed the maps into the crate as a head appeared around the side of his door. "No one's going to want it, you know."

Hoffner looked over to see Gert Henkel stepping into the office. Henkel was fortyish and rather dapper in his Hauptsturmführer uniform, the double chevron and braided circle making him someone to be taken seriously, willingly or not. The insignia placed him somewhere between the old Kriminal-Kommissar and Kriminal-Oberkommissar designations—or maybe somewhere above them both; Hoffner had given up trying to follow it all. Oddly enough, for all his Nazi trappings, Henkel was a decent fellow. It was still unclear how much of the party line he swallowed: too good a cop not to see it for what it was, but too ambitious not to keep his mouth shut. Hoffner wondered how long that would last.

Henkel said with a smile, "When was the last time you cleaned the place?"

If not for the glaring shine on Henkel's boots, Hoffner might even have called him friend. "How old are you, Henkel?"

Henkel kept his smile. "A good deal younger than you." When Hoffner continued to wait, Henkel offered, "Forty-two."

Hoffner nodded and went back to the crate. "Then I'd say the last cleaning was just before you set off for Gymnasium." Hoffner tossed several more scrawled-on pads onto the pile. "You did go to Gymnasium, didn't you, Henkel? Or are you one of those uneducated but terribly hardworking little butcher's sons who caught the eye of some well-meaning cop and so forth?"

Henkel's smile grew. "Never took you for an elitist, Nikolai."

Hoffner picked up the last of the pads. "I'm not. I just like a bit of schooling. Your uniform can be rather misleading on that."

Henkel snorted a quiet laugh and stepped farther into the office. "My God, you're getting out just in time, aren't you?"

"Too late to turn me in, then?"

"Not my style." Henkel settled in one of the chairs along the wall.

Hoffner continued to flip through his pad. A photograph of Martha with Sascha at five or six years of age had somehow wedged itself into the pages. It was a dour-looking thing, mother and son both moodily sunburnt, probably taken at the beach one of those summers before Georg had come along. Still, she had been pretty.

Hoffner slid the photo back in and placed the pad in the crate. He looked over at Henkel. "Not your style? You might want to ask yourself why sometime."

Henkel spoke easily. "That was your generation, Nikolai. It's answers now, not questions."

Again Hoffner bobbed a nod. "Is that meant to be clever or charming? I'm never quite sure with all these new rules."

Henkel looked momentarily less charmed before the smile returned. "I'd never really taken you for a Jew."

How quickly word traveled, thought Hoffner. "Neither had I," he said. "But that's just it. Your boys have left me no choice."

"Early pension, and at full pay? They're actually doing you a favor at the moment."

"It's not this moment that worries me."

Henkel snorted another laugh. "Gloom and doom. I was wrong. You really are a Jew." When Hoffner said nothing, Henkel pressed. "Oh, come on, Nikolai, don't take it so personally. No one's going to let an old bull cop like you get caught up in any of this." The humane Henkel was making an appearance. "It's just putting things in order. They make a show with a few of the more arrogant types, and then everyone settles in. Better for the Jews to live their own lives, anyway. Probably what they want themselves." He smiled. "Now, if you happened to own a shop or, God forbid, actually had a little money, then . . ."

Hoffner tossed another handful of scraps into the wastebasket. "I might need to take it a bit more personally?"

"No, Nikolai, you wouldn't." Henkel leaned forward. "This is politics. They're saying what they know people want to hear. So they've taken it a bit far. They'll pull back. Trust me, six months from now, no one will be talking about any of this."

Hoffner swept the remaining clips into his hand and deposited them in his pocket. "They," he said, as he brushed the grit from his palms. "Your friends might not like hearing that from someone wearing their uniform."

Hoffner thought he might have overstepped the line but Henkel was in too good a mood. "It's me, Nikolai," Henkel said, sitting back again. "I'm the one who's getting it. I'll probably have to bring in a fumigator, but who wouldn't want the great Nikolai Hoffner's office? There was quite a pool for it. Somehow I won."

For the first time, Hoffner smiled. "Somehow," he said. He took his hat from the rack. "Then I suppose it's yours to enjoy."

He started for the door, and Henkel said, "You're forgetting your crate, Nikolai."

Hoffner stopped and looked back. He stepped over and pulled out a pen. Scratching out the word "desk," he wrote "trash" below it. He then pocketed the pen and moved out into the hall.

MENDEL

It had taken some getting used to, living among the refined. Even now, Hoffner could feel the eyes from across the street with their tidy disdain—sneering at the brown suit, brown hat, brown shoes. Brown was not a shade for the rich, at least not the brown Hoffner was sporting. Still, it was good to have a successful son. Georg's house was large, his lawn well-kept, and his flowers always a jaunty yellow or maroon, even after too much rain: remarkable how wealth could absorb even the dullest of colors.

The one blemish on the otherwise flawless façade was a tiny streak of fresh paint on the doorjamb. Hoffner stepped up to the veranda, lowered his umbrella, and stared at the spot where the mezuzah had hung. Not that Georg had grown up with anything remotely Jewish—he had grown up with nothing—but the boy had fallen in love with a girl, and such girls demanded these things. She had even gone so far as to demand (ask, hope) that Georg might move himself up on the Judaic ledger from quarter Jew to full-fledged. Only twenty at the time, Georg had submitted without a blink, a year's worth of preparation happily weathered to make him fit for marriage. Hoffner was now sandwiched between a dead mother and a practicing son, both of whom had returned to their roots without a single thought to the living family tree. Odd how, thus far, Hoffner was the only one to have paid for his lineage.

The mezuzah had come down after the latest spate of street beatings. Until recently, the punch-ups had always taken place in the seedier parts of town or outside synagogues. Even so, all but a few of the houses along the street were now festooned in swastika flags: national pride, they said, the German Olympic spirit on display. Those conspicuously unadorned—the Nazis had forbidden Jews from flying the Reich colors—drew stares enough. Why advertise beyond the obvious?

Hoffner pushed through the front door and into the foyer. He slid his umbrella into the stand and then opened the door to the house. Almost at once the smell of boiled chicken and potatoes wafted out to meet him.

Luckily, Georg's Lotte was an excellent cook. Hoffner followed the smell past the sitting and dining rooms (too much velvet and suede), along the carpeted corridor (very Chinese), and into the white-white tile of the kitchen. At least here there was something of the familiar. Lotte was at the stove, standing beyond the large wooden table and leaning over a pot that seemed to be sending up smoke signals. Very quietly, Hoffner said, "Hello."

She was known to jump. Several meals during his early days in the house had spilled to the floor with the simplest of greetings. Hoffner cleared his throat and again spoke in a calming tone. "Smells very nice."

"I heard the door," she said, without turning. She continued to stir. "A messenger came with another note. That makes three. It's on the table."

Hoffner saw the ripped-open envelope with the now-familiar Pathé Gazette rooster in the top corner. The note was stuck halfway back in.

"And?" he said, pulling out a chair and sitting.

She seemed to take comfort in the heat on her face. "They don't feel there's any need for alarm, at this point." The last phrase held just the right touch of resentment. " 'It's mayhem,' 'what Georg thrives on,' 'the only one who can get it on film,' so forth and so on." She dug through for a piece of something, scooped it up, and tossed it into the sink. "They're doing what they always do. They're being pricks."

Hoffner liked this most about Lotte. In fact, he liked almost everything about her. She was lovely and fine-boned, very good to Georg, and so clever when it came to seeing things as they really were. Georg had needed a girl like this, a girl just as clever as himself. And while Georg might have had a bit more empathy for the world beyond them—Lotte was never one to suffer fools—it was only a bit. By some miracle, the world had allowed them to find each other.

It was her mouth, though, that Hoffner marveled at. There was an honesty to the way she used words like "prick" and "shit-brain." They weren't meant to shock, just define. Hoffner imagined it was her precision that made her so endearing.

He said, "I don't think they're doing it on purpose."

"Of course they're not doing it on purpose," she said, stirring again. "That's what makes them pricks. They know exactly where he is. They just don't want to tell us."

Hoffner nodded and asked, "Is the boy about?"

"Still," she went on, "I imagine they're expecting some really wonderful reels of war-torn Barcelona, bodies and red flags, rifles in the air. And all by the end of the week. Isn't that exciting?"

Hoffner had told himself to wait until dinner to bring things up but, truth to tell, he had never been much good at waiting. He said, "I suppose I'll just have to go and find him, then."

"He's up in your rooms," she said. "Where else would he be? I think he's got something special planned for you today."

Hoffner waited and then said, "I wasn't talking about the boy."

It took her a moment to follow. When she did, she continued to ladle through the meat.

"Oh, I see," she said. "You meant Georg. Going to Spain and bringing him back. Yes, that would be very nice of you. And some eggs while you're out. We're running low."

"They've given me the sack at the Alex." He waited for her to turn. "This afternoon," he said. "It's a few years early, but they think it's for the best. After all, I've had such a nice career up until now."

She was still holding the spoon. He noticed a glint of Georg's empathy register in her eyes: it was nice to see it. She said, "I'm so sorry, Nikolai."

He shook his head. "No reason. Not much police work going on at the place now, especially for a half-Jew cop." She tried an awkward nod, and he said, "So I'll go see this Wilson fellow tomorrow. The one who runs Georg's office. He's always seemed nice enough. Let him know what I'm planning to do."

There was an uncomfortable silence before she said, "What?"

Hoffner continued easily. "I'm sure he knows where Georgi was filming last. No reason to put any of that in the notes. I'll start there." The spoon began to drip and Hoffner pointed. "You might want to watch that."

Her silence turned to confusion. "You're not being serious?" Chicken stock splattered to the tile but she ignored it. "You know, I don't find this funny." When he continued to stare at her, she said, "They may be pricks, Nikolai, but they're right. He's followed someone up into the hills. That's what this is." She found a dishrag and crouched down to clean up the spill. "He'll get the footage he wants and come back down. And then he'll come home." There was an unexpected frailty in her need to believe what she was saying. "It's the Spanish. Do they even have telephones?" She stood and turned on the faucet.

Hoffner watched as the dishrag now began to get the worst of it. He said, "We both know Georg's never gone this long without a wire or a letter." When she said nothing, he took hold of the envelope, pulled out the note, and—glancing through it—realized she had managed it almost verbatim: "mayhem," "thrived."

"'Incomplete communications,'" he said, reading. "That's a dangerous little phrase." He waited and then added, "If you need me here, I won't go."

"Need you?" she said; he heard the first strains of anger in her voice. She turned off the faucet and said, "That's not it and you know it."

She continued to stare into the sink, and Hoffner suddenly realized how badly he had missed it. This wasn't anger. This was fear. It was a cruel sort of stupidity that had let him think she might actually be encouraging, even excited at the prospect. All he had done was to make the danger acutely real for her.

He set the page back on the table. "No one else is going after him, Lotte. No one else wants to think they have to." And for some inexplicable reason: "There's probably a better story in it if they don't." He was too late in realizing how deeply this had cut her. Instead, he found a bit of grease on the table and began to rub his finger along the wood.

Her eyes remained on the faucet. "So you just get on a train and go to Spain, is that it?"

His fingers had become sticky. He looked for something to wipe them on. "I've a friend who can fly me in."

"A friend?" she said in disbelief, turning to him. "So this has been in the works for some time."

Hoffner let the silence settle. "Yes."

"Of course it has," she said. "And getting the sack from the Kripo—that just makes it easier, doesn't it?"

"I was going anyway."

She tossed over the dishrag. "I'm sure you were."

"As I said, I won't go—"

"Yes, you won't go if I tell you I'm too weak to let you. Would that cause some real misgivings, Nikolai, a moment of genuine concern? But then I've never played the martyred wife with Georg, so why should I try it with you?"

At twenty-four, she already had more resilience than he would ever know in himself. And courage. It took a kind of courage for bitterness to stand up to fear. It was something he had seen only in women. Or perhaps it was what he provoked in them. Either way, it made him feel small in its presence.

He focused on the rag as he wiped off the grease. "It's more chaos now than—" He stopped himself. Than what, he thought—killing? How much more could he possibly mangle this? He looked at her. "They haven't drawn the battle lines. There aren't any fronts to be held. They're picking sides, and a man can get lost in that, no matter how noble his intentions. A man like that needs someone to come and find him." And, perhaps trying too hard to redeem himself, he said, "If it were you, Lotte, I wouldn't need to go at all. You'd be just fine."

She held his gaze. It was a strained few moments before he caught the flicker of surrender in her eyes. Another moment and she pointed to the rag. "They're still pricks," she said.

"Yes," he agreed, tossing it back. "They are."

It was enough for both of them.

She turned to the pot and, with one more unexpected kindness, said, "He'll be impossible if you don't go up now. Just try not to get him too frantic before dinner."

The walk across the back lawn to the carriage house was mercifully dry. Hoffner kept his head down, careful not to notice the tiny pair of eyes following him from the second-floor window. He pulled open the door, mounted the steps, and instantly heard the scurrying of Mendel's little feet above him. At the top of the railing, Hoffner saw Elena, the boy's nanny, who was standing behind a lamp. To a four-year-old, a woman of her size—thick in all the right places—could actually be hidden behind such things. There was a stifled giggle from the blanketed lump on the sofa.

"What a long day I've had," Hoffner said. "How nice it is, finally to be alone. I'll just stretch myself out for a nice rest."

He tossed his hat onto a chair and began to ease himself down onto the sofa. Instantly, the boy's hands gripped Hoffner's shoulders with shrieks of "Not alone! Not alone! Not alone!"

Hoffner went through all the required confusion—"My goodness! Who's that? The sofa's alive! Help me!"—as they ran around the room, Mendel clinging tightly to his back. Finally, Hoffner pulled the boy around to the front and they both slumped back to the sofa with a smothering of kisses for Mendy's neck and belly.

This was, with only minor variations, the routine every day, down to the last few gurgles of laughter before Hoffner finally let go. Mendel quickly leaped to the ground and raced over to the drawing table in the corner.

Elena, well practiced, now stepped out from behind her lamp and said, "We spent a good deal of time on this one, Herr Chief Inspector. A little trouble getting all the letters of your name to fit over your head, but we finally managed it."

She was always very good with the prompting. Not yet forty, Elena might have been the perfect opportunity for a healthy father-in-law living within arm's reach, but both of them had been smart enough not to play out that farce. Hoffner nodded, trying to catch his breath as the boy raced back to the sofa and thrust the page onto his lap.

The only thing even remotely familiar on the paper was the drawing of a silver-star badge—or at least that was how it was described. It had recently become Mendel's signature piece and was about two-thirds the way up on a big black blob, which meant that the blob was Hoffner. A few weeks back, the boy had been given a book on cowboys from Lotte's father, an insufferable fan of the American West. With very little encouragement, Hoffner had pointed out that a sheriff was a kind of policeman, whereupon Mendel had instantly assigned that role to him. Lotte's father remained less than pleased.

As to the "letters" Elena had mentioned, there were various scrawled lines and curls above the blob, the nearest thing to German an upside-down *A*, that looked more like a capsized boat than anything else. Still, it was three little clumps of something, with the *A* at the end.

"'Opa,'" said Hoffner, reading. "How wonderfully you've drawn it."

The boy dug himself into Hoffner's side as he peered at his own work. "And that's your badge there," he said.

"Yes, of course. I saw it at once. Thank you, Mendy. We'll put this one up with the others."

"Can I see it?"

This, too, was part of the ritual, the handling of the badge. Instinctively, Hoffner reached for his pocket before he realized his badge was no longer there. He might have felt a moment's regret—his first and only for this afternoon's events—but instead, he chose to ignore it. Even so, he had grown fond of watching the boy gaze at the thing, hold it up to his shirt, bark out orders. Pride required so little in the very young.

Hoisting himself up, Hoffner said, "I think it's time we get you your own badge, Mendy. A deputy's badge. What do you say to that?"

So much for not riling up the boy. The moment of primal excitement quickly gave way to an equally deep despair as Mendy was told that the promised badge was, as yet, unpurchased. Hoffner's only recourse was to give in to the nightly plea: eating dinner with the boy, or least sitting with him while he struggled to master a fork.

Fifteen minutes later, Mendy sat on a high stool at the kitchen table— Hoffner seated by his side—as Elena put the last of the little meal together. Mendy placed his hands on the table and began to teeter himself back and forth. Instantly, Hoffner grabbed hold of the stool.

"I won't fall," said the boy. "I'm balancing."

Hoffner kept his hand on the stool. "Not a good idea, Mendy."

"But I won't. I promise. I won't."

Elena set a plate of tiny chicken pieces, potatoes, and spinach in front of the boy. She then placed a glass of beer in front of Hoffner.

"Eating time, Mendy," she said. Her tone was one that everyone in the house had learned to obey; Hoffner quickly took a sip of his beer. "If I see you balancing again," she said, "we go to the quiet place. Understood?"

Hoffner had never visited the quiet place—a closet under the stairs— although he had heard tales of it. According to Mendy it was filled with shadows, creaking wood, and even a few monsters. Mendy, however, had learned not to mention the monsters. They had not impressed Elena.

"Is it good?" said Hoffner, as the boy speared a second piece of chicken and shoved it into his mouth. Mendy had a remarkable talent for fitting an entire plate's worth of food inside his cheeks before starting in on the chewing. Hoffner saw the boy going in for a third, and said, "I'd work on those before taking another, don't you think?" Hoffner bobbed a nod toward Elena, who was at the sink washing up. "You wouldn't want to . . . you know."

Mendy thought a moment, then nodded slowly as he pulled back his fork. Chewing, he said, "She likes it when I finish quickly."

Hoffner said, "She likes it when you don't choke."

This seemed to make sense. Mendy nodded again and, continuing to chew, said, "Did Papi have a quiet place when he was little?"

It was always questions about Georg these days—badges, forks, trips away: did Opa go away quite so often when Papi was little? This happened to be a particularly reasonable one. The trouble was, Hoffner had never spent much time with Georg at this age—at any age, truth to tell. It made the past a place of reinvention.

"Yes," said Hoffner, "I think he did. Right under the stairs, as a matter of fact." There had been no stairs in the old two-bedroom flat.

Mendy swallowed and whispered, "Did it have monsters?"

Hoffner leaned in. "Not after we got rid of them."

The boy's eyes widened. "Really?"

Hoffner nodded quietly. "Maybe you and I can do that sometime." Before Mendy could answer, Hoffner plucked a piece of chicken from the plate and popped it into his own mouth.

Mendy said loudly, "Opa is eating my food." Hoffner put on a look of mock panic as Elena, without turning, said, "Opa can go to the quiet place, too, if he's not careful."

Mendy stabbed at a clump of spinach, studied it, and shoved it in. "If she sends you, I'll go with you," he whispered. "That'd be good for both of us."

Hoffner brought his hand to the boy's face and drew his thumb across the chewing cheek. Mendy continued unaware and drove in another piece of meat.

It was all possible here, thought Hoffner. His only hope was to find his way to dying before he learned to disappoint this one.

•   •   •

Hoffner's suggestion that he have dinner out was met with little resistance. Lotte's parents—the Herr Doktor Edelbaums—had called to say how concerned they were with Georg still out of the country: wouldn't it be best if they all dined together, Friday night after all? They would be over in half an hour.

Together, of course, meant just the family. There was always that moment of feigned surprise from the Herr Doktor when the "lodger"—Edelbaum's infinitely clever title for Hoffner—put in an appearance: "No murders to be solved tonight, Herr Sheriff? So you'll be joining us?"

Frau Edelbaum was a good deal more pleasant, though without any of the tools necessary to inject some tact into the proceedings. She would smile embarrassedly, say how lovely it was to see him again, and sit quietly with her glass of Pernod while her husband—perched at the edge of Georg's favorite chair—played trains with Mendy. Hoffner would look on from the sofa and try desperately to time the sips of his beer with any attempts to engage him. And while this was perfectly unbearable, it was Mendy's departure for bed, and the subsequent dinner conversation, that took them over the edge. In the end, Hoffner was doing them all a favor.

He stood with Lotte in the foyer as he slipped on his coat.

She said, "They won't be here much past ten," smoothing off one of his shoulders. "I'll make sure."

"Not to worry. Gives me a chance to see a few friends." He pulled his umbrella from the stand. "It's not as horrible as you think."

"Yes, it is. You detest him."

Hoffner fought back a smile. "Tell him they let me go for being a Jew. That should cause some confusion."

"He's more frightened by all this than you know."

Hoffner shook the excess water from the umbrella. "He has good reason to be." He buttoned the last of his buttons. "I'll be sorry to miss the chicken. You'll save me a piece?"

"It's already in the icebox."

He leaned in and kissed her on both cheeks. "They won't treat me nearly as well in Spain, you know." He saw her wanting to find the charm in this, but it was no good. "I shouldn't tell them about any of that," he said. "I'd hate to have your father pretending concern for me just for your sake." Not waiting for an answer, Hoffner opened the door and stepped out into the rain.

ÜBER ALLES

Rücker's bar hadn't changed in nearly thirty years. Any given night it was the smell of burned sausage and over-sauced noodles that wafted out to the street and made the last few meters to the door so familiar. The sounds from inside came a moment later, old voices with years of phlegm in the throat to make even pleasant conversation sound heated. Hoffner found something almost forgiving about walking into a place where he wasn't likely to see a face younger than fifty. Even the prostitutes had the good sense not to be too young; teasing the old with what was so clearly out of reach would have been cruel. The new girls learned to steer clear quickly enough; the ripe ones came to appreciate a clientele that preferred to talk, have a few drinks or a laugh, before trundling upstairs for more sleep than sex. To an old whore, a night at Rücker's had the feel of a little holiday. It might not be much in the purse, but it was easy and quiet and at such a nice pace.

The barman placed a glass in front of Hoffner and pulled the cork from a bottle of slivovitz.

"Let's make it whiskey tonight," said Hoffner.

The man recorked the bottle, reached for another, and smiled as he poured. Hoffner took his drink and scanned the tables.

Eight o'clock was still early for the usual crowd. Dinner with the wife, followed by all that endless chatter about a day spent up on the girders or underground digging new track, could keep a man home until almost half past eight. The ones without families knew it best to straggle in even later, keep the rest guessing as to where they might have gotten to in the last few hours. The smartest always had a hint of perfume on the clothes, that watered-down swill a man could buy for himself and spray onto a collar just before coming through the door. It was the surest way to get the conversation going: "What do you mean, what do you smell?" The quick sniff of the shirt, the look of surprise, the overeager laugh, and finally the confession: "Damn me if she doesn't use the cheap stuff!" Roars of laughter after that, even if everyone knew the game. Still, why spoil a man's last chance at pride?

Hoffner spotted Zenlo Radek sitting in the back. Two of his men were hunched over a series of plates piled high with beef, potatoes, and sausage, while Radek glanced through one of the newspapers stacked at his side. Radek might still have been somewhere in his early forties—maybe even late thirties—but his face had long ago given up on youth. It was its lack of skin, or rather the stretching of the skin across the bones, that made it so perfect for the surroundings: gaunt and pale blurred even the sharpest of eyes. Then again, it might have been his homosexuality. That aged a man, too.

Radek continued to read as Hoffner drew up.

"The streets won't be nearly as safe now," Radek said, flipping the page. He had unusually long thin fingers. "But I'm sure they sent you off with something nice. A cigarette case, a gold watch. Let you listen to the time slipping by. *Tick, tick, tick.*"

Hoffner was never surprised by what information Radek had at his disposal. "Never took you for the sentimental type."

"Don't confuse pity with sentiment, Nikolai." Radek closed the paper and looked up. A taut smile curled his lips, but the eyes told Hoffner how glad Radek was to see him. "And here I thought you might not be putting in an appearance before your trip." Hoffner looked momentarily confused, and Radek said, "Toby Mueller. He's got a plane all gassed up out at Johannisthal. Heading off to Spain, I hear, and with you in tow. Daring stuff, Nikolai."

Or maybe there was room for surprise. Hoffner had to remind himself that as Pimm's onetime second—and now boss of the city's most notorious syndicate—Radek was tapped into every conduit in Berlin. Even the Nazis came to him when they needed information. There was talk, of course, that Radek had been the one to give Pimm up to the SS—"Make it quick, painless, a single shot to the head"—but that was absurd. It might even have been insulting. Truth to tell, Radek had never wanted this. He was simply too smart, and too loyal, not to be the one to take it all on in the end.

"Running the Immertreu," he had once joked to Hoffner, drunk. "Tell me, if I've been spending all this time trying to kill myself, isn't this a much better bet than the needle ever was?"

As it turned out, Radek had proved too resilient even for heroin. It was years now since he had lost himself to the attic rooms on Fröbel and Moll Strassen. The rooms were long gone—who among the war-ravaged was still alive to fill them?—but Radek had given them a good try: veins streaked that deep pumping blue, boys at the ready for whatever was asked of them, and always the empty hope that he might somehow forget he was no longer a man—images of a single grenade rolling through the French mud, skin and trench wood flying everywhere, and his trousers drenched in blood.

The medics had saved him. Of course they had saved him. Keeping death back had become such an easy thing, just as easy as teaching a man how to piss through a tube.

For now, Radek was done with death, or at least his own. Instead, he read his papers, watched his men eat, and dictated every instance of corruption in his city. And who wouldn't call that a life?

Hoffner pulled over a chair and sat. He took a drink.

Radek said, "He won't find it noble, you going after him, Nikolai. Georgi knows you too well."

Hoffner set his glass on the table. "You're giving me too much credit."

"Am I?"

Hoffner pulled his cigarettes from his pocket. "So it's the big ideas tonight—pity and nobility. And here I thought I'd come in just for a drink." He bobbed a nod at the two large men who were working through their plates. "Gentlemen."

The larger of the two, Rolf, said, "Sausage's not so good tonight. You can have ours if you want."

Hoffner waved over a passing waiter, ordered a plate of veal and noodles, and lit his cigarette. "You should come with me, Zenlo. Spain's perfect for you these days. Black market and civil war. What could be better?" Across the room a woman started in at the piano.

"And deal with all that chaos?" said Radek, as he leafed through the stack. He pulled out the "BZ". "That's nice for a man with a truck and a cousin down at the docks. Those of us with a little more at stake have to think differently." He found the Grand Prix results and folded back the paper. "The desperate never buy for the future, Nikolai. No market stability. Order and fear—with maybe a little strong-arming thrown in—that's what gives you a future." He pulled a pen from his jacket pocket. "Berlin suits me just fine right now."

Hoffner looked over at the smaller man. "So he's off the Freud and Jung, is he?" The man continued to sift through his plate, and Hoffner said, "Tell me, Franz, what's he reading now?"

Franz brought a spoonful of potatoes up to his mouth. "Keynes," he said, before shoveling it in.

This required a moment. "Really?" Hoffner said. "That's—ambitious." Franz chewed, and Hoffner said, "He's getting it wrong."

"Is he?" said Franz, swallowing. "We should all be getting it so wrong."

Radek continued to read as he spoke. "It's the new psychology, Nikolai. Primal urges. Consumer desires. Totted up in columns and graphs. And this time it's all scientific. Here." He showed Hoffner the page he was marking. "Rosemeyer and Nuvolari. Auto Union and Alfa-Romeo. Clearly the two best drivers in the world. Barcelona last month—Nuvolari one, Rosemeyer five. Nürburgring two weeks later—Rosemeyer one, Nuvolari two. A week after that in Budapest, and they're one and two again, only this time reversed. Milan, it's Nuvolari, and finally Rosemeyer takes the German Grand Prix last week. And on and on and on. We know there are ten other premium drivers out there every week—Chiron, Caracciola, Trossi—yet these are the two who come up with it every time."

"I'll make a note," said Hoffner. "What does it have to do with economics?"

Radek ignored him. "Is it because they have the best cars? No. Half the drivers are with Alfa-Romeo. And I don't have to tell you what it takes to handle that tank of an Auto Union thing. Sixteen cylinders. Have you seen it, Nikolai? You have to be a beast of a man just to keep the car on the road."

"So Rosemeyer and Nuvolari are reading Keynes?"

"Shut up, Nikolai. The point is, you'd be an idiot not to put your money on one of these two. And yet, even with the odds, people don't. Half the money every week finds its way onto Farina or Varzi or Stuck, and these are good drivers, don't get me wrong. But the chances, if you look at the trends"—he shook his head in disbelief—"almost impossible. So you have to ask, Why do people do it?"

It took Hoffner a moment to realize that Radek was waiting for an answer. "Primal urges?" he offered.

"Exactly," said Radek. "They buy something with no real possibility of a return because they want to *believe* it can have a return. And the oddsmakers *tell* them to believe it can have a return. 'This week,' they advertise, 'Farina will do it. He has to do it. You have to *want* him to do it.' And they trust this because they live in an ordered world where, if things go wrong, they can try again the next week and the next and the next. They buy a product they shouldn't want to buy because they so desperately want it. And that, Nikolai, is economics."

Hoffner sat with this for a few moments before reaching for his whiskey. He took a drink. "So it's the oddsmakers who are reading Keynes?" Hoffner expected a smile but Radek said nothing.

Franz, now running his fork through the remains of his beef, said, "I wouldn't push it on this one if I were you."

Hoffner smiled and looked at Radek. "We're taking this latest theory very seriously, are we?"

Radek said, "You enjoy being an idiot, don't you?"

"Not really a question of enjoying," said Hoffner. "I think I liked the sex theory better, though. I've never bet on car racing."

"Last I checked," said Radek, "you weren't doing much on the sex front, either."

Hoffner laughed to himself.

Radek set down the paper and took his glass. "You have any idea where he is?" He drank.

Hoffner lapped back the last of his whiskey. "Barcelona," he said. "Somewhere in there." He raised his empty glass to a waiter. "I think everything's happening up on hilltops right about now."

"And he's alive?"

"He has to be, doesn't he?"

"It'll be hot."

The waiter appeared and took the glass. "Yes," said Hoffner. "It will."

"Georgi's good in spots like that. He always has been."

"You've met him twice, Zenlo." There was an unexpected edge to Hoffner's voice. "You have no idea who or what he is." It was an awkward few moments before the food miraculously arrived, and Rolf and Franz were forced to stack their plates onto the empties so as to make room. Finally Hoffner said, "He's always liked you, though. Liked that you never tried to corrupt me."

Radek was glad for the reprieve. "How much more corruption could you take?" When Hoffner started in on the noodles, Radek said, "You like Gershwin, Nikolai?" Hoffner focused on his plate and Radek said, "I do."

Hoffner nodded as he chewed.

Rolf said lazily, "It's not Gershwin." He was working his way through a mouthful of potatoes.

"What?" said Radek.

"The piano," said Rolf, swallowing. "It's not Gershwin. You're thinking of the wrong thing." He shoveled in another forkful.

"I'm not."

"You are."

"No," said Radek. "I'm not." There was a quiet menace in his tone; Rolf, however, continued to chew. "This is"—Radek became more serious as he thought—"*Crazy Girl*," he said triumphantly. "'Embraceable You' from *Crazy Girl*."

"*Girl Crazy*," Rolf corrected. "And, no, it's not. This is 'Night and Day' from *The Gay Divorce*. Cole Porter." Rolf took a drink of beer and swallowed.

Radek watched as Rolf dug back in. "I have the phonograph," Radek said.

Rolf nodded. "Good. Then you have the phonograph of *The Gay Divorce* by Cole Porter." He raised his hand to a waiter, made some indecipherable gesture with his fingers, and went back to his plate. "I'm getting the spätzle, Nikolai, if you want some."

This, evidently, was the way an evening with Berlin's most dangerous trio took shape: elementary economics and Tin Pan Alley.

With anyone other than Rolf or Franz, Radek would have found a reason to press things, even when he knew he was wrong. He had once told Hoffner it was good for a man to learn how to cower every now and then. This wasn't cruelty. It was therapeutic, even better if the man recanted the truth just so as to save himself. Radek called it the psychology of order: men liked knowing where they stood; they liked even better being told where to stand. No wonder he was finding Berlin so comforting.

"Finish up," said Radek. "We're heading west. I've got a treat for you."

Half an hour later, all four were crammed into the back of Radek's Daimler saloon, Franz and Rolf perched precariously on the two jump seats.

"You were a fencer, weren't you?" said Radek.

Hoffner tapped his cigarette out the window and watched as a floodlit Unter den Linden raced by. The avenue had once been famous for its dual column of trees down the center. Not now. The Nazis had insisted on building a north-south U-Bahn to impress their Olympic guests. That meant digging and destruction and the temporary loss of the trees. But not to worry. There were always plenty of flagpoles and light stanchions at the ready to take their place, row after row of perfectly aligned swastika banners fluttering in the rain.

Berlin was now nothing more than an over-rouged corpse, gaudy jewels and shiny baubles to distract from the gray, fetid skin underneath.

Hoffner said, "It's going to smell like this for a while, isn't it?"

The avenue was jam-packed with the city's esteemed visitors, guzzling their beer and munching their sausages—most of them good little Germans, small-town folk, who had been arriving by the trainload for the past week. The foreign contingent—all that promised money from abroad— had proved something of a disappointment. Still, at least most of these knew how to speak the language.

Radek said, "Gives it a nice rustic feel, doesn't it?"

They drove past the Brandenburg Gate, and the light in the car intensified. Hoffner said, "So how much have they laid out for all this?"

"Why?" said Radek. "You thinking of chipping in?"

Hoffner turned to him. "How much?"

Radek shrugged. "No idea."

"Really."

Radek shook his head. "I'm telling you, we had the stadium—that's it. The electrics went to Frimmel. The Sass brothers took the village complex. They get catering on that, so they'll be making some nice money, although they've had to deal with the Wehrmacht, and I wouldn't wish that on anyone. And Gröbnitz got waste disposal."

Franz, who was staring out the window, laughed quietly to himself.

"Franz likes that Gröbnitz will be up to his arms in it," Radek said. "What Franz doesn't realize is how much money there is in shoveling someone else's shit."

Hoffner said, "Refreshing to see all the syndicates working so nicely together."

"It's the Olympic spirit," said Radek. "Everyone's been asked to sacrifice."

"And in your pocket?"

Radek smiled. "Isn't there a little pride somewhere in there, Nikolai? Something for the German greater good?"

"Tremendous amounts," said Hoffner. "How much?"

Radek's smile grew as he bobbed his head from side to side, calculating. "A hundred thousand seats in the stadium . . . Maifeld—that's over twenty-eight acres of open ground—the practice facilities . . . Maybe"—he shot a glance at Franz—"what do you say, Franz? Twelve, fifteen million?"

"Twenty-seven," Franz said blandly, as he continued to stare out.

"Twenty-seven million?" Radek's disbelief was matched only by his cynicism. "Really? That much? Just imagine getting a cut of that."

"Yah," said Hoffner. "Just imagine."

"They want to throw away the city's money on this, Nikolai, I'm happy to help them." Hoffner tossed his cigarette out and Radek said, "So you didn't think of pulling out the old saber? Helping the great German cause?"

The thought of dragging his ancient legs onto the strip forced a dismissive snort from Hoffner. "I think Fräulein Mayer rounds out the token half-Jews on the team, don't you?"

It had been in all the papers, the girl's "special dispensation" from the Reich's Committee. Mayer, a former world champion now living in

America—and a Jew only in name—had been made an "honorary Aryan." It seemed demeaning, no matter which way one leaned.

"She's not doing them any favors," said Radek.

"Who," said Hoffner, "the Jews or the Reich? My guess, she wins something, she'll have to give it back anyway."

The Reichssportfeld sits on over three hundred acres of Grunewald forest in the far west section of town. From central Berlin, it is a relatively easy trip past the Tiergarten if one makes sure not to take the truck roads out to the Halske or Siemens factory sites—unless, of course, one is desperate for a rotary engine or any number of other electrical engineering devices. If one keeps to the low roads, the first behemoth to appear on the horizon is the stadium itself. It looms at the end of the wide Olympischer Platz, stone and granite leading all the way up to the double columns of the Marathoner Gate, with the five rings pitched in between. Though ostensibly the brainchild of the March brothers—Werner and Walther—the entire complex has the feel of an Albert Speer design, the thick limestone and wide columns telltale of the Reich's architectural wunderkind. There was a rumor that the Führer, on hearing of Werner's plans to create a modern wonder—steel, glass, and cement—said he would rather cancel the games than have them take place in "a big glass shitbox." But that was only rumor.

Next are the Maifeld parade grounds—vast, wide, green, resplendent—surrounded by nineteen meters of elevated ground, two meters higher than the stadium itself. Originally slated to hold over 500,000 people, it manages only half that (much, again, to the Führer's dismay), but there is the hope that, with the new health incentives—and the aim at a "fitter, sleeker, trimmer" German—the grounds might actually squeeze in close to 300,000 in the not-too-distant future.

And finally there are all those squares—August Bier Platz and Körnerplatz and Hueppeplatz (absolutely vital to name one of them after the German Football League's first president)—but the real gem is the Langemarck-Halle. It is a series of cavernous rooms built to commemorate the gallant singing student soldiers (*"Deutschland, Deutschland über alles"*) who gave their lives in the early days of the war, charging in full chorus against the hordes of ravaging Belgians, who were bent on destroying the mythic German spirit. That the battle took place at Bixchote (so much harder to spell, and not really all that German-sounding) never deterred the planners from immortalizing both the place and the moment of the century's first spilling of Aryan warrior blood. The caverns sit under the Maifeld grandstands and directly below the bell tower. Someone had suggested early on that they call it the Führer Tower, but Hitler himself had vetoed that. Why overstate things?

The place was oddly quiet as the car pulled up. Hoffner noticed the requisite guards and policemen roaming about. There might have been more security elsewhere, but no one would have been stupid enough to stop Radek's Daimler. These were his grounds; even the SS knew to leave him alone.

The car stopped and the four men stepped out onto Olympischer Platz. Somewhere off in the distance a crackling light from a welder's torch cast shadows against a far column. Hoffner wondered if perhaps Werner March himself might be somewhere about, chiseling out the last bits and pieces. March had promised a dedication ceremony for early May. Instead, he had quietly announced the stadium's completion about two weeks ago: AND NOT A MOMENT TOO SOON, the *BZ* headline had read. The editors had hoped to run a cartoon of March holding up the back of the stadium on his shoulder, a wide smile on his sweating face, but they had received a note from the Reich's Propaganda Office advising them that such a display—"humorous as it was"—might be seen as beneath the paper's dignity. How anything might be seen as beneath the *BZ*'s dignity remained open for debate.

Radek stepped around to the back of the car, pulled open the boot, and removed a bag. "The boys are going to stay here," he said, refastening the latch, then bobbing his head toward the gate. "How'd you like to see the stadium, Nikolai?"

They walked in silence along the lamplit arcade: the place seemed to demand that kind of reverence. Flags from the competing countries hung limply from their poles. Searchlights shone high onto the stadium's façade, arching up and over and misting into the gray of the sky.

Hoffner stared up as they passed under the gate. A few stars had managed to break through the cloud cover, but for the most part it was just swirls of black hovering above the iron rings.

Two or three guards strolled along the plaza beyond; all were careful not to notice Radek and his companion.

Hoffner said, "Do you smell that?"

"What?"

"Bad beer and piss."

"I do," said Radek.

"And that's not a problem?"

"Not much they can do about it when the wind shifts."

Hoffner was surprised at the ease of the answer. "So this happens all the time?"

"Three times a day."

Hoffner was waiting for an answer.

"Strength Through Joy Village," Radek finally said. "The thing's about half a kilometer from here. It's even got its own train station."

"You're joking."

"Would I joke about that?"

They made their way between the central columns and into the stadium's main entryway. Their footfalls began to echo.

Radek said, "It comes equipped with Strength Through Joy Beer Halls, Strength Through Joy Children's Tents, Strength Through Joy Crappers. There might even be some Strength Through Joy Tits thrown in, but I think those girls are reserved for the pure Aryan clientele. That's something you don't get on the cruises."

The Strength Through Joy recreation camps and holiday cruises had been set up by the Reich as a thank-you to the working class of Germany. The simple folk were, after all, the very spirit of the Reich. And such spirit—pungent as it was—deserved a little knockwurst and dancing on the cheap.

"Your boots are good?" said Radek. "It's going to be wet."

They mounted a stairway, arrived on the second level, and then moved down a short tunnel. Somewhere toward the middle of the tunnel, the stadium grounds began to come into view.

If Hoffner had hoped to find something clever or demeaning to say, he couldn't. The place was overwrought, militaristic to a fault, self-consciously classical, larger than any other space he had ever seen, and breathtaking.

The curve of the stands pressed up and outward like the perfect ripple of a stone dropped into a still lake. The color was somewhere between the cream white of porcelain and the rough green-gray of sanded limestone. Empty, the seats looked like flawlessly laid tracks—twenty, thirty, sixty of them, circling the field in a series of infinitely rising loops. Everything was bright from the overhead lights, and yet there was no glare. Most remarkable, though, was the field itself, broad and masculine, its grass tufted and thick, glistening from the rain as if its own exertions had produced this rugged sheen. The smell, full and green, lingered, with just a taste of polished stone in the mouth. Hoffner stood in silent wonder.

"It's even better on the grass," said Radek, as he started down the steps. Hoffner had no choice but to follow.

Reaching the bottom of the stairs, both men stepped up onto the low wall and then jumped down to the field. Hoffner felt a slight twinge in his knee. He did what he could to ignore it as they made their way across the six lanes of cinder track and out to the infield. At the far end, the top of the bell tower loomed through the wide and solitary opening in the stadium wall. Even the sky seemed more immense here.

"That's where he'll be coming through tomorrow," Radek said. "Arm up, strutting, *Heil Hitler!*" He flipped his hand in a mock salute. "We might even see a smile."

"I thought you liked Berlin just now?"

"What's not to like?"

They made it to the center of the field and Radek stopped. The silence and size of the place came together in a single rush; odd to feel dizzy without moving.

Radek set the bag down. "And despite what you've heard, he asks for girls." He knelt down and opened the bag. "Young ones. You never want to know what he does with them. The girls never say a word after. It's unpleasant, but he pays well."

Hoffner was still finding his bearings. "I didn't know you'd taken to pimping," he said. "Or are the economic trends good there, too?"

Radek pulled a bottle of champagne and two glasses from the bag. "It's one client, Nikolai. I don't think that makes me a pimp." He stood and handed a glass to Hoffner. "A marked man, yes, but not a pimp."

"So he'll kill you one day."

Radek snorted a laugh. "He's going to kill a great many people one day, Nikolai. At least I'm getting paid."

Radek stepped back and let go with the cork. The echo brought a stream of guards running out onto the first-tier balcony—small, shadowy figures from this far off—and Radek shouted, "Champagne, gentlemen! No worries!"

His voice continued to echo as the men disappeared as quickly as they had come.

"Like trained dogs," said Hoffner.

"They're terrified," said Radek, as he filled Hoffner's glass. "Sabotage. They think some Russian or Jew is going to infiltrate the place, set off a bomb, ruin their fun. Truth is, there's nothing they could do to stop it, but the SS likes to show an effort." Radek poured his own. "No uniforms. You saw that?"

"I did."

Radek smiled and raised his glass. "It's all so damned ridiculous."

Hoffner raised his as well. "And this is for . . . ?"

Radek shook his head easily. "An end. A beginning. Whatever you'd like it to be." He drank.

"The poet pimp," said Hoffner. He drank as well.

"We're going to nip that one in the bud, Nikolai. No more pimp, all right?" Radek finished off his drink and, staring into the glass, said, "You could come work for me. Now that you're done at the Alex."

Hoffner nearly choked as the fizz ran up into his nose. He coughed before answering. "I appreciate the joke."

Radek poured himself a second. "It's no joke."

The two men stared at each other until Hoffner finally said, "Yes. Yes, it is."

Radek needed another few moments before tossing back his drink. He then nodded. "I'm glad I waited, then. Wouldn't have looked so good if you'd said no at Rücker's." He crouched down and set the bottle and glass on the grass. "Pimm said he was waiting until you were done with the

Kripo to give you this stuff." He reached into the bag. "I'm sure he had something pithy he wanted to say before handing it over. I don't."

Radek pulled out half a dozen canisters of film. Each had a small strip of adhesive attached to it, with a name and an initial written in fading ink. He set them on the grass.

"Jesus," Hoffner said in a whisper. He was stunned at what he was seeing.

"Yah," said Radek. "Turns out they never knew he had them. There's some nice stuff of Hess and Streicher. Apparently old Julius shares the Führer's tastes."

The films had been made in 1927 by members of the then fledgling National Socialist German Workers Party, long before they had decided to trim the party name. At the time, the films were innovative, some of the first to take a crack at synchronization of sound. They were also remarkable for having broken new ground with an unimagined kind of depravity—violent and sexual. Hoffner had spent months trying to forget them. His boy Sascha had been in one.

"I thought Pimm burned these," said Hoffner.

"And give up this kind of leverage? He wasn't stupid."

"A lot of good they did him."

Radek said nothing as he continued to stare into the bag. Finally, standing, he said, "Yah." He looked at Hoffner. "You get in trouble, you can always ask Streicher if he wants to run an editorial in *Der Stürmer* on little girls, ropes, and needles. My guess is he'll take a pass."

They stood like this for what seemed a very long time before Radek said, "You want to take a run around it?"

Hoffner was still digesting the last few minutes. "Pardon?"

"The track, Nikolai. A lap."

Radek was being serious; Hoffner half smiled and said, "So the films weren't enough of a treat?"

"Standing in the middle of my legacy is the treat, Nikolai. The films are what they are. The run—that's if you've always had some pathetic dream of breaking the tape. Don't worry, I'll cheer you on at the end, if you want."

Hoffner laughed quietly. "And I deserve all this because . . . ?"

"Don't go to Spain."

"You'll miss me that much?"

"You'll die there."

Hoffner saw the concern in Radek's eyes. It was genuine and therefore all the more unnerving. "You're probably right," Hoffner said.

"It's rifles and bullets, Nikolai. Maybe even some German rifles and bullets."

"Really?"

Radek's gaze sharpened. "Trust me, Nikolai. Two weeks ago we had a crack squad of Wehrmacht troops training out at the Olympic Village. No one knew it, and now they're gone. Makes you wonder where they went with all their desert gear and machine guns. Not much need for desert gear in the Rhineland, is there?" Radek waited for the silence to settle. "This isn't some dustup, Nikolai. You haven't heard from Georg in ten days not because he's up on some hilltop. It's because he's dead. You want to tell his pretty wife and little boy that you tried, fine. But unless you're planning on spending your time sitting in a café in Barcelona drinking the health of the Republic, I don't think you come home." Even Radek's caring had a cruelty to it. "I got off the needles. That's on you. I'm telling you not to go to Spain. That's on me."

Radek leaned over and picked up the bottle. He took a long swig as he walked off. "So is it a lap or not?" he said, gazing off into the stands.

Hoffner stood staring after him, the wide expanse beyond them suddenly small. "Wrong shoes," he said.

Radek looked back. "Fine." He started for the track. "Then pick up your films and let's get out of this shithole."

Hoffner was in a good drunk by the time he made it back to Droysenstrasse. The lights were out in the house, but Lotte had been kind enough to leave the back path lit. He wove his way through the yard, found the door to the carriage house, and hoisted himself up the stairs.

As it turned out, the lecture out at the stadium had been just the tip of the iceberg. Radek, in full political lather, had spent the last three hours taking everyone through the latest reports coming out of Spain and the Rhineland. On Spain he was a bit spotty; his sources were having trouble getting through. Imagine that? But on the rearming of the Rhineland, there he was fully informed.

"Five months and no one's raised a finger against us." He liked to slap his own down onto the table for emphasis. "And we went in on bicycles, for Christ's sake. They'll let us do whatever we want, and it'll be the same in Spain."

It was unclear whether this was good or bad news to Radek. He had fallen asleep before explaining. The fact that his pillow had been the chest of a very fat and very naked girl made it clear that he had no idea where or who he was at the time.

Hoffner steadied himself at the top of the stairs. He did his best with a few of his buttons before finally just pulling the shirt over his head. His shoes and trousers dropped to the floor without too much effort as he fumbled his way onto the bed. Had he been any less drunk he might have jumped at the sudden sight of Elena looking back at him.

"I hear you're going to Spain tomorrow," she said.

Hoffner took a moment to appreciate the very fine pair of breasts staring up at him. He nodded.

"So you might be killed," she said. "And then we'd never have done something this stupid."

He needed another few moments before saying, "I'm drunk."

"Yes," she said. "Is that going to get in the way?"

This required no thought. He shook his head.

"Good."

She pulled back the rest of the covers and invited him in.

CLIMBING BOOTS AND SHORT PANTS

At 8:00 a.m. on the dot, the band of the Berlin Guards Regiment sounded *Ein Grosses Wecken*—a grand reveille—outside the Hotel Adlon. Luckily, Hoffner was far enough removed across town to sleep through it.

The members of the International Olympic Committee, however, were not. Given just over an hour to wash, shave, and eat—always avoid the rabbit crepes at the Adlon—they were then shuttled off to either the Berlin

Cathedral or the Church of St. Hedwig (Protestants on the left, Catholics on the right) for an hour of religious observance so as to fortify themselves for the day's events. While they prayed, thousands of children—all across the city's recreation fields—began to perform in exhibitions of group gymnastics, obstacle races, and synchronized club twirling: the object here to show the many athletic pursuits of Berlin's schoolchildren. Mendy, having watched the neighborhood children prepare for these displays over the last weeks, and eager himself to twist and leap and bend along with them, had been told he was too young and too Jewish to be included. Lotte decided to keep him inside for the day.

Still later, as Hoffner stirred from a remarkably deep sleep (retirement and robust late-night exertions will do that), an honor guard from the Wehrmacht, along with various uniformed Hitler Youth detachments, looked on from Unter den Linden as the Belgian delegate—a Monsieur Baillet-Latour—laid a wreath at the Tomb of the Unknown Soldier; so nice to have all the hostilities between the two countries long forgotten, even better to see military sacrifice as the prelude to amateur sport.

By mid-morning, it was Hermann Göring—always so dapper in his sky-blue uniform—welcoming the IOC members and his Führer to the Old Museum in front of the Royal Palace a few blocks down. While Hoffner shaved, thousands of SS men and ever more Hitler Youth regaled them by singing:

Hoist up our flags in the wind of the morning!
To those who are idle, let them flutter a warning!

No one was even remotely idle as the dashing Baldur von Schirach—twenty-nine and leader of the Youth—stepped to the podium and addressed the crowds with the truly inspirational words, "We, the youth of Germany, we, the youth of Adolf Hitler, greet you, the youth of the world." Unter den Linden erupted in applause and cheering as the torchbearer finally appeared.

There was a quiet intensity along the avenue as the white-clad young man jogged slowly to the museum, lit the flame, and then jogged back across the square, where another pyre awaited him. The "flames of peace," so Göring had promised, would burn throughout the games. No one had mentioned Berlin's good fortune to have several libraries and bookstores in the immediate vicinity, should the flames need feeding.

Lotte was at the kitchen table reading through the *Tageblatt* when Hoffner finally appeared at the door. She kept her eyes on the paper. "You'll be joining us for lunch?" she said.

He was still feeling the whiskey at the back of his throat; it was enough just to nod. He noticed Elena by the sink, washing and peeling something. Mendy was under the table with a train.

Lotte continued to read. "Yes or no?"

Hoffner managed a croaked, "Yes."

Lotte looked up and said, "If you could fix another plate, Elena, that would be very nice."

Elena dried her hands and moved to the stove. "Bit of a cold, Herr Chief Inspector?" she said.

"No," he said. "Just getting old."

"You've a long way to go there, Herr Chief Inspector," she said. "Don't let anyone tell you otherwise."

Hoffner caught Lotte staring at him for a moment. Just as quickly she leaned under the table. "Lunch, Mendy." She looked back at Hoffner. "We're all done playing."

It was nearly half past one before Hoffner made it to the middle of town. The crowds were already out at the stadium, the athletes due to arrive within the hour, Hitler by four. To keep them all entertained, the Olympic Committee had enlisted the services of the Berlin Philharmonic, the National Orchestra, and—how could they go on without them?—the Bayreuth Wagner Festival choir, all three en masse with soaring renditions of the *Meistersinger* overture, Liszt's *Les Preludes*, and anything else with lots of trumpets and trombones. The stadium had yet to open its beer and wine concessions, so the louder the better.

Hoffner stepped down from the tram, crossed Kaiser-Wilhelm-Strasse, and pushed through the door at number 17.

The Berlin office of the British Pathé Gazette Company was three rooms at the top of a rather sweet if old five-floor walk-up: one secretary, four filmmakers, and all of them with the singular task of covering Germans in the news. Hoffner had stopped in twice before: the first time three years ago, to see Georg's new digs; the second last month, when Mendy had been rushed to the hospital after falling down the stairs. The telephones at Georg's had somehow gone out. Luckily, Hoffner had been at the Alex, only a fifteen-minute walk—or ten-minute run—depending on the traffic. Papi and Opa had arrived at the hospital to find Mendy unbroken and utterly delighted to be sporting a very long bandage on his leg. He had limped for two days after—each day a different leg—until Lotte had told him to knock it off.

Anthony Wilson was leaning out an open window behind his desk, peering off into the distance, when Hoffner stepped into the office. Hoffner shut the door, and Wilson ducked his head under his arm to see who it was.

"Hallo there, Inspector."

Wilson was a young thirty-two, with too much enthusiasm for a man his age. He continued to peer back in this odd position before saying, "Join me?" Wilson returned to his viewing, and Hoffner had no choice but to step over, remove his hat, and inch his head out. The damp was oddly thick up here.

Wilson said, "A fellow across the way on four says that when the street's clear, you can actually hear the music." He was straining his ear westward. "Out at the stadium, I mean."

Even his German sounded like public school English. Hoffner imagined all those years Wilson had spent working on the "Bosch" while his friends had been struggling through Horace and Sappho. Not much newsreel work, though, in ancient Rome and Athens.

The wind picked up, and Hoffner said, "You know that's not really possible, Herr Wilson."

"Oh, I know," he said. "But they get a nice kick out of seeing the Englishman stick his head out the window. They're placing bets on it. How long I can go. They don't think I know about it. They'll be wondering who you are in a minute or two."

"So we'll be out here that long?"

Wilson looked over, then smiled. "Fair enough." He ducked under, and Hoffner followed. Immediately, Wilson began to smooth back what little hair he had. He was tall like Georg, but with an inordinately narrow head. "Someone on the fourth floor's just won a bit of money." He smiled again, motioned Hoffner to a chair, and took his own behind the desk.

Hoffner stepped over and sat. He was trying to convince himself that Wilson's airy mood was a good sign. Then again, the man might just have been an idiot.

"Any word?" asked Hoffner.

Wilson's face did its best with a look of seriousness: the mouth remained closed even as the jaw dropped a bit. Was it possible for the face to grow longer?

"'Any word,'" Wilson repeated pensively. He looked across at Hoffner. "No. No word, Inspector. But I shouldn't be too concerned."

The English were always so good with an empty phrase. Hoffner waited and then said, "The trouble is, Herr Wilson, I am."

There was some quick nodding from Wilson as he retreated. "Yes, yes, of course you are. I am as well. Naturally. I just mean it's still early days. Everyone involved with POG was moved to a safe—"

"Pog?" Hoffner interrupted.

Wilson seemed surprised by the question. "POG—People's Olympic Games?" When Hoffner said nothing, Wilson added, "Why Georg went?"

Another favorite of the English: the meaningless acronym.

Georg's reason for going to Spain was, of course, not news to Hoffner. In fact, it had been impossible to be in Berlin over the past few months and not hear all the updates on the highly controversial, if equally pointless, *Protestspiele.* Barcelona for the people. Barcelona for the Games of Protest. Ludicrous.

"No," Hoffner said. "I know why Georg went, Herr Wilson. I just didn't know the games were called"—he hesitated—"POG."

Wilson flipped open a cigarette box on his desk and offered one to Hoffner. "Well, technically, it's just a few of us here at Pathé Gazette, Inspector. Makes it so much easier in wires and the like. POG this. POG that. You understand." He lit Hoffner's cigarette and took one for himself. "No point in using it now, though, is there? Still, as I said, everyone was moved to a safe spot once the trouble began." He lit up.

"And where exactly do you find a safe spot in Spain these days, Herr Wilson?"

Wilson let out a stream of smoke. For an instant Hoffner thought he saw something behind the eyes: it was strangely familiar and then just as quickly gone. Wilson said, "That's probably a very good question, Inspector."

"And yet I shouldn't be concerned."

"Georg wanted to go on filming. Do you blame him? We both know he's gotten himself out of deeper holes than this."

"Has he?" Hoffner saw it again in the eyes. He let it pass. "And how does one lose track of a man eager to go on filming?"

"It's a war, Inspector." The tone was mildly sharper. "It takes time for things to settle in."

It was a callous answer, and not in keeping with the Wilson of only moments ago. Hoffner took a long pull and said, "By the way, it's no longer inspector. Just Herr Hoffner. My papers went through yesterday."

"Really?" Wilson said. He leaned in and, focusing on the glass, began to curl his cigarette into the ashtray. "Good for you."

And there it was: the eyes and the voice coming together. Hoffner was struck by how obvious it seemed.

It was the way Wilson had said it—"Good for you"—that went beyond mere congratulations. There was a relief in the voice, as if making it to the end of a career unscathed deserved a nod of admiration. As if, one day, Wilson hoped he might make it there himself.

Hoffner continued to watch as Wilson played with the ash. "Yes—it is," he said. "I imagine you'd like to get there one day yourself."

Wilson stayed with the cigarette. "Pardon?"

"The job. It can be rather dangerous. Nice when you survive and get the pat on the back at the end." Hoffner watched Wilson spend too much time with the ash. Finally Hoffner said, "Which branch?"

Wilson took a moment too long before looking up. "Which branch . . . ? I'm afraid I don't understand." The amiable smile was really quite a feat.

"War Office or Admiralty? Or is the British Secret Intelligence Service all under the same roof these days?" When Wilson said nothing, Hoffner added, "Thirty years, Herr Wilson. I think I know when I hear a cop."

A car horn from the street broke through, but Wilson continued to stare. His smile became more masklike as the eyes began to sharpen: rare to see intelligence growing on a man's face.

"Just like that," he said. There was now a quiet certainty in the voice.

"Like what?" said Hoffner.

"Georg said you were uncanny at what you did. Hard to believe that good." There was nothing accusatory in it. "When did he tell you?"

"Tell me what?"

Wilson crushed out his cigarette and then nodded to himself. "Fair enough." He sat back. "We can play it that way. He's too useful to us to care one way or the other."

Hoffner watched the self-satisfied indifference across the desk.

Georg—an agent of British Intelligence. Hoffner was torn between a feeling of pride and terror.

"How long?" he said.

"How long what?"

"How long has Georg been with you?"

Wilson looked up. "What is it you want, Herr Inspe—" He caught himself. "Herr Hoffner?"

"He wouldn't have told me. You know that."

Wilson continued to stare. "No, I suppose he wouldn't have." He waited, then reached down to the bottom drawer. He returned with a bottle and two glasses and placed them on the desk: it seemed every office in Berlin was fitted with a set. "You really had no idea, did you?" Hoffner said nothing and Wilson poured. "Amazing how he fell into our laps. But then, everything got tossed around in 'thirty-three, didn't it?" Wilson recorked the bottle, took his glass, and sat back.

"I'm sure it's easy to see it that way, from a distance."

"No, no, I know," Wilson said blandly. "I'm sure Georg was devastated. Angry. Six years with Ufa and they throw him out." Hoffner's eyes remained empty. "Ufa-Tonwoche has always been a second-rate newsreel studio," Wilson said. "Georg was too good a cameraman and director to be stuck there. He was lucky to move on."

"So you made him your offer before they found his work too degenerate?" Hoffner took his glass. "Or was that later when you recognized his talents and his anger?" He drank.

Wilson took another cigarette from the box and lit it. "I think I'm going to continue calling you inspector, Inspector. It'll make me feel so much better about all this."

"Is that in some manual someplace?"

Wilson smiled as he exhaled. It was his first honest expression in the last ten minutes. "I'm sure it is." He took another pull. "You're expecting me to say that my father was some old beat cop, tough, hard-drinking, and this is my way of making him proud."

"No," Hoffner said. He finished his own cigarette and began to crush it out. "Your father was a banker—Harrow, Eton—the same places you went. The only moment of real disappointment came when you chose Oxford over Cambridge—or Cambridge over Oxford—whichever let him know you were your own man." Hoffner let go of the cigarette. "He finds the whole newsreel business silly, but if he only knew what it was you were really doing . . . Closer?"

To his credit, Wilson had kept his smile. "It was Winchester, then Cambridge."

"My mistake." Hoffner brushed the ash from his hands. "Old beat cops don't produce men like you, Herr Wilson. They produce the boys who go and die for your principles."

Wilson's eyes showed a moment of genuine regard. Both men knew it had no place here.

Hoffner said, "I've been thinking of taking a trip to Spain."

"Have you? Bit dodgy there right now."

"I'm going after him."

"No, I don't think you are."

"And why is that?" Hoffner watched as Wilson took a drink. "Where was he filming, Herr Wilson?"

"The retired Kripoman decides to go and—"

"Yes," said Hoffner. "I know. Get himself killed. I've been warned."

"Oh, I don't care if you get killed." There was nothing malicious in the voice, not even a hint of that very brave English self-sacrifice. Wilson was simply trying to move them beyond the obvious. "I'm sure that would be tragic in some meaningless way—and isn't that always the worst sort of tragedy—but I just don't think you'd be much good. Do you even have Spanish or Catalan?" Hoffner said nothing, and Wilson continued. "Nothing better than seeing a nice little German in his climbing boots and short pants, sweating his way from one café to the next, asking about his boy gone missing: 'Excuse me, señor, do you speak German?'"

"And I imagine Georg was fluent?"

Wilson gave nothing away. "Now if the boy happened to be some sad-sack Communist or socialist out to fight back the new fascists, I doubt anyone pays much attention. More troubling when the boy works for a British newsreel company—and a Jew to boot—and his daddy starts asking around. You see where I'm going with this?"

Hoffner looked at the bald pate across from him; even the shine seemed more credible now. "You really think the SS doesn't know exactly what you are?"

"What the SS does or doesn't know isn't my concern. I just don't like helping them along. And if they're interested in Georg, so much the easier to let his sixty-year-old father lead them right to him."

"I'm glad I inspire so much confidence." Hoffner set his glass on the desk. "And why would the SS be so concerned with Georg?"

"The Spanish fascists haven't a chance if they don't get help from the outside; we both know that. And we both know where that help will be coming from. The trouble is, we're all promising not to get involved in Spain—England, Russia, Italy, France. Even the Germans are willing to make that promise. Imagine if someone starts nosing around and finds out that the Nazis won't be keeping their word. Especially when they're the ones throwing the big international party out at their new stadium. Not so good for the image. Not so good for Georg." He took a last pull and crushed out the cigarette in the ashtray.

"So what did you send Georg off to find?"

Wilson flicked something from his finger and sat back casually. "I didn't send him off to find anything."

Men like this were always so effortless with a lie, thought Hoffner. "I see—because of that promise you'll all be making not to get involved."

"We *won't* be getting involved."

"Yes, I'm sure that's true."

Wilson was no less glib. "We do happen to be running a news organization, Inspector. On occasion that means having to film the news. Barcelona and its Olimpiada—that was news. So Georg went."

"And he just happened to be in the right place at the right time."

"Whatever the reason he went, there's nothing I can do to stop you from going after him now. I'm just hoping you understand what's at stake."

"Georg's life, I think."

"Oh, is that what you think this is about—a single life?" Wilson set his glass on the desk. "If you're that naïve you won't make it out of the Friedrichstrasse Banhof."

"I'm not much on trains."

"Then he'll be dead by the time your boat docks."

"I've always found flying much more efficient."

For the first time Wilson hesitated. It was the silence that held him.

"You have a plane," he finally said. "That's good. That's very good." He took another cigarette and lit up. "Don't tell me how or where. Unregistered planes are a rare thing to get hold of these days."

Wilson stared at Hoffner for another few moments and then was on his feet. He pulled a set of keys from his pocket and stepped over to the floor safe. Kneeling down, he used two of the keys to open it. He retrieved a single sheet of paper and shut the door. He set the page in front of Hoffner. There were five words written on it:

HISMA: BERNHARDT, LANGENHEIM; HANSHEN: VOLLMAN

"His last wire," said Wilson. "Five days ago from somewhere in Barcelona. It's impossible to say where."

Hoffner continued to stare at the sheet. "And you've decided I should have this now?"

Wilson sat. "We don't have enough people in there to send someone looking for him. You know that. Not that sending someone in would be much good. But since you're taking that trip . . ."

"These are German names. I'm a German."

Wilson was now leaning back, his eyes fixed on Hoffner. "I'll keep that in mind. We think these are the names of contacts he made or locations. The trouble is, we need to keep a low profile. As I said, not the time for us to be digging around. Hisma and Hanshen might be names. More likely they're not. That's where I'd start."

"Very generous of you."

"Yes—it is. Of course, you don't have to go if you don't want."

It was Wilson's strongest card: giving Hoffner a way out and knowing he would never take it.

Hoffner picked up the sheet. "From the look of it, Bernhardt and Langenheim are connected to Hisma. Vollman to Hanshen."

"I agree. So that should make it easier."

Hoffner had no idea why Wilson thought that. Nonetheless, he folded the paper and placed it in his coat pocket.

"And when I find him?"

"You'll bring him back."

Hoffner saw a drop of whiskey in his glass. He picked it up and tossed it down. He stood.

He was at the door when he turned and put on his hat. "By the way, I don't own a pair of climbing boots."

The amiable smile returned. "How very nice for you."

His valise was already packed and waiting by the foyer door when Hoffner got home. There was no point in checking through it; Lotte would have thought of everything. He followed the sound of her piano-playing into the sitting room.

She was working through a rough passage of something. He dropped his hat onto a chair as she continued to play.

"Long meeting," she said.

He moved a cushion on the sofa and sat. "Yes."

"And he was helpful?"

"Enough."

She was making a complete mess of the left hand. She tried a few more times and then stopped. She looked over. "You told him you were going?"

Hoffner nodded. He thought she might launch into something else, but she just sat there, staring at him. Finally she said, "Good." She stood and stepped out from behind the piano. "Do you have time for an early dinner?"

"I think so, yes."

"Mendy wouldn't nap." She was crossing toward the hallway. "You might want to go up."

As she passed, Hoffner said, "Wilson seemed very confident."

She was inside the archway when she stopped. She turned. Her eyes told him nothing. "You don't mind leftover chicken, do you?"

Hoffner shook his head.

"Good. We'll have that then." She tried a smile before moving off down the hall.

Upstairs, Mendy was at his writing table, deep into a drawing.

"I hear we lost the nap again," Hoffner said.

Mendy continued to draw.

"Maybe you're getting too old for that." Hoffner stepped over and cocked his head to see what the boy was drawing: blob and badge were front and center. "Not such a bad thing to be too old for a nap."

The pencil continued to move, and Mendy said, "Does that mean I can go?"

"Go where?"

"With you and Papi?"

Hoffner pulled over another small chair. His knees were almost to his chin as he sat. "I don't think so, Mendy." He expected the little face to turn, but the boy was showing some resolve. Hoffner said, "Papi always brings you something nice. I can bring you something, too."

"I don't want anything."

"How do you know when you don't know what it is?"

Mendy finished his drawing, handed it to Hoffner, took another piece of paper, and started in again.

Hoffner watched as the little hand moved, the other pressed down on the page to keep it in place. He couldn't see the face, not that it would have helped. It was nearly half a minute before Hoffner decided to look again at the drawing he was holding. He then stood.

When he reached the door he said, "Thank you for the picture." Mendy kept to his drawing, and Hoffner said, "I'll see you downstairs."

Mendy never made it to dinner. In fact, he stayed in his room even after the cab arrived. The worst of it came during the walk down the front path. There was still enough sun in the sky to catch a little face and eyes in the window, but Hoffner refused to turn.

Even so, the thought of them stayed with him for the forty-minute ride. It would have been longer had the cabbie not been clever and taken them south from the start. Anything else and they would have hit traffic heading west to the games. Luckily Johannisthal was far enough south, and far enough east, to keep it immune. Tempelhof, where all the big aeroplanes had been landing, was a zoo now. Mueller had been smart to keep himself out here.

"My tires blow on this," said the cabbie, "and you'll be the one paying for the spares. Understood?"

The man had been grumbling for the past ten minutes. Most of the roads around Johannisthal were little more than stomped-down grass and ruts. The modern touches—tarmac and lighting—were reserved for the airstrips: this time of night, the cab's headlights were no match for the sudden dips and turns.

When the cabbie finally reached his limit, he pulled up about fifty meters from the old air show bandstands and reached back to open the door. They were sitting in the middle of a deserted field, the beams from the headlights spilling out like two narrow pancakes. "You're close enough," he said.

The big hangars were beyond another field, but Hoffner was happy enough to let the man go. He stood and watched the taillights bounce along the grass—the engine's grind a thinning echo—before he picked up the valise and headed across the mud. The smell of sewage and sulfur seemed to follow him. By the time Hoffner stepped into the last of the hangars, his shirt was damp through to the waist.

The place reeked of gasoline, even with the doors wide open. The cement floor was a trail of brown and black puddles, with tire marks crisscrossing the entire landscape. Twelve or so aeroplanes were parked along the walls—German, French, English—most of them stripped of parts in aid of the others. Elsewhere, pieces of engine were neatly laid out on sheets, while wheels and the like rested against walls and toolboxes. As far as Hoffner could tell, there were no signs of life.

Stepping farther in, he recognized a few antiques among the four or five untouched planes: a Sopwith Snipe in nice condition; better still was the single-seater Albatros fighter, 180-hp of liquid-cooled speed. Hoffner remembered how Georg had been able to recite the specifications from memory: little wooden models dragged off to a park or set in rows along a windowsill. Hoffner even recalled helping the boy with one of them. Or two. Or not.

"You've lost weight."

The voice echoed, and Hoffner tried to locate its source. He set his valise down and said, "Hello, Toby."

"I hope that doesn't mean you've stopped drinking?"

Toby Mueller appeared from behind the tail of one of the pilfered planes. Mueller was of average build, but the limp in his right leg made him seem shorter. He had lost part of the foot, along with several fingers, during the war. Neither had stopped him from flying.

Hoffner said, "You've quite a collection."

"Yah," said Mueller, as he rubbed a bit of grease off his good hand: the fingers on the other held the rag like two pincers. "Didn't think I'd actually be seeing you."

"Sorry to disappoint."

They had known each other for over twenty years, Mueller the gimp World War I ace and Hoffner the cop who made sure he never got caught for smuggling. They had met on a hillside in the Tyrol, toasting Victor König, Hoffner's onetime partner and Mueller's squadron leader. Two months later they had buried König. It was a bond impossible to break.

"No, it's good for me," said Mueller. "Eight—ten hours. Bit long on my own."

"So you were going anyway?"

Mueller's smirk held just the right mix of disbelief and mockery. "No, Nikolai, I'm doing all this for you. Here, let me get your bag." Mueller remained where he was and nodded over to a single-propeller biplane. "We're taking the Arado. You can put it in the bomb hold."

Hoffner picked up the valise and made his way over. The plane was two seats in tandem set behind the twin wings, the whole thing maybe eight meters in length, two and a half meters in height. Hoffner had expected them to be taking the beauty next to it, a red single-wing affair, with room for at least four, and who knows what else in the undercarriage. If Mueller was planning on making this a business trip, the red one looked to have far more room for merchandise.

Mueller saw where Hoffner was looking. "She's nice, isn't she?"

Hoffner found the latch on the Arado and shoved his valise inside.

Mueller said, "They've clocked her at nearly three hundred kph. And that's not even in a dive. It's like riding cut glass."

Hoffner had no idea what Mueller meant but nodded anyway as he started over.

Mueller said, "She'd have us there in six hours, maybe less."

"But she's not yours, is she?"

"Oh, she's mine. Had her down in Marseilles last week for some very nice fishing."

"I'm sure the catch was good."

"The catch is always good, Nikolai."

Whatever Mueller was smuggling, Hoffner knew not to get involved in the details. "She's just not for us," he said.

Mueller's smirk reappeared. "It's a night flight, Nikolai. The Lockheed might be quick, but she's not so good after dark. Trust me. The little Arado is a much better bet."

Hoffner was rarely impressed by Mueller's acquisitions, but this was something even for him. "How the hell did you get your hands on an American plane?"

Mueller's smirk became a broad smile. "Well, there might have been a girl or two, and some French Air Corps mechanics involved, but I can't really say."

"Or," said Zenlo Radek, who was now standing at the hangar's entrance, "he might just have walked in here one day and found the plane waiting for him."

Both Hoffner and Mueller looked over to see Radek in a dinner jacket and bow tie, his hair slicked back: hard to imagine the skin on his forehead looking more strained than usual, but there it was. He was carrying a small satchel.

Hoffner turned back to Mueller, and Mueller's smile reemerged. "Well, it might have been something like that, too." Mueller patted a few fingers on Hoffner's shoulder and began to limp off toward the Arado. "Evening, Herr Radek."

Radek was now making his way over. "She's all gassed, Toby?"

Mueller nodded and ducked under the propeller. "All gassed."

Hoffner turned again to Radek and said, "Very nice. Casino night?"

"Big party out at Göring's."

"And you're bringing the girls?"

Radek drew up and held the satchel out to Hoffner. "Here."

Hoffner hesitated before taking it. He pulled back the flap and saw two or three thick rolls of Spanish pesetas, the same in German marks and English pounds. There were perhaps ten packs of cigarettes. Tucked in at the bottom was a Luger pistol and several boxes of ammunition.

Radek said, "No idea if the peseta is still worth anything, but the marks and pounds should do you all right. I was thinking of throwing in some francs, but no one ever wants francs, do they?"

Hoffner closed the flap. "Didn't know Toby was on the payroll."

"He likes it that way."

"So what's he taking to Spain?"

"You."

"And bringing back?"

Radek laughed quietly. "Toby thinks he deserves a holiday—gimping around Spain with a few bandages on his shit hand and leg. He thinks it'll have all those girls eager to soothe his pain."

From somewhere Mueller's voice rose up. "I'll be a regular war hero. *¡Viva la Revolución!*"

"It's a civil war, idiot!" Radek shouted back. He looked at Hoffner. "He also heard you needed a lift."

"And you couldn't convince him otherwise?"

"I might not have tried all that hard."

There was a chance Hoffner might give in to the sentiment. Instead, he said, "Then I'll try not to get myself killed."

Twenty minutes later, Hoffner felt his stomach lurch as the plane climbed over Berlin. He peered out at the lights and saw the brightest of them off in the west. They were circling the stadium in a ring of fire, Nazi spectacle at its best. He stared at the flames, as they wavered and pitched, and imagined them washing over the city whole. He then turned his eyes to the night and did what he could to forget them.

3

FINGERS SO RAW

It was like climbing through sifted dust. The heat smelled of the sea, but it was only a tease. Worse was the sand that kicked up from the path and clung to the skin like dying ants. Mueller seemed to be enjoying it.

"I'm not impressed," Hoffner said, as Mueller continued to hum. "You're baking in this the same way I am."

Mueller placed his good hand on the rock face and ducked around a jutting stone. "How's that valise holding up?"

Mueller had been kind enough to rig a few ropes around the thing, with the satchel tied on at the back. Hoffner was wearing them like a rucksack, although the valise was far too long for his back.

"Fine," he said.

"I'm sure it is."

They had left the plane fifteen minutes ago. Mueller had waited for first light before bringing them low into the coast. It was clear that this was the usual drill, a strip of beach south of the city, far enough removed to be of no practical use to anyone except the truly gifted. Hoffner had kept his eyes closed for the last two minutes of the flight, certain that the water or the rocks would be making quick work of them. Instead, Mueller had brought them down, with two short bumps and a quick turn. Even with his eyes opened, Hoffner had been unable to fathom the speed, drop, and length of the landing. He had been equally amazed to discover the sand-colored tarpaulin awaiting them in a nearby cave: five minutes to drape the Arado; another five to rig the valise. Now, from a vantage point high above the beach, Hoffner had no hope of finding the plane.

"It's up here," said Mueller, as they came to the top of the scarp. Something resembling a road lay a few meters off, with a thick copse of trees beyond it. Mueller started through the shrub grass. It was only then that Hoffner remembered the limp.

"You make that climb look easy, Toby."

"Rocks are uneven," said Mueller. "We balance each other out."

There was no such luck under the trees: roots and branches were particularly rough on Mueller, but he said nothing. Twenty meters in they came to an opening and a second tarpaulin. Mueller pulled it off to reveal an old Hispano-Suiza: a four-seat, open-back saloon with two oversized front lights and an undercarriage that poked out beyond the grille like a giant tongue. The windscreen was folded down onto the bonnet and gave the entire thing the look of a long-faced priest caught in a state of permanent terror.

" 'Twenty-two Torpedo," said Mueller. "Not bad for fifteen years."

"Bit stingy of Radek."

"Why?" Mueller said, tossing the tarpaulin into the back and propping up the windscreen. "She runs better now than she did when I got her." He slid behind the wheel while Hoffner disentangled himself from the valise; his shirt was a thin layer of perspiration. "We pass through a few towns; then it's open road for about an hour. After that it's walking again, just outside the city."

He started the engine as Hoffner settled in.

"You might want to have your pistol on your lap," Mueller said. "Up to you. I don't mind if you sleep." He put the car in gear and maneuvered them out through the trees.

Talk of the gun had been a joke. The coast road to Barcelona was empty, not that there was any safety in it. The thing snaked above the water like curled twine and clung to the shrubland and rock as if any sudden movement might spill it into the sea. The glare was no less daunting and made anything more than a few hundred meters ahead fade into the rust and sand-washed rise of the hills. There might have been a rifle—or two, or twelve—fixed on them from above; then again, there might have been nothing.

Mueller kept his good hand on the wheel, his other limp in his lap. Changing gears required a sudden explosion of energy, good foot and bad foot tangoing along the pedals, while the gap-filled hand struggled to find its grip on the gearshift. Hoffner was glad for the few stretches of straight road.

The first signs of life appeared around one of the curves. A line of ageless women walked in twos along the siding, each carrying a large straw basket, eyes locked on the plodding regularity of their feet: if there was a civil war some thirty kilometers up the road, they had yet to hear of it. Mueller took the car wide, and Hoffner stared back as two of the women glanced up. Their lips were parched and red and full with unknowable smiles. There was a heat to these women that seemed to mock the sun. One of them waved, and Hoffner brought an awkward hand up.

"You'll have to do better than that," Mueller said, his eyes fixed on the road.

Hoffner watched as the last of the faces slipped behind the curve. "What?"

"They were laughing at you. You know that, don't you?"

Hoffner settled back in. "Were they?"

"The wave." Mueller smiled. "That was precious, Nikolai."

The car began to climb, and Hoffner realized how raw the scars would always be with Mueller: an unseen kindness taken for betrayal, a woman's smile the prelude to humiliation. There was no escaping that kind of self-damning.

Hoffner peered into the haze of the sky. "It's a different sun now." Even the blue of the water seemed to pale under it.

"Is it?" Mueller snorted. "More of a punch here than on Droysenstrasse? Wait till you head inland."

Mueller downshifted, and a village appeared in the distance around another turn. Hovering behind it was a wide surge of rock—Herr Wilson's balding pate in limestone and brush—which rose some two hundred meters from the base of the hills and made the houses below look like tiny pieces of bone tumbling from a shattered skull.

"Not Berlin," said Hoffner. "Here. Different from what it was. Different from the way a boy sees it."

For the first time Mueller glanced over. He saw the sweat peeling down Hoffner's cheek and neck. He turned back to the road. "Never pictured you as a boy." Hoffner said nothing, and Mueller added, "Take a drink, Nikolai. You're going red."

The road began to dip, and Hoffner heard the waves over the churning of the engine. "We came in the summers," he said. "A month at a time." He found the canteen. "Calella. It's about two hours north of here."

"I know the place."

"It was for my mother's health, I think—or mine. I don't remember anymore." Hoffner took a swig. "The Kripo gave that kind of time back then. They didn't pay, but they let my father go."

Mueller took the canteen. "Long way to come for health."

"Yah." Hoffner was still staring out.

"He had a girl in Calella, your father? Waiting for him?" Mueller drank. Hoffner nodded absently.

"You knew?"

Hoffner caught sight of a bird diving into the water. The wings and beak drew to a fine point and then were gone. An instant later the bird reappeared and flew off. "I suppose," he said. "Not much need for discretion with an eight-year-old." He took the canteen and drank deeply.

"And your mother?"

Hoffner screwed the cap on until it was tight. He remembered her standing in a doorway, her arm bloodied, the sun streaked across her face as she stared out through dry, unfeeling eyes. There was nothing else to it—no moment before or after to give it meaning—save perhaps a boy's untried compassion. Even now Hoffner couldn't tell if he was recalling or inventing it.

"I ate a lot of rice," he said. "And fish. And I learned how to bend hooks for the fishing boats. You can't imagine your fingers so raw."

Hoffner was too late in realizing what he had said, and Mueller said, "No, I suppose I can't."

The sea disappeared behind a rise in the earth, and within a minute the road had narrowed to a single lane. The first hovels appeared on either side, with the smell of sour milk in the air. Hoffner recalled that, too, and wondered how he had ever managed to forget it.

"Jesus!"

Mueller jammed his foot on the brake as they took the next curve. A small barricade, made up of chairs, rugs, and whatever else had been scraped together, stretched across the road. A man with a rifle over his shoulder—his face pale from the heat—emerged from one of the crumbling houses, his hand raised in an unpolished authority. He pulled up to the car as a second figure stepped out from the doorway. Both were in shirtsleeves, with suspenders to draw the trousers high on the waist and red neckerchiefs tied loosely at the throat. The man kept his rifle on his back as he held out his hand.

"*Vale*," he said, as if this were a formality.

Hoffner expected a spray of broken Spanish from Mueller, the offer of a thick wad of bills. Instead, Mueller reached into his pocket and, no less casually, pulled out a crumpled piece of paper. Hoffner sat amazed.

Mueller handed the paper to the man and said in a perfect Spanish, "You've moved it up the hill. That's a bit rough. I might have driven right into it."

The man continued to glance at the page. He handed it back and nodded over at Hoffner. "Another German *socialista* come to fight?"

"Something like that," said Mueller. He reached under the seat and pulled out a bottle of brandy. He handed it to the man. "I'm guessing there's still that ban on alcohol."

The man said, "And it matters?" He turned and tossed the bottle to his friend, who caught it and pulled back part of the barricade—room enough for a car to drive through. The man then turned to Mueller. "The stamp on your pass comes due tomorrow. A cartload of brandy won't help you then."

"I'll keep it in mind."

The man stepped back. "They've moved the checkpoint on the other side as well." He nodded for Mueller to drive on. "Don't run into that one."

Mueller put the car in gear, and Hoffner waited until they were out of earshot. "Old friend of yours?" he said.

Mueller remained silent as he continued to stare ahead. He took them down into the town square, where a pious if haggard-looking church stood at one end, immune to the filth and disarray of the skiffs and fishing nets lazing at the other. The sea and the docks opened up beyond them, but there seemed to be no sound coming from the waves. It was just the smell of salt and wet fur. Lines of drying sheets blew in the breeze, but the place was strangely empty. Mueller followed the street up to where the second barricade appeared, just beyond the last of the houses. Another bottle, and they were back on the coast road.

Hoffner said, "They're not going to win this thing if all it takes is a few bottles of booze."

Mueller reached for the canteen. "That's a courtesy, Nikolai." He had the spout to his lips. "You and I don't have that piece of paper, we're lying on the side of the road back there, a single bullet hole through the back of the skull for each of us." He drank.

"Good that you had it, then."

"Yes."

"And they're selling these pieces of paper in Marseilles?"

Mueller held the canteen out to him. "You haven't met these boys, Nikolai. These are the true believers. Nothing's for sale with them."

Hoffner took a drink. "So you just asked for one and they gave it to you?"

Mueller stared ahead, his smile at once coy and obvious. "Some of us didn't have to ask." The road straightened, and Mueller pressed down on the accelerator.

It was nearly an hour before they turned in from the coast, a dirt path that ran through thick grassland dotted with carob, olive, and fig trees. They were heading up toward Montjuïc—Jew Mountain, according to Mueller— one of those ancient hills on which ancient cities plant themselves. Mueller had promised a fortress at the top that had seen ancient Romans or Muslims or whichever invading conqueror the Catalans had so bravely sent back into the sea, time and time again. Hoffner had always thought cities like this too comfortable in their pasts to make any present-day swagger seem more than a borrowed vanity: the fading libertine—wrinkled, bronzed, and smelling of a too-sweet cologne—drawing strength only from memory.

And yet it wasn't all that long ago that the hill had known sheep and cows and goats and, somewhere off in the distance, those long stalks of yellow wheat that a woman could thresh and grind into whatever might keep a family alive: twelve hundred years of tradition rooted out by a city once again desperate to move beyond itself. The world had come to Barcelona in 1929, and sheep and cows and goats were not what the world was meant to see. Instead, it was a mechanical fountain that swayed under the lights; a grand palace to rival any of the most lavish in Europe; pavilions to tease with tastes of Galicia, Valencia, and Andalucia; and views of the city to make even the worst kind of frippery seem worthwhile.

The World's Fair had transformed Montjuïc, or at least that part of the hill which faced the city. It was now a glowing tribute to Barcelona's past, present, and future. For Hoffner, though—coming up on it from the backside—it was little more than a rise of brush and thick trees, with a few tracks leading nowhere.

"Bit of a risk, leaving the car up here," Mueller said, as he downshifted and willed the old sedan up the slope. They were well into the tree cover now, grateful for a respite from the sun. "We'll do a little painting before we go. Find it a good spot."

It was impossible to mount Montjuïc head on. Instead, they lumbered up one of the slaloming paths until, about fifty meters from the top, they stopped. Mueller pulled up hard on the hand brake before stepping out to find a few rocks. He wedged a handful behind each of the wheels and then headed back to the boot.

Hoffner was lighting a cigarette as he gazed up the hill.

"Smells like sugared beets," he said.

"Does it?" Mueller found a small jar of something and placed it on the fender. He went back to his rummaging.

Hoffner said, "At least the sun's not making it through here."

"At least." Mueller reappeared with a small paintbrush and limped around to the side of the car.

"The path's still good," said Hoffner. "We could take it up a bit farther."

"We could." Mueller knelt down. "If you like cracked axles and blown tires. We'd also hit the cliff. At least that would make it easier coming down."

Mueller unscrewed the top of the jar. Mixing the paint with the brush, he began to slather the doors in some sort of design. Hoffner tried to decipher it upside down, but the dripping made that impossible. He got out on the driver's side and stepped around the car.

It was letters: CNT-FAI.

"Anarchist trade union," Mueller said, admiring his work. "Leave it to the Spanish to unionize the one group bent on tearing the whole works down. 'Don't like anything that smacks of organization? Come, join our organization . . .'" He took some water from the canteen and washed off the brush. "Must have a hell of a time collecting dues."

When he had everything back in the boot, Mueller closed it and started up the hill. Hoffner had no choice but to grab the rucksack and follow.

"So you just leave it there?" Hoffner said, doing what he could to adjust the ropes on his shoulders. "No one touches it?"

Mueller nodded without turning. Even with the limp he was putting distance between them.

Hoffner said, "A few letters on the side and everything's fine?"

Again Muller nodded.

When Hoffner began to feel it in his legs, he said, "So why didn't we paint it in the first place, avoid the hill altogether, and just drive into town?"

Mueller continued to walk. "Right foot giving you a little trouble, Nikolai? Tough going on the rocks and roots?"

"I was just asking."

Mueller slowed, then stopped. He looked up as if he were thinking something through. Hoffner took the opportunity to stop as well. "Why didn't we drive into town?" Mueller said. "What a good question." He looked back at Hoffner. "You'd think a cripple would be smarter than that."

Hoffner started walking again. "Fine. There's a reason. Just walk."

Mueller let Hoffner pass him before saying, "You don't want to be driving a car into Barcelona these days, Nikolai. They'll either take it and burn it or pull you out so they can beat you before they take it and burn it."

"And they do this to people who have those mysterious pieces of paper?"

"A car requires a different piece of paper," Mueller said, as he started up the hill again. "So we walk."

A small falcon hovered high on the wind ahead of them, its head pressed down, before it banked and sped toward the ground.

They were beyond the trees now, almost to the top, where the grade of the hill grew steeper. Off to the right Montjuïc was sheer cliff, two hundred meters of rock face to the sea. Hoffner wondered if the bird might some-how misjudge the sudden rise—fail to pull itself up in time—but that would have required a different kind of instinct, a daring built on fear. It was the bird's effortlessness that saved it from anything human. The wings came within a half meter of the ground and swept up again, with some-thing small and wriggling caught in its talons.

"They like the rocks and the fortress," Mueller said, as he brought them to the summit. "Kestrels. Don't know what it is in Spanish."

"*Cernícalo,*" Hoffner said. He had no idea how he remembered it.

Mueller was only mildly impressed. "Smart little birds. Rats never see them coming."

The fortress spread out along the summit like two cocked arms, with a long stone tower rising from one of the elbows. The surrounding walls were all angles and points, little diamonds poking out to make any kind of frontal assault an impossibility. Hoffner had expected to see more by way of recent damage—bullet holes, walls breached—but for the most part the fortress was perfectly intact. It was also a product of the eighteenth century, with an enormous cannon on a rotating wheel peering out from one of the turrets. Oddly enough, from the look of things, it was completely aban-doned. Hoffner had expected at least one rifle-toting caballero to make an appearance, another silent nod at the crumpled paper. Even the bird was eating quietly.

"You're an idiot, Toby." Hoffner unloosed the rucksack. He let it fall and followed it to the grass. It was years since he had felt this kind of ache in his legs. "The only Romans who've seen this place have come on holiday to take photographs. The big gun might have been the giveaway."

Mueller snapped his two pincer fingers together: he needed a cigarette. Hoffner tossed over the pack, then the matchbox. Remarkably, Mueller caught them both. "Ancient Romans didn't have rotating cannons?" said Mueller. He lit up and tossed back the pack. "Really? I'll have to make a note." He pocketed the matches. "It's no tourists these days. Rumor has it they had some Nationalists locked up inside, but then who'd want to make the trek up here to feed them?"

"You're assuming they were getting fed."

Mueller took another quick pull on the cigarette and said, "We need to be down the mountain before it gets too hot."

He stepped over and picked up the rucksack. He spun it onto his back and started to walk. "We need to go." He then limped off across the grass—sloped trees to one side, fortress to the other—and Hoffner found a moment's relief in the absurdity of it.

Hoffner forced himself to his feet. "Not sure how much more walking I've got in me, Toby."

Mueller tossed the cigarette to the grass. "Then this is your lucky day."

They were bicycles, black, at least ten years old, but with enough leather on the saddles to make them workable. Mueller had them chained to a tree on the far side where the rutted paths, such as they were, led down into the city.

Hoffner stood a few meters behind and above as Mueller pulled open the lock.

"You're joking," Hoffner said.

Mueller double-looped the chain under the seat and pulled up the taller of the two bicycles. He stood waiting for Hoffner to take it before pulling up the other. Both had the letters CNT-FAI painted across the handlebars. Hoffner also noticed how the right-hand pedals on both were fitted with a block of some sort to compensate for Mueller's limp.

"I always keep a spare," said Mueller. "Told you it was your lucky day."

Mueller slotted the valise-cum-satchel into the rack and began to limp with the bicycle over to what passed for a path. He was surprisingly agile as he jumped onto the seat and let the slope take him. Hoffner watched as Mueller's head bobbled with increasing speed—down, around a turn, and gone. Hoffner shouted after him, "You're a son of a bitch, Toby!" then stepped up, climbed on, and found some speed of his own.

Hoffner had no reason to worry about the oversized pedal. He was simply holding on as best he could, his grip firmly planted on the hand brakes as the wheels seemed to take every root and rock with miraculous finesse. There was a strange familiarity to it, a thousand years of cigarettes and brandy tossed aside by something almost impatient. Hoffner began to smell the rubber on the tires, and gently released the brakes until he found himself letting go completely. He was actually managing the thing: more than managing it, he was gaining on Mueller. Somehow the bumps were a help as well, relieving the strain from the valise in his lower back. Hoffner might even have heard himself laugh.

"Enjoying yourself?" Mueller shouted over his shoulder.

Hoffner hadn't the courage to answer as the turns came more quickly. It was nearly fifteen minutes of catching his breath until the taste of sugared beets began to recede, the canopy of trees was thinner—then gone— and the path became smooth. The glare from the sun took several seconds to adjust to as Hoffner looked down: to his amazement he was staring at pavement. He looked up again and saw a massive building farther down the slope—domes and steeples tinted by the sun—and, beyond it, the city and its harbor.

Mueller slowed, and Hoffner gently squeezed the brakes. The two were now side by side as they rode.

"Palau Nacional," Mueller said. "No guns inside so they left it alone. It'll be the People's something-or-other by next week. Could be now."

Hoffner might have been drawn to the sight of its wide fountain, or its endless steps, or its twin pillar gates planted at the far end of the plaza— these, in their perfect symmetry, were meant to hold the eye—but instead he saw only the city stretching out beyond them. It was a sea of white stone and tiled roofs.

"Bring your knees in, Nikolai," said Mueller. "You're beginning to look like an old priest."

JOSEP GARDENYES

It was another twenty minutes before they came to even ground. Hoffner was grateful for the cramped feel of the side streets. The smells coming from the open doorways might have left the taste of boiling wool in the mouth, but at least the buildings were packed tightly enough together to make direct sunlight rare: six stories on either side, with balconies draped in red and black. His head was throbbing from the heat or thirst or lack of booze—or maybe just the thought of continued exertion—but whatever it was he knew he needed to get off this horrible machine and find something without wheels to sit on.

It didn't help that at almost every intersection it was a test to see how well he and Mueller could wend their way around the barricades that littered the streets. Most of the sandbag and brick obstructions were unmanned, although there had been one a few blocks back where they were forced to bring out Mueller's magical piece of paper. Their interrogator had been without a gun, only a sack on a rope over his shoulder and an airman's cap stitched with the letters FAI along one side. He stood atop a bullet-strafed sandbag in a white shirt—sleeves rolled high and neat to the upper arm—and an elegant pair of pleated dress trousers, his shoes fine if slightly worn. He would have looked the perfect part—cigarette dangling from his lips, a few days' growth of beard—had he not been, at best, ten years old. Even so, he spoke with an authority that made the boys back on the coast road look like amateurs.

"You know why we must destroy the fascists?" the boy said, as he glanced across the paper. It was unclear whether he knew how to read.

Mueller nodded vigorously and Hoffner did the same.

The boy said, "So that Spain can be free."

Mueller pulled a wrapped bar of chocolate from his pocket—Hoffner wondered what else might be inside should he go looking for himself—and handed it to the boy.

"*Salud*, friend," Mueller said. "*¡Viva la Libertad!*"

The boy pocketed the chocolate and nodded them along. Half a block later, Mueller pulled a second bar from his pocket and handed it to Hoffner. "You weren't thinking that was real, were you, Nikolai?"

Hoffner peeled back the wrapping and took a bite. It was good Swiss chocolate. "I'm glad he didn't have a rifle."

"He's got one somewhere. It doesn't work, but he's got one."

"That's encouraging." Hoffner handed the bar back and Mueller pocketed it.

"They're all so damned sure of themselves," Mueller said, with a tinge of bitterness.

The streets began to grow more peopled. Men and women—all with the red neckerchief—walked in small groups, bags with food, newspapers. They were inside stores or leaning from balconies, conversations and laughter, caps and hats arrayed in the various emblems of their new-won power. It was a city on a Sunday, like any other, except here there had been no prayers to God or hopes of salvation. They had left those behind. And of course the guns—a rifle over a shoulder or a pistol at the waist. They carried them with the same easy certainty one wears a new pair of shoes: moments here and there to recall the novelty, but always that sense of purpose and pride. That these had been used to kill other Spaniards ten days ago hardly seemed to matter. Or perhaps that was what mattered most of all.

Mueller smiled at a girl in a doorway. She smiled back, and Mueller continued to walk. "One day to take the city, and now it's boys playing at soldier."

Hoffner was thinking about the chocolate; he could have used another bite. "So you're telling me that wasn't a checkpoint back there?"

Mueller laughed quietly. "With a boy standing guard? They may be arrogant, Nikolai, but they're not stupid." He spat something to the ground. "Ten days ago—maybe that was the genuine article. Now it's for a boy to run out when his friends dare him to stop the two foreigners and see if he can get a bit of chocolate. He's a hero today. When we find a checkpoint, you'll know. Trust me."

They had come to the far end of the Conde del Asalto, a narrow strip of road identical to the rest except it marked the edge of Poble Sec, a workers' district. The Paralelo—a wide avenue that had seen its fair share of the fighting—was a stone's throw away, and Mueller found a nice big tree to rest the bicycles against.

"You thirsty, Nikolai?" he said, as he pulled the valise out of the rack.

Hoffner leaned his bicycle up as well. "You won't get the chain around this, you know."

"I wasn't planning on trying."

"So the painted letters manage it again?"

Mueller handed the valise to Hoffner. "No one takes a bicycle, Nikolai. It's not the way they do things here."

"But a fifteen-year-old car—"

"A banker or a judge or some old *marqués* used to drive one of those. Have you ever seen a banker on a bicycle? The letters, they're just—" Mueller smiled and shrugged.

"They make sure the girls know who you're fighting for?"

Mueller kept his smile as he led them across the street. "You'll like this place. Quiet, serene. *Tranquilidad.*"

On the far corner was a café, tables outside, with just enough tree cover to make sitting out worth the heat. A few were occupied, though it was too early for food. Glasses and bottles with something a deep yellow stood on most of them. Two men—one with a nice full mustache, the other trying desperately to grow one—were at one of the back tables, and Mueller headed toward them.

Hoffner said under his breath, "You know them?"

"Everyone knows everyone in Barcelona these days." Mueller raised a hand and said, "Gabriel," loudly enough to draw the mustached man's attention. The man smiled at once and raised his hand as he stood.

"Toby!" he said, as he stepped around the table toward Mueller.

Gabriel was barrel-chested, though not tall, with the thick arms of a man who had spent his life doing someone else's heavy work. The cheeks were round, the nose pug, and the thick, thick mustache—on closer inspection—had a ruff of tobacco-dyed hair at its center. His lips curled around a cigarette even as he spoke.

"Finally some German reinforcements. You've brought—what?— thirty planes, twenty tanks, ten thousand rifles?" He didn't wait for Mueller to answer before pulling him in for a full embrace. "You smell of sweat and beets." Gabriel let go. Somehow the cigarette remained fixed on his lip.

"You came down from Montjuïc, didn't you? Idiot." Before Mueller could answer, Gabriel turned back to the table. He motioned for the younger man to come over. "You know him, I'm sure," he said under his breath. "The mustache is a mistake, but you can't say anything."

The younger man was strangely small and with unusually pale features for a Spaniard—light eyes, ginger hair. The hands were also soft and slender. If not for the long narrow nose it would have been hard to place him in this part of the world. There was age in the face that made the patchy stubble above the lip even more of a curiosity. He was called Aurelio, and he shook hands with the kind of firmness of a man one was meant to trust.

"They came down Montjuïc," Gabriel said to him. "On bicycles. In this heat."

"Good tough Germans," said the little man, "but not terribly bright." He smiled and led them back to the table. "We'll need a drink."

Hoffner had tried Coca-Cola—once. It had been enough. Gabriel drank nothing else. Café Tranquilidad had somehow kept a healthy stash of it. Anarchists, it turned out, liked their American fizzy drinks. Luckily, Aurelio preferred wine.

The little man refilled the empties and set the wine bottle back on the table. "You don't sound like a socialist, Nikolai, let alone an anarchist."

They had been through the antifascist arguments—intricate explanations of the cause and its meaning and its essentialness—an animated tour de force that had brought Gabriel's cigarette out of his mouth for a single moment as he had stabbed at the air with it. Queipo de Llano. Son of a bitch.

Hoffner said, "It's hard not to be one these days, isn't it?"

Aurelio's smile became a quiet laugh, and he brought his glass to his mouth. "Sitting with two anarchists in the middle of Barcelona," he said. "Each with a pistol on his belt. Yes, I'd say you're right." He took a sip. "Did he tell you it was Jew Mountain?"

Hoffner was holding his glass on the table, staring at it. It took him a moment to answer. "Pardon?"

"Montjuïc," said Aurelio. "Did Toby tell you it was called Jew Mountain?" Hoffner had no reason not to nod, and Aurelio said, "Are you a Jew?"

The question caught Hoffner off guard. He waited, then picked up his glass. "Odd question from a godless Spaniard. Or are you trying to make me feel more at home?" He took a drink.

"Don't worry. It's not Berlin. No, I was just wondering if he told you because he thought it would make you feel more—I don't know—connected. Toby has that sort of sentimentality."

Mueller was finishing off his second glass of wine. He shook his head and swallowed. "The Spaniard accusing the German of sentimentality. That's rich."

Hoffner said, "Half-Jew—my mother—so, yes—in Berlin. I didn't think it mattered here."

"It doesn't," Aurelio said. "But if it did—matter to you, that is—I'd hate to be the one to disappoint. It's Jupiter Mountain, not Jew. Common mistake. Toby knows it, I think."

Hoffner looked across at Mueller, who shrugged, and Hoffner said, "Then he'd know it wouldn't make any difference to me, one way or the other."

Aurelio glanced at Gabriel and tossed back the rest of his drink. He stared into the empty and said, "Then why are you here?" It was another few moments before he looked directly at Hoffner. The gaze was hard, and Hoffner suddenly felt very much aware of the pistol that was hanging somewhere off the little man's belt.

Hoffner finished his drink. He placed the glass by the bottle and nodded as if in agreement. "I see. No anarchist, no socialist, no angry Jew. So what am I doing in Barcelona?"

Gabriel said, "It's a curious place to be these days otherwise." He looked over at Mueller. "Not that we don't trust you, Toby, but—" The Spanish shrug had so much more to do with the chin and the tilt of the head than the German.

There was a heaviness in the silence that followed. It lent a truth to what Hoffner said. "I'm looking for someone."

Aurelio lapped at the last of his glass. "Better that than being looked for, I suppose."

Gabriel opened a third bottle of the Coca-Cola, and said, "You're a policeman?"

Again Hoffner looked across at Mueller. There was nothing there. Hoffner picked up the bottle of wine. "Was. Yes."

"The shoes," said Gabriel. "I imagine that's universal."

"I imagine it is." Hoffner poured himself another.

"The Germans who've come have all been wild eyes and young or dripping with nostalgia. I'm sure you'd recognize them." He drank. "The first are useless. They think we'll take on Hitler once we're through here, the great International rising again. They don't know Spain at all, do they?" He began to play with the bottle cap. "The second—also useless, but with years and years of dreamed-up arrogance to stand on. They've been through it before, they understand how to organize. That was quite a success all those years ago, your little Rosa Luxemburg and her band. They took Berlin for—what?—ten minutes? But then these Germans see it differently.

"Luckily," he said, tossing the cap into a bucket on the floor, "they're all happy to kill fascists, so we drink with them, and listen to their empty tales of struggle—workers of the world with their pretty houses and gardens and weekends by the sea—and know they haven't the slightest idea of what it is to live every day with a boot clamped down on a throat." Gabriel looked directly at him, and Hoffner wondered where the amiable man of only minutes ago had gone. "You seem to be neither, so you can understand our interest."

Hoffner thought about drinking the wine. For some reason, though, he was wanting water. He looked around for a waiter.

"My son's the Jew," he said. The waiter was nowhere to be found. "We've worked it in reverse—half to full. He came to film the games, and he went missing." Hoffner looked back at the table and found a canteen in front of him.

"The waiter," Aurelio said. "He'll expect you to have brought your own. It's a miracle they had the wine."

Hoffner nodded his thanks and drank.

"My son could be one of your young Germans," he said, "but I doubt it." Hoffner screwed the top on and handed it to Aurelio. "Not that I care as long as I get him out of here."

Gabriel said, "So an old German with no politics, and a young Jew with no sense. It's a compelling story."

"You seem overly concerned in a city draped in red."

"Euphoria's a nice thing for a day or two, but I'm not so convinced this is as finished as everyone seems to say."

"So, a Spaniard with sense."

The round cheeks squeezed up and around the eyes, forming a smile. "I can guarantee you Toby's thinking the same thing."

Mueller had been running one of his pincer fingers along the table's edge, staring at it as it went back and forth.

Gabriel said, "He knows better than to trust any of this good fortune, don't you, Toby?"

Mueller looked up. He bobbed an indifferent nod.

Gabriel said, "It's because you're a criminal, isn't it, and criminals always know better."

Mueller said, "Is he around today?"

"Tell me, Toby," said Gabriel, "do you think the fascist generals are done for? Are we anarchists as unstoppable as we think we are?"

It was clear Mueller was uncomfortable with this, and not because he was any less savvy than the rest. He just didn't like the distraction. "Is he in the back?" he asked.

Gabriel said, "Toby can tell you who's the best man to get a voucher from, where you can still find a bit of ammunition, and how to get a truckload of whiskey down the coast. He's always been good with those sorts of things." His cigarette had lost its flame; even so, it stayed on his lip as he continued. "You remember that banker we pulled from his car—paying off scabs to work during one of the general strikes? What was that—'thirty, 'thirty-one? We needed to know which gas station he used on Fridays. Toby figured it out. That's why he got to keep the car." Gabriel laughed—it was tobacco-laced, and he pulled the dead cigarette from his mouth. A fresh one was in its place and lit within seconds. "What Toby won't do is look into the future. I haven't decided which I admire most. Yes, he's in the back. I wouldn't take too long with it."

Mueller stood and reached into his pocket. Hoffner stood as well, and Mueller placed two pairs of women's nylons on the table.

"We ask for guns and you bring us this," Gabriel said. "You're a good man, Toby. Maybe you *can* look into the future."

Mueller said, "It'll take more than a pair of these for the two of you to catch a girl. They're all wearing trousers these days, anyway."

Aurelio reached over for his and stuffed it in his pocket. "Every little bit helps."

Mueller squeezed a hand on Gabriel's shoulder. "Live to enjoy this." He nodded at Hoffner to follow him.

Hoffner stepped out. "Good luck with your boy," Gabriel said.

Hoffner picked up the valise and satchel. "Good luck with your war." He turned and began to weave his way through the chairs toward the café door.

Josep Gardenyes—no one ever remembered his real name—sat at a table in the back against a wall and ate hungrily from a bowl. It looked like soup, but who would have been crazy enough to eat soup in this weather, except maybe Josep Gardenyes, whose real name no one could ever remember.

Hoffner stopped and set his bags by the bar while Mueller made his way between the empty tables. This time he had been told to stay back. Mueller pulled up, and Hoffner watched as the two men spoke.

Gardenyes was a weathered forty and not one for embraces or warm smiles. His thin glance at the bar, though brief, was enough to make clear how beautifully Gabriel and Aurelio had played it: despite himself, Gardenyes needed protecting. He might have resented the caution but he accepted the loyalty.

Mueller nodded to Hoffner, and Gardenyes pushed the bowl to the edge of the table. This was as much of an invitation as he was likely to give. Hoffner went over and pulled back a chair.

Gardenyes said, "For a policeman you have interesting friends."

Whether it had been Mueller or the shoes, Hoffner decided on a lazy smile. "Former policeman," he said.

"I don't think there is such a thing." Gardenyes was now speaking Catalan.

"You do find them from time to time," Hoffner answered in kind. He sat.

A faint light of respect played in Gardenyes's eyes. "A German bull—ex bull—with Catalan. I'm even more concerned." The eyes began to show a smile.

"I spent time here as a boy," said Hoffner. "Not that difficult to pick it up." He looked into the bowl and found a few empty mussel shells, the remains of an overcooked potato, and the skin from a fish resting high on the rim. "Were the prawns fresh?" he said, as he picked up the potato and squeezed it in his fingers.

The smile reached Gardenyes's lips. "I can have them make you a plate."

Hoffner nodded and dropped the potato back in. He picked up a knife and continued to sort through the food. He said, "You like *suquet*, Toby?"

Mueller had found two more glasses and was pouring the wine. "Fish stew? Fine by me as long as they don't put beef in it." He set the bottle down. "No beef this time. That was disgusting."

Hoffner was still with the knife, propping up and examining the underside of the skin, when Gardenyes said, "You spent time north of here?"

"Yes," said Hoffner. Even the bones had been eaten.

"And now you've lost your son."

The smile remained on Gardenyes's face even as Hoffner looked over. Hoffner said, "Not yet, I hope."

"That's a bit cold."

"Why? It's what you wanted to hear me say." Hoffner set the knife down. "I can guarantee you my son isn't dead, if that's what you're thinking. As for lost, that would mean he was mine to lose. He wasn't."

Gardenyes studied Hoffner's face before looking past him to a man standing by the door to the kitchen. Gardenyes motioned for two more and Hoffner brought out his cigarettes. Gardenyes took one and Hoffner lit it.

Gardenyes said, "Not every day you get to light the cigarette of a dead man."

"You'd be surprised," said Hoffner.

Mueller set the bottle down, took hold of his glass, and said, "They're not going to kill you, Josep." He drank.

"Oh, yes, they will. And when they do, Gabriel and Aurelio will tell them I was a criminal, too dangerous, and they'll save themselves."

Hoffner said, "And here I thought it was your anarchists who were running things now."

"You're in Spain," said Gardenyes. "There are anarchists and there are anarchists."

Hoffner lit his own. "I imagine you'll be up on a cross at the time, begging for water?"

Gardenyes gave into a quiet laugh. "Up on a cross. That's good. I've heard He was a bit wild, too. And dangerous. Although you wouldn't know it to see Him these days."

"If anyone's actually looking for Him."

Smoke trailed from Gardenyes's nose. "Oh, they're looking for Him. Trust me. There's probably half a dozen nuns and priests hiding in plain sight just the other side of the road."

"I must have missed them."

"You can tell them by the little gold chains underneath the neckerchiefs. Ragged trousers, white shirts, little berets, and always with the loudest ¡Viva la República! as they pass you by. But it's that chain they can't quite bring themselves to tear off. They'll lie through their teeth as long as little Jesus is still dangling close to their hearts. Such a short walk from anarchist to savior, not that they'd know it."

"And yet you're convinced your men will betray you."

"Betray me?" A wry if uncertain smile crossed Gardenyes's eyes. "I'm the one who's told them to do it. No reason all three of us should be dead."

"Very noble."

Again Gardenyes studied Hoffner. "You don't sound convinced."

"No, I probably don't." Hoffner took a pull and caught sight of Mueller out of the corner of his eye. It was nice to see Toby this uncomfortable.

Luckily Gardenyes seemed to be enjoying it. "I was thinking your balls must be sore—riding all the way down from Montjuïc—but here they are, on display."

The plates arrived. The man from the kitchen pulled two spoons from his apron and was gone as quickly as he had come. Mueller sniffed warily at his food; Hoffner set his cigarette in the ashtray.

"It used to be they called me a criminal—a common criminal—because it was easier for them," Gardenyes said. "Toss me in prison, exact their re-venge in the name of order. It gave their law, meaningless as it was, a sense of moral purpose. There's your God again, even if He was being used to strip away anything human from the people He was sent to protect."

Hoffner was wiping the spoon with his thumb. "Am I in for the full soapbox, or can we water it down a bit?"

Gardenyes's smile, if not completely lacking in cruelty, was at least gen-uine. "And I didn't even mention the word 'bourgeois.'"

"Don't worry," said Hoffner, "you've got time." He was leaning over the bowl, smelling the freshness off the steam. "Monkfish," he said. "And hake. We never get them this nice." He filled his spoon and blew on the broth, then winced as he swallowed.

Gardenyes said, "Pimm liked this stew. Same as you. Odd for a cop and a criminal to have such similar tastes."

Hoffner winced through another sip. "And why is that?"

Gardenyes shook his head easily. "I don't know. You just don't think they should. Easier if it's all"—he thought for a moment—"what's the German, *Ordnung*? Neat and clean."

"And you like neat and clean?"

"Not at all."

"So you knew Pimm?"

"Of course I knew Pimm. Now Radek. And one day it'll be Little Franz taking over. The Berlin syndicates have always been so well orga-nized, perfectly filed. *Ordnung*."

"Not the Spanish way."

"Not the anarchist way," Gardenyes corrected. "For Pimm, crime was crime. Profit. Power. He made good money here in Spain. For us, it's al-ways been a tool of politics. A way to create something new. The crime—if in fact it's crime at all—is just the means."

"Like pulling a banker from his car." Hoffner was sifting his spoon through the liquid.

"Exactly." Gardenyes nodded at Hoffner's bowl. "The clam," he said. "Always start with the clam. Underneath." Hoffner flipped everything on its end, and Gardenyes said, "Pimm thought I was a common criminal. I let him believe it. Radek probably thinks the same, although maybe he sees things differently, now that it's an actual war." Gardenyes looked over at Mueller. "What do you say, Toby? Is this different from the old days—stealing from a payroll, knifing a factory boss? Is it permitted now because we have rifles and wear uniforms? Or is crime still just crime with you Germans, whatever its purpose?"

Hoffner had the clam resting on the back of his tongue. It was smoky and soaked in garlic, its texture perfectly soft. It seemed unfair to swallow. He took a drink and set his spoon after a prawn. "You're going to tell me there's no such thing as good and bad people. Only people who are good and bad at different times." He found the prawn. "If it's going to be the entire manifesto, I'll take some bread with it."

Gardenyes waited and motioned to the man by the kitchen. He then tapped his ash to the floor. "Pimm said you saw crime differently, criminals differently. It's why he liked you. I think he said it made you incorruptible." Gardenyes took a pull. "Is that right? Are you incorruptible?"

Hoffner separated the prawn from the rest of the stew. It was fat and pink, and he ran the edge of his spoon through the meatiest part of it. The metal clanked on the bowl. "The clam was good," he said. "Nice and soft." He brought the wedge of the prawn to his mouth, smelled the brandy and salt on it, and slipped it in.

Gardenyes said, "Am I a criminal?"

"Not for me to say."

"Was Pimm?"

Hoffner took another sip of the broth. "Of course."

"And yet—"

"And yet nothing. He was a pimp and a thief. He supplied narcotics, he killed men—"

"And he was the only friend you had."

Hoffner hated Pimm for this moment. Not that anything Gardenyes was saying was less than the truth, but such truths weren't meant for a man like Gardenyes. Hoffner set the spoon in the bowl and took his cigarette.

Gardenyes said, "I don't think he meant you were incorruptible in the noble sort of way."

"No, he wouldn't have."

"But there was something—what did he say?—something you saw that was bigger than the crime, bigger than the idea of order itself. Something that was worth protecting."

Hoffner took a pull and then crushed the cigarette in the ashtray. "Imagine Pimm saying that."

"Well, maybe not exactly that."

"Maybe not."

"Still, one wonders what it was that had a cop seeing beyond crime and order. What it was that could be worth so much to him. That he'd willingly sacrifice so much for."

Hoffner picked up the spoon. It was all he could do to keep his focus on the bowl.

"I've never been to Berlin," said Gardenyes, his cruelty now effortless. "Never seen its streets, heard its crowds, smelled its air. Is it really as remarkable as people say?"

Hoffner clutched at the spoon as he stared into the bowl. "It was. Once."

"How terribly sad that must make you."

This was why the anarchists had taken the city so quickly, thought Hoffner. Men like this. Men who could conceive of nothing beyond Barcelona's streets and her hills and the taste of her too bitter water. Hoffner wondered if Gardenyes would meet his own despair with the same resilience should his city ever cease to be what he needed her to be. Hoffner wondered this of himself.

The man arrived and Gardenyes said, "We'll have some bread. Butter, if there is any."

The man moved off and Hoffner set down the spoon. He needed a drink. He poured himself a glass and drank.

He said, "They won't have the butter, will they?"

"No. They won't."

Hoffner was done playing. "I imagine you were something of a hero in those old days. Pulling bankers from cars. The noble bandit. Defender of the defenseless. It has such a familiar ring. Funny, but I don't remember Pimm ever mentioning you, so I'm guessing you're right. He probably thought of you as—what?—a good knife, a petty thief, someone smart to have on the payroll. He did have you on the payroll, didn't he?"

It was the first moment of hesitation in Gardenyes's eyes, long enough to feel the venom behind them. Gardenyes said, "You have a strange way of asking for help."

"Help from a dead man. Now that would be something, wouldn't it?"

It might have been a sudden pushing back of a chair or the waving of a pistol in the face, but Gardenyes remained perfectly still: whatever violence he felt lived in the silence. He took a last pull, tossed his cigarette to the ground, and leaned forward.

"You have no idea." For the first time his voice had no interest in masking its bitterness. The stare was almost hypnotic.

"And yet you'll help me find my son," said Hoffner. There was nothing in his tone. "For old time's sake."

Gardenyes's stare became a half grin, then something far more unnerving. The smile was completely empty of thought.

"*Incontrolats*," Gardenyes said. It was as if the word carried no weight. "You know what these are? No—I don't think you do." He rocked his chair on its hind legs, and his head rested against the wall. There was an unwelcome easiness in the way he leaned back and looked over at Hoffner. "Uncontrollables," he said, his voice too calm, its menace too refined. "Men beyond hope. Men beyond the revolution. Anarchists calling their own such a thing. Can you imagine it?"

It was everything Hoffner could do to keep his gaze fixed on Gardenyes's.

"You see, I thought the whole point was to tear down the control, keep tearing it down. But now, of course, they have it. They won't admit it, these anarchist friends of mine. They say, 'Look at us. Look at the revolutionaries who told the socialists, No, we don't want a part of your government, even if you hand it to us—even if you *beg* us to take it. We've given you the state, freed you from the fascists, but no, we want nothing that tastes of leadership or popular fronts or control.'" Gardenyes's head turned slightly and his eyes drifted: it left the small table feeling unbearably exposed. "I'll give them that," he said quietly. "They did say no."

He looked back at Hoffner, the eyes now too focused.

"The trouble is, you let yourself be seduced by your own order, *your* control, and everything goes on its head. Now they say, 'Don't go too far, don't embarrass us, don't commit acts that are'"—he stared into Hoffner's eyes as if the words were somewhere behind them—"what was it? . . . 'contrary to the anarchist spirit,' counter to the 'revolutionary order.'" The eyes flashed momentarily and he came forward, the chair landing on the stone with an unexpected force. "Revolutionary *order*?" He leaned into Hoffner, and Hoffner let him lean. "What exactly is that supposed to mean?"

Hoffner had been holding the spoon against his thigh, and a small oval of liquid had seeped into the cloth. He felt the tackiness underneath, on his skin. Gardenyes slowly pulled himself back and Hoffner smelled the Spaniard's breath still between them.

"I have some names," Hoffner said. "You can see if they mean anything to you. And you can tell me where they're keeping the injured Germans."

Gardenyes picked up his glass. It took him a moment to realize it was empty before he set it back down. He continued to stare at the table. "The fascists don't have such problems," he said. "One mind, one body with them. Makes it so much easier." He looked over at Hoffner. "Maybe soon enough I won't be the only dead anarchist in Barcelona."

The bread arrived with a wedge of butter on a plate.

Gardenyes put out his hand. "I'll see those names now. For old time's sake."

HANSHEN

Mueller opted out. He had done his bit, getting Hoffner to Gardenyes. If Gardenyes hadn't killed him by now, Hoffner would probably be fine on his own.

"I said probably." Mueller was resting his gimp foot on the car's running board as he took the last few pulls of a cigarette. Most of the smoke was trailing in at Hoffner through the window.

The Modelo 10 was a recent addition for Gardenyes, a four-seater out of Ford's Barcelona plant that, up until the July fighting, had been churning out cars at an unusually healthy clip. It was unlikely that any of the driving enthusiasts who had bought the Modelo 10s or 8s had realized that they were sporting around on a German-made chassis and brakes and any number of other German components. Back in January, Ford London had sent down the word that Herr Hitler wanted better results out of his Ford Deutschland plants. So, to appease the Führer, Ford Ibérica had been told it was suddenly in the market for large stocks of automotive parts coming from Dagenham and Köln. This, in turn, had kept the London office happy, which had kept the American office happy, which was doing everything it could to keep the German office happy. So much happiness churning out of so few moving parts. It seemed to bode well for the future of international détente.

As it happened, this particular Modelo 10 had belonged to a rather successful dentist who had had the very good sense to send his wife, two small children, household staff, dental assistant, and mistress ahead to northern Italy on the night before all the trouble began. He had gotten wind that something was brewing from his brother-in-law, who was married to an older sister living in Morocco, and who was involved with something to do with the export of large metal tubing (he had been in Granada before that, but there had been talk of an incident with a woman connected to the postmaster). The brother-in-law had sent a cable saying he had heard something from someone (no names written down), and that certain events and certain "expediencies" (this was, in fact, the very word he had used, although slightly incorrectly) were "in the works" and might mean a change for the better in Barcelona—the brother-in-law being a staunch fascist and assuming only the best, which is what someone who has never been to Barcelona will always assume. The dentist, knowing better, had acted accordingly.

He had been pulled from his car on the nineteenth while trying to find the coast road. His driver had abandoned him at the first sound of shots, and the dentist, always at sixes and sevens when it came to navigating the roads in and around the city, had gotten lost. Two women and a rough man had beaten and then shot him. The dentist had lain very still for nearly an hour before the loss of blood had finally killed him. One of the women had given the car to Gardenyes in exchange for five completely useless Russian rifles, while the other had cursed her friend for being so stupid. In the meantime, both wife and mistress continued to wait patiently, certain that they would soon be resuming their previously well-balanced lives, albeit with a vaguely Venetian flair.

Hoffner was examining a stack of rubber-banded wooden tongue depressors he had found in the pocket next to the backseat when Gabriel turned on the engine. Aurelio was in the seat next to Gabriel, Gardenyes still in the toilet.

Hoffner said, "He doesn't use any of these, does he, when things go south? I'm thinking he's more of a bullet-to-the-head sort of man."

Mueller tossed his cigarette to the street and leaned in as two spears of smoke streamed from his nose. "That'd be my guess, but you never know. I wouldn't be all that eager to find out." Mueller leaned in closer and spoke quietly. "Nothing stupid, Nikolai. You don't know these boys. I don't know them, and I've spent time with them. I'd like to be at each of their funerals."

Gardenyes appeared at the café door and quickly made his way over to the car.

Mueller said, "They'll know where to find me." He stood upright as Gardenyes got in the other side and settled in next to Hoffner. "Three days," said Mueller.

He was saying something else, but the car was already in gear.

The third-floor corridor of the Hospital Clinic was like any other—stark, white-walled, and overly sanitized. Hoffner had always found something incongruous in the heavy silence of such places: life-and-death decisions behind each door, and yet never more than a whisper from those making them. Even the air moved hesitantly, peering slowly around each corner, as if coming face to face with a forgotten gurney or a figure slumped listlessly across a chair might be too much. Gardenyes walked with purpose, but it was a false bravura that led the way. He, too, was doing his best to keep the healing stench from his lungs.

The double doors at the end of the corridor were fitted with two square windows, level with the eye and large enough to give a hint of the vast ward that lay beyond them. The word RECUPERACIÓN was set above the doors in thick black tile, though the letters seemed to be mocking themselves, saying, "You won't find it in here, and you know it." Gardenyes pushed through and Hoffner followed.

The smell was at once sweeter, and the air seemed to widen as if it were reaching for the corners of the ceiling high above. Eight rows of cots, perhaps twenty in each, stretched to the back wall, where three enormous windows—each a collection of iron-rimmed square panes—tinted the sun a gray-yellow. There were pockets of hushed exchanges between the four or five nurses scattered about, none in white, but what else would they be? The door swung closed behind Aurelio, and the squeak of the hinge echoed before it vanished into the dust.

A woman was sitting behind a desk. She had a rifle propped up against it, but there was little chance she knew how to use it. She wore a green short-sleeved shirt, and when she stood, a pair of brown trousers appeared that hugged her narrow waist. They were held in place by a thin leather belt that ran too long through the loops. Her arms were equally slender, everything long and fine, although the hair was short and too carelessly held to just above the shoulders. Hoffner would have expected the jet black from the coast road this morning, but this had a lighter tint to it and seemed a much better fit for the pale, suntanned face and blue eyes. She might have been thirty, but the eyes had her older.

"*Salud*," Gardenyes said indifferently. "We need to see a doctor."

The woman looked at all four men. "Is someone injured?"

"No," Gardenyes said, scanning the room behind her impatiently. He looked at her. "Does this hospital employ doctors?"

"It does."

"Then I imagine you can go and get us one." When she continued to look at him, Gardenyes said, "My name is Josep Gardenyes. When and if you find a doctor, he'll know the name. Tell him I'm waiting to talk to him." When he saw her still standing there, he drew up his shoulders. "Well?"

Again she looked at the others. "Of course." She saw Gardenyes reaching for his cigarettes and added, "We don't permit smoking in here. Not with all the open wounds." She moved smoothly past them and out the swinging doors.

Gardenyes pulled the cigarettes from his shirt pocket, put one to his lips, and lit up.

Gabriel—who had been complaining about hospitals and the sick and the stink of formaldehyde since the drive over—shivered with too much drama and said, "Someone's dying in here. You can smell it. It was worse two weeks ago, I can tell you that. Now it's just the old dead, not the fresh kind."

Aurelio said, "She's from León." He was at the desk, sliding his fingers along the few papers that were spread across it. "The hair and the eyes. People always think I'm Castilian. I'm not, but they always think it. She was pretty." Finding nothing of interest, he began to open the drawers.

"Leave it," said Gardenyes. He seemed unable to smoke the cigarette fast enough. He was at the door, staring out, then not. Gabriel might have put a voice to it, but it was Gardenyes who truly hated this place. "What takes so long?" he said, as he dropped the cigarette to the floor. He lit another, and Hoffner stepped over and picked up the stub.

Hoffner said, "So where is it you're from?"

All three looked over as if he had asked the most idiotic question imaginable. Aurelio shut the drawer, Gardenyes looked back out through the window of the door, and Gabriel simply shook his head in disbelief. Hoffner had no idea why.

Gardenyes suddenly stepped back and moved to the desk. He dropped the half-smoked cigarette to the floor and hid it under his boot as the door squeaked open. Gabriel and Aurelio quickly moved into line. It was like watching three schoolboys waiting for a caning. The woman reappeared, holding several small vials in her hands.

"I've found you a doctor," she said, as she moved back to her chair and sat. She placed the vials on the desk. "Unfortunately, she has no idea who Josep Gardenyes is." She looked at Hoffner and pointed to his hand. "I told you not to smoke in here."

Hoffner realized he was still holding the butt. He nodded apologetically. "No, of course not," and dropped it into the can at the side of the desk. "My mistake."

She looked up at Gardenyes. "What is it I can do for you?"

Gardenyes was still trying to digest the last few moments. "You're a doctor?" he said.

"It would seem so, yes."

"You're a woman."

She nodded. "That would also be right."

Gardenyes was still struggling. "We're—we're looking for Germans."

She said, "Well, that's two out of three. I know a little Dutch, if that helps?"

Hoffner couldn't help but smile, and she looked over at him. He thought she might return it, but that would have done neither of them any good. Instead, she looked at Gardenyes and said, "By the way, I've saved fascists. The first day, the day after that, yesterday. We all did. We all have. We make no distinctions. So if you're here to round up—"

"You misunderstand," said Hoffner. She looked at him, and he explained. "Not Germans. *A* German. I was hoping you might have records from the last week or two."

She seemed remarkably at ease with the three bandit anarchists standing over her. It was the strange one at the end—with his even stranger valise and satchel—that was causing the hesitation. Had Hoffner been looking for it, he might have seen something of the familiar in the gaze. Deep and abiding loss was so readily apparent to those who shared it, but Hoffner had long ago given up looking for such things. It was enough for her to blink it away.

She said, "And I would hand over these records to you because you happen to be in the company of Josep Gardenyes, onetime leader of the anarchist *patrullas* to whom half of Barcelona owes its safety and undying gratitude." She looked at Gardenyes. "Yes, I know who you are. I can't speak for the other half."

Gardenyes was rather too pleased with himself at this. To his credit, he indulged it only a moment.

She looked again at Hoffner. "It wouldn't make any difference even if you had Buenaventura Durruti himself standing here. This is Barcelona. We're led by anarchists. We have no records."

Gardenyes had fully recovered; he was once again on solid ground. "So you'll help my friend, then?"

She was still looking at Hoffner. "You call Gardenyes a friend?"

Hoffner recognized the toying disdain in the eyes. Men like Gardenyes were a necessary irritation to a woman like this—a woman who could sit perfectly straight in a ward filled with the dying. It gave her an uncommon strength.

"He calls me one," said Hoffner. "You can take that as you like."

Half a minute later the three Spaniards were on their way back to the car. Gardenyes assured Hoffner that he would look into the names and locations Wilson had provided—"Yes, yes, of course, no worries, we'll be in touch." It was a flurry of empty promises, leaving Hoffner alone with the desk and the woman behind it.

She called herself Mila, and he had been right to think her older. Not that much older, but enough distance from thirty to make sense of the steadying compassion she showed as they walked along one of the rows. It was one thing to reassure with a well-schooled, naïve precision. It was another to understand the terror that a bleach-soaked sheet and a paper-thin blanket could bring to a man staring hopelessly up at an endless ceiling.

One of the men propped himself on his elbows as she came closer. His face was full with color, healthy even, and held a look of unbridled hatred. His right hand was thickly wrapped. He glanced at Hoffner and, for a moment, seemed uncertain whether he would say anything. Mila came to the end of his cot, and the hatred got the better of him.

"Did you decide on it?" the man said. "Was it you?"

She stood there, allowing him to stare through her. "Yes," she said, "it was. It's a terrible thing. I'm sorry."

There was a silence, and the man again looked unsure. He had expected more, a reason—the details for why his leg was no longer his. A man would have comforted with such things and forced the hatred to run its course.

"The other will be fine," she said. "And the hand. But it doesn't make any more sense of it, I know."

The man continued to stare up at her; then he turned his head, and his eyes seemed to search for something. Finally, he began to shake his head slowly. "You're sorry," he said, but the hatred was already draining from him.

"I am. It's a terrible, terrible thing."

Hoffner saw it at once: she knew this one would never give in to self-pity. It was why she could console. She began to walk and Hoffner followed.

Ten beds down, she stopped again. "If he's here, he'll be in with these. I heard German from a few of them."

She left him to it. There were six men—boys, really—all with various degrees of injuries, the worst with half his face covered in white bandages. Traces of red had seeped through where the eye would have been. Georg was not among them.

The interviews were brief. One of the boys had, in fact, been involved with the games, a javelin thrower now living in Paris whose left leg was in plaster up to the mid-thigh. He had taken a bayonet somewhere along the Diagonal but had managed to get a round off before his attacker had done more damage. The loss of blood had kept the boy in bed for over a week.

"Bit ironic," the boy said. "A bayonet. Just imagine what it would have been if I'd been a hammer thrower."

Hoffner was glad for the resiliency. "And you were part of the German team?" he said.

"I'm a German. What else would I be?"

The boy remembered no one resembling Georg, no filmmakers. It had all been catch-as-catch-can, half the team making it only as far as Paris before being told to turn back (to wherever they had come from) as a war had broken out. Hoffner ran through the names from Georg's wire. It was pointless. None of the boys recognized a single one.

Mila was writing out something when Hoffner drew up.

"I thought there were no files," he said, through a half smile.

She continued to write. "We'd have nowhere to put them even if this was one." She quickly finished with it, set it to the side, and looked up at him. "Was he your German?"

Hoffner found himself taking a moment too long with the gaze. "No." He nodded back at the beds. "Nice boy. He wants to get in on the fighting. That's a shame."

"Is it?"

"Yes—it is."

She seemed surprised by the answer. "He'll have his chance."

"Really?"

"A leg like that—young and healthy—takes about three weeks. You think we'll still be singing in the streets three weeks from now?"

"I wasn't planning on being here."

"No, I'm sure you weren't."

For some reason Hoffner had his pack of cigarettes in his hand. He shook one to his lip and saw her staring up at him. "Right," he said, and removed it.

She looked over her shoulder and said to the nurse nearest her, "I'm taking five minutes. I'll be outside." She opened the drawer, slid the sheets in, and stood. "I'm assuming you have more than one in the pack?"

It took a bit of muscle to hoist up the window at the far end of the corridor, but she managed it. She stepped out onto the roof, and Hoffner followed.

The view was mostly trees with a few buildings cut in between. The heat lay across the black-tarred roofing like exhaustion and seemed to rise to just below the chin. Hoffner felt his neck instantly wet. He lit her cigarette, and she let out a long stream of smoke.

"You've come a long way for one German," she said, as she stared out across the trees. "You think he'll mean as much to you when you find him?"

Hoffner lit up. "Nice to hear *when*. There's been a lot of *if* with everyone else."

"I might have said *if*, but that wouldn't make me much of a doctor, would it?"

"Woman doctor. That's uncommon."

She ignored the obvious. "So where in Germany?"

He wiped his neck and his fingers grew slick. "Berlin."

"That's not a nice place to be these days"—she looked over at him—"or maybe it is? Is it a nice place to be?"

He took a long pull and nodded out at the buildings. "I'm guessing these saw a lot of the fighting."

She stared at him until she knew he was growing uncomfortable. "No," she said. "Everyone needs a hospital. They left it alone."

"You must have been busy."

"Yes." She continued to look at him. It was impossible not to let her. "Finding someone in Spain these days. That's—" The word trailed off. He expected her to say more, but she did well with silence.

He said, "He's not here to fight. I'm thinking that should make it easier."

"Easier to keep him alive or easier to find him?"

Hoffner had yet to figure out why she had taken him out here. He imagined it was an answer he might not want to have. "Both, I think."

"Such is a father's love." The words were almost indifferent. She took a pull as she looked out again. It was several long moments before she said, "You speak a beautiful Spanish."

Hoffner was studying the face. There was a thin line of perspiration above the lip. It pooled in tiny beads. She showed no thought of brushing it away. "Thank you."

"That's also uncommon." She took a last pull and dropped the cigarette to the roofing. It hissed at the touch of the tar. "Are the rest of the clothes in your valise as ridiculous as the ones you're wearing?" She gave him no time to answer. "A decent pair of boots, a hat?" She ran her toe over the cigarette. "And I'm sure you've got a place to stay?"

"I appreciate the concern."

"Do you?" She looked directly at him. "You'll need that and the clothes if you want to find this nonfighting boy of yours. Why did he come, by the way?"

"Does it matter?"

He felt her eyes across him. She offered a quiet smile. "You can't trust Gardenyes."

"I think I know that."

"Good. We have an extra room. And some clothes."

The suddenness of it caught Hoffner off guard. "You're being very generous."

"This is Barcelona. This is what we do."

"Is it?"

She drew her hand in the air across his chest. "They'll be a bit big for you here, but the rest should be good."

"And your husband can do without them?"

"There is no husband."

"Brother?"

There was a moment in the eyes, and she started for the window. "I'll write down the address. There should be some food. You look like you could use some sleep."

The key for the building proved unnecessary. A woman—small, veined, and gray—sat perched on a low stool that stood propping open the front door. She held a pile of green and red peppers on her lap and was slicing them into a bucket. She held the knife by the back of the blade and moved through the peppers with alarming speed. Even when she looked up to see Hoffner staring at her, she continued to slice.

The street was like most of the rest, narrow, and with buildings no more than five or six stories high. They seemed to be leaning into each other with rounded shoulders, as if the whole thing might collapse with a little push. Or maybe it was this woman who was holding them in place? She wiped the knife on her skirt for no apparent reason and went back to her slicing.

Hoffner said, "I'm going to number four. I have the key."

She reached into the bucket and dug through for something.

Hoffner pulled the valise-cum-satchel off his back. His shoulders were going stiff. "The doctor—" It struck him only now that he had no idea what her proper name was. "I have the key from her."

The woman brought out a slice of red pepper and held it out to him. The knife was still in her fingers.

"Have it," she said.

Hoffner took the wedge. It was crisp and wet, and the sweetness settled at the back of his throat. He nodded as he swallowed. "Thank you."

She moved her legs to the side. It was a token gesture, and he picked up his bags and sidestepped inside.

The staircase was almost completely dark. Hoffner smelled almonds and garlic, and something else he couldn't quite place, but it seemed to go well with the taste still in his mouth. At the second landing, a dim bulb sprouted from the wall and gave off just enough light to bring out the metal 4 on a door halfway down the hall. He stepped over and slotted the key into the lock.

The place was charming enough, walls a bright yellow, windows with sheer drapes in white and pale green. Beyond them stood a wrought-iron balcony that ran the length of the wall. A low sofa sat across from the windows, along with a few chairs and pillows scattered about. There was a table, a bookcase—small things of meaning set along one of the shelves—and an archway that led off to what might be a kitchen. It was neat, inviting, and showed nothing of the life being lived inside it.

Hoffner set down the bags and moved across to the drapes. He pulled them back and noticed that one of the windows had been left open. There was hardly any sound from the street, but for some reason the smell of almonds was stronger here. A window across the way showed a woman sleeping in a small room. She was lying on her back, her hair billowing from some unseen fan. The rest of her lay perfectly still until her hand came up and wiped at something on her cheek. Just as easily the hand fell back to the bed. The stillness returned, and Hoffner wondered if she would remember it ever happening.

Hoffner turned back to the flat and now saw through to the kitchen. There was an icebox, sink, stove, small table, and a man seated at one of the three chairs. He was older than the woman from the street, though not much bigger, and he was peering over at Hoffner. An opened newspaper lay across the table.

The man said, "You have a key." It was a statement, nothing more.

Hoffner needed another few moments. "Yes," he said. "The doctor—she gave it to me."

The man continued to peer across at him. The face showed no fear, no distrust, not even curiosity. It was a look devoid of content. "Are you English?"

Again Hoffner needed a moment. "No."

"German?"

"Yes."

The man nodded. "You look German or English. I don't mean it to offend."

"It doesn't. Does she do this often?"

"Do what?"

"Allow people to stay."

The man thought a moment, then shook his head. "Not that I'm aware of, no."

"And you live here?"

"Yes."

"Then you'd be aware of it."

The man waited. This seemed to make sense. He pushed the chair back and stood. He was a good head shorter than the doctor. "I have some hard eggs in the shell," he said, "if you're hungry." He stepped over to a cabinet, pulled out a plate, and set it on the table. He went to the icebox.

It was always small men who gave Hoffner trouble when it came to age. The back was ramrod straight, but even then he put him at close to eighty. The hair was a fine white.

"She mentioned some clothes," said Hoffner. It seemed inconceivable that they would have once belonged to this man, but given the circumstances and the last few minutes, Hoffner was open to anything.

The man placed two eggs on the plate. "There's a closet in the other room. I can show you." He placed a kettle on one of the burners, lit the gas with a match, and then pointed Hoffner in the direction. "It's through here."

Hoffner followed him down a short corridor and into a bedroom. A simple metal-spring bed jutted out from the far wall, with a small table, washing pitcher, and basin next to it. A wooden armoire stood along the near wall. The man unlatched the armoire and pulled open the doors.

He said, "They might be wide in here"—he ran his hand across his chest—"but otherwise they should fit well enough."

Shirts and trousers hung on hangers, with two pairs of boots wedged underneath. The man stared at the clothes and then placed his hand on one of the sleeves. He stood quietly for several seconds. He closed the doors and said, "You'll want a bath first."

Hoffner stood in the doorway. "I'm called Nikolai."

The man looked over. It was the first sign of emotion to reach his face. "You have a Russian name."

"Yes. My mother."

The man showed a moment's surprise, then approval. "Mine as well," he said. He seemed to grow taller with this. "I'm called Dmitri Piera. I am the father of your doctor. I'll go run that bath."

Hoffner slept first, two hours—maybe more—long enough to feel a different kind of heat when he woke. This one left pockets of cooled air to breathe and made sitting remarkably pleasant. He had bathed in the tub and now wore a shirt, suspenders, and trousers from the armoire as he sipped from a glass at the kitchen table. Both father and daughter had been right about the chest.

Piera offered coffee but said tea would be better. He also explained the other smell. Hazelnuts. He was guessing someone had peppers.

"It might be *calçots*," he said, "but the onions are hard to find these days."

Hoffner set his glass on the table. "I need to thank you for all this."

Piera set his glass down as well. "She gave you the key, and the clothes were here. She'll tell me why when she gets home."

"You have great faith."

It was the first hint of a smile to cross Piera's face. "You're in the wrong house for that."

"She's a good doctor."

Piera dropped a piece of sugar into his glass. "Were you injured?"

"No."

"Then how would you know?"

"She's not?"

Piera stirred the tea with a spoon and set it by the glass. "Not easy for a woman to be a doctor."

Hoffner thought it brave to show this kind of pride in a child. He said, "The clothes—there was a husband?"

Piera took a sip. "There was, but they aren't his. He was small like me. That's a long time ago." Piera was happy to leave it at that. He was on his feet again, opening a drawer at the counter and pulling out a thick wedge of bread. He found a slab of butter inside the icebox and brought it to the table. An old army knife appeared from his pocket. He opened it and began to slice the bread.

"She doesn't like that I use this," he said. "She has a proper knife, but what can you do?" He smeared a piece with butter and handed it to Hoffner. He did the same for himself and took a healthy bite. The sound of the door opening brought a momentary lift to the air. Both men listened as the door clicked shut. Piera ran his tongue along his teeth and swallowed. He said, "We're in here."

Mila appeared at the archway. She held a bag filled with something, and her hair was now loose and pulled back over an ear. Hoffner imagined the skin had a remarkable smoothness. She stepped over and gave her father a kiss on each cheek. She looked at Hoffner.

"You found the clothes," she said. "And a bath. That's good." She set the bag on the counter and began to pull out the contents: vegetables, fruit, something in a brown paper wrapping.

"You should sit," said Piera.

Mila continued with the food. "They had fish and escarole. And we have fruit and some cream."

Hoffner was on his feet. "I can help with that. I also have to thank you—"

She shook him off easily. "No, I enjoy it. And no, you have no reason to thank us. Just sit." Hoffner did as he was told, and Piera took another sip of his tea. Mila said, "They're changing the vouchers again, so tomorrow I need to stop down at Casa Cambo and see what we can get."

Piera said, "You'll tell them you're a doctor?"

"I always do." She reached up for a pan hanging over the stove. "Did you tell him about your son, Nikolai?" She might have spoken with the same ease of only moments ago, but Hoffner heard something else in it. She set the pan on one of the burners and said, "Nikolai has a boy. How old did you say he is?"

This wasn't something she was likely to have forgotten. More than that, Piera was suddenly rigid in his chair, staring at his glass.

Hoffner said, "Twenty-five. You're sure I can't help you?"

Mila poured a drop of oil in the pan and unwrapped the fish. "He was filming the Olimpiada," she said, too casually. She rinsed the pieces under the tap. "And now he's gone missing. Nikolai has come to find him. His son." She lit the burner with a match and gently placed the pieces in the pan. "I usually do just a bit of garlic and salt. That's all right?"

Piera's jaw clenched. "That's enough," he said quietly. He stood and moved out from behind the table.

Mila pressed the back of a fork onto the fish. She stared down into the pan. "The clothes look good, don't they?" she said, but her father was already past her. He was in the living room when she finally looked up. It was impossible not to see the frustration and sadness in her eyes.

Hoffner stood quietly. For some reason, he felt shame. Not that he knew what role he had played in getting them here, but the knowing or not knowing was never essential. Shame relied on a kind of empathy—deep, blind, and unthinking until the moment it was too late—and all the more startling because it was so rarely his. That he felt it now, standing awkwardly in a kitchen with a woman he hardly knew and who was unable to meet his gaze, struck him as both exhilarating and terrifying.

He said, "The fish—it's smoking."

She looked over at him. The oil popped, and she turned to the pan and quickly flipped the pieces. She said, "Did you sleep?"

"Yes."

She nodded and sprinkled some salt. "And no word from Gardenyes?"

She knew there wouldn't have been. Still, it was better to ask than chance the silence.

"No," Hoffner said. "He'd know to find me here?"

"He'd know how to find you. That's all." She lifted one of the pieces with the fork and bent closer to smell it. She set it back in the pan and added more oil.

Hoffner said, "You might have told me."

"Told you what?"

"Whatever it is I'm doing by being here." He watched her flip the pieces again. "I'm not in the habit of making old men so uncomfortable."

She took the pieces out of the pan and laid them on a plate. "That's not for you to worry about."

"Still—"

"Still nothing," she said, as she brought the fish to the table. "You have a meal, a bed, and clothes." She laid a cloth over the plate. "And tomorrow you'll go and look for your son."

"And these clothes I happen to be wearing?"

She was now tearing at the escarole and placing the strips in the pan. When she finished, she took a jar from the bag and, opening it, poured in white beans. She stirred them quietly.

Piera's voice came from behind Hoffner. "She has a brother." Hoffner looked back and saw the small man holding a bottle; it held a pale liquid. "He wears a different uniform now."

Piera stepped over and placed the bottle on the table. He went to the shelf and brought over three glasses.

"Knives and forks are in the second cabinet," he said, nodding to the one by the sink. Hoffner stepped over and found them. He set three places.

The silence waited with them until they were all seated. Mila pulled the cloth from the fish and placed a piece on each plate. She did the same with the escarole and beans, while Piera filled the glasses; she then took her fork and began to eat. The men followed.

"Where is he now?" Hoffner said.

He saw Mila run her fork through the escarole as she stared at her plate.

Piera said, "He fights for the fascists. He's not my concern." Piera scooped up some beans.

"Zaragoza," she said, as she reached for her glass. "At least that's where they say he was three days ago."

Piera took his time chewing and swallowing. "Your son is a journalist?" he said.

Hoffner watched Mila as she drank. "Yes," he said. "Newsreels."

"Very interesting." Piera sucked at something at the back of his teeth and took another forkful.

Mila said, "My father is a Communist. So was my brother—a long time ago. Communists aren't very forgiving."

Piera picked up his glass. "Nothing to forgive," he said plainly. He drank.

"He means nothing he *can* forgive." Mila brought up another piece of fish. "He thinks it makes him clever to say it." She ate.

Had Hoffner known the quickest way over the balcony and down to the pavement below, he would have taken it. Instead he was left to jab at a few beans with his fork.

He said, "I also have a son who fights for the fascists."

Both father and daughter looked over. The same stare of betrayal filled their eyes.

"No," Hoffner said easily. "Not the one with the newsreels. He also has a brother." Hoffner went back to his fish. It was uncanny how moist she had kept it in the pan.

Mila said, "And he fights here, the other one?"

Hoffner shook his head as he ate. "No. The older boy is in Berlin—I think. I haven't seen him in quite some time."

"And you regret it?"

There was very little subtlety with her now. It made her somehow more endearing.

Hoffner said, "Not for me to regret what he is."

"No, I meant—"

"I know what you meant," he said, and took his glass. He drank. He then looked at Piera. "I don't know this wine."

Piera needed a moment. "Penedès," he said. "Light. Nice with fish."

Hoffner nodded and finished his glass, and Mila said, "And the younger one—does he regret it?"

She showed no backing down. There was no point in not answering.

"The younger boy is a Jew," Hoffner said. "By choice. His brother is a Nazi. There was some unpleasantness. They haven't spoken in several years. It's not all that complicated."

"But you come for the young one when the other is outside your back door."

Hoffner set down his glass and took the bottle. He began to refill the glasses. "I don't have the luxury to care about their politics. I know which one will take my help. That makes the decision much easier."

"Easier for whom?" she said.

"For the one who'll use it," said Hoffner. He finished pouring.

"Or for yourself."

Piera cut in angrily. "Of course for himself." It was the first raw emotion to reach his voice. "What kind of question—easier for whom? You think he does this out of spite, to punish the other? He helps the one he can. This is a simple thing to understand."

Piera realized too late how forcefully he had spoken. It was several moments before he went back to his fish.

Hoffner said, "I don't know why I mentioned it. I'm sorry."

Mila was looking at her father. "No," she said, "I'm the one who is sorry." Piera's face softened even as he refused to look at her. She turned, and her eyes seemed to smile. The brightness in the face was all the more staggering given the last half minute.

"You'll find him," she said.

She sliced her fork into a piece of escarole. Hoffner watched as she drew it up to her mouth. She glanced at him, and it was all he could do to find the fish again on his own plate.

Two hours later he stared out from the balcony, glass in hand, as he listened to the distant sounds of music and voices from the street. Mila sat behind him on a low chair, her knees drawn to her chest. Her head was cocked lazily to one side as she listened as well. Piera had gone to bed.

Hoffner said, "I'll try and find the place tomorrow."

"He'll want to go with you," she said. "He'll insist."

Hoffner nodded.

An hour ago, Piera had given him Hanshen.

It had been something of a fluke, really, or maybe not—or maybe it was just Hoffner's turn for a bit of good luck. In any event, it was going to save him some time.

Georg's wire had indicated Hanshen was a German word. That, apparently, was not the case.

The name had come up during the third glass of Orujo and the second game of chess with Piera, a game that had not gone terribly well for Hoffner.

"You've played before," Hoffner said.

"A bit." The booze and the game were taking the edge off. Piera was smiling.

"Next you'll want to put some money on it."

"I'm a Communist," said Piera. "What would I do with it if I won?"

"You'd figure something out."

Hoffner made a move and quickly lost a bishop. He tried to convince himself that he was letting Piera win.

Mila was sitting on the sofa, reading a book. "You need to tell him," she said.

Piera kept his eyes focused on the board.

She repeated, "You need to tell him, Papá." When Piera continued to stare, she said, "My father was a chess champion. Quite famous. He's probably working through a different game in his head while he's playing you."

"And that's supposed to make me feel better?" said Hoffner.

"No," said Mila. "It's supposed to make him feel worse."

"You're not bad," said Piera. "Not good, but not bad. You should come tomorrow. I play every day. At my club. We could find you an eleven-year-old. You wouldn't beat him, but it would be good for his confidence."

His club—renowned as the best in the city—was a little room over a Chinese café, down in the Raval section of town. It was called Han Shen's. Everyone knew it.

Now Hoffner knew. He asked about Vollman, the name linked to Han Shen in the wire. Piera didn't recognize it.

A boy in the street shouted something over the music. A breeze cut across the balcony, and Hoffner turned to see Mila with her knees still pulled up close to her chest. She said, "I need to sleep."

Hoffner watched as she uncurled herself from the low chair and stood. She drew up to him and kissed him on both cheeks.

She said, "You need sleep, too."

She placed a tired hand on his chest and then moved to the balcony door. He watched her step inside and turned back to the city. He looked down to the far end of the street and wondered if there was still enough courage for this left inside him.

THE GOOD GERMANS

Mila was gone by the time he awoke. Piera was in the kitchen, waiting with coffee. There was also a note. It was not from her.

"A little ginger-haired man," Piera said as Hoffner took it. "I told him there was no point in waking you."

"Did he say how he found me?"

"He said he came from Gardenyes." Piera watched as Hoffner opened the envelope. "There was no reason to ask."

The note confirmed Han Shen. *Chess club at a Chink café,* it read. The club was in the back and up some stairs. Gardenyes gave the address.

As for the rest, Gardenyes had found a Karl Vollman on the Olimpiada rolls. A German. He was a chess player.

Perfect, thought Hoffner.

There was nothing else on the man.

The name Bernhardt had proved more interesting, or at least more plentiful. According to Gardenyes there had been nine Bernhardts listed at the Barcelona telephone exchange as of January. Two were printers (brothers), both of whom had left three weeks after the Popular Front victory in February. They had taken five other Bernhardts (sons) back to Germany with them. The last of the listed Bernhardts was a writer living with a Frenchwoman down by the water. Gardenyes had actually dealt with the man. He was a drug addict and most likely dead, but Gardenyes was sending one of his boys to look into it. As for the name Langenheim—and whatever Hisma might be—Gardenyes had come up empty.

Piera said, "You've found your boy?"

Hoffner folded the page and slipped it into his pocket. He had the Luger on his belt. "I'm assuming we can walk to this place from here."

The smell of garlic followed them as they passed the storefronts and drawn metal gates of the Raval's cramped streets. Why half the shops were closed remained a mystery. According to Piera, a joint order had come down last week from the anarchist CNT and the Communist POUM for everyone to head back to work: the city needed to move again; a few days of gunfire wasn't going to stand in its way. Workers' committees were now running the factories, collectives shipping the goods in and out. Then again, maybe the Raval had always been exempt from such things. Places built on corruption and defeat rarely take notice of the world flickering above them.

Even so, Hoffner had expected something a bit more exotic—animal parts dangling from hooks, barrels filled with God knows what—but there was something disappointingly tame to it all. Barrio Chino was little more than a few token lanterns on taut cords and gates here and there with those perfectly upturned oriental roofs; the whole thing felt a bit insincere.

Odder still were the little men and women standing outside or in, sporting their red neckerchiefs in an act of utterly indifferent solidarity. They wore them for security, nothing else. This week it was anarchists. Next it might be fascists. No doubt they had the appropriate colors waiting somewhere in their back rooms.

Piera walked with a stick, the wood as veined as the hand that gripped it. His neck was already beading from the heat.

"I bought this somewhere in here," he said. "The Chino do well with wood. You can't speak to them—maybe five words of Spanish among them—but the work is good."

"They seem to like the neckerchiefs."

Piera smiled. "It's ten years since they've come here. Can't see them staying much longer. Mostly roll carts, flophouses, the occasional shop. They work for almost nothing—at least up until a few weeks ago. Don't imagine the whores get much out of them."

As if to make the point, a woman emerged from one of the darkened archways. Her dress was pulled down low on the shoulders, the rest too tight around a figure that could best be advertised as replete with extra cushioning. Still, the face looked young even if the hair and skin had both gone an unnatural white—one from a bottle, the other from too many hours lost to needles and men—and there was a kind of girlish enthusiasm in the way she walked and smiled: big pouty lips encircling a remarkably straight set of teeth, and a chest with enough heft to smother a small cat. It might have been the heroin or the pills or whatever else was coursing through her body, but Hoffner let himself believe she took a pleasure in knowing that, despite the recent upheavals, she had never packed it in.

She steadied herself against a wall, brought her foot up to adjust the strap of her shoe, and broadened her smile for Piera. The little man offered a surprisingly robust nod that seemed to catch even the woman off guard. Piera continued to walk.

"That's why the anarchists are idiots," he said. "You think they'll get a girl like that off the streets?"

Hoffner looked back as they walked. The woman was still watching them, a handkerchief dabbing at the moist folds of skin on her neck. She seemed so much more impressive than a German whore, as if she had expectations of her own: not enough just to hand her the money; there had to be something in it worth her time.

Piera said, "You see."

He was pointing his stick at a poster plastered across one of the storefront gates. It showed an intoxicated woman in a classic red dress drawn in hard angles, a cigarette dripping from her fat gray lips, her hand roaming into the jacket pocket of some faceless man. Across her chest was written the warning, THE WHORE IS A PARASITE! A THIEF! LET'S GET RID OF HER!

Someone less troubled by the apparent threat had more recently drawn her other hand: it was reaching a bit lower down on the man's leg, with the words PLEASE! ROB ME! ROB ME! ROB ME! scrawled across the logo for the CNT.

Piera said, "The anarchists promised to close down the brothels."

"That's a sad sort of promise."

"Not to worry. It's their boys who fill the places every night."

Hoffner followed him down a few steps and into an open courtyard. Two young boys and a man were kicking around what passed for a ball. The man had set his rifle against a wall.

Piera said, "It's not so much that they're hypocrites." The smell of the garlic had soured. "They are, but that just makes them anarchists. The question is, Why bother with morality at all? She harms no one—"

"Except perhaps herself."

Piera dismissed the idea. "A man in a coal mine harms himself. A man who breathes fumes in some factory all day long harms himself. Work is harmful. What shattering news. It's still necessary. As is what she does."

"From each according to her ability—"

"Laugh all you want, but if you need a morality beyond that, find a priest. To go looking for it with an anarchist"—Piera shook his head—"that makes you a fool."

It was heartening to hear this kind of mutual support among the newly victorious.

They moved through to another narrow street and Piera raised his cane and pointed to an archway. Chinese symbols were printed in thick black ink above the door, along with a more Spanish rendering of the name: HAN SHEN. Below it the cobblestones ran with the remains of some recent spillage; tiny yellow bubbles clung to the stone and gave off the distinct smell of onions and chicken fat. Hoffner was careful to step around them.

Inside, two old Chinese sat silently at one of four tables in the dim light, peeling little stalks of something and tossing the beans into a barrel on the floor. The air was damp, cooler than on the street, and smelled of day-old flowers.

A woman was standing in a long black smock by the stairs that led up to the back room. She had what Hoffner imagined to be the widest face he had ever seen. It was as if someone had taken the skin and bones and hammered them flat until the nose had all but disappeared; likewise the eyes and mouth seemed to crease to the very edges of the flesh. To make matters worse, her skin was a kind of mottled gray, and her hair looked as if it had been planted on the scalp in tiny clumps of baled black hay. Hoffner might have taken her for one of those sideshow curiosities one sees for a few coins at a country tent, but there was too much of the familiar in the way she stared across at them to make that mistake.

He said to Piera, "Café's a kind way of putting it, isn't it?"

Hoffner had seen enough of these faces back in Prenzlauer Berg not to appreciate the stamp of opium. On a German complexion, the needles and pipe left a kind of sticky residue; yellow and smooth, it sank the cheeks and narrowed the pupils to blackened pinpoints. With a Chinese, the face flattened and grew pale. It might have been bloating or bone disintegration, but whatever the reason, the addict was no less recognizable. This, however, was the most pronounced case Hoffner had ever seen.

He said, "You're sure it's only chess they play here?"

"The chess is upstairs," said Piera. "What they do in the basement is someone else's business."

The woman was now walking toward them. Her head teetered from side to side but thus far remained planted on her neck. Piera reached into his pocket and pulled out a coin. He placed it in her hand, and they stepped past her to the stairs.

It was a long narrow room above, bare wooden floors and the kind of stone walls that seemed to undulate from too many coats of white paint. A row of small windows were open at the topmost edge of the far wall; they made the air breathable. Fifteen or so tables filled the space, each with a hanging bulb above, along with a small colored shade in deep reds and oranges. There was probably something Chinese to the design, but Hoffner didn't recognize it. Much to his relief, the place smelled of tobacco and sweat.

Only four of the tables were occupied, a pair of men at each, except for the nearest, where a young man sat by himself, staring at his board. Every few seconds he glanced up at the chair across from him with a look of mild confusion; he seemed genuinely surprised to find it empty.

Piera said, "They used to bring the addicts up here when the *asaltos* came to arrest them. Those long coats and perfect buttons, with their little truncheons in their hands—and staring in here with no idea who was on the drugs and who was simply crazy."

"Until someone vomited or passed out," said Hoffner.

"You've never played tournament chess, have you?"

The young man stood and moved over to the empty chair. He looked at it for several seconds before muttering something to himself and sitting. Again he began to examine the board.

"Does he ever win?" Hoffner said.

"Every time, I imagine."

One of the men a few tables down looked up, not quite so young, rail thin, but with dark slicked-back hair. There were bruises on his face, along with some scabbing on the forehead. Evidently not everyone in the streets had fought with bayonets and guns. The man recognized Piera. He nodded and went back to his game.

Piera said, "He once drew three games with Capablanca. Rome, 1921. Remarkable player."

Hoffner had given up following chess a long time ago, but even he recalled the great Cuban player.

Piera said, "He can tell you every move of every game, show you how Capablanca held the pieces before he moved them—forefinger and thumb, middle finger and thumb, entire palm—and how much time he took with each piece in the air. It's like watching a film."

"And he's one of the sane ones?"

"He runs the place."

The other two tables were deep into games. Hoffner said, "Do you recognize everyone in here?"

"No."

"Good. Stay here."

Hoffner made his way over to Piera's friend and stood hovering above the table. Neither of the men playing bothered to acknowledge him. Finally Hoffner cleared his throat.

Piera's friend reached for one of his rooks—there was more bruising on the knuckles—and said, "Yes, we know you're there." It was Spanish, but the accent was from elsewhere. "The idea was we didn't care." He placed the rook along the last rank and went back to studying the board.

Hoffner said, "You run this place, a room over an opium den?"

The man showed no reaction as he continued to scan the pieces. "You're not Spanish, so I'm thinking I don't have to care what concerns you."

Apparently even the chess club boys were getting to play it tough these days, although there was something too comfortable in the way this one doled out his aggression. Hoffner wondered how much time the man was splitting between his upstairs clientele and those in the basement.

The man across the table ran the back of his fingers through his beard and then slid a pawn forward one square. Piera's friend stared a moment longer, peering over at a completely different area of the board before sitting back. Only then did he look up at Hoffner. He took a moment and said, "He has a pretty daughter—Piera. Have you met her?"

"I'm impressed," said Hoffner. "You'd think you'd be able to smell it up here."

"What, Piera's daughter? I hope not."

In a different place, a different time, Hoffner would have cracked the man across the face, but that kind of brutality was too easy now. Instead, Hoffner picked up one of the pieces on the side of the board.

"You're a long way from home, aren't you?" Hoffner said. When the man continued to stare, Hoffner added, "I was thinking Polish from the accent, but the face is wrong. Maybe Czech or Romanian. You boys are always good with chess."

It might have been animal instinct, but the bearded man across the table now slowly pushed back his chair. He took out a pack of cigarettes and moved off, happy to go smoke in a corner.

Hoffner said, "Your friend's accustomed to stepping away from the game?"

"Usually with his king down."

"Oh, that's right," Hoffner said, as he set the piece down. "You're quite the hero. Drawing with Capablanca. Very impressive." It was nice to see the jaw tighten. "I've never understood that. No winner, no loser. It's as if the game never happened, so why bother remembering it?"

The man's tone was equally tight when he spoke. "What do you want?"

"Don't worry—it's not about the drugs." It might have been. Gardenyes's note had mentioned the writer Bernhardt and his predilection, but Hoffner knew that could wait. Georg's wire had been very clear: Han Shen was connected to Vollman. Better to keep things simple and start there.

"Germans," said Hoffner. "You've had a few of them playing in here the last few weeks."

"Have I? We don't check papers at the door."

"Not good for business."

"No."

"Bit of a drop-off since the fighting started?"

"What fighting?" The man spoke with a goading insincerity. "I haven't heard any shots today, have you?"

Hoffner regretted not having slapped him. "So, business as usual?"

The man set his hands on the table. "Something like that." He started to get up, and Hoffner quietly gripped the shoulder and arm and held them in place. The man sat back down.

Hoffner said, "I'm going to give you the benefit of the doubt and say you're too clever to be in deep with what's going on downstairs. You turn a blind eye and they make it worth your while. No crime in that."

The man said coldly, "There is no crime in Barcelona these days—

haven't you heard?" Hoffner tightened his grip and the man said, "It's as a courtesy to Piera I'm talking with you."

"The same courtesy that's keeping your arm from snapping in two. We understand each other?"

The man winced, then nodded.

Hoffner said, "There's a man named Vollman. From the Olimpiada. I need to find him."

The answer was too long in coming. "I don't know him."

"Yes, you do. He would have been in here a few days before the games." Hoffner turned the elbow and watched as the man's eyes tried to fight back the pain.

The man said, "I wouldn't know where he is."

"We both know that's not true."

The man chanced a look at his friend, who was still smoking in the corner. Almost at once, the bearded man tossed the cigarette to the ground and bolted for the door. He was surprisingly agile and might have made it had Piera not whacked his cane across the man's kneecap. There was the expected yowling, the looks of pain and panic—all the trappings of men caught up in something well beyond their means.

Hoffner said, "That was remarkably stupid. Where is he?"

The sight of his friend sprawled on the floor brought a final tensing of defiance from the man in the chair. Just as quickly his shoulders dropped. He stared down at the board and said, "You're scum to help these people, Piera."

Piera looked particularly daunting standing over the bearded one. "This from a man who helps the Chinks run their poison up from the south."

The man said bitterly, "So it's not just your son, Piera, is it?"

Hoffner was having trouble following the sudden turn in the conversation. He was, however, quick enough to keep Piera's cane from landing on the man's skull.

Hoffner said, "Enough. We all take a step back."

Hoffner waited and then released. It was another few seconds before Piera slowly brought the cane down.

"What people?" Hoffner asked.

The man snorted to himself, then mumbled something in a Catalan only vaguely familiar. Finally he said, in Spanish, "No, I'm sure you have no idea."

Hoffner noticed the four sets of eyes peering over from the other tables. Piera was staring at him as well. Oddly enough it was Piera's expression that was most unsettling. Hoffner did his best to ignore it. He turned to the man and repeated, "What people?"

From behind him Piera said, "You haven't made a fool of me or my daughter, have you?" There was a quiet accusation in the voice.

Hoffner turned to him. "What?"

"It's a simple question," said Piera.

The silence only deepened Hoffner's confusion. "No," he said. "I haven't."

"Then why does he think you're hunting down this Vollman for the fascists?"

The thought was absurd. Hoffner continued to stare, and Piera said, "He believes we are also fascists."

Hoffner was doing what he could to make sense of the last half minute. He turned to the man, the eyes now fixed on the far wall. Hoffner saw their contempt and instantly understood why.

"Who else has been in here asking about Vollman?" said Hoffner. When the man refused to look up, Hoffner again grabbed him by the arm. "Who else?"

The man took his time. "Germans," he said. "Germans—like you."

"Not like me. Who?"

"Yes, like you." The man continued to stare straight ahead. "Twisting arms, beating faces, breaking knees. Exactly like you."

The hatred in the eyes was now unassailable. It was no match, though, for the sudden revulsion Hoffner felt for himself. He slowly released the man and said, "That's not who I am. I thought you were—" Hoffner shook his head. "You know what I thought you were."

The man turned to him. "Do I?"

Hoffner was having trouble matching the gaze. "The drugs. I assumed—"

"What? That Communists can't peddle drugs? We run it as a collective, if that makes you feel any better. Are even the good Germans like this now?"

Hoffner found himself staring into the man's eyes even as the words gutted him. "No," he said quietly. "They're not."

"And you believe that?"

It was all Hoffner could do to answer. "I'm trying to find one of the good ones. My son. I assume your Vollman is another."

The man studied him. There was a moment's uncertainty. "Your son?"

"Yes. A filmmaker."

Again the man waited. Hoffner saw another moment in the eyes before the man said, "The boy from Pathé Gazette?"

It was said so easily, and yet Hoffner felt it to his core. Georg had been here. Hoffner nodded.

The man thought something through and then turned to Piera. "Your son, Piera," he said. There was regret in the voice. "I was sorry to hear about that."

"So was I," said Piera. "You know where this Vollman is?" The man nodded and Piera said, "Then you're lucky. I would have broken the arm."

The man knew every twist and bend of the Raval's back alleys. Piera had stayed behind. The morning's events had taken it out of him. Still, he was in better shape than the one with the beard. The knee was already the size of a melon. Piera offered no apologies.

They drew up to a building and the man pulled out a set of keys. The alley was empty. Even so, he peered off in both directions. Satisfied, he unlocked the door and ushered Hoffner in.

Four worn wood stairways later they stood in front of a single door, and it was through here that they discovered the sleeping Karl Vollman.

The room was a nice molting of chipped plaster and paint, with a tiny sink and spigot wedged into one corner. Water stains—browns and yellows—provided what color there was, while an angled window looked out on endless lines of clothes drying in the heat. Everything smelled of rust. Had there been an easel and a few stacks of drying canvas, Hoffner might have hummed the first bars of "Che gelida manina," but the place was too hot for frozen little hands, and there didn't seem to be much hope in it, even if Vollman was sleeping soundly.

Vollman was in undershirt and trousers, with his shoes neatly at the foot of the bed. Even sleeping, there was a power to the body, the arms pale and muscular. Most distinctive, though, was the shock of white hair on a man no more than fifty.

Hoffner's guide stepped toward the cot and placed a hand on Vollman's shoulder. Vollman remained absolutely still until he took in a long breath and suddenly bolted upright. The sinew in the chest tightened and then released.

The man said, "Karl." He spoke in German.

Vollman stared straight ahead. He rubbed his face briskly and began to nod. It was only then that he noticed Hoffner.

"Monsieur," said Vollman. "Je suis soulagé que vous soyez ici. Êtes-vous prêt à partir?"

Hoffner needed a moment. "What?"

The man from the club said, "He's saying—"

"I know what he's saying," said Hoffner. "He thinks I'm taking him to Paris."

Vollman spoke in German. "Yes."

Hoffner said, "You think it's not safe for you here."

"No."

"And why is that?" Hoffner always felt a moment's regret watching a man's eyes give in to the truth.

Vollman said, "Who is this?"

Hoffner pulled out his cigarettes and offered one to Vollman. "My name is Hoffner." He took one for himself. "I believe you know my son."

Paris faded.

Hoffner thought he would see a few moments of calculation in the eyes—how else were chess men meant to react?—but Vollman showed nothing. He just sat there, remarkably well-shaven, although his shirt and trousers did show several days of sleep and sweat.

Hoffner said, "You're here because of my son."

Vollman focused. He looked over, reached for the cigarette, and placed it in his mouth.

Hoffner said, "I'm sorry for that."

"Is he dead?"

Hoffner lit Vollman's cigarette, then his own. "No."

"You know that for certain?"

Hoffner let the smoke stream from his nose. He said nothing.

Vollman stood and headed for the sink. "I ran out of German cigarettes about a week ago," he said. "Don't much like the Spanish ones." He placed the cigarette on the edge of the sink and pulled a hand towel from some unseen hook. He began to wet it. "Leos here doesn't smoke, so he doesn't care."

The man from the club said, "I've different things to care about."

Vollman ran the cloth along his neck and forehead. "That's always a good excuse, isn't it?" Vollman rinsed his mouth, placed the towel back on the hook, and retrieved his cigarette. "He has no idea why he's protecting me. That makes him a good friend, so I forgive him the cigarettes. You've come all the way from Berlin, so you must have a great deal that needs forgiving."

Hoffner felt oddly at home with a man like this.

Vollman said, "You should go, Leos."

The man from the club waited and then looked at Hoffner. He said, "I'll take Piera to the Ritz. Two hours. If you don't show, I'll kill him. Fair enough?"

Hoffner liked when things were made this clear. He nodded.

"And you give my friend here your cigarettes," the man said. "So I don't have to hear him whine about it anymore."

Hoffner tossed the pack onto the cot as the door pulled open and shut behind him.

Vollman was not a Jew. It was the least surprising thing about him, even if he did come from a long line of true believers—years spent organizing in the working-class districts of Berlin, with a few scars on his right arm to show for it. He had been at school in Switzerland with all the best revolutionaries and had even spent time with Lenin before the mad dash to Moscow. That Lenin had gotten it completely wrong, and paved the way for Stalin and his thugs, hardly had Vollman giving up on the Soviet experiment just yet. Stalin would have his chance to make things right here in Spain; all would be forgiven if the tanks and planes and men began pouring in.

That said, it wasn't all that unusual a story until Vollman decided to explain why he was in Spain. He had come as a special envoy of the Unified State Political Administration, working with its foreign department, what he referred to as INO through OGPU. Hoffner stared blankly, and Vollman simplified: he was, for lack of a better term, an agent of Soviet Intelligence. And while that might have been staggering on its own, it seemed even more implausible that Vollman should feel the need to share the information with Hoffner. Yet even that seemed reasonable enough.

"What else would I be?" Vollman said easily, as he lit his third cigarette. He was sitting on the cot. "Why else would Georg and I have been in touch with each other? Birds of a feather."

Hoffner took a long pull and nodded as if this made any real sense to him.

Vollman said, "I'm not saying anything you don't know."

Hoffner realized it was in his best interest to agree. "It's a recent piece of information, but yes. I knew why Georg was here."

Vollman reached for his shoes. "You haven't made some horrible mistake, have you?"

"I don't think so."

Vollman began to lace up. "It's rather funny if you think about it. Three Germans in Spain—a civil war—one working for British Intelligence, one for Soviet Intelligence, and one"—he finished lacing and looked over— "one looking for the other two."

Hoffner felt the slightest threat of violence slip into the room. "I'm looking for just one," he said.

"And yet you've found the other."

There was nothing to be gained in retreat. Hoffner dropped his cigarette to the floor and began to crush it under his shoe. "You could get to Paris any time you like, couldn't you?"

"And why would I want to do that?"

"Your friend Leos seems to be going to great lengths to get you there."

"He does, doesn't he? Did you take a few cracks at him yourself? He's been very good at letting people thrash him on my behalf."

"It's very kind of you to let him."

Vollman's gaze turned to a smile. It was an odd reaction, odder still to see genuine warmth in it. "It's a sweet little line—the kindness of my cruelty. I imagine it once had a place."

There was nothing mocking in Vollman's tone, more nostalgia than derision. Hoffner was moving well beyond his depth.

Vollman said, "It's only cruel if that sort of cruelty still exists—the one where a man uses another, wittingly or not, in the name of some larger cause. 'I will sacrifice you, Leos . . .'" Vollman watched as the words floated out the window. "It's such a dangerous thing to rely on—sacrifice. Even more ridiculous to ask it of someone. Are we such fools as to think there's nobility in any of this?"

Hoffner imagined Georg standing in his place, sifting through a conversation built on unspoken truths and unadorned lies, and only then did he realize that he had no idea what his son might be capable of.

Hoffner said, "So, a German socialist working for Soviet communism—and there's no great cause? I find that highly unlikely."

"My cause was Germany. Same as yours. That's long gone. It's now just making sure the world keeps things balanced."

"Comrade Stalin never struck me as such a pragmatist."

"Who said anything about Stalin?" Vollman flicked a bit of ash to the floor. "A grotty little attic—never been the place for ideologies and five-year plans, has it?"

Hoffner was thinking another chair would have been nice right about now. "So the true believer turns out to be not so true. I imagine there's something sad in that."

"Why? Would you really want a zealot holed up in here?"

"It's a long way from this to a zealot."

"Is it? All it takes is the word 'truth' or 'message' or 'cause'—or 'sacrifice.' I don't much cotton to those. For me it's always been much easier to look at the more practical side of things. Guns, tanks, planes. Who has them, how they get more. That's why Georg was here. That's why I'm here. To see how these Spanish generals plan to wage their war. And who they plan to get their weapons from. The practical. That's why he told me you'd be here."

Hoffner was getting tired of meeting himself through other people's eyes. "I'm surprised he mentioned me."

"No, you're not. He said you'd come if things went sour. He was actually proud of that."

Hoffner needed a moment; there was too much caught in his throat to find an answer. "So things have gone sour?"

"He's been out of touch for what—four days, maybe five?"

"A week."

Vollman's eyebrows rose as if to make his point. "That's not good."

"No."

"And you think you'll just go off and find him?"

"I found you, didn't I?"

Vollman liked the answer. He moved past it quickly. "The world has never been so ready to declare its allegiances. They'll all be shipping themselves into Spain by the truckload in the next weeks, months, and every one of them with his arm raised in whatever salute suits him best. It's a terrible thing to know how pointless it's all going to be."

"And yet here you are."

"Of course I'm here. Who else is going to make sure all those theories and truths don't muddy what really matters?"

Hoffner nodded quietly. "That balance you and Georg and all the rest of your attic-dwelling friends are keeping safe for us. How lucky for me to be able to thank you in person."

There was no ruffling Vollman. "Georg might tell you he sees something more in it, something nobler—that can get a man in trouble—but I wouldn't hold it against him." Vollman finished his cigarette and began to crush it against the metal leg of the bed. "As for the rest of us, we know exactly why we're in Spain. We've come for the dry run. Germany, Italy,

England"—he dropped the butt to the floor—"Comrade Stalin. We're here to see how it all works before moving onto the big stage. The Spanish have always had such remarkable timing."

"Your sacrificial lambs."

Vollman's smile returned. "They've led themselves to the slaughter. There's no sacrifice in that."

Hoffner wondered how long it took a man to rid himself of any feeling for the world beyond him: a month, a year, a lifetime watching his own truths ground down to nothing? Easier, then, to toss them all away and damn the world for still trying.

"So your friend Leos," Hoffner said. "He thinks he's protecting a frightened little chess player up here, even though the anarchists are running the streets. So what's he protecting you from?"

Vollman reached for another cigarette; it was clear why he had run out so quickly. "I'm just a poor helpless refugee," he said, as he lit up. "Leos thinks I might have overheard something or seen something at his club. I need to get out of this war-torn country."

"And yet here you sit—waiting."

"Barcelona's always been much better after dark."

"And he has no idea what you do then, after dark?"

"It's all a bit loose—Leos doesn't press—but there might be a few people who've taken an interest in me."

"And how long have the SS been in Barcelona?"

Vollman spat something to the floor. "A week, ten days. Not early enough to have saved it for themselves."

"But early enough to have known about Georg?"

Vollman took another pull and let his head rest against the wall. He waited until the smoke had streamed from his nose. "You wouldn't still be clinging to any hopes of something noble in this, would you? That would be a disappointment."

"I asked about Georg."

"Of course you did. And of course they knew. There are never any great surprises in this. Not for those of us who sleep in shithole attics. It comes down to who gets the guns and where they get them from. And how long they can keep it a secret. We know it. The British know it. The Nazis know it. That's why ideology is meaningless. Something else Georg said you'd understand."

The truth, once untapped, was such an easy thing for men like this. They used it like a weapon. "So he's looking for guns?" said Hoffner.

"And planes and tanks and ships and anything else they might try to get through to the generals in the south. Franco has thirty thousand troops sitting in Morocco. He needs to move them across the water to the mainland, and he needs something for them to fight with once he gets them across. It's a little game. The Nazis say they won't send in the guns, and everyone says they believe them. And then we all go looking for the way the Nazis will send in the guns. It's more about the where and the how than the what."

"And Han Shen's?"

Vollman stared across at Hoffner. It was another few moments before Hoffner saw it.

"The opium lines," Hoffner said.

"Nice little network for delivery, if you think about it."

Hoffner hadn't. "And the Nazis—they think they can use the drug lines to supply guns for the fascists?"

"They did a week ago."

"And now?"

Vollman shrugged, took another pull, and tossed the match to the floor. "That depends on whether they know who's running it. If they think it's still the Chinese, the Nazis will send the guns. Naturally they won't know it's Leos and his Communists who'll be getting them. That'll make the Barcelona anarchists stand up and take notice of their clever little Communist friends. Duping Berlin. Nice twist, don't you think?"

"And if the Nazis have figured it out?"

"Then there'll be a lot of dead Chinese and dead Communists. That's the way things always go at the beginning. Trial and error."

There wasn't even a hint of feeling. "And Georg knew all this?"

Vollman took another pull. He seemed to be deciding whether to mislead or enlighten. "He was following something south," he said. "Down to Teruel. Something to do with the guns. That's my gift to you."

"So who are Bernhardt and Langenheim?" Hoffner thought it time for a little strafing of the truth of his own.

Vollman had been at this too long, though, to show any kind of reaction. He continued to stare across before taking a final pull. "You should get to the Ritz. Leos isn't one for idle threats."

"And Hisma?" said Hoffner.

The silence this time was too long. Vollman said, "You should go."

"I imagine Georg expected me to pass those names along."

"He's a clever boy."

"It's b-e-r-n—"

"Yes," said Vollman. "You'll need to head south if you want to find him."

"And you'll be here in Barcelona?" Hoffner knew there would be no answer. He waited and then moved to the door. He had the handle in his grip when Vollman said, "Pawn to queen bishop three. It's the Caro-Kann defense. My specialty. Leos likes to know I'm safe."

Hoffner had his back to him. So this was what safety felt like, he thought. He nodded and opened the door.

The wide avenue of the Rambla was up and moving as Hoffner made his way through the heat. Open-backed trucks carrying men and rifles, men and grain, men and pigs, trundled between the lines of trees, careful to avoid the still uncleared piles of brick and stone. A week ago trucks like these, then filled with boys eager for the fight at Huesca or Zaragoza, or maybe even as far west as Madrid, had been cheered on by the thousands. Even now the frenzy of those first few days hung in the branches—hats and scarves tossed high and abandoned—but who could deny the sound of victory still echoing in the leaves?

Vollman had talked a great deal; he had said almost nothing. It was clear he recognized the names in the wire: Langenheim and Bernhardt. Hisma might have been something new to him—or maybe Hoffner just wanted to think that—but at least things were now on the table. This was about guns and the way the Nazis would get them into Spain. And Georg had been sent to expose that. In a world gone mad on truths and malice, ideologies and sacrifice, this was nothing more than a boy's playground game. Smack the bully and make him cry. That tens of thousands of Spaniards might have to die in the process hardly seemed to matter.

It was a sobering thought as Hoffner came to the Ritz, its ten stories of palatial stone and glass filling the entire block. The curved rise of the façade and the blackened windows did little to soften the appearance; even the row of balconies above seemed to sneer down at the plaza through gritted teeth. Hoffner imagined this to have been the breeding ground for Barcelona's elite, with chandeliers and dinner jackets and crystal glasses set across endless stretches of brocaded linen tablecloth: all those photographs of withering smiles, men and women staring up in perfectly seated lines of privilege and decay.

It would have been enough to smell the hair tonic and toilet water if not for the riddling of pockmarks along the stone from recent machine-gun fire. Likewise, the ragtag group of trucks parked outside—men hauling carcasses of beef and pork through the front door—cast out any lingering sophistication. Most glaring, though, was the awning where the words HO-TEL GASTRONÓMICO NO. 1 severed all links to the past. The Ritz was now a UGT/CNT canteen: so nice to see the socialists and anarchists working hand in hand to feed the people.

Hoffner crossed the plaza and joined the line heading in. The man in front of him was reading the latest issue of the *Solidaridad Obrera*, most of the newspaper's front page a description of the fighting in Aragón: a pilot by the name of Gayoso—anarchist or socialist was still unclear—had coasted down to 150 meters and dropped a bomb on Our Lady of the Pillar in Zaragoza. The "purring of the engines," so the article read, had been unfamiliar to those in the streets, but both church and city had escaped any real damage when the bomb failed to explode.

The man in front snorted and shook his head.

"They think Jesus saved their little church," he said. "You get us some bombs that work, and General Mola will be wishing he never left Navarre."

Hoffner was expecting more of the history lesson, but the line began to move. Four minutes later he stood in one of the grand ballrooms, now teeming with diners. It was humanity at its chewing best, a long narrow table at the side running some thirty meters to the back wall; large and small round tables filled the rest of the floor. The chandeliers were still above—most without bulbs—but the light pouring in from the ceiling-high windows made them almost an afterthought.

If there was an empty chair to be found Hoffner couldn't see it—mothers with children bent over bowls of soup and bread, waiters in white coats or shirtsleeves darting in between, and above it all the hum of eager silverware and untamed conversation. These might have been the recently dispossessed, but Hoffner suspected the room brought its own brand of self-satisfaction to those inside. Even eating was a kind of triumph in the new Barcelona.

A man approached through the maze of chairs. "You're alone, friend?"

It was a single motion to call Hoffner over and send him off toward the long table where the next chair in line stood empty. Hoffner thought to explain, but there was too much movement behind him—in front of him, to the side of him—to stand in the way of progress. He sidestepped his way through and took his seat.

The man next to him was shoveling the last bits of rice onto a fork. He had yet to look up. "*Salud*, friend," he said. "He'll be by in a minute. Best to have your voucher out."

This was the sticking point. Hoffner realized his time at the Ritz might be short-lived. He turned to have a look around and was nearly flattened by a waiter carrying a large silver tray.

"Watch yourself, friend," the man said as he buzzed by, and Hoffner pulled back. When he looked out again, Hoffner saw Mila a few meters off, standing directly across from him.

She was in a different pair of trousers, slightly lighter blouse, but the belt, hair, and eyes were exactly the same. She was smiling at him.

She walked over. "You always do what you're told?"

The shock of seeing her left Hoffner momentarily at a loss.

"We're down here," she said, "but you're welcome to stay with your new friend if you like."

Piera, Leos, and a third man—with oddly drooping eyes and a scar across his left cheek—were working through several bowls of beans and chicken when Mila and Hoffner drew up.

Hoffner said, "Pawn to—"

"Yes." Leos cut him off as he continued to eat. "He likes all that. You wouldn't be standing here if he wasn't tucked away."

Mila sat, and Hoffner took the chair next to her. He said, "I didn't expect to see you."

"And I didn't expect to find my father being held hostage." She was smiling.

Leos had his glass to his lips. "That's unfair," he said.

"You would have killed him, wouldn't you?"

"Yes."

"So what else would you call it?"

Leos thought a moment, shrugged, and drank.

Hoffner said, "You just happened to stop by the Ritz?"

She poured them both some wine. "Workers' Canteen Number One," she corrected. "And no. When my father goes to the club, I bring him lunch. When he gets kidnapped, I tend to follow along."

Leos said, "So now it's kidnapping." He chewed through a bone. "I suppose next you're going to tell me I actually killed him."

Hoffner was struck by how easily they tossed this all about. Leos would have shot Piera without a thought. He was just as likely to share a bowl of chicken with him. Evidently instinct worked minute to minute these days.

Piera pushed his bowl forward and sucked something in his teeth. "Did you find your son?" he said, with no real interest.

There was a commotion by the door, and they all turned to see the head man shaking his head. One or two others in line were doing the same. Finally the head man threw up his hands, stepped back, and little Aurelio— shirt and ginger hair matted in sweat—moved past him. The man with the droopy eyes was instantly on his feet.

Aurelio drew up and stared, his breathing heavy.

The standing man began to shake his head, as if to say, Well?

It took Aurelio another moment to focus. When he did, his voice was quiet.

"*Patrullas*," he said. He seemed almost confused by it. "No papers. Nothing." He looked at Hoffner, then Mila, then Hoffner again. "They took him. On the street." It was as if he were watching it play out in front of him. "The butt of a rifle to the head and gone. There won't even be enough of him left to bury."

4

PASE DE LA FIRMA

In the early spring of 1919, while Detective Inspector Nikolai Hoffner recovered from his investigations into the murder of Rosa Luxemburg, General Severiano Martínez Anido arrived in Barcelona to quell the more dangerous elements within the anarchist Sindicato Unico. The Sindicato was the most powerful union in the country and had recently begun to encourage some of its members to explore alternative measures when dealing with work stoppages, lockouts, and industrialists in general. It seemed that bold words and tossed rocks were getting them only so far. The leadership wanted something more permanent. Thereafter, bullet and garroting-wire sales rose dramatically throughout the city.

General Martínez Anido, a mild soft-spoken little man, had been sent on direct orders from the prime minister, Don Eduardo Dato. Dato's exact words—if his secretary's memory can be trusted (she had somehow remained on the telephone line while Dato made his intentions clear)—were to "get yourself to that rat-infested Catalan pisshole, cut off the balls of every last swine-fucking anarcho, and feed them to the bastards' wives." Martínez Anido, never one to take an order at anything less than face value, immediately set about infiltrating the dark and murderous secret society of the Unico with men of his own. By December he had rounded up thirty-six of the worst of them—including their leader, Roy del Sucre—and had them all rotting behind bars in the always inviting Fortress of Mahón in the Balearic Islands. Rumor had it that one of these detainees had been accidentally castrated (although how one is accidentally castrated is anyone's guess), but Dato's secretary was less than forthcoming on that front. The rest of the inmates languished fully intact, one of them a twenty-two-year-old Josep Gardenyes, although no records show anyone of that specific name on the prison rolls at the time. His cellmate had been a droopy-eyed man with a scar on his left cheek. When, fifteen months later, the two managed to avenge themselves by ambushing and machine-gunning Dato in Madrid's Plaza de la Independencia (by then Gardenyes had taught himself to steer a motorcycle with his knees), they became brothers in blood.

The sole surviving brother was now sitting in the corner of a dank bar six blocks from the Ritz, his fourth whiskey already gone, his droopy eyes unashamedly weeping. He had felt a moment's hesitation crying in front of the woman, but she was a doctor and no doubt had seen worse. The two Communists had lived through bloodlettings of their own: who were they to fault a man his passion? And Aurelio was probably more drunk than he was himself. As for the German—he would be dead within a week, so what difference did it make?

Leos pushed the bottle toward the man and hoped one more glass might be enough to stop the wailing. Remarkably, the man was managing to cry even while drinking.

"It would be pointless," said Aurelio. He had been working through a canteen of water and was in full command of his faculties. "I didn't recognize any of the boys who picked him up, and I know them all."

Leos said, "So how do you know these were *patrullas*?"

"Because they told us," Aurelio explained. "'We're with the *patrullas*,' one of them shouted. 'We won't put up with this kind of disgrace! You have us to thank. The true spirit of anarchism.' On and on. Then they smacked the rifle across the back of his head and tossed the body into the car. They weren't even carrying the right kind of pistols."

Hoffner, who had been listening for the better part of the last five minutes, finally spoke. "So you think they took Gardenyes for another reason."

Aurelio reached for his canteen. "Whoever they were, they were sloppy."

"How?"

Aurelio took a drink. "You have one on your belt. Put it on the table."

Without hesitation Hoffner pulled the Luger out and set it next to his glass.

"That," said Aurelio. "That was what one of them had."

"Which means?" said Leos.

Aurelio looked across at Hoffner. "Those names on the list—the ones you gave him—Gardenyes found one of them."

Vollman had been right, thought Hoffner. The SS had wasted no time in getting here. They had killed Gardenyes for poking around. "I know," said Hoffner.

"No," Aurelio said. "Not the chess player, the drugs. Bernhardt. Another German. That was what had these *patrullas*-not-*patrullas* looking for him. It's why Gardenyes sent my crying friend here to find you at the Chinaman's." Aurelio glanced over at the man. "All right—it's enough already."

The man went on undeterred and Aurelio looked back at Hoffner. "I'm guessing you knew that would happen—the *patrullas*."

"I didn't."

"And I'm supposed to believe that?"

Hoffner picked up his glass. "The pistol's there. I'm sure no one would mind if you used it." He drank.

Aurelio nodded over at Mila. "She would." Hoffner thought he saw a moment of color in her cheeks before Aurelio said, "She's the one who'd have to clean it up."

Leos tossed back the last of his glass and set it firmly on the table. He was done. "I'm sorry your friend is dead," he said as he stood. "*Patrullas* or not, I have to get back."

Hoffner was peering into his glass. "New kind of deliveries to be made?" He lapped at the last of his whiskey and then said, "I'd be careful there."

It was clear Leos understood exactly what Hoffner was talking about. Leos stared for several seconds before saying, "What else did Vollman overhear?"

"You'd have to ask him that yourself, wouldn't you?" Hoffner now felt every eye at the table on him; he continued to gaze at Leos. "He thinks it goes through Teruel."

"Then he thinks wrong."

Hoffner waited. This wasn't misdirection; this was a reclaiming of control. For better or worse, Leos was speaking the truth; the drug/gun conduit didn't run through Teruel. The question was, What had Georg found to send him there?

Hoffner said, "You be sure to tell him that."

Leos stood silently. He then swept a glance across the table and said, "*Salud*. You have my condolences." He turned and headed off.

Aurelio watched him through the door before turning to Hoffner. "What the hell was that?"

Hoffner leaned forward and took hold of the bottle. "He runs drugs. It's a dangerous business."

"So what's in Teruel?"

Hoffner poured himself another glass and set the bottle down. "Evidently not drugs."

With surprising speed Aurelio reached over and grabbed hold of Hoffner's hand. The whiskey in the glass spilled to the table. For such a small man, Aurelio had a remarkably strong grip.

Hoffner said, "If you'd wanted a glass, I'd have been happy to pour you one."

Aurelio tightened his grip.

Hoffner said, "It's an easy hand to break. It's been broken before."

"What's he moving?" said Aurelio. Hoffner said nothing, and Aurelio's gaze grew more severe. "This is what got Gardenyes killed," Aurelio said, "so I think I'd like to know."

Hoffner was beginning to feel a deep ache up his wrist and into his forearm. Aurelio had done this before. Even so, Hoffner said, "He was already dead—isn't that what he told me?"

Aurelio brought the thumb tighter into the palm, and the ache moved past the forearm and into the elbow. Hoffner shut his eyes momentarily from the pain, and the grip suddenly released. He opened his eyes and saw the Luger held just above the table and aimed at Aurelio.

Hoffner had been wrong at the clinic; Mila looked very comfortable with a gun.

"Put it down," Hoffner said.

She was staring across at Aurelio: the little man hadn't moved. "He was going to break your hand," she said.

"He might have broken it already," said Hoffner. He was stretching the fingers and wrist. There would be pain but nothing else.

Piera, silent to this moment, said quietly, "Put the gun on the table, Mila."

The sound of her father's voice did nothing to shake her. It was several long moments before she turned and held the gun out to Hoffner. Reluctantly he took it. She sat back and he set the gun down.

Hoffner said to Aurelio, "You can take your hand off your own gun now, or you can shoot me. It's up to you."

Aurelio remained absolutely still. He then slowly brought his other hand up from under the table. It was clear Mila had not been aware of this. Aurelio said, "I wasn't going to shoot you."

"I know that," said Hoffner. "She didn't. So now we all know." With his good hand, Hoffner poured a glass and placed it in front of her. The color had yet to return to her face. Mila took it and drank, and Hoffner said, "So—about this Bernhardt. Gardenyes found him?"

Aurelio was still studying him. He slid a glass to the center of the table and watched as Hoffner filled it. "His place," Aurelio said. "Not what you'd expect. Down by the docks. Too nice for the neighborhood and much too nice for a drug addict."

"But no Bernhardt."

"No." Aurelio took the glass.

"And nothing else?"

Aurelio drank.

Hoffner said, "So now they come looking for you and Gabriel?"

Aurelio finished the glass and held it out for another. Hoffner refilled it.

"They've made their point," Aurelio said, "but who knows? The CNT will take credit. This is what they were going to do anyway. They like statements like this—a man tossed in a car, beaten, a bullet to the neck, no trial, no discussion. It keeps the socialists and Communists thinking we anarchists can be trusted. That we can take care of our own loose cannons. Whoever did this knew how to play it." He drank. "Leos is moving guns?"

Hoffner appreciated how easily Aurelio got to it. He recapped the bottle. "He's trying to."

"And your son is helping?"

Hoffner felt Mila's eyes on him. He ignored them. "No. That's not why he's here."

"A great many people will be coming to Spain for one reason and leaving for another. You know your son that well?"

Hoffner pulled out a cigarette and set the pack on the table. "I need to go south." He lit up.

"That requires papers."

"Then it's lucky I'm sharing a drink with you."

Aurelio leaned forward, took one of the cigarettes, and waited for a light. He sat back through a stream of smoke. "You know the terrain?"

"No."

"Then it's suicide."

Mila said, "That's why he'll be needing two sets of papers."

The table was suddenly quiet. Even the man with the scar stopped crying. Piera let out an audible breath and Hoffner turned to her. She was staring across at Aurelio.

The little man returned her gaze and then looked at Hoffner. "What is she saying?"

Hoffner was still fixed on her. "I have no idea."

She turned to Hoffner. "Do you know the terrain?"

There was something so familiar in the gaze. "Stop it," he said.

"Stop what?"

"This. Whatever you think you're doing."

Piera let out another long breath, and Mila turned her head to him. "You knew it would be this the moment he walked in the house," she said. "The moment you heard him speak."

Piera was reluctant to answer. "No," he said. "That's not true."

"Then with the boy," she said. "When I told you about the boy. You knew then."

Again Piera tried to hold himself. "Yes," he said at last. "It doesn't mean a thing. You kill yourself if you do this."

"I kill myself if I don't."

Hoffner was done catching up. He had been there for everything they were talking about, and yet he hadn't the slightest idea what any of it meant.

"Knew what?" he said. Mila continued to look at her father and Hoffner repeated, "Knew what?"

She turned. The eyes were now completely unknowable.

"You love your son," she said. "I love my brother. Gardenyes could get you a pass out of Barcelona, and you'd need someone to show you the way. That would get me to Zaragoza."

Aurelio said, "Zaragoza isn't the way you get to Teruel."

"It is now," she said, as she continued to stare at Hoffner.

He was expecting a look of victory, the conceit a woman holds in reserve for those moments beyond a man's control, but there was nothing so cunning in the eyes. Mila's gaze carried only its strength of purpose.

"Who's to say I'll take you?" he said.

"Who's to say there are any other volunteers?"

Hoffner wanted more—stifled hope, desperation—but she gave him none. He would have given none either, and it was why he said to Aurelio, "You can get us two sets?"

Aurelio was weighing something behind the eyes. "Yes."

"Two sets to get us through," Hoffner said, "and another two to square us with the Nationalists. You can do that?"

Aurelio said, "I think you'll want to avoid the Nationalists."

"Can you do it?"

Again Aurelio stared at Hoffner. It seemed a very long time before he slowly nodded.

"Good," said Hoffner. He looked at Mila. "I'm assuming you have a gun."

The details proved surprisingly simple. It was just a matter of finding space on a truck, stuffing a canvas bag with the necessities—Hoffner's empty satchel and suitcase remained at Piera's—and then meeting up with Aurelio.

The choice of meeting spot, however, was another matter. At a little before six, the message came through from one of Gardenyes's—now Aurelio's—minions that he wanted them out in the Plaza d'España within half an hour. And not just on the plaza. He wanted them at the far side, along the westernmost gate of the Arenas bullring. To Hoffner this seemed slightly bizarre; to Mila it made perfect sense. The man had a car waiting downstairs.

They drove in dead silence, probably a good thing, since Hoffner was forced to keep his palm planted firmly on the ceiling to make sure he remained inside the car: Why speak and tempt even a moment's break in the man's concentration? Mila sat between them in the front seat, her shoulders bouncing back and forth, her expression devoid of concern. Evidently this was the way one drove through Barcelona—corners taken to the sound of screeching wheels, pedestrians nimble and happy to skip out of the way no matter how narrow the streets. That the sun was perched on the horizon so as to blind them made the prospect of hitting someone—or being hit—slightly less problematic: there might be a thud or a bump, but at least it would come as a complete surprise.

In the rare moments of manageable speed, Mila tried to point out some of the more interesting spots along the way: a palace with some exotic ironwork that looked like a fat scorpion climbing between the two front archways; a music hall with scars still dug into the stone from a decades-old anarchist bomb; a movie house with a Spanish-print poster for *Hop-a-long Cassidy*—extended through July 24—although Hoffner was guessing that the "yarn with a kick like a loco steer" might be waiting quite some time for its next showing. After that it was a straight shot up the Paralelo, across the plaza, and over to the arena.

The place had the look of any number of killing pits, two vast coliseum tiers behind countless arches, although these were more Moorish than Roman. The red brick was another distinguishing mark, as was the strange little dome atop the main entrance tower, a red cupola more fitting for a mosque than a bullring. Large posters from the most recent combats were still plastered to the front walls. The most daring was of a torero, Marcial Lalanda, painfully suave and a far cry from the six-shooting Señor Hop-a-long. Lalanda was staring down the back of a bull, his haunches raised high—Lalanda's, not the bull's—in a pose of ultimate courage: the motionless *pase de la firma*. According to the lettering, the fight had been to benefit the city's newspapers in a "sumptuous manifestation of artistry." If Lalanda's hindquarters were any indication, the crowd had not gone home disappointed.

Hoffner slammed the car door shut, and the man sped off in a grinding of tires on gravel. Mila was already heading across to the entrance gate, where a long tunnel led down into the ring. Standing inside and in half shadow was Aurelio, with a rifle over his back. He stepped out.

"Did you sleep?" he said.

"No," said Hoffner, as he drew up.

"That was stupid."

Aurelio led them down the tunnel—the ground was now packed earth and rock—through torn papers and pieces of metal wire strewn across. The papers were snatches from recent programs and posters, but the wire was a complete mystery. Odder still were the tire tracks that crisscrossed everything, and the walls—chipped stone and brickwork—that seemed to be sweating with the smell of gasoline. The light at the end was a dull orange, filled with aimless clouds of grit and dust rising from the ring.

Everything came clear as the three emerged. It was cars everywhere, in every shape, size, and state of disrepair. They were parked at odd angles, up against the wooden fencing or in klatches across the ring. A few were burned out, most stripped of their tires. The glare off the windscreens made it necessary to bring a hand up. They were Spanish, German, American, and even one of those Dutch Spykers with its ludicrously heart-shaped grille. This particular one had lost its front axle and looked as if it were kneeling in prayer or, better yet, waiting for a swift kick to the backside; even it understood this new Barcelona. Elsewhere a group of about ten saloons stood in an oval, lost in some frozen rally race, eternally waiting for the one just ahead to step on the gas.

These were the remnants of a now extinct race—the bourgeoisie—branded and on display. The markings were simple, the letters CNT-FAI meant to codify and classify for future generations.

Hoffner said, "I'm guessing we can have our pick."

Aurelio moved them across the ring as he spoke. "You bring one of these back to life," he said, "it's yours for the taking."

They passed a man who was rummaging through the open bonnet of an old Mercedes. Half the engine parts lay in piles in the dust, another piece of metal tubing finding its way onto the heap as the man tossed it to the side.

Hoffner said, "He has no idea what he's doing, does he?"

"With the car?" said Aurelio. "Of course not. To melt it down and make it into something that fires a bullet? That he knows how to do."

Hoffner looked back and saw the man toss out another large piece of something. "Clever," he said.

"Very—if he can find some bullets."

Aurelio nodded them over to one of the openings in the fencing and ushered them through. The light was now in the form of hanging lamps along the vast scaffolding maze underneath the seats. Deeper in, Hoffner saw two enormous water tanks with a truck that looked almost roadworthy nestled in between. Aurelio led them over, and the smell of gasoline became suffocating.

"Best station in the city," said Aurelio. "The cemetery out there might give the boys something to play with, but it's the gas that's the real prize." He shouted over to the truck. "You're loaded?"

"Loaded," a voice shouted back.

"How many jars?"

"Six." The voice became Gabriel's as he stepped out from behind the truck. "Enough to get us out and back."

He looked exhausted. Worse, his left ear was bandaged, and the right eye and cheek were swollen. The gashes were deep and well-placed: something metal, thought Hoffner, maybe even brass. Whoever had done this had planned to take their time killing him.

"It's not as bad as it looks," Gabriel said. Even with the swelling, he still had a cigarette tacked onto his lip. The thick mustache was all but swallowing it.

"Good to hear. Same men who took Gardenyes?"

Gabriel ignored the question and stepped over for Mila's bag. "Doctor." The hand was also black and blue, and two of the fingernails had been torn off.

Mila said, "I should have a look."

"At what?" Gabriel took her bag and headed to the back. "I've had a bit of a sore throat, but aside from that . . ."

Hoffner followed Gabriel as Aurelio helped Mila into the cab. "You're lucky to be alive," Hoffner said.

Gabriel reached the back and pulled up the flap. "Not so much luck." He tossed the bag in.

Hoffner drew up next to him and saw the two dead bodies laid out against the jars of gasoline. Both were dressed in the usual getup—suspenders, trousers, neckerchiefs—except these had small bullet holes just below the right eyes. From the tiny shards of glass, one of them had worn eyeglasses. The back of the heads had been completely torn off.

Gabriel said, "The Nazis are going to have to send in better than these if they think they're going to help the generals win the thing. I mean, how clever do you have to be to remove a gun from its holster before you try to torture and beat a man to death? Guns stay outside the room. It's the first rule, isn't it?"

Hoffner saw the stacks of rifles, rolls of bandages, and packages of food strewn haphazardly throughout the hold. He looked back at the Germans. "They're quick learners," he said.

"That's a pity."

These two couldn't have been more than twenty-five. Hoffner noticed the Bifora wristwatch on one of the arms and thought, They really have no idea what they're doing, do they?

Hoffner said, "You took the gun when one of them leaned in to pull out the fingernails. Lots of screaming and distraction." He didn't need to turn to sense Gabriel's appreciation.

"Yes," Gabriel said.

"You shoot well with your left hand."

"Close range. Not that difficult."

"And you keep them as souvenirs?"

Gabriel took hold of Hoffner's bag and tossed it in. "Better if they're missing. A dead body gets replaced by someone not as good at dying. Let them wonder for a few days where their friends have gotten to." He let go of the flap and started back to the cab.

Hoffner asked, "They wanted to know if you'd found Bernhardt?"

Gabriel stopped at the door and took the handle. He looked back. "Have I?"

"Not yet," said Hoffner, "but you will."

It was three hours later, and a hundred kilometers of safe Republican territory behind them, when Gabriel shut off the headlights.

The sun was long gone, but he continued to drive. Not that there had been much to see since the outskirts of the city. It was fields and hills and, somewhere in the distance, mountains, but even with a full moon there was little chance of seeing any of it as more than vague shadows. Towns had come and gone as pockets of light, with the occasional barking of a dog to remind them of lives being plotted and endured along the way. They had passed two checkpoints. The men at each had gone through their papers; the dead Germans had been admired and forgotten.

After that, Hoffner, Mila, and Gabriel had settled into an easy silence. The constant jolts to the chassis, and the grinding of the gears, continued to beat out a comforting rhythm.

Hoffner stared out through the windscreen. It was a road incapable of holding its line for more than thirty meters at a time. Now, with the light gone, he was strangely aware of the smell of manure. He hadn't smelled it before but knew it must have been there.

"You know the road?" he said.

Gabriel's left hand was resting on the steering wheel in a pose far too casual for the speed. Mila sat sleeping between them.

"Let's hope." Gabriel lit his next cigarette. He set it on the edge of his lip and tossed the match out the window.

Hoffner said, "It seems very peaceful."

"It does."

"But you don't believe it."

"I don't."

"You do know you're winning the thing."

"Yes, so I've heard."

"Tell me," said Hoffner. "What is it that makes me so lucky to have found the one group of anarchists in Spain who can't enjoy the taste of victory?"

Gabriel fended off a smile. "Common sense?"

"That's never it."

"Then an instinct for your own kind. You wouldn't know what to do with it either."

A curve forced them to the left, and Gabriel brought his full focus to the road. He ground the gears until the cab hitched at the loss of speed. Hoffner gripped the dashboard and placed an arm across Mila. She continued to sleep.

Hoffner said, "I think this is different."

"Then you'd be wrong. It's never different. Not when you've been through it before."

Hoffner waited for more. Instead, Gabriel reached his hand down to a small tin box on the floor. He flipped open the lid, pulled out a Coca-Cola, and handed it across to Hoffner. For the fifth time in the last two hours, Hoffner opened a bottle and handed it back. This was the last of the stash Gabriel had brought.

Hoffner said, "A Spanish anarchist and his dedication to the American capitalist dream."

"It tastes good. That's all."

"I've seen this stuff take the rust off a tire bolt in twenty minutes."

Gabriel nodded and took a swig. "Just think how clean my insides must be."

For the first time since Hoffner had met him, Gabriel pulled a healthy cigarette from his mouth. He held it in the hand with the bottle. He was thinking something through. Finally he said, "You know Asturias?"

Hoffner had never been to the northwest of Spain. He shook his head.

"Very beautiful. My family has been there a long time. Gijón. On the coast."

Gabriel set the cigarette back on his lip and placed the bottle between his legs on the seat. He downshifted as the road began to climb.

"Two years ago we had a miners' strike. Very bloody. Strikes weren't popular back then. Right-wing government. The miners tried to take the capital. They marched on Oviedo. They were gunned down. Three thousand killed, another twenty-five thousand thrown in prison. And the man the government sent to break the back of Asturias? Franco. The same

Franco who now sits in Morocco and waits to do the same to Spain. Not so different."

Gabriel spat something out the window, and Hoffner said, "You were there?"

"In the streets, at the barracks, in the hills—of course." Gabriel took the bottle from between his legs. "I told my wife to spit on my picture when the *asaltos* came looking to arrest me. I haven't been back since. Now I go home." He drank.

"And she knows you're coming?"

Gabriel remained quiet for nearly half a minute. "Yes," he finally said; if there was regret in his voice, he refused to admit it. "She knows."

Hoffner watched as Gabriel tipped the bottle all the way back before setting it on the floor.

Gabriel said, "I hear our doctor pulled a gun. Impressive."

Mila was now leaning against Hoffner's shoulder, the heat from her back and neck full against him. She had shivered once or twice in sleep— from a dream or a memory—but now lay perfectly still.

Hoffner said, "I'm sure Aurelio was impressed."

"She's too slim for Aurelio to be impressed. You'd think he'd like them that way—little as he is—but he never does."

"I was talking about the gun."

"Anyone can pull a gun. It's the shooting that makes the difference."

"And you think she can do that?"

"What? Shoot a gun?" Gabriel took a pull on the cigarette. "Why not? Don't worry. She'll get through. She's a doctor. Everyone needs a doctor."

"If they believe her."

"Why shouldn't they believe her? It's you they won't believe." Gabriel was baiting him.

"You think I'm going with her?"

Gabriel tried a laugh, but the pain in his cheek got the better of him. "No, of course not. You'll be letting her slip into Zaragoza all by herself. By the way, did she sleep alone last night?"

Hoffner let Gabriel sit with this one before saying, "I've no idea."

Again Gabriel snorted, and again the pain was too much. "I imagine she likes them older."

And Mila said, "I imagine she does."

Her eyes were still closed, her arms folded gently across her chest. Gabriel was lucky to have the road in front of him; Hoffner stared out as well and tried to piece together the last half minute. There was a chance he had made an ass of himself. Cleverness was never much of a virtue in his hands.

Mila said, "Where are we?" Her eyes were open now as she straightened herself up.

Gabriel said, "Coming up on Barberà."

She peered out. "And he likes a bigger woman, something to grab onto?"

Hoffner expected a look of embarrassment from Gabriel, but all he saw was the smile underneath the mustache. The cheeks rose and Gabriel suddenly coughed through a laugh. This, evidently, was worth the pain. "Something like that," he said.

She looked at Hoffner. "Would you have guessed that, seeing how little he is?"

She was giving him a way out. She might have been giving him more, but Hoffner knew not to take it. "He's keen on guns," he said. "A girl like that—more space to hide one."

Gabriel's laugh became a throaty growl, and Mila said, "What happened to the headlights?" It was only now that she seemed to notice.

Again Gabriel spat something out the window. "Not so good to advertise through here."

"I thought it was safe up to the Durruti line?"

"It is—mostly. Just not through here."

"And they won't hear us?"

Gabriel downshifted and the truck began to climb. "They've been hearing us for the past ten minutes. Hearing, seeing—either way it's not so good, but why take the chance? Even a blind pig finds the mud sometime."

"This is Republican territory," she said.

"Is it? My mistake. I must have missed the day they brought the mapmakers out, pictures for everyone nailed to the doors. You be sure to tell the boys guarding the church up ahead that they're breaking the rules."

The road leveled off and the truck took on speed. There were lights somewhere in the distance—candles, judging by the flickering—but most impressive now was the moon. It was directly in front of them, its glare spreading out across the fields like foam on lifeless waves. It was only a momentary pleasure.

"Duck down," Gabriel said. "They won't hit anything, but just in case." He tossed his cigarette out the window and accelerated.

Without thinking, Hoffner pulled Mila close into him and the two slid low on the seat. Gabriel held the wheel with two hands and angled his head back against the cab wall as far as he could take it. Hoffner imagined them caught like a rat in a lantern's beam, scurrying toward the darkness and helpless against the naked light. Then again, a rat has an instinct for survival: not much chance of finding that in a truck heading west to the hills of Zaragoza.

The first *ping* came from behind them, then beyond, then in a wild series that seemed to stretch out in all directions. Hoffner's eyes darted aimlessly with the shots until he found himself fixed on a spot outside Gabriel's window. It was off in the distance, turrets, ancient and stone, clawing at the sky like raised talons. He felt Mila's body against him. She, too, was staring out.

Gabriel swung the truck hard to the left and the turrets vanished. A last wave of shots flew by and then fell away. Hoffner waited another half minute before pulling himself up. Mila sat with him.

"What was that?" he said.

Gabriel tried his best not to mock. "Boys with guns?"

"No," said Hoffner. "On the hill. The turrets."

Gabriel flipped on the headlights, and Mila said, "Montblanc. The old city wall."

"And they don't mind the shots at night?"

Gabriel said, "No one's shooting at them." He downshifted, and the gears ground out with a sudden kick.

"Besides," said Mila, "they've had worse. They say it's where Saint George killed his dragon. You live through that, you live through anything, don't you?"

A MAN IN THE GROUND

At just after midnight, Gabriel shut off the engine. Three jars of gasoline remained, but he knew he would have to keep a watch on them. Gasoline had a tendency to go missing with so many militiamen roaming about. Not that they had much use for it—a fire burned better with wood, a kerosene lamp might explode from the added heat—but these were anarchists. They had spent a lifetime scavenging. Why should a bit of freedom get in the way now?

Truth to tell, Osera de Ebro was not the most logical place to have set up the front. Zaragoza was still another thirty kilometers on, but this was as far as the weapons had taken them. Even so, Buenaventura Durruti— the great anarchist leader, the man who had given them Barcelona and would send Franco back into the sea—was insisting he could mop things up. The rebels had at most fifteen hundred troops inside the city. They were *requetés*—beret-wearing, priest-toting Navarrese monarchists who saw this as a last holy crusade—but why be daunted by that? Truth and fashion stood in equal measure on either side of the line. No, it came down to discipline and experience and weapons, and while these were all firmly in the hands of the *requetés* as well, Durruti still had one card to play. He had numbers, twice as many men—four times that by the end of the week—each fighting with something perhaps even more essential: a sense of the inevitable. Barcelona had proved that God had forsaken His own. Discipline and weapons be damned.

Remarkably, even the *requetés* knew this of their foes. In fact, the only person who seemed unaware was a Colonel José Villalba. Sadly, Villalba was the leader of the Republican forces and spent most of his time shuttling back and forth between Barcelona and his Aragón headquarters in Bujaraloz. Bujaraloz was another thirty-five kilometers behind the Osera line; in order to reach it, Villalba chose to take the train. The railroads were still under the workers' control, and he reasoned that he could use the time to study maps and charts and piece together what little information he had on the men who might be dying for him. Had he decided to look out the window he would have seen that the fighting along the way was more skirmish than full-on battle, but Villalba kept the curtains drawn. It was better for the heat, he said. Reading his reports, he decided it was too early to bring the other Republican columns up to the front. He told Durruti—a colonel telling a man who disdained rank, commissions, an equal among equals—that, valiant as he was, he had plowed on too quickly. They would have to strategize together. And so Durruti began to spend much of his own time shuttling back and forth between Osera and Bujaraloz in order to convince the colonel that the time was ripe. There were no trains this far out, which meant that, with all the driving, Durruti needed to get his hands on some gasoline.

Gabriel decided to sleep in the back of the truck.

The smell of day-old flesh woke him at just after six. Gabriel looked over at the dead German nearer him and noticed that a string of flies had made camp below the right eye. Odd that they would have begun there, he thought. The back of the head was so much easier a way in.

He hoisted himself up and pulled back the flap. The heat had yet to take root, but it was already stale enough to bring a sheen to the face. Outside, the small square proved only slightly better in daylight. A few cars and motorcycles stood in a not-terribly-convincing line; two large guns— French 75s, he guessed—sat on the back of trucks, looking as if they hadn't been fired since the last war; and surrounding it all was a huddle of two-story buildings, hunched and leaning toward defeat. It might have been the burden of insignificance or the thought that they might actually be called upon to serve some larger purpose, but either way they carried their future like the weight of an unwanted boon: Why us, why now—why?

Gabriel saw a bit of movement across the square. It was inside the house that had promised beds for the German and the woman last night. He hopped out of the truck and headed over.

As it turned out, the beds were nothing more than a few flat sections of floor with a collection of equally disappointing straw mattresses laid over them; the word "mattress" might have been kind. There were perhaps eight of them placed at odd angles, with men strewn across in various states of sleep.

Hoffner was just opening his eyes when he saw Gabriel step through the door.

"Did you sleep?" said Gabriel.

Hoffner propped himself on an elbow and shook his head.

Gabriel said, "Is she up?"

They had set up a small barricade around Mila's piece of the floor. She said it was unnecessary—she would be sleeping in her clothes—but the woman whose house was now the makeshift barracks had insisted. It might be a new kind of war, but not that new.

Hoffner pointed over to the chest of drawers—with the three chairs and blankets spread over them—and said, "She's in the master suite."

Gabriel stepped over and rapped a hand against the wood. "Good morning, Doctor."

He rapped again, then a third time, and Mila's voice came from behind him. He turned to see her coming through the front door. She was carrying a tray.

"I've found some coffee," she said, "and something that looks like cheese. They said it was cheese. I'm hoping it's cheese."

Hoffner sat up. She looked clean, as if she had found a washbasin. The face, though fresh, showed the weight of the night, the age lines more creased as they edged out from the eyes. She had taken care with little else, her hair pulled back to mask its wildness, and the neck speckled pink from exhaustion or the sun. It was a completely unadorned Mila who maneuvered her way through the beds, and it was this careless, untended beauty that brought a tightening to the muscles in Hoffner's gut.

She set the tray down and handed him a cup. He found himself staring into the dark liquid.

"You're up early," he said.

"Four was early," she said, as she gave another to Gabriel. "You didn't hear the boy come in?"

Hoffner shook his head.

"He was whispering through the blanket before he finally pulled it back," she said. "I think he was hoping to catch a glimpse of something."

"Did he?" Hoffner drank. The coffee tasted of cheese.

"It was dark," she said, "but let's hope." She pulled over one of the chairs and sat. "There was an arm that needed patching. They have a sniper—at night—somewhere up in the hills. It wasn't so bad."

Hoffner said, "And they don't have a doctor of their own?"

"I'm guessing he likes his sleep."

This was something he would have to remind himself of. Places like this held no surprises for her, at least when it came to the doctoring.

She picked up a wedge of cheese, sniffed it, and took a bite. "I told them I needed to get into Zaragoza. They said it was impossible. I mentioned you." She sipped at the coffee as she stared at Hoffner. "They said they're very eager to meet you."

With no basin or water in the barracks, Hoffner was forced to do what he could to rub the sleep from his face. His eyes felt swollen and his mouth tasted of red onion as he followed Gabriel and Mila across the square and into a one-room shack. Funny, but he hadn't had onions in days.

The place was dirt-floored and smelled of cooking oil and something sweet—crushed sugarcane or three-day-old sweat, it was impossible to say which. A woodstove stood at the back, tin cups, and a coffeepot resting on top. The exhaust pipe drove up through a hole in the ceiling that was just too wide for its spout. Had it been raining, there would have been no point in lighting it. Then again, it was August; why light the thing at all?

Three men stood leaning over a small table near the stove. Their backs were to the door, and they were pointing at various positions on a map. From the look of the clothes and the rank smell in the air, Hoffner was guessing they had been up all night.

The tallest of the three was the first to turn. He was somewhere in his twenties with a handsome face, a wild, full beard—a beard that inspired confidence—and arms the size of unstripped logs. The hair was thick there as well, as were the tufts climbing up through the top of his open shirt. Two thin suspenders kept his trousers above his narrow waist.

The man kept his eyes on Mila for a moment too long. Hoffner chanced a side glance and saw it in her face as well, a look of complicity, recognition in the light of day. Neither showed regret. Neither showed anything beyond this single moment.

The man turned back and said to one of the others, "Tura. He's here."

Hoffner chafed at his sudden feelings of betrayal. They were ludicrous. He had said nothing to her, nothing to himself about her, except perhaps that she was his to protect. And maybe that was most ludicrous of all. He forced himself to keep his eyes on the men at the table.

The man called Tura continued to speak quietly to the third in their company: there was an occasional murmured response, a shake of the head, but this was how it passed for nearly a minute. Hoffner thought the big one might interrupt again, but instead they all stood waiting until the third man finally nodded and headed to the door. Only then did the one called Tura reach for his cigarette—a weedy, self-rolled thing propped on the edge of the table—and turn to the room.

It was a hard face, square and lined, and with a day's growth to make the cheeks seem even more brittle. There might have been something oafish to it—the wide brow and high forehead—but the eyes were too focused and the color too deep a brown to hide the raw intelligence. This was a stare of perfect conviction. It held Hoffner's gaze even as the cigarette smoke drifted past him.

"You're the German," the man said. It was a peasant voice, guttural and crackling.

"And you're Buenaventura Durruti."

Hoffner had seen too many of the posters across Barcelona, photographs in every newspaper from Moscow to London, not to know him at once. Strange to come face-to-face with the soured breath of an ideal.

Durruti looked over at Gabriel. "Sleep hasn't improved you, Ruiz."

Gabriel nodded. It was as much as he had brought to the conversation.

Durruti took a pull on the cigarette. "So. You have a son in Zaragoza, and you'd like to find him."

Hoffner took a moment. "No," he said.

Durruti was not one to show surprise. The eyes moved to Mila, then back to Hoffner. Smoke trailed from Durruti's nose. "You have a son?"

"Yes."

"But not in Zaragoza."

"No."

Durruti took another pull and nodded. "I must have misunderstood."

"Yes."

Durruti finished the cigarette and dropped it to the floor. "And yet you're eager to make your way into a city garrisoned with more than a thousand rebel troops." He crushed it out under his boot. "That would be reckless even by my standards."

Hoffner said, "The doctor has a brother—"

"Yes," Durruti said. "I know. The doctor and I are old friends." He pulled back his shirtsleeve and showed the bandage; the bullet had hit him just below the elbow. "The fascists have good aim. They're also smart with a target. I've been told they're even better in daylight." Stepping to the stove, he picked up the coffeepot; he kept his back to Hoffner as he poured. "So this son—the one not in Zaragoza—he knows something about guns. Tell me about these guns."

Hoffner looked again at the big one; he was standing by the map, his arms crossed at his chest. He, too, was forcing himself to keep his eyes on the table. Hoffner said, "I'd take a cup of that coffee if you have it."

Durruti handed him the one he had just poured and looked at Mila. "Doctor?" She shook her head, and Durruti went back for another. Again he kept his back to them.

"They're German," said Hoffner.

"Yes," said Durruti, "I know." He took hold of a can and dripped some thick milk into the coffee. "And they're in Zaragoza?"

"I told you, my son isn't in Zaragoza."

"That's right." Even with something this simple, Durruti was taking no chances. He stirred the coffee. "But they do have guns in Zaragoza. German guns."

"I wouldn't know."

"I would." Durruti set the spoon down and turned. "That's why I'm telling you—so when you take your doctor in to find her brother, you won't be surprised when you get shot by one of your own."

Hoffner watched as Durruti drank. Hoffner said, "You know where they're coming from?"

"What, these German guns? My guess: Germany."

Anywhere else, Hoffner would have resented the taunt; here it seemed justified.

He took a drink and then said, "Teruel. My son is in Teruel."

"With guns?"

Hoffner said nothing.

"And you know this for certain?"

"No."

Durruti nodded once for emphasis. " 'No,' " he repeated. The eyes sharpened as he stared across. "You're very close to being helpful, then not. Why is that?"

"Tell me what it is you want to hear."

An unexpected half smile creased the thick lips, and Durruti set the cup down. "Well—I might like to know that you'll be bombing the munitions factory once you're inside, or that you've a trainload of rifles up the road. Or that maybe you're doing all this because you truly believe in the revolution and not because it's something so meaningless as saving a boy's life. But you can't tell me any of that, can you?"

Hoffner gave Durruti the moment. "No, I can't."

The smile remained. "At least you're honest."

"I'll take the explosives if you want."

"Will you? That's kind. I don't have any, so I'll save you the trouble."

Durruti's power lay not in his arrogance but in his utter lack of pretense. It was an honesty not meant to impress.

Hoffner pulled out his cigarettes. He offered them to Durruti and Durruti took one. Hoffner lit it, then lit his own.

"That's good," said Durruti. "At least you know the first rule." Hoffner said nothing, and Durruti explained. "A stranger in Spain—you should always offer a man tobacco."

"And the second?"

Durruti took a pull. He glanced at Mila, then back at Hoffner. "You're not so good on that one."

Hoffner held the pack out to Mila, even as he said to the big one by the table, "You know these rules too?"

The man looked up. It was clear now how much of a boy he still was. He glanced at Mila but said nothing.

Mila took a cigarette and said to Durruti, "He's fine on both." She let Hoffner light hers. She gave nothing away. "So, can you get me inside the city?"

Durruti had watched all this with mild disinterest. He took another pull and said, "They'll shoot you, then him, and then where will his son and those guns be?"

Mila said firmly, "In Teruel. He won't be coming with me. You'll get your guns."

"Ah," said Durruti. "So now they're *my* guns." He nodded slowly. "There *are* no foreign guns in Spain. You know this, of course." He seemed to take pleasure in showing his cynicism. "The French won't come in— Blum's already said it—not with the Rhineland slipping away. Why provoke more of that? And the English?" He took a pull and shook his head. "Not much money to be gained here either way. They'll leave it alone. Which leaves us with the Russians." Even the smoke seemed more aggressive through his nostrils. "They'll be the ones to send us rifles and colonels, just to make sure we know how to be good Bolsheviks, but the guns will be shit. So will the colonels. They've all signed their pieces of paper, those promises to stay away. They're doing it to keep the Germans and Italians out. Wouldn't want it to break into a real war, now, would they? And we all know how good you Germans are with a promise." Durruti took another pull.

Hoffner had expected another bandit anarchist—bullets and ideology ablaze—but Durruti showed a much subtler mind. He knew that his Spain, anarchist Spain, was on its own.

Durruti said, "So no, they won't be *my* guns. The only hope I have is to end this war before all those German guns find their way through."

Mila said, "He's not coming with me."

"But that's not true," Durruti said. He took a last pull and dropped his cigarette to the floor. "He's the only way I get you inside Zaragoza." Not waiting for a response, Durruti looked past Hoffner to Gabriel. "You're sure you want to do this?"

Gabriel had been leaning quietly against a wall. He pushed himself up and said, "I was sure last night. Why should it be different now?"

Durruti nodded. He looked back at Hoffner. "You still have the German clothes you came in?"

It took Hoffner a moment to answer. "Yes."

"Good. You'll need to change."

It made perfect sense. Hoffner was looking for fascist guns and he was looking for Germans. Why not be a German fascist and see where it took him? Mila was less convinced.

"And Gabriel?" she said.

Durruti was placing bricked explosives inside a hollow in the backseat of an old Mercedes sedan. He leaned farther in. "You'll need someone to shoot the checkpoint guards if the passes fail," he said. He was making sure each one had a fuse.

Mila stood outside the door. "I could do that."

"No—you couldn't." Durruti brought the cushion down and bolted it by pulling a lever near the window; it looked like a hanging strap. "Neither could your German. It's why you need Ruiz."

Hoffner was sitting back against the car's bonnet. He was almost half-way through a pack of cigarettes and it wasn't even ten o'clock. At some point in Barcelona, Mila had washed his shirt. It smelled of lavender. The rest of him wasn't quite so floral.

She stepped over and sat next to him. They had said nothing to each other since the shack. Closing her eyes, she tilted her head back and let the sun fill her face. She said, "He's wrong, you know."

Hoffner tossed his cigarette to the ground and stared over at a group of men who were in line for something—food, toilet, maybe both. They each had a rifle slung over a shoulder or a pistol strapped to a belt. There were berets, metal helmets, an airman's cap that had frayed at the back, but nothing to say they belonged together. They didn't stand like soldiers. They didn't smoke like soldiers. But they talked like soldiers—that hushed, half-joking pose of false hope and unexamined fear. It was good to be brave, thought Hoffner, good to believe in this beyond all else. He looked again at Mila. It was good to believe in something.

Durruti closed the door and stepped over. He took a cigarette from Hoffner's pack and leaned in for a light.

Hoffner said, "And you really don't care where we set them off?"

Durruti pulled a piece of tobacco from his tongue and flicked it to the ground. "You won't have enough to do any real damage. You do it to make them know we can. The real destruction will come from the aeroplanes."

"If the bombs ever manage to go off."

"That was bad luck."

Mila still had her eyes closed. "For whom?" she said.

Durruti forced a tired smile. "Don't make me think twice about this."

"I'm glad you've thought about it at all."

Hoffner shook out another cigarette; what else was there to do? He lit up. "You really want to bring it all down to rubble, don't you?"

Durruti was now looking over at the men. There was nothing in the eyes to show the pain or pride he felt. "I want a free Spain," he said. "I want collectives—purpose. I want all of what was to be gone. This socialist government won't give me that. They might even kill me once I get rid of the fascists for them. So it all has to go."

"And then?"

"We rebuild." This was something Durruti had thought long on. "We destroy because we're capable of building. We were the ones who built the palaces and the cities. We'll build them again, this time better. We're not afraid of ruins. We have a new world—inside—in our hearts."

A man emerged from a nearby building and spoke as he made his way over. "It's Colonel Villalba," he said. "He's on the telephone."

Hoffner said to Durruti, "They have a telephone here?"

Durruti said under his breath, "It's why we picked the town." He looked at the man. "Do I need to take a drive?"

"He wants to come here."

For the first time, Hoffner saw genuine surprise in Durruti's face. Mila opened her eyes.

"And why is that?" said Durruti.

The man did his best to hide his disgust. "He wants to see what the enemy looks like up close."

"You're joking."

"It was my fault," the man said. "He asked what we were up against."

"And?"

"I said the rebels."

"And?"

The man shrugged. "He wanted to know who exactly, what forces, how many cannons and machine guns, do they have cavalry?"

They all waited until Durruti said, "And what did you tell him?"

"I told him that they're the enemy because they don't report their troops or forces. Otherwise, they wouldn't be the enemy."

Hoffner couldn't help a quiet laugh, and Durruti said, "I thought you were a baker, not a comedian."

The man said, "I'm a soldier."

"Bravo. A soldier keeps his mouth shut. Tell him I'll come to the telephone. Don't let him hang up."

The man headed off, and Hoffner said, "He has a point."

Durruti tossed his half-smoked cigarette to the ground. It was his only moment of frustration, but it was enough. "I should be in Zaragoza by now," he said. "Villalba knows it. All this waiting." He looked around. "Where the hell is Ruiz?"

Gabriel had insisted on burying the Germans. He had taken three men with him almost an hour ago.

Hoffner said, "It takes time to put a man in the ground the right way."

"It takes time," Durruti said sharply, "because he'll want the same for himself. Gabriel might not believe in a God but he believes in a balance to things."

Up to this moment Hoffner hadn't known what to call it with Gabriel, but this made perfect sense. He said, "And he thinks he'll be with the fascists when he needs burying?"

"He knows it." Durruti had no reluctance for the truth. "He's dead if he goes back to Barcelona. The *patrullas* or your German friends will finish him—or track him here. There's not much good in that. So he'll take you to Zaragoza, get you in, and while you and the doctor find what you need, he'll plant the fuses. And when you get yourselves out, he'll set them off. If he tries it earlier, he knows none of you make it out. Now you know why he takes his time."

Durruti spat a piece of tobacco to the ground, and Mila—realizing what Durruti had meant—said, "He's heading home. To fight in Gijón."

"Yes. But first he fights here."

"You mean first he dies here."

Durruti took his time before answering. "He'll set off the fuses. He'll get out. And then he'll fight in Gijón."

"I don't think you believe that."

"No?" said Durruti. "I'll tell him when he gets back. I'm sure that'll make a great deal of difference to him."

Hoffner said, "There's no reason for that."

"There's no reason for any of it," said Durruti, "but none of us have that luxury."

As if to save them all, Gabriel appeared from around one of the houses across the square. Three other men were with him, and Gabriel raised his hand in a single wave.

Durruti started out toward him, but the sudden *ping* of bullets forced him instantly to the ground, two shots, then a third. Hoffner grabbed hold of Mila and pulled her down behind the car as Durruti began to crawl his way back. The square was filled with shouting. Half the line of men were diving through doorways and windows. The other half stood frozen. Another two shots, and then silence. Durruti drew up next to them and leaned his head against the car.

"Our sniper's getting bold," Durruti said. "Broad daylight." There was a hint of respect in the voice. He shouted over to the men who had yet to move. "Get down!"

The men quickly ran for cover, but there was no point. Ten seconds was as much mayhem as the sniper could muster. Nonetheless, Durruti edged his way up to the bonnet and began to fire out into the trees. He was joined by several others along the houses until he shouted, "Enough. Save your bullets."

The echoes faded, and Durruti listened for another half minute. He continued to look out beyond the village.

"He's running," he said. "That's what I'd be doing." He stood upright and stepped out from behind the car. Slowly, others began to make their way out.

"It's done!" he shouted. "We need a patrol."

Durruti waited for more of the men to move into the square before he turned and extended a hand to Hoffner.

"It's fine," he said. "Just be glad he didn't hit the explosives."

Hoffner took the hand, then helped Mila to her feet. She seemed completely unruffled.

She said, "You're all right?"

Hoffner nodded. He was about to say something when he saw a single figure lying unmoving in the square. The body had fallen forward, the shot clean to the back of the skull. A line of blood had curled down to the mustache.

Even a blind pig.

Hoffner stared at Gabriel's body and knew that Mila, too, was staring out with him.

AN ACT OF FAITH

"No," said Hoffner. The force in his tone surprised even him. "We still go."

"Then you take my man," said Durruti.

"No."

They were in the shack. The bearded twenty-year-old stood silently at the door. Mila was sitting by the stove.

Durruti said, "Then you don't find your son."

Hoffner looked over at Mila. She was refusing to help him. She was agreeing with Durruti.

Hoffner said, "Gabriel was willing to kill himself for this. Fine. Your man isn't. It would be for show—you said it yourself. The explosives stay here."

"And I give you a car and gasoline and bullets because I'm feeling generous? No. You take the explosives—with or without my man—and you plant them. What you do after that is no concern of mine."

"My son—"

"You think your boy is more capable than Gardenyes or Ruiz?" Durruti let this take root. "They took Gardenyes. They had Ruiz. They nearly killed him. These guns from the Germans will find their way into my country no matter what you or your boy do. We're done." He looked at his man. "When the others return, send them out to find the shooter. They buried Ruiz. They'll want his killer."

The man nodded and headed out. Durruti turned to the table and, with as much focus as he could, began to study the map.

Hoffner said, "So either I let you sacrifice your man, or I sacrifice myself and the doctor. That's quite a way to win a war."

Durruti refused to turn. "It's the way we win this war."

"I've heard. Men charging at cannons, refusing to dig trenches." And with perhaps too much bitterness, "Better to be shot full in the chest, in plain view, than to survive like a coward."

Durruti stood unmoving. When he turned, his face was empty, the heat gone from him.

"These men," Durruti said. "My men." It was a rare admission. "For every fifty, I have one who knows how to fight. The rest have passion, daring—what they take for quality. Arrogant men because they fight with ideals, not guns. And it's these ideals that tell them not to think, not to question, not to die. Sit them down in a trench—where they can learn to flatten themselves against a wall at the first sound of an aeroplane engine or feel the terror of hours trapped in a mudhole with guns and fear staring back at them—and they become nothing. Then they *are* nothing but sacrifice. And if that's what they are, this war is already lost."

Hoffner had misjudged Durruti. The venom wasn't pride; it was a need to shut out the inevitable. "Then turn them into soldiers."

Durruti snorted dismissively. "A German speaks. We haven't time for that. We have numbers—now—and somewhere we have guns: Spanish, Russian. The rebels inside Zaragoza—those troops with all their years of training and killing in Asturias and Morocco—they're happy to wait. Happy because while they wait my bricklayers and bakers and peasants come to understand what they themselves truly are. So I sacrifice one, and he sacrifices himself, and the passion and daring go on."

Hoffner stood with no answer. There was no answer for any of this, and Mila asked, "Did you know Gabriel well?"

It took Durruti a moment to remember she was in the room. He looked at her. "Yes."

"And Gardenyes?"

Durruti hesitated. "Why do you ask this?"

"Because I didn't," she said, "and I feel the pain." She stood. "We do it ourselves, and you keep your man. Show us on the map."

She stepped passed him. There was a moment between Hoffner and Durruti before they both stepped over. Durruti picked up a wax pencil and began to mark.

She had changed into a silk dress, flower print, sleeves long to the wrist. And her hair was pulled up in a bun.

Durruti had shown them how to get north of the city. It would have made no sense to soldiers at an outpost to have a car coming from the east: How would a German fascist and his lady friend have made it through? Durruti had promised two hours, maybe three, of dirt that passed for tracks and roads, but at least they were avoiding the river.

It was a puzzling terrain, flat and open, at times barren and then wild with green. There were rises here and there, little houses, but more often than not it was the sudden looming of a castle in the distance—ancient and decayed—that traced the path Durruti had given them. Twice they heard gunfire; twice they maneuvered around wagons pulled by mules. Hoffner noticed no neckerchiefs. These were peasants, smart enough to keep their loyalties to themselves. If Durruti pushed through, so be it. Until then, they would wave and nod to anyone passing by.

It was nearly half past one, and the heat in the car was making quick work of the little air coming through the windows. Mila had brought lipstick. She gave her lips a brown-red coating and looked at herself in a small mirror. As if anticipating his question, she said, "They'll expect it. Anarchists have bland lips. Fascists have red ones. Not too red. It's a fine line for God."

Hoffner nodded but said nothing. He had said very little since the shack. She put the lipstick in her purse and stared out. She, too, had said almost nothing.

The road was suddenly bounded on both sides by fields of sunflowers, each turned up to the midday sun. The smell was strong, the heat stronger.

"The boy," she finally said. "Last night. He was young. I let him hold me."

Hoffner focused on the twin line of ruts ahead of him. He felt his throat go dry. Again he nodded.

She said, "He was a chemist."

"Why are you telling me this?"

She looked at him. "Why do you think I'm telling you?"

Hoffner hesitated before turning to her. There was nowhere for the car to go but along the track.

Her face showed nothing, no longing or need. And yet it was strange to see this intimacy given so freely. It was the loss behind her eyes that reached out to him, and made plain—only now—why he himself felt the longing. It had never been about her beauty, raw and fine as it was. It was this. And while he could find nothing safe in it—its pull no less daunting than if she had offered him love—Hoffner let it take him. She placed a hand on his cheek. She held it there, then brought it down and looked out again to the road.

She said, "It's your son who's not here—the one you don't follow—that makes you this way. Why is that?"

Hoffner stared at the powder on her cheek, the soft ridges she had failed to smooth. He turned, and his eyes settled on the fields in the distance. They swayed with a momentary wind.

"You know this for certain?" he said, trying to sound too cavalier.

"I do."

There was no hope of distracting her.

"He's called Sascha," he said. "He hasn't been a boy for quite some time."

"And he knows the pain it gives you?"

"He thinks I'm not capable of feeling it."

"But he tries anyway."

"He did—once. Not for a long time now."

"But that doesn't matter, does it?"

They were halfway through a canteen of water. Hoffner picked it up and unscrewed the top. He drank. When he looked out again, he was relieved to see what Durruti had called the Ontinar Crossroads just over a rise—two or three houses and another dirt track coming in from the west.

Hoffner had kept his collar buttoned, his tie tight to the neck. The jacket was soaked through, down to the waist. Still, better to be the bitter German sweating his way through Spain than a man comfortable with the Aragón summer. He noticed the telephone wire sprouting from the roof of one of the small buildings. It was exactly as Durruti had described it.

"No," he said, "it doesn't."

He slowed the car as they reached the buildings. It might have been due to the three Nationalist soldiers standing with their rifles raised, or the sandbag barricade that was clearly a recent addition. More likely it was the sight of the Renault tank perched behind them. The tank was old, maybe not even a match for the big guns back in Osera, but it made its point. Hoffner pulled up to the barricade and turned off the engine.

Two of the men kept their rifles raised as the third now walked over. He was wearing the green and tan uniform of a *requeté*, with the dual leather straps that cut across his shoulders and chest. The belt buckle was well polished, although the three leather bags that clung to the belt—ammunition, cigarettes, papers—looked as if they had seen better days. A silver crucifix was pinned just above the heart, with a red barbed X sewn onto the pocket. The jodhpur pants were narrow at the shin and looped over the boots. He wore a crimson beret angled to the forehead and without a hint of panache.

There was no mistaking these for soldiers. The one approaching pulled his pistol from its holster and cocked the barrel. He held it at his side.

"Out of the car," he said, when he had positioned himself just beyond the grille.

Hoffner opened the door slowly, stepped out, and put his hand back for Mila as she slid across. He took her hand. The two stood and waited.

The man said, "This road is closed."

"I have papers," Hoffner said calmly. His Spanish was now simple, halting, and with a distinct German accent.

The man stared. "This road is closed."

"I have papers."

The man looked at Mila for the first time. Hoffner wanted to turn to her, but he kept his eyes on the man, who looked back and said, "How do you come to be on this road?"

"I am not a Spaniard," said Hoffner. "I do not know these roads. I have come down from the north. My driving instructions were poor. I am going to Zaragoza."

The man glanced again at Mila, then at Hoffner. He held out his hand. "Show me these papers."

Hoffner slowly reached into his jacket pocket. He retrieved them and held them out. The man took them and, with the pistol still in hand, unfolded them. He read.

"Where did you get these papers?" he said.

"Berlin," said Hoffner.

The man quickly looked up. Despite himself, he showed a moment's uncertainty. "This is a Safe Conduct."

"Yes."

"Signed by Nicholas Franco."

"Yes," said Hoffner. "The General's brother sent it by dispatch eight days ago."

"To Berlin."

"Yes."

The man was finding himself well beyond his capacity, but still he held his ground. Durruti had been wise to be so precise with the story.

"Your passport," said the man.

Again Hoffner reached into his jacket. He handed the papers to the man and chanced a look at Mila. Her face was moist from the heat, but she stood without the least sign of discomfort. It was a remarkable pose of submissive indifference.

The man looked up from the papers. "And the woman?"

Before Hoffner could answer, Mila said, "My papers are in my purse." She turned to the car, but the man stepped over and raised his pistol.

"No, Señora," he said. "Where is the purse?"

Mila looked at the man. Hoffner couldn't be sure if this was genuine fear in her eyes or not. She said, "I was only trying to get them."

"Yes, Señora. Where is the purse?"

Mila pointed to the seat and the man called over to one of the others. The second man quickly walked up, leaned his rifle against the car, and reached in through the passenger window for the small purse. He held it up, took his rifle, and brought it around.

The first man opened it. He looked through and brought out a small crucifix on a chain of prayer beads. He looked up at Mila.

"This is yours, Señora?"

She nodded and he held it out to her. She took it and kissed it.

"There are no papers, Señora."

Mila's look of panic was only momentary before she quickly turned to Hoffner. "You have them," she said. "Remember? The man gave them both to you when we left the last post. You put them in the other pocket."

Durruti had been very specific on this. A woman—a good Catholic woman—in distress was almost irresistible to a soldier of God. And the man able to save her—His obvious emissary.

Hoffner nodded, relieved, as if he had just remembered. He reached into his pocket. "Yes, of course. I'd forgotten. I'm sorry to have caused any trouble."

He handed the papers to the man, who quickly glanced through them.

"Another Safe Conduct."

"Yes," said Hoffner.

The man continued to look through them. "How did you get on this road?"

Hoffner waited for the man to look up. "There was gunfire," Hoffner said. "I was stopped and told to drive around. The soldier said it would meet up with the first road. He was mistaken."

The man held the papers out to Hoffner. "And why do you go to Zaragoza?"

Hoffner took them, placed them in his pocket, and said, "That I cannot say."

This, more than anything, seemed to convince the young *requeté*. He said, "We'll need to check the car."

Three minutes later, Hoffner drove them past the barricade and into Nationalist Spain.

Augustus Caesar, born Gaius Octavius Thurinus, son of the she-wolf Atia Balba Caesonia, adopted nephew of the tyrant Gaius Julius Caesar, husband of the harridan Livia Drusilla, and first Emperor of Rome, hated Spain. He had fought there against Pompey as a boy, at the side of his uncle, and had developed a "horrible burning" in his *meatus urinarius* after an evening spent with two young women from the Tarraconensis province. The burning eventually subsided (a doctor familiar with the women suggested a combination of herbs and minerals), but young Octavian never forgot his days of agony in the city of Salduba. In later years he even went so far as to blame his inability to produce an heir on the peoples of Hispania. That Rome would have to suffer through the likes of Tiberius, Caligula, and Nero was hardly the fault of two welcoming young virgins (or so they described themselves), but who was really to say? In an act of contrition, and with the hope that Spain might seem more than a cauldron of filth and whores to the people of Rome, the men of Salduba renamed their city after the young Octavian when he ascended the throne. They called it Caesaraugusta, which, over time—and due to dialect and the influence of the conquering Moors—became Zaragoza. It seemed highly unlikely that now, under the watchful gaze of the *requetés*, the city might offer a glimpse into that distant past. Then again, Zaragoza was filled with soldiers. Even the holiest of men needed something for which to repent.

Hoffner brought the car to a stop. A barricade stretched along the entrance to an ancient-looking bridge, with the thick brown water of the Ebro swirling below it. Wide enough for perhaps two trucks to pass, the bridge was six stanchions in limestone brick—a pristine nod to Rome in the vaulted archways in between—and looked untouched by the recent fighting. Not that there had been much to speak of. Zaragoza had followed the Seville approach to self-defense: Let the soldiers take what they will and never—never—hand a rifle to a worker. It had saved the city from any real scarring, though not so much the workers. Those who had fought with their shouts of *¡Viva la Libertad!* had been rounded up, shot, or worse. It was a terrible blow to Zaragoza, as the city had always been known as a hotbed of CNT activities. Passion without guns, though, has a tendency to end badly. It had in Zaragoza, and it was why the Puente de Piedra—after five hundred years surviving Moors and floods and the occasional rumble from the French—stood whole. Perhaps it had been saving itself for this unit of *requetés* now standing atop it.

Watching them from the car, Hoffner suspected that the young soldiers making their way over were thinking much the same thing.

"Señor," one of them said. "Papers, please."

Things were more relaxed here. They were twenty kilometers inside Nationalist territory, with fifteen hundred armed men just the other side of the bridge. A cordial "Señor" was the least one of them could offer.

Hoffner handed both sets of papers to the man and waited. If the boys at the Ontinar Crossroads had used their telephone correctly, this would be a quick stop, after which Hoffner would be ushered through to meet someone with real questions. If not—well, "if not" wasn't something to dwell on these days.

The man with the papers told the others to wait while he returned to the small shack by the barricade. At just after three o'clock, Hoffner and Mila drove across the bridge.

It was good to be out of the open country; the sun through the windscreen had made the air almost unbreathable. Now looming above them and providing shade—perhaps for the province as a whole—was the basilica of Our Lady of the Pillar, a massive and unwavering reminder of God's bountiful dominion. Palatial walls sat below four fortresslike towers, each standing sentry over the Roman dome and tiled cupolas within. If this was a place to inspire quiet devotion, it was for a God dressed in full armor. Hoffner suspected that even had the bombs exploded, the spires themselves would have risen up to slap the aeroplane from the sky.

Mila stared up as they drove. "Welcome to Aragón."

A motorcycle led them into the plaza, which stretched out behind the basilica. The square was large enough to land a plane, the buildings surrounding it a collision of Roman and Moorish design, with a few that seemed forever lost in the struggle. At the far end stood a second cathedral— why a square should need two was something only Zaragoza could answer—and a church tower that made the hunched houses of Osera seem perfectly upright by comparison. A line of military trucks was parked at the center, with two more of the Renault tanks thrown in for good measure. There was a starkness to it all, and not for the presence of the guns. It was the emptiness. A few soldiers stood at various posts, but the heat and God and common sense were keeping the rest of Zaragoza indoors. If this was victory, thought Hoffner, it was a far cry from the kind he had seen in Barcelona.

The motorcycle pulled up in front of a building and the soldier kicked out his stand. The place was one of the newer ones on the square, eighteenth or nineteenth century, and with the wrought-iron balconies and ornate stonework of a municipal courthouse. Two soldiers with rifles flanked the entrance. Hoffner turned off the engine, and the motorcyclist led them through and into the enclosure of a wide receiving hall.

It was all stone and wood, vaulted ceilings—and surprisingly cool. Doorways and corridors led off toward more doorways and corridors, while a staircase climbed along the walls to the upper floors. Peppered throughout were men in uniform who moved with a look of deep concentration. This was the hushed feel of newly minted authority—muffled conversations and telephone bells ringing from above. Hoffner might have been mistaken, but he thought he caught the smell of sweet incense drifting down from on high.

The motorcyclist led them up the stairway and, somewhere on the third floor, took them into an office that looked like a small banquet hall. The wall facing the street was a series of long, narrow windows that stepped out onto equally narrow balconies, each with a singular view of Our Lady of the Pillar. It was unclear which of the buildings was keeping watch on which, but Hoffner imagined that the man at the far end of the room— desk, bookcase, and telephone—readily deferred to the will of the Holy Mother across the square.

A second man in uniform approached. He and the motorcyclist exchanged a quick salute, and the motorcyclist retreated. The man then motioned Mila and Hoffner toward the distant desk—a sudden and almost jarring "Señor, Señora" to break the Spanish silence—before leading the way.

The other man stood as they drew up. He was tall, with a chiseled face, a nobleman in the most recent guise of Spanish privilege. He was no more than twenty-five, his hair black and slicked above a high forehead, his uniform perfectly pressed. Where Durruti had defined hunger and passion, this showed centuries of refinement. The only flaw was a red patch of skin under the right eye. Something from birth. Something to cause shame.

He was a career officer, only weeks removed from his betrayal of the Republic. He wore his treason with the easy assurance of a divine right.

"I am Captain Doval." The voice was nasal and lingered on the words. "I have been expecting you, Señor, though not expecting you."

From the slight curl of the lip, Hoffner imagined this to be some form of humor.

Hoffner offered a clipped nod. "Captain." His Spanish was once again fluent, though no less Germanic. "What we have to discuss does not concern the señora. She has a brother in your garrison whom she wishes to see. The last name is Piera." He looked at Mila.

"Carlos," she said. "First Sergeant Carlos Piera, under General Cabanellas."

The curl inched toward a smile. "We are all under General Cabanellas, Señora, but I shall see what I can do." Doval nodded to the second man, who retreated to a small desk and a telephone. The conversation was brief and successful.

The second man said, "Your brother will be in the Gran Café within half an hour. The señora is welcome to wait in the anteroom just here"—he motioned to a door beyond the desk—"until an escort can be found to take her to the café."

Hoffner said, "I'd like to see this anteroom." He removed his papers from his jacket pocket and placed them on the desk. "You may examine my papers while I'm with the señora."

Hoffner took Mila by the elbow. He had been swimming in Nazis for the past three years; it was easy enough to strike a convincing pose. The Spaniards offered their own clipped nods before Hoffner led Mila to the door and through.

The room was small, one window, a few chairs, and with a second closed door that led out to the corridor. Hoffner shut the door behind him and held his finger to his lips. Waiting perhaps fifteen seconds, he suddenly pulled the door open. As expected, the second man was only half a meter off, ostensibly reading through a file.

Hoffner said, "A glass of water for the señora. And one for myself. And perhaps a few crackers. I'll take mine at the desk."

He waited for the man to move off before closing the door. Mila was at the far end by the open window. Hoffner joined her.

"You're very good," she said quietly. "You've even got me believing you're a son of a bitch. You know what you'll say to them?"

"No."

It had been a long time since he had seen admiration in a woman's eyes. It was there only a moment before she said, "The captain seems young."

"He does. How long do you think you'll need?"

"Not long. Half an hour."

"Good."

A small wind came through the window and she looked up at him. Hoffner was learning to trust her silences. She slowly brought her hand to his cheek and pressed her lips to his. When she pulled back, he was still staring at her.

"That would take longer," he said.

It was good to see her smile. She rubbed her thumb across his lip and said, "A handkerchief would be better."

Hoffner pulled one from his pocket and wiped off what lipstick remained.

She said, "You didn't need me to get you through last night or this morning. You could have gone south on your own. You knew it in Barcelona."

"Zaragoza needs guns," he said. "Coming here helps me find my boy."

"Yes," she said, something too knowing in her eyes, "I'm sure it does."

She stared up at him, and he felt his hand move to the soft of her back. He kissed her again, her lips parched but smooth. She drew him in closer and he released. There was a rapping at the door.

Mila said, "Don't underestimate them."

Hoffner used the handkerchief again and turned to the door. "Come."

The door opened, and the second man stepped through with a plate of crackers and cheese and a glass of water.

Hoffner said, "Good." He turned to Mila with a nod. "Señora. I'll see you at the café." With nothing else, he headed into the office.

• • •

"You came through Barcelona?"

Captain Doval sat behind his desk. He held Hoffner's papers casually in his long fingers, which showed a recent manicure.

"Yes," said Hoffner. He placed his empty glass on the desk and reached for another cracker. The cheese was surprisingly fresh.

"And you encountered no difficulties?"

Hoffner dabbed his finger at the crumbs on his shirt. "You wear a red neckerchief, raise your hand with a *¡Viva la República!* and Barcelona is your friend." He licked at the crumbs.

"I wish it were all so easy."

"It will be." Hoffner finished the cracker and brushed off his hands. "So. I can expect your help in finding this man?"

Doval's expression remained unchanged. "Your German. Herr Bernhardt."

"Yes."

There really had been no other choice. If guns were coming in, this was where they would be heading. Besides, it was always best to bring a bit of truth to the table with a man like Doval. And arrogance—German arrogance—with crackers, brushed hands, and a thoroughly polished indifference.

Doval placed the papers on the table. He rubbed something off one of his nails, and said, "Papers are an easy thing to come by these days, Señor Hoffner. Especially in Barcelona."

Hoffner showed nothing. "I imagine they are."

"A Safe Conduct is impressive."

"Especially one signed by Señor Franco."

Doval seemed less convinced. He waited before saying, "Your Spanish is excellent." Even a compliment seemed a sneer.

Hoffner could see where this was going. Papers wouldn't be enough. Funny, he thought: where better than Nationalist Spain to be forced to have it all come down to an act of faith. It was now just a matter of waiting for the right moment. Hoffner continued, "But not your German."

"No—I don't speak German."

"Odd," said Hoffner. "I would have expected a bit more from the Reich's liaison."

"Odd is having a member of the Reich appear without warning."

Hoffner appreciated Doval's impatience. It was coming now. "You're going to waste both our time, aren't you?"

"I have a man with the woman at the café."

"I'm sure you do."

"He can detain her if need be."

"Or shoot her. Or you could shoot me. There are so many possibilities for you."

Doval tried to match Hoffner's effortlessness, but it came off as preening.

"You will admit it's surprising," said Doval. "A German with rare yet ideal papers arriving with a Spanish woman. She was also in Barcelona?"

"She was."

"And you just happened to be carrying a second Safe Conduct for her?"

Doval was taking them closer and closer. Hoffner pulled out his cigarettes. He chose not to offer one. "You ask very good questions."

"I hope they're not wasting your time."

"Not at all." Hoffner lit up and let out a long strain of smoke. "When we speak about Bernhardt, I'll be happy to explain it to you."

"Assuming I know who this Bernhardt is."

Hoffner took another pull. "But that's not the point, is it—whether you know."

The power of German arrogance lay in its cruelty; Spanish arrogance relied too willingly on dignity. It placed Doval at a considerable disadvantage.

Hoffner said, "The better question is why do *I* know about Herr Bernhardt, and why do I choose to come to a rebel stronghold to talk about him. The rest is meaningless. I'm assuming you can set up a direct telephone line to Berlin."

Doval needed a moment. He had never imagined the request coming from across the desk. "Yes."

"How long will it take?"

Again Doval hesitated. He was convincing himself of the logic. "Twenty minutes," he said.

"Good. And you have someone here who speaks a perfect German?"

"I have."

"Then I'll save us both some time." Acts of faith require so little preparation, he thought. "You're to have your man contact Gruppenführer Edmund Präger at the SS offices of the Sipo in Berlin. Präger. With an umlaut. I have the number, but coming from me you'd question it. So we'll sit together while your man tracks it down. When he has the Gruppenführer on the line, I'll tell your man what he needs to ask. And then you'll tell me what I need to know about Bernhardt. We're clear?"

Eighteen minutes later the telephone on Doval's desk rang through. Hoffner had spent the time drinking a second glass of water and finishing the cheese and crackers.

Doval said nothing. Instead, he chose to watch Hoffner. It was an old technique and not terribly effective in the hands of a man still green with his own power.

Doval nodded to the man who had promised a perfect German, and the man picked up the telephone.

"Hello?" The man's eyes darted as he listened. "Yes . . . slower please . . . yes . . . thank you . . . I can wait." The eyes settled on the rind of cheese before suddenly refocusing. "One moment." He cupped the receiver and looked at Doval. Doval looked across at Hoffner, and Hoffner said in Spanish, "You're to tell the Herr Gruppenführer that SS Hauptsturmführer Nikolai Hoffner is in Zaragoza, Spain, at the Nationalist headquarters with a Captain Doval."

Doval nodded to the man. The information was relayed in German and Hoffner watched as the man continued to listen. Either Präger would understand or Hoffner would be dead. It was as simple as that.

The man with the perfect German said in Spanish, "I think he's asking why you've contacted him, Captain."

Doval again looked at Hoffner, and Hoffner said, "You're to say this and only this: 'Braunschweig.'"

Doval again nodded and the man said hesitantly into the receiver, "Braunschweig." There were several more seconds of darting eyes, and the man said in Spanish, "SS Hauptsturmführer Hoffner has the Gruppenführer's complete authority. Contact is not to be made again." The man listened for more and then said, "Hello? . . . Hello?" He held the receiver out to Doval. "The line has disengaged, Captain."

Doval was looking across at Hoffner. "Set it down, Lieutenant. You're dismissed."

The man placed the telephone in its cradle, saluted, and moved to the door. Doval waited until they were alone.

"I've never heard of this Präger," said Doval. His caution remained.

"No," said Hoffner, "I'm sure you haven't." It was nice to know that two old bull cops could still wreak a little havoc. "The Gruppenführer's immediate superior is SS Obergruppenführer Reinhard Heydrich. That, I suspect, is a name you're more familiar with. We can put a call directly through to the Obergruppenführer if you prefer."

Doval had evidently spent time enough in the company of the SS not to give way to this kind of bullying. Instead he said, "Langenheim never mentioned Braunschweig."

Langenheim, thought Hoffner. All the names from Georg's wire were finding their way onto the table. Granted, Hoffner had no idea how Doval knew Langenheim—or who Langenheim might be—but at least they were heading in the right direction.

"No," said Hoffner. "I'm sure not."

"And the woman?"

Hoffner pulled out his cigarettes. This time he offered one to Doval. "The woman is no concern of yours." Doval took one and Hoffner lit it. "She has a brother who fights for you. That should be enough." He lit his own and sat back. "When was Bernhardt here?"

Doval was doing what he could to reassert control. He sat back as he stared across through the smoke. "He wasn't," he said.

Hoffner knew to tread carefully. Any moment this could all come crashing down. He began to feel a dull throbbing at the back of his neck. He took another careless pull on the cigarette and said, "Really?"

"But I would have assumed you knew that."

Doval was proving surprisingly adept. Hoffner let the smoke trail from his nose. "Would you?" he said. His only choice was a quiet contempt. "And when would I have learned this, Captain, having been in Barcelona for the past four days? When I telephoned to Berlin from the Ritz? I'm sure no one at the anarchist telephone exchange would have thought to ask why." And with no time for a response, "I need to know when Bernhardt was here. Do we understand each other?"

Doval might not have found the sweating German—with his half stories and vague papers—compelling, but Hoffner had brought something else with him: the aura of Nazi infallibility. It was enough to cut through any lingering concern.

"It was the nephew," said Doval. "The boy from Barcelona. No doubt you've met him."

Nephew, thought Hoffner. The drug addict was a nephew. Which meant there was a second, older Bernhardt. Hoffner had spent a career being told things he was meant to know. It made revelations like this quickly digestible.

Hoffner said, "I don't trust anyone involved with that. Opium is a mind without control, too easily persuaded. When was he here?"

Doval flicked a bit of ash into the ashtray. "Six days ago. He said he was having trouble establishing contacts."

"The Chinese were being less than accommodating?" Hoffner let this settle for only a moment. "As I said, I don't trust any of it. I haven't from the start." Hoffner finally saw what he had been hoping for: an instant of mutual understanding. They would find common ground in their distaste for the drug lines. Hoffner said, "Bernhardt thinks he's helping the nephew. I'm here to make sure he understands that's no longer in his best interests. Where was the nephew heading?"

"South."

"And the elder Bernhardt knew this?"

"I assume so."

Hoffner decided to take a chance. "You assume so? You have wires to this effect?"

It was not a good choice as Doval looked momentarily puzzled. "I don't think I follow."

The throbbing became a dull ache. Hoffner retreated to frustration. "The elder Bernhardt. Did he communicate this to you?"

Doval was no less forthright. "He made it clear we were no longer to continue in this direction."

"With the Chinese and the drugs?"

"Yes."

"And the nephew knew this?"

"Yes."

"He knew the guns were still coming from the south?"

Doval's hesitation returned. The SS never asked; they gave orders. This was too many questions. Regardless, Hoffner had swum well beyond his limits; there was no point in worrying about getting back to shore now.

"The elder Bernhardt," Hoffner pressed. "He made it clear that the drug lines were no longer a possibility, that the new routes were to go through Teruel."

Doval showed a moment's pause. This had struck a nerve.

Hoffner said, "I've said something that confuses you, Captain?"

Doval kept his eyes fixed on Hoffner. "No, Hauptsturmführer, you haven't."

The answer was too weak, and with nothing behind it. "You're aware of Teruel, Captain?"

"Yes," said Doval. "Of course."

"You're not filling me with tremendous confidence. I need to see these wires."

"You continue to refer to routes, Hauptsturmführer." Doval spoke with an unexpected resolve. "What routes would those be?"

The gaze across the desk showed none of the weakness of only moments ago. Mila had been right. These were not men to be underestimated. Hoffner wondered if this was where Doval had been leading him all along.

Hoffner waited. He took another pull on his cigarette. He let the smoke spear through his nostrils. And then he did what any good Nazi would do. He smiled.

"You don't speak German," said Hoffner. His voice carried a newfound respect. "Now I see why." He leaned forward and slowly crushed out his cigarette. "Ambition is a far more vital quality."

Doval showed nothing, and Hoffner knew it was only a matter of time before there would be a second telephone call to Berlin.

Hoffner continued. "Bernhardt chose not to tell you about the routes, Captain. I have to accept that. My mistake was assuming you knew, Teruel notwithstanding. If that means you take me outside and shoot me, so be it."

Doval sat remarkably still. Hoffner returned the gaze and understood the reason Gabriel and his kind had taken no time for celebrations: if this was Spain's future, there would be no Spain worth remembering.

Doval said, "I wouldn't bother taking you outside, Hauptsturmführer. The walls in my office are sturdy enough."

Hoffner gave in to another smile, and Doval opened the top drawer of his desk. He reached in and pulled out a thin file of papers. He handed them across and sat back while Hoffner read.

A WAY THROUGH

The air outside was remarkably fresh. Or perhaps it was just that Hoffner felt himself breathing again for the first time in the last hour. The young lieutenant assigned to escort him to the café walked with no such appreciation for the air.

Hoffner said, "Your German was excellent on the telephone."

The young lieutenant nodded once. He spoke again in German. "Thank you, Hauptsturmführer."

"In the coming weeks, Captain Doval will need you more than he knows."

"Yes, Hauptsturmführer."

Hoffner found himself lighting a cigarette as he walked.

He suspected Doval might be telephoning to Berlin at this moment, perhaps even to Langenheim. That said, there was very little in the wires to concern Doval—at least in showing them to someone who had mentioned routes and guns and Teruel.

As far as Hoffner could tell, the wires served as confirmation: the nephew had been in Barcelona; he had come to Zaragoza; he had gone on to Teruel. After that, he was due to head west, stopping along the way in places now, or soon to be (God willing), in fascist control: Cuenca, Tarancón, Toledo, Coria, and finally Badajoz on the Portuguese border; a straight line across the heart of Spain.

More than that, there were contact names in each of the towns and cities, along with addresses for each man. Hoffner had written them all down.

The travel itinerary was the elder Bernhardt's way of assuring Captain Doval and his fellow liaisons across the country that mechanisms were being set in place to guarantee the steady flow of guns and ammunition from Germany into Spain. How they hoped to accomplish that—and how these contact names played a role—remained the mystery.

Hoffner was guessing Georg might be trying to piece that together himself.

"Here we are," the young lieutenant said.

Hoffner tossed his cigarette to the ground and followed the boy to the café door.

The Gran Café was wall-front windows and wooden pillars throughout, with the smell of fresh coffee and garlic hanging in the air. Mila was at a table at the back, beyond the bar. A man in the uniform of a *requeté* sat with her. He was reading through a letter.

Only two of the other tables were occupied: a trio of officers sat knee to knee as they sipped silently through bowls of something brown; closer to the door an old priest was reading a newspaper and drinking from a glass of yellow liquid. He looked up with a gentle smile as Hoffner stepped inside. Mila's own escort stood by the bar with a cup of chocolate and a plate of churros. The strips of dough were powdered and had left white specks under his nose. They made the man's sharp nod to Hoffner's lieutenant somewhat less imposing.

Hoffner drew up to Mila's table. The lieutenant was now with his friend at the bar, delicately trying to inform him of the powder. There was a flurry of nose activity over Hoffner's shoulder, and Mila said, "Everything all right?"

Hoffner nodded. The brother looked up with the same features as his father, although here they were hidden behind a neatly cropped beard and mustache. It was unclear whether he had been crying, but the eyes showed a heaviness. He stood. He was tall like his sister.

Hoffner said, "Sergeant Piera."

"Señor Hoffman."

Mila corrected. "Hoffner."

Piera looked at his sister. His mind was clearly elsewhere. He looked again at Hoffner. "Yes, of course. Señor Hoffner. My apologies."

Hoffner motioned to the chairs, and the two men sat. Mila said nothing, and Piera went back to his letter. Hoffner noticed a loose stack of perhaps twenty on the chair beside him, a brown piece of twine at the side. Three of the letters had already been opened and read.

Mila kept her eyes on her brother as he flipped to the back of the one in his hand, read it, and set it down. He stared for several moments before saying, "That's the last?" His eyes remained fixed on the table.

"Yes," said Mila.

Piera's eyes moved as if he were reading something only he could see. "She wrote well."

"She did."

He nodded. His mind was struggling to find its way back. The eyes filled and his breathing became heavier, but he refused to cry. Mila placed her hand on his.

She said, "I don't like the beard."

Even his smile showed pain. "Then you're lucky you don't have to see it that often." He looked at Hoffner. "Forgive me. A friend has died. I've just been told of it."

It was clearly more, but Hoffner knew to say only, "I'm sorry."

Piera tried to move past it. "You've been to see Captain Doval?"

"Yes."

"And you've come from Barcelona?"

Hoffner nodded. He had no intention of opening this up, but Piera saved him by saying, "Thank you, then. For bringing Mila. I won't take any more of your time."

Piera stood. He reached down and collected the letters, and Hoffner noticed how large the hands were. Odd to notice that, he thought. He watched as Piera embraced his sister. Mila was not so good with the tears. She rubbed her eyes against her brother's shoulder. Piera released her and said, "It's a bit strange, isn't it?"

She stared into his face. "Yes. It is."

"To see each other this way."

They were finding anything to keep him from going. She nodded. "Yes."

Piera looked at Hoffner. "She's a doctor, you know. Did you know that?" Hoffner nodded and Piera tried a ragged smile. "Of course you knew. We could use doctors this side, too." He looked at his sister and seemed momentarily confused.

Her eyes filled, and she said, "Be well, Carlos. God be with you."

Piera stared a moment longer and then nodded. He looked again at Hoffner and went past him. As he walked to the door, Piera set his beret on his head. He opened the door and stepped out onto the street.

Mila watched him through the glass, even when she could no longer see him.

She said, "I asked him to come with us."

Hoffner could only imagine that moment.

"We should go," he said. He turned to the soldiers at the bar. "Lieutenant." He was once again the man from Berlin. "Bring my car around. And I'll have a cup of the chocolate with the—" He pointed to the strips of dough.

"Churros," the man said.

"Yes. And call ahead to the city's southern barricade. The road to Teruel. Tell them to expect us in the next half hour."

The sky took on a deep blue just before sunset, softening a landscape that was growing more desolate by the hour. The few patches of green now came as sudden eruptions, clumps on a hillock or straggling weeds of wild brush that seemed beaten down by earth and rocks. It was a place unchanged for centuries, and it made the past a kind of comfort.

There had been no further contact with Captain Doval. The car had appeared fully gassed; the two lieutenants had been sent on their way. Nonetheless, it was now more than an hour, and Hoffner was still expecting to peer into the rearview mirror and see the dust of an approaching car rising in the distance.

Mila was staring out, her head resting back against the seat. She had slipped in and out of sleep, barely moving, not even to swat the fly that seemed incapable of finding its way to an open window. The thing battered itself against the dashboard, and she began to follow the lazy line of telephone poles, one after the other after the other.

Hoffner was fighting off his own exhaustion, the strain from his performance still knotted in his neck. Even the miracle of having come through did nothing to help. His head felt light, and there was a tackiness at the back of his throat. He imagined that nausea would follow, but for now he focused on the road.

Again he glanced in the mirror, and Mila said, "Either they're coming or they're not. Staring in the mirror won't change it."

She was suddenly aware of the fly. She followed its flight, cupped it in her hands, and held it before releasing it at the window. She closed her eyes and let the last of the sun stretch across her face.

It was nearly a minute before she said, "Do you ever miss her—your wife?"

Hoffner felt the back of his neck compress.

He had been foolish just beyond the city. He had let her ask questions. More foolish, he had answered them. Now she had Martha's death and Sascha's hatred to toss back at him. Seventeen years removed and he still felt the stale taste of his own arrogance in his mouth. The Nazis had been nothing then—nothing but a distant rumbling from Munich and the south. And yet he had underestimated them. He had dismissed them as thugs and charlatans, and they had murdered his wife. To have his son blame him for her death and to let them steal his Sascha away—maybe that was what lingered in his throat.

He had no strength for that past.

"The girl in the letters," he said. "She was his wife?"

Mila took a moment before answering. "Near enough. It was a long time ago." She opened her eyes and stared out. "She never sent them. She was killed in the fighting last week." She looked over at him. "Do you ever miss her?"

Hoffner peered into the mirror. "No," he said. He focused on the road ahead. "I don't think I do."

She nodded quietly and turned again to the window. "He was a doctor, my husband. At a clinic in the Raval. I was a terrible nurse."

Hoffner was glad for the lift in her voice. "I don't believe that."

"I was. It's what you get when you have a twenty-year-old who knows better than everyone else. They all hated me."

"Except for this doctor of yours."

"Yes."

"He fell in love with you?"

"He did."

"And he trained you?"

She smiled, recalling something. "No. He was much more of an idealist than that. He married me and took me to Moscow."

"How romantic."

The smile remained. "The Revolution was good for opening all those doors. He found me a place at one of the medical academies: Sechanov— old, prestigious. He was at a prison hospital: Butyrki, I think. Funny how you forget those things."

Hoffner glanced in the mirror again. Not so hard to forget.

"It must have been cold," he said. "Moscow—for a Spaniard."

"It wasn't the cold that was the problem." A pack of cigarettes lay bouncing on the seat and she took one. She lit it, placed it between his lips, and did the same for herself. "He began to write," she said. "Always a mistake. A pamphlet on medical reforms. They arrested him." She spoke as if she were reading from a manual. "He was sent to build roads in a work camp near Ukhta, in the north. March of 1930. He died three months later."

Hoffner thought to say something consoling but managed only, "I'm sorry."

"Yes." She was staring down at the cigarette in her hand. "Do you think you ever really loved your wife?"

Hoffner had told her almost nothing, and yet he now wondered how much she had heard. There was never any safety in this.

She wasn't expecting an answer, and said, "I loved my husband. Very much, although it's hard to imagine it now. I suppose you either choose to forget quickly or not at all. I chose to forget."

Hoffner needed them past this. "And then you came home?"

There was a vague sad smile on her lips when she looked up. "No. Carlos wouldn't be in Zaragoza now if I'd managed to make it home then." She took a pull and spared him the question. "They arrested me a month later and sent me to a camp: Siblag, also in the north." She thought of something and shook her head. "There was a letter I'd written, nothing in it, but I was the foreign wife of a foreign counterrevolutionary. It was easy enough." Her voice was distant as she turned to the window. "A year in prison for two lines in a letter."

Hoffner glanced over. She was so matter-of-fact, and yet the eyes were full as she stared out. He watched as she let the wind dry them. It was the only moment of hardness to find her face. He saw it drain from her, and she said, "It doesn't make me callous not to remember, does it?"

What an unfair question, he thought: you only remember the pain, nothing else, so why not shut it all out? He looked out at the road and said, "No. It doesn't."

She seemed to agree and took another pull. "When I came back, things were bad. Carlos blamed my father—Russia, Stalin, Communism, my father again. Me." It was another moment before she said, "And one day he said God would never have let it happen. God. Can you imagine? What could be crueler than that, until he actually began to believe it?" She tossed the cigarette out the window. "Not much God to be had in Barcelona." Her head found the back of the seat again and she stared out at the poles. "So he left."

Hoffner was glad for the silence. The sun had turned a blood red; he watched as it dipped lower on the horizon.

She said, "They look like giants, don't they? Stubby arms all in a row."

It took him a moment to understand. He bent his head closer into the windscreen and glanced over at the poles. He leaned back and nodded. Again he turned to the mirror.

She said distantly, "No knights to fight off these days." She looked over at him and, with a sudden energy, hitched herself around and stared back through the rear window. "There's nothing, Nikolai. No one's following. No dust rising from tires or hooves. You pulled it off. And now you can find your son and not worry that some distraction might have thrown it all away."

She was looking directly at him. Her hair had slipped from its knot, and her face was pale. It was an endless few seconds before she sat back and stared out at the road.

She waited for him to answer until she finally said, "It wasn't for luck or courage, that kiss. You know that."

Hoffner knew almost nothing. He was having trouble enough keeping up, but this—it was such a long time since any of this had made sense to him. And to have it here, now. It seemed beyond his grasp and made him feel weak.

Without warning, he jammed his foot on the brake and brought the car to a sudden stop. Mila bounced against the seat and instantly glanced back, expecting to see something on the road, but it remained empty. She looked at him as if she thought he might reach for her, but instead, he turned back and pulled on the strap that released the backseat cushion.

"What are you doing?" she said.

He opened his door and stepped out. "Slaying giants."

"What?"

He opened the back door and took out one of the brick explosives. He then stepped around to the nearest telephone pole and, crouching down, set the brick against its base. He looked over at her in the window. "What do you think, three or four?"

She was staring at him. "What?"

"Three or four of the poles? Would that be enough?"

"You're not serious?"

"Very serious."

"Then you're not thin enough to be playing the part."

"Thank you. No, this is for Durruti and our friends back in Zaragoza. They decide to call ahead, I need them not to get through." He stood and moved to her door. "You'll drive so I can light them before jumping in." He opened her door. "Move over."

She sat staring up at him. "You're going to light the fuses and then jump in the car?"

"Yes."

"And then I speed us away so you can light the next one?"

"Yes."

"And this does what?"

"Did Sancho Panza always ask so many questions?"

"Yes."

"Well, at least we're true to form. Move over."

She drove them to each of the four poles. Hoffner set the bricks in place, and she took the car back around to the first. She watched him as he stepped out. "This is madness," she said.

"Yes." He leaned over. "Ready?" He looked back to see that she had the car in gear. She nodded and he lit the fuse. He then ran and jumped in.

"Ride, Sancho, ride!"

Dust and earth kicked up as she accelerated, then more smoke as she screeched to a stop at the second pole. Another match, another mad dash. It was just as Hoffner was diving back in the car for the fourth time that the first of the bricks exploded.

She drove off, looking back through the mirror, while he angled his head and shoulders out the window.

It was a wonderful thing to see, the pole ripped from its roots, the wire limp to the ground. Suddenly the second exploded and the pole jumped into the air, tearing at its mooring and keeling over. The third and fourth followed suit, the last stripping the wire with such force that it snapped across the ground like the lash of a whip. Mila stopped the car, and they both got out.

Pale clouds hovered above the four felled poles, the remaining stumps jagged shards of wood cutting through the plumes of smoke. The standing poles at either end of the gap stared helplessly across at each other, as if they could conceive of nothing to fill the chasm between them: one world at an end, another begun.

Hoffner listened. There was absolute silence, not even the sound of settling dust. It was such a small thing—four meaningless poles of wood—yet he felt a surge of energy. Even the knot at the back of his neck was gone. Mila drew up next to him.

"Are we done?" she said, no less gratified.

He watched for another few seconds and said, "Get in the car." He stepped around and slid in behind the wheel. They drove and he glanced back in the mirror, this time for the sheer pleasure of it.

That night, they stopped twenty kilometers from Teruel. It was late and they were exhausted. They found a tavern with two rooms above. Mila took a bath while he smoked. Hoffner bathed while she went for a second bottle of wine. And they shared a bed and knew that this was how they would find their way through.

5

TERUEL

She was still asleep when his eyes opened. There was the sound of plates or cups being stacked on a shelf somewhere beyond the door and down the stairs, but Hoffner lay quietly. She had pulled the sheet to just above her waist, her bare back to him, curved to the pillow, and her hair loose against her neck. The shoulder rose almost to her cheek, and he saw the two long scars he had traced with his fingers through the darkness last night. She had said nothing, his thumb gliding along the small of her back and across the spine, the raised skin like jagged lines of wire against the pale smoothness of the rest. He brought his face toward her neck, and she said, "You hardly move when you sleep."

She turned and looked up at him. It would have been so easy to show the expectation of a kiss, that dizzying and ageless hope of a first morning together, but instead they simply stared. It was effortless, and Hoffner nearly mistook it for the hollow comfort of a shared loneliness. That at least would have been familiar. But this was other. It brought a softening to his face, and she smiled, and he felt its warmth like the distant pull of an unknown faith.

"I thought you were dead," she said. "I had to listen to make sure you were breathing."

"I'll remember to make more noise." He gave her a kiss on the forehead and brought his legs over the side. He sat.

"Coward," she said.

He looked back and was thankful for the smile. "Yes. Petrified." He stood and pulled on his shorts, then reached for his cigarettes. He tapped out two and lit them. "Do you think they'll have eggs? For some reason I'm wanting eggs."

She pulled back the sheet and propped her head on an elbowed hand as she rolled on her side. He imagined he had never seen this kind of perfect beauty, not for the litheness of her shape or the delicacy of her face, but for the absolute peace she felt in her own uncovered body. It brought him back to the bed, and he sat, and she took a cigarette.

"Thank you," she said.

"For what?"

"The cigarette."

"Oh—yes."

"What else did you think I was saying?" This was payment for the kiss on the forehead. "Was the young captain helpful?"

Hoffner took hold of the water jug and poured out a glass. He handed it to her. "Yes."

"You must be very good at what you do."

"You don't need to be so good."

She took a drink. "You should stop saying that. It's not the truth, and it's not all that endearing. He would have shot you." She finished the glass and held it out to him. He poured a second, and he drank.

She said, "I'll need to find a place to wash some clothes." She sat and moved to the edge of the bed. She picked up her chemise and dress from the floor. "I can do it in Teruel while you"—she had to think a moment—"do whatever it is you'll be doing there."

Hoffner watched her slip the clothes over her shoulders. She reached back to button the collar of the dress, and he said, "You don't have to come, you know. It's probably safer if you head back to Barcelona." At least he was trying to sound noble.

She reached for her hose and began to slide them on. "So it's this you're not terribly good at." She finished and looked back at him. "I don't want to go back to Barcelona, Nikolai. And I don't think you want me to, either. Do you?"

He waited and then shook his head.

"You see? That wasn't so hard." She stood.

Hoffner was suddenly aware he was sitting in nothing but his shorts. He stood, found his shirt, and began to button the buttons with a new-found resolve.

She reached over and picked up his pants. She held them there and waited. "There's no rush, Nikolai. The pants aren't going anywhere."

He nodded absently, took them, and slid them on.

She said, "You're not going to tell me you don't do this sort of thing, or that you haven't for a very long time, or ever—are you?"

He looked across at her and, not wanting to betray himself, again shook his head.

"Good." She moved closer and brought his suspenders up and over his shoulders. She smoothed them against his chest. "Even if it's true, what would be the point in saying it? Love isn't meant to stand back and stare at its past."

She gazed up at him and then stepped over to her shoes. She slid her feet in and bent over to buckle them, and Hoffner—aware of a sudden and deep numbing at the back of his head—stared across at her and let himself believe in all things possible.

Teruel was in a state of mild panic. Sitting a thousand meters above sea level—and now with no telephone lines to the north—it had become an island of misinformation at the southern tip of Nationalist Aragón. The Civil Guards who had secured the city for the rebels strode about in their capes and tricorn hats as if the future of Europe lay in the balance. They coughed out orders, looked out through field glasses onto an endless hori-zon, and smoked cigarettes that gave off the smell of soured bark. All this was understandable. They had spent the better part of the last week staring off in the other direction toward Valencia—another pointless exercise— where rumor had it that anarchists were opening up the prisons and filling their ranks with rapists, murderers, and thieves. It might not have been the truth—most of the inmates were of the political variety—but always good to parade out the apocalypse when trying to stir up a bit of vigilance. Now, with Teruel's imagination well beyond reason, the Guardia had positioned fifty of their own and one hundred of the town's bravest caballeros inside buildings, along the old aqueduct, and atop the red ceramic roofs. Three hundred eyes, give or take, stared out silently at the Zaragoza road.

Remarkably, Hoffner and Mila drove up the slope without a single shot being fired. It was either a miraculous show of self-restraint or a level of cowardice as yet unknown in Spain. Hoffner was undecided as he sat behind the wheel and spoke with the sergeant in charge.

"Yes," Hoffner said, "the road was completely empty." For some reason Teruel was a good ten degrees hotter than anywhere else in Spain. "The telephone lines were untouched."

"And you left Zaragoza this morning?"

It was the third time the man had asked, although this attempt came off more as a hope than a question; the Safe Conduct papers and the mention of Captain Doval had placed Hoffner on something of a pedestal. Hoffner was a man with connections, prestige, which meant he had answers. For a sergeant in the Guardia it was simply a matter of asking enough times before he heard what he wanted to hear.

"No," said Hoffner, a bit more forcefully. "Not this morning. Last night. We were at a tavern this morning."

"In Albarracín."

"Yes," said Hoffner. "That's right. In Albarracín. You can telephone—" He caught himself. "Obviously you can't telephone. We left there an hour ago. No one was on the road. I need to see your commanding officer."

"So you think sending out a group would be all right? To check the lines?" The man's hope had become faith in this German.

Hoffner knew it would take them two hours to find the downed poles, another two to remount them—if, in fact, they were clever enough to take shovels, wire splicers, and whatever else one needed to resurrect the dead. That would give him until early afternoon to find Georg in a town filled with anxious Spaniards. Then again, Captain Doval might already have sent out a crew to fix the wiring, but what was the point in worrying about that?

"Good, yes," Hoffner said. "Send out a group. Absolutely. Now, where do I find someone in charge?"

The man shouted over to one of the other guards. "The colonel here says the road is clear."

Hoffner hadn't mentioned a rank; still, it was nice to hear he had merited a promotion.

"Take five men," the sergeant continued, "rifles, a spool of wire, and find someone who knows what he's doing with the lines." He looked back at Hoffner and said quietly, "They like to think it's coming from someone with clout. You know—a little pull." Hoffner understood why the SS would have no trouble fitting in here. The man said, "You'll want Alfassi. He'll be having something to eat down in the Plaza del Torico. Ferrer's. Straight on. You can't miss it."

Maybe it was the heat or the height or the horror of what lay just beyond the walls, but fascist Teruel was showing a good deal more spirit than had Zaragoza. The square was cluttered with people and animals; stands were filled with fruit and foods, some of which Hoffner had never seen—large gourds, and thin stalks with a kind of yellow flower sprouting along the sides. He imagined they were all edible, but why shatter the mystery? Planted in the middle was a small fountain and column, with a bronze bull standing atop it. A few children were howling up at the bull, while a young priest, dressed in full cassock, sat on the edge of the fountain and rinsed his eyeglasses under one of the spouts. Without warning, the priest howled back, and the children darted off. Laughing, the priest shouted after them and a woman crossed herself as she walked past. The priest nodded piously and began to wipe his glasses on his sleeve. Murderers at the gate, and this was all the comfort Teruel required.

Hoffner had parked the car on one of the side streets. He and Mila were now walking toward a narrow building on the far side of the fountain. As with everything in this part of the world, it was an odd mixture of styles, thin alabaster columns along the second floor façade, and a pink Mudéjar tower peeking out at the top left. As the floors climbed, the windows moved from simple rectangles to arches to half-moons, with the usual ironwork balconies stretching out below them. It was the perfect place to meet a Spaniard called Alfassi.

Hoffner opened the door and Mila led them inside. The thick stone walls resembled a fortress grotto, damp and cool, although here there were hanging bulbs and tables and chairs, and a wooden bar that ran the length of the wall. Animal parts hung from metal hooks above, with two large pig heads the centerpieces of an otherwise ragtag display. As in the square, Hoffner was hard-pressed to define what most of this was—a few legs of something that seemed caught between a cow's and a goat's—but the conversation was light, the smells surprisingly good, and the presence of the Guardia almost nil. There was only one, sitting across from a gray-haired woman, his tricorn hat propped on the table between them. She was dressed all in black and, except for the face and hands, showed only two slivers of skin on each of the wrists. From the expression on the man's face, she seemed to be in the midst of a nice harangue. Even with the rifle leaning against the table, he looked utterly helpless.

Hoffner followed Mila through. There were the expected stares, none more than a few seconds, before they arrived at the table. The woman was instantly silent, and the man looked up. Not wanting to offend, and not sure how the Guardia divvied up their ranks, Hoffner stole a page from the sergeant at the gate.

"Colonel Alfassi?" he said.

The man continued to stare. Hoffner thought he might have over-reached—did the Guardia even have colonels?—when a voice a few tables back said, "Did you say Alfassi, Señor?"

Hoffner turned and saw a small spectacled face, tan summer suit, gold cuff links, and a thin red tie sitting over a bowl of soup. The man was perfectly bald, save for the neatly cropped strip of hair just above the ears. After a week of anarchists and soldiers, Hoffner found it almost jarring to see a man of wealth, especially in these surroundings. No surprise, then, that he was sitting alone. He held a newspaper which, from the look of the weathered edges, was at best a week old.

Hoffner said, "Yes, Señor," and the woman went back to her harangue.

Hoffner and Mila stepped over, and the man introduced himself as Rolando Alfassi, a timber merchant whose time was now spent as chief member of the recently established Committee of Three for Public Honor. It was why the sergeant had sent them to him. Hoffner suspected that the honor in question might have more to do with the purging of Teruel's remaining leftists, but why argue semantics with a man who had just ordered them a plate of *jamón* and two more glasses of lemon water? The pulp was thick enough to chew when the glasses arrived.

"From Zaragoza?" Alfassi said, as he cut slowly through a thin slice of the ham. He ate with great precision. "You know, we lost all telephone contact with Zaragoza last night." He sniffed at the meat and ate it.

"Yes," said Hoffner. "The sergeant at the gate mentioned it once or twice."

Alfassi smiled. It was a simple straightforward smile. "And you've heard nothing about the south?"

The telephones were clearly not a concern for Alfassi. He was reading a week-old newspaper: Whatever information was meant to find him would find him.

"No, Señor," said Hoffner. "We've been only in the north."

Alfassi nodded as he worked through a second piece of the ham. "Then you've seen the atrocities, the nuns and the desecration. They say it was terrible before the soldiers stepped in." He ate.

It was an odd place to begin a conversation: the quality of the road, the weather, the number of burned carcasses strewn across the church steps. Hoffner could have told Alfassi that, only yesterday, he had refused a tour of Zaragoza's bodies still awaiting burial—the slaughtered workers with their union cards pinned to their shirts—but that might not have gotten Hoffner a second plate of the ham, which was really quite delicious.

"No," said Hoffner. "I was traveling with the señora."

"Of course." Alfassi seemed genuinely remorseful. "Forgive me, Señora." Mila said blankly, "Have you buried your own?"

Alfassi stared for a moment, and it was only then that Hoffner realized Zaragoza had been very different for her. She had thought only of her brother: the truth of the war had been set aside for an afternoon. Here, she had no such luxury. He was inclined to remind her of the washing she had promised to do, but instead he said, "The señora is a doctor. She's been attending to the wounded. She worries about disease."

"A doctor finds all killing horrific," said Alfassi. It was surprising to hear the compassion in his voice. "It must be difficult."

"Yes," she said, "it is."

Alfassi leaned in and said quietly, "I find it all quite horrible myself." It was as if he knew he wasn't meant to admit it. "We have many, many bodies. Soon we'll have more. It's a terrible time." He sat back and took another piece of the ham on his fork. "It's never really a question of knowing God's will, is it? But at least He's there. To say He isn't, or never has been, or shouldn't be—" He slipped the fork into his mouth and shook his head. "Some choose to act impetuously, I know—every war has its excesses—but surely God has a right to protect Himself. What is Spain without God? What is God without Spain?" Alfassi swallowed and said, "Have they buried the bodies in Zaragoza?"

To call wholesale murder impetuous was unforgivable. Even so, it was clear that Alfassi's fight was not about control or power. It was about fear— the simple fear of losing his God. And, as with all men who live through fear, he was looking for guidance. Holy vengeance was something new, at least in this century. Cleaning up after it was still open to debate.

Hoffner said, "I wouldn't know."

Alfassi nodded and cut another piece. "It's a good point—disease. There's enough to think about without that."

"And these bodies," Mila said. "How many exactly?"

Hoffner tipped over his glass—an accident—and water spilled to the lip of the table. Instinctively Mila pulled back, and Hoffner quickly apologized. He tried to stop it with his napkin.

"You're all right?" he said. She said nothing and Hoffner looked at Alfassi. "It's very good. The lemons are fresh."

"Yes," said Alfassi. "Don't worry. Someone will clean it."

A man appeared with a rag and quickly mopped up what remained. He poured Hoffner another glass and moved off.

Hoffner said, "I'm not a Spaniard, Señor."

"Yes, I know. A thousand years ago, neither was I. The name: it means 'from Fez.'" He enjoyed this little nugget. "You're a German."

"Yes."

"We've had quite a few of you through here in the last week."

"None causing any trouble, I hope."

There was a roll on his plate. Alfassi took it and ripped it open. "Am I to be expecting more of you?"

"I'm interested in just one, Señor, a journalist with the Pathé Gazette Company. He would have been carrying a moving film camera. He was sent to bring back newsreels."

Alfassi buttered the roll and took a bite. He nodded. "Also called Hoffner. I don't think that's a coincidence, is it?"

Hoffner tried not to show a reaction.

Alfassi had known all along, and he had taken his time. It was now unclear whether this had all been for show—a bit of pious propaganda for a visitor—or something more sinister. Hoffner wondered if the Guardia with the rifle was always just a few tables down.

Hoffner said, "No coincidence, Señor. You met him?"

Alfassi continued to chew. "Briefly. I don't trust foreign journalists. It's always so easy to pass judgment from a distance." He swallowed. "At least with our own, we know if they're right or wrong before we read them."

"My son isn't the kind to judge."

Alfassi reached for his glass. "That would depend on what he chooses to film, wouldn't it?" He drank, and Hoffner waited for the conversation to take its unpleasant turn. Instead, Alfassi added, "I don't think he was in Teruel long enough to have made many choices. Three or four hours. He didn't eat the ham."

Hoffner had the strangest sensation, an image of Georg sitting across from Alfassi, probably at this very table. That Georg was already gone was only a momentary disappointment. The boy was alive. That was enough for now. Georg would be heading west, along the route outlined in Doval's wires. Hoffner was less clear on where Alfassi might be leading them.

"His loss," said Hoffner.

"Tell me, Señor." There was something caught in Alfassi's tooth. He ran his thumbnail through it. "Why is it that all these Germans are interested in your journalist son, and why do they all come to Teruel to find him? Surely Zaragoza, Barcelona, or Madrid are far more interesting these days."

Alfassi's tone was almost impenetrable. The words seemed to threaten, then not. Hoffner couldn't decide if this was charm or guile or simply the residue of an unflappable faith. What he did know was that the SS was tracking Georg—"all these Germans."

Hoffner said, "I'm not a journalist, Señor. I wouldn't know. How many Germans exactly?"

Alfassi took the last of the ham on his fork. "You're both so interested in numbers." He sniffed and ate.

"Yes," said Hoffner.

"I have a son," said Alfassi. "Not much younger than yours." The faint echo of compassion returned. "I suppose I would ask the same questions, follow the same course."

"I suppose you would."

"And when you find your son, Señor, you'll take him out of Spain? Immediately?"

Hoffner was trying to understand the last few moments. This was more than compassion, and while he had no idea how much Alfassi knew, or wanted to know, it was clear that the man was struggling with this. Whatever the reason, Hoffner nodded.

"Good." Alfassi also nodded. "There were two Germans. One four days ago, the other yesterday—an unusual German, that one. And now you."

"And you told them—"

"Neither was his father. I told them nothing." Alfassi's eyes grew more focused; when he spoke again, he made clear why every Guardia and every visitor to Teruel knew exactly where to find him. "We won't win this war without the Germans. We know it. That doesn't mean we become like them." Again he picked up his glass. "You ask about bodies, Doctor. How many more do you think we'd have if we'd listened to these Germans? Not that any of us needs encouragement these days, anywhere in Spain. We can kill each other quite well on our own. But we know why we do it, and why it will stop, one way or the other." He drank and set the glass down. "These Germans see it differently. For them it's terror, not truth; power, not faith. And while I'd be foolish to say that terror and power don't serve other ends, they can't be the only reasons we do this. At least not in my Spain." He looked again at Hoffner. "I don't believe this is your war, Señor, nor the señora's—at least not here. More important, I don't believe I want your son getting in the way of it. We understand each other?"

Alfassi knew exactly who they were and why they had come. He was also a man of conscience, limited as it might be. That he was choosing to find his penance in Georg was all that stood between Hoffner, Mila, and the rifle two tables down.

Alfassi said, "He was looking for a Major Sanz, a new man. I don't know him. He's at the Guardia Station. I'm sure you can find him there."

There had been no mention of a Sanz in the contact list from Captain Doval's wires. In fact there had been no one to contact in Teruel. Maybe, thought Hoffner, that was because Teruel was already fully under fascist control.

Hoffner nodded and said, "Thank you."

Alfassi picked up his newspaper. "Get out of Spain, Señor. Quickly." He was already reading, and Hoffner pushed back his chair and followed Mila to the door.

She pulled her arm from his hand the instant they were outside. He knew to keep his eyes ahead of him as they walked.

"You treated him with such respect," she said, the disdain stifled but raw. "The great man who finds killing impetuous. You have no idea what this war is about, do you?"

"He knew who we were."

"He knew nothing."

They walked along a cobblestone ramp, smooth and yellow like an old man's teeth. Above, iron flakes peeled like dead skin from the rusting balconies, while washing hung loose in the courtyard below. It laced the air with the taste of vinegar. Somewhere, the muffled pitch of a mass was being sung.

"It was my mistake," Hoffner said. "A woman doctor. He knew that could mean only one thing."

"You think he did this out of compassion? One father to another? Are you really that blind?"

Hoffner stopped and took her arm. He held her there, afraid to see the hatred—or, worse, the betrayal—and all he could think to say was, "Yes. I am. What would you have me do? He's letting me find my son. If that doesn't earn him a little something—" Hoffner hadn't thought this through. Her eyes were growing unbearably distant. How long had it been since he had felt this need? "Don't do this," he said. It was the ache in his own pleading that took the breath from his voice. "Don't make me defend what I do to find him."

Hoffner stared into her eyes, not knowing if in this infinite moment he had condemned himself to a life he already despaired of. To have it this close—

She said, "Do you think that's what I'm asking? Do you think I don't see that?"

Hoffner had no bearings for this. His head was suddenly light, the sound of voices behind him—somewhere—beginning to vibrate unrelentingly. He felt his arm go weak, then his legs. He let go of her and reached for the wall, the scarred stone scraping into his hand, the pain a momentary relief. He heard his own breath—deep and heavy—saw himself crouching, then sitting on the stone. He had an instant of nausea and then great thirst. His eyes tried to find their focus, movement somewhere in front of him, when he saw her, on her knees. She was doing something with his neck or throat or tie. It was the tie. And then the cold tin of the canteen on his lips, and water, the stream of it flowing down to the pit of his stomach. He looked at her as she doused his handkerchief with water and set it at the back of his neck. His head throbbed.

She turned to the courtyard below and said, "The heat. He's not used to it." Hoffner noticed people behind her. They were staring, nodding. She said, "I'm a doctor. It's fine."

They moved off, and Hoffner felt his arms again. "It's not the heat," he said.

She moved the handkerchief to his brow and squeezed it, and the water ran down his face. "I know," she said. "But maybe it is just a little."

He took her hand and felt the dampness of it.

With her other, she placed two fingers under his jaw and felt for his pulse. Hoffner looked into her face, the color gone, the beads of sweat creasing her cheeks and lips. He said, "I won't choose—"

"You should stop talking."

"You don't understand." He needed her to know this. "I won't have this be a choice."

"I'm not asking you to."

"No. You have to see what I'm saying, what I need from you."

She stopped and stared into his eyes. "What you need from me you have. What you need from me isn't a question. There are no choices."

"I have to find him."

Her gaze softened. "You really don't understand this, do you?" Hoffner tried to answer, and she said, "Of course we find him. What did you think—just because I tell you you're an idiot when it comes to a man like Alfassi it means more than that? You *are* an idiot when it comes to Alfassi, and you have no idea what this war is about, but why would that change anything? Wouldn't it have been worse if I hadn't screamed a little after that?"

Hoffner felt a relief he had no hope of understanding. "I thought—"

"Yes. I know. But I'm allowed to tell you how sad and desperate this war makes me, Nikolai. And I need to know you won't collapse every time I do." She handed him the canteen again. "But I'm glad you thought it was a choice. Now drink."

Hoffner drank and felt his strength returning. He waited another half minute and drank again.

She said, "You're all right?"

He took a last drink and handed her the canteen. He nodded and got to his feet.

He said, "It's nice to know I'm an idiot." His legs felt heavy but at least they were there.

"He's a Spaniard with a conscience. It's easy to be fooled." She took a drink and saw something down in the courtyard. She slipped her arm through his. "We should get you something with salt. I could use some my-self." They began to walk.

He said, "So when did conscience become such a terrible thing?"

"You've been living in Germany too long. The fascists there don't bother with it."

"And here?"

She slipped her hand farther down his arm and took his hand. "Here Alfassi has God and truth and what he takes for compassion. His is a fas-cism that breeds inspiration." Her fingers curled through his, and Hoffner gripped at them. "If he manages to win this war, you can be sure he and his friends will be here long after your thousand-year Reich is dust. Alfassi knows it—brutality as brutality runs its course—but a man of conscience, gentility, kindness? He can breathe life into brutality again and again and make it seem almost humane. It's a particularly Spanish cruelty and we've had centuries to become very, very good at it."

They came to a little awning, two tables and three chairs. A curtain, made of strings of bamboo beads, hung across the open door to keep out the flies. They sat, and Mila said into the curtain, "Two beers and an order of *migas*, please."

A voice grunted acknowledgment. Hoffner didn't know *migas*.

"Bread crumbs," she said. "Like porridge, with bacon or chorizo or whatever they have lying around. It'll be good for you."

He nodded and pulled out his cigarettes.

"I wouldn't," she said. "Not until you get something in your stomach."

Hoffner set the pack on the table. He kept his eyes on it as he placed his hand on hers. The knuckles were wonderfully smooth.

He said, "You don't expect this, do you?"

He waited for her to answer. When she didn't, he looked up. She was staring across at him. Hoffner felt his head go light again, until he saw the smile curl her lips.

She said, "And what is it you didn't expect?"

For some reason he had no idea what he had been meaning to say. None. He shook his head quietly, and watched as her smile grew.

"It must be terrible," she said easily, "to feel something and not have the courage to admit it, even to yourself. I'm not asking you to. I have no such cares about love. It doesn't make me weak or sad or hopeful or carefree. I'll leave that to the young. All I know is when it comes. And how rare it is. And that makes it even more certain."

Hoffner felt her hand under his, and he found his voice. "Yes," he said. "That's right. I think . . . that's right."

The bamboo beads swayed, the plates arrived, and they ate.

Major Sanz proved to be a man of little conscience. He was cut from the same cloth as Captain Doval and kept his interviews brief.

And so, knowing that the telephone lines might reengage at any moment—and perhaps still a little lightheaded—Hoffner barreled on. He showed Sanz the Safe Conduct papers, he mentioned Alfassi and Doval, and he explained his role with the contact names in each of the cities to the west.

Naïvely, Sanz said he thought Georg had been a journalist. Hoffner quickly disabused him of this: Georg was a member of German Intelligence—why not? The SS had lost track of him. He had been heading into Republican territory to secure the routes and the contacts.

Major Sanz was only too happy to confirm them.

More remarkable, though, was Sanz's request for thinner crates. Naturally, Hoffner had no idea what the man was talking about.

"For the rifles," Sanz said, as if speaking to a child. "You're getting twelve—not even that—into each one." Hoffner's expression prompted further details. "The wood is too thick. Use a thinner wood and you get maybe eighteen, even twenty inside. It's not so important here in Teruel. We can leave the crates out in the open, have as many as we like. Who's going to care? But you go west—Cuenca or, my God, think of Toledo—and the more crates you have, the more difficult it will be to keep them hidden. You see what I'm saying?"

Hoffner did not, until Sanz showed him the printed packing slip that had accompanied the crate.

At the top, in an official script, was the crate's origin: Tetuán, Morocco. Just below, in the same script, was the name of the company that had shipped it: Hispano-Marroquí de Transportes, Sociedad Limitada. Elsewhere on the slip, the company was simply referred to as Hisma.

Hoffner stared at the word. It was the final name from Georg's wire, the name connected to Bernhardt and Langenheim.

Hoffner said, "You have other papers from the company, Major?"

The man hesitated.

"In your files," said Hoffner. "I need to make sure you have the proper paperwork, should anyone come asking for it." What could be more convincing? thought Hoffner. A German asking for paperwork. He looked directly at Sanz. "You see what I'm saying?"

Again Sanz hesitated before he began to nod. "Yes—yes, of course. I have it all here."

Sanz retrieved various sheets from the bottom drawer of his desk and handed them to Hoffner.

"I believe that's everything."

Hoffner quickly peeled through the stack until he came to the fourth page. It was there he read the announcement of incorporation for the Spanish Moroccan Transport Company, a company intending to ship medical supplies and engine parts and farming equipment—the list went on and on. It was a general partnership, with a Johann Bernhardt as its chief officer. The funding, though vague, had come from Berlin. How or when this had happened was, of course, not made clear on the pages in front of Hoffner. Perhaps that was where Langenheim had played his role.

That said, it was Bernhardt who had created a legitimate private company as a front for supplying weapons. Along with the shipments from Germany to the primary base in Morocco, Bernhardt and his cohorts were planning on sending rifles and ammunition directly to recently formed Hisma outposts throughout Spain. Teruel had been the testing ground. So far, three shipments had passed through unimpeded. The weapons were coming encased in old turbine and piping crates, some even in medical supply boxes. Thus far it was only enough for two or three squads, but expand it to the other cities on Doval's list—that straight line across Spain—and Hoffner could only imagine what a few thousand stockpiled rifles could do for a conquering army. Franco would simply need to get to the city gates, and the guns would be waiting for him—or, better yet, turned on the men still inside.

"Thinner crates," Hoffner said. "Of course. I'll put it in my next report."

A LONG, LONG SWIM

There is a kind of madness that lives on the plains of La Mancha. It settles on the mind in the last of the afternoon, when the sun perches between the passing sails of the windmills and seems to wink with every turn of the blade. It isn't the billowing itself that sparks the delusion—that, they say, requires a nobler kind of madness—but the sudden and unrelenting sense that this might be the last time the sun will make such an effort. La Mancha begs for indifference, or at least a disregard from anything still clinging to life. Even the trees know it. Hobbled by their own weight and bent toward senility, they peer out across the burned earth and laugh through parched bark at anyone foolish enough to remain out under this sky. It is, if He would admit it, the only place where God gazes down and wonders if even He has something still to learn. Maybe, then, the madness is His, for what else could God possibly have to learn, especially from a strip of land ready to shred itself on the truth.

Driving through the heat, Hoffner gazed into the bleached red of the sky, the color of blood mixed with water, although here it was clouds sifting through a dying sun. He had lost track of time, more so of which Spain he was in. This far east, La Mancha gave no aid in defining lines of defense or offense. It was simply men in the distance, a signal to pull over, rifles and pistols raised, and a determined effort to produce the right papers. Neckerchiefed soldiers became uniformed ones became neckerchiefed ones again, even if the stares and faces all looked the same. A wrong turn and it might have been another platoon of young *requetés*—a few more hours lost to the fitful infancy of war—but at some point Mila convinced him that they had seen the last of the Nationalists. They changed their clothes. Hoffner scratched a large CNT-FAI across the car door. And Mila found a well and filled the canteens. They were back in Republican Spain, although Hoffner had a sense that there was little hope of finding Barcelona's arrogance anywhere in here.

In those timeless stretches of road, Hoffner began to see where Georg had been leading him. Han Shen had given him Vollman. Vollman had sent him to Teruel. Teruel had given him Major Sanz and the names and the cities where Hisma would be setting up shop. Hoffner ran through those names in his head, over and over, until a single image began to form: Cuenca, Tarancón, Toledo, Coria—a straight line of some six hundred kilometers to the Portuguese border. Add Badajoz to the list and the shape took on the form of an inverted skillet, with Badajoz at the base of its handle, and Madrid perched just above at the center of the pan. Madrid.

The key to Spain. Arm these hidden pockets of rebellion with rifles and ammunition and they would crackle like tinder to light the flames and swallow Madrid whole.

Somewhere in those six hundred kilometers was Georg. It was now a race to Badajoz.

Oddly enough, Hoffner and Mila seemed to be the only ones moving with any urgency. Where the coast road to Barcelona had seen fish and fruit baskets carried in twos, here it was mule trains, three or four in a line, with carts in tow painted all manner of bright colors. They overflowed with charcoal and firewood, wineskins and gossip, and, while the wheels were as tall as a man, they never seemed to move more than a few kilometers an hour. They had known Spain well before Hannibal, well before God, and looked none the worse for it: men with flat Siberian faces, heavy coats even in this heat, and never so much as a glance for the Mercedes as it raced by. Why show wonder at something as momentary as an elephant warrior or a suit of steel? "This too shall pass" seemed to echo in the plodding groan of the wheels.

Two hours in, Cuenca came and went. To Hoffner, it was a city unlike any he had seen before, a modern Babel perched high on a slab of rock between two narrow ravines. Where reason would have told it to build bridges so as to step beyond the rock, Cuenca had chosen to climb ever higher, its buildings spiraling up to hang like wireless birdhouses over the water below. Unsteady as they looked, they gave a perfect view of the bodies now lying across the bottom of the ravine—Guardia, landowners, priests. There was always a priest.

Hoffner and Mila had sat in one such place, a tavern of sorts, and listened to the story of a man called Guzman, a good honest tradesman, who had treated his workers with justice and had thus survived the first days of the fighting. Somehow, though, poor Guzman had been found hiding holy objects taken from the cathedral. Clutching at these little crucifixes and chalices, he had said it was a simple misunderstanding. He was planning on melting them down. He was a businessman, after all, not a fascist. So, taking him out into the square, the militiamen had insisted he do so—now, at this very moment. Guzman had nodded several times, looked at his wife, and broken down and prayed. He cursed the rabble, told them they would burn for their heresy, and refused to give up even one of his treasures until he was beaten senseless. He was then shot and tossed over the wall.

This was only one of a handful of stories making the rounds, but luckily it was the first Hoffner and Mila heard. Guzman was the contact name on Captain Doval's list, the name confirmed by Major Sanz back in Teruel. Guzman was the Hisma liaison. Had Hoffner gone asking for this man, he and Mila might now be resting alongside him on the rocks.

There had been no point in looking for Georg. Guzman had been dead days before Georg could have gotten there. With no Hisma liaison to question, Georg would have moved on.

Surprisingly, Georg's absence was not the reason they were now back on the road. Mila had refused to stay in the city for the night. Hoffner thought it an odd reaction, especially given her outburst about Alfassi, but he kept it to himself. He knew she would be finding fewer and fewer places to sleep if stories like these continued to trouble her.

The first stars came quickly through the dusk. It was only minutes before they filled a sky the color of charred cork, with a moon so low on the horizon it looked as if it might loose itself and roll across the plains and hillocks. The air was cooler, and the smell sweet like pressed grass.

It was pointless to think they would find beds tonight. Tarancón was still another sixty kilometers on. Arriving in the middle of the night in a Mercedes driven by a German, no matter how pure his Spanish, would only complicate things. And the villages along the way wanted nothing to do with anything or anyone unknown. It left the backseat of the car as the only choice until Mila said, "There," and pointed out into the middle of the darkness.

Some fifty meters off, a small fire was burning at the center of some rocks. In the shadows stood three mule carts, the mules tethered to the side.

"You won't get a word in," she said, "but they'll let us sleep. You'll also drink the strangest wine you've ever tasted. Flick the lights and stop the car."

Hoffner did what she asked and then followed her across the brush grass toward the flame. The coolness in the air had turned to chill. He draped his jacket across her shoulders.

Two men sat around the fire. They were interchangeable save for the misshapen hands, fingers broken at odd angles, badges of honor from the hoof of a mule or a wheel rolling backward in the mud. How they managed to keep a grip on anything remained a mystery. They were drinking from a *porrón*, a glass bottle with a pointed spout. Tipped up, it remained just beyond the lips—much to Hoffner's relief—and sent a thin jet of wine spurting into the mouth. They passed it back and forth while a tin pannikin sat over the fire and cooked something smelling of meat.

"*Salud*, friends," Mila said, as she and Hoffner drew closer.

Neither man looked over. One drank while the other stirred. The one stirring said, "Tonight it's '*Salud*.' Last night we had 'Most gracious señors.' I think I liked last night better."

Mila said, "You ate with soldiers last night?"

"We drank with soldiers last night. And you?"

"A bed in a tavern."

"Very nice. Nicer than this."

The other stopped drinking and handed the *porrón* up to Mila. She took it, drank, and handed it to Hoffner. He drank and handed it back. The taste was like oranges left too long in the sun, with a burning at the base of the throat. Hoffner knew this was more than wine.

Mila said, "May we sit, friends?"

The one stirring said, "What do you bring?"

She drew her arms closer across her chest and said, "Warm bodies and conversation."

The one stirring smiled and said, "Not so warm." He nodded over to the other. "Get them blankets."

The other stood and walked slowly back to the carts. Mila and Hoffner stood close by the fire. When the man returned, the blankets were a soft wool—softer than Hoffner expected—and smelled of camphor oil. Mila and Hoffner both sat on the same one and pulled the other over their legs.

The one stirring said, "A man who lets a woman do all the talking." The smile remained. "I'm not sure I like this kind of man."

Hoffner said, "It saves time."

Only now did either of the men show a reaction. They both turned and looked at Hoffner. The stirring stopped, then slowly started again. The one stirring said, "You speak a Spanish not of Spain."

"Not of Spain, no," said Hoffner.

"Hers has a Catalan," said the man, "but she's sat like this before. Not you. She knew to drink first, then sit. You're lucky to be with a woman who knows these things."

The hands might have been battered, but the ears were remarkably fine-tuned. Hoffner nodded. "Yes."

"Have you come to fight these soldiers? They're very eager to fight."

"No," said Hoffner.

"They tell me they have only a few more weeks of this, and then the fighting will stop. They'll have taken what they want."

"They're soldiers," said Hoffner. "They have to believe that."

"Yes," said the man. He stopped stirring and gingerly pulled the tin from the flame. "The others say Franco is dead, so it's hard to know who to believe."

The name of Franco was the last thing Hoffner had expected to hear. Evidently the war was not so young if it had reached this place.

Mila said, "Franco is dead?"

The man tipped the meat onto another dish and passed it to the other. "Drowned trying to come across from Africa. It's a long, long swim." He set the pannikin over the flame and pulled something from a leather bag. "Goat. Tough but fresh."

"Good," said Mila.

The other passed Hoffner the *porrón* and began to gnaw at his meat. Hoffner drank. It was already finding his head. He handed it to Mila and she passed it to the one stirring.

He said, "Next go-round you'll drink again."

"Yes," said Mila.

The one who stirred talked and talked—about the age of his mules, the men in Jábaga who had refused to let him enter the town—"But you *know* me . . ." "We know no one"—and the rifles he had seen stacked along the walls and ready to be fired, if only they could find a way to scrub thirty years of rust from a barrel. The other chewed and swallowed, swallowed and chewed, and glanced at Mila each time his friend mentioned guns or dying. They had seen their share of it, men left for dead in cars, propped up behind a wheel at the side of the road and still gasping for breath. Rich men, with wide neckties and fat cheeks and mouths dried with blood where the butt of a rifle had taken out the teeth. And when Mila finally shivered from the cold, he stopped and told her to drink and sent his friend to the cart for a wrap to sleep in.

"Franco is dead," the man said again. A car passed in the distance. "That's what I tell them. It makes the men think twice about what they do."

The wrap folded over on itself and had a zip fastener. Inside was flannel.

"We have only one," the one who stirred said. "It can fit two." His friend was already by the carts. They had slung hammocks between the wheels, and the other now dropped himself into one.

The stirrer built the rocks higher around the flame and then, in a way Hoffner had never seen, brought the flame low, though not completely out. It was suddenly much darker, but he could still feel the heat. The man stood and weaved his way to his hammock. Hoffner thought, All men should speak so well this drunk.

Hoffner pulled off his boots and slid in next to Mila. He reached down and pulled the fastener up and felt her body press close against his. He lay back, and they stared up at a sky infinite with night.

She said, "If the sun comes again, you'll forget it can look like this. The ground will forget as well."

"The sun will come."

"It seems a shame, though, doesn't it?"

Maybe it was the wine, but the stars momentarily shuddered, and Mila turned on her side to him and pressed her lips to his cheek. Her hand moved across his chest, then her arm, her torso until she was slowly above him.

She saw it in his eyes and said, "They're already sleeping."

Her lips found his again, the warmth of them and the coolness of the air, and beyond a cradling of stars, and Hoffner let his hands glide across the smoothness of her back, her legs, the clothes unloosed and his own body freed, and he felt her chilled skin across his own like the pale breath of absolute need.

He would love her. He knew this. He would find this life and he would love her.

•   •   •

They arrived in Tarancón by mid-morning. Hoffner learned to play a game with a stick, something with the words *dedo* and *pelota*, although even the men and boys who played with him seemed to have any number of opinions as to what it was called. They sweated under the sun in the court-yard of a small clinic—little more than the front room of a house—while a woman and a girl lay dying inside of burns from a house fire. It had been a terrible thing, quick, and nothing to do with the fighting. In fact, Tarancón had seen almost none of the fighting. The Guardia had quickly pledged themselves to the Republic and had even stepped in to make sure the killing was kept to a minimum. Tragedy remained a thing of fires and falling trees and a boy drowned in early spring—as it had been for as long as anyone could remember. It was so much easier to understand than the news of the horrors sprouting up everywhere around them. The two inside were dying. Infection had set in. And the comfort of a woman doctor—so strange and yet perhaps a miracle (although no one would have called it such a thing)—gave them peace as they slipped quietly away through the morphine.

It was hours before Mila emerged from the house, walking with a man a good deal older. He had come the night before from Cuenca. He was a doctor as well, but the woman and the girl had already been fight-ing the burns for five days—why had it taken so long to send a boy on the two-day ride for him?—and there was nothing he could do. He hadn't slept and was grateful that Mila had been there to take the two to the end.

Hoffner tossed the ball to one of the boys, then ran his handkerchief over his neck as he walked toward her.

"They're both gone," she said.

"I'm sorry," said Hoffner.

"No, it's better. It should have happened three days ago." She intro-duced the doctor. He said he was tired of watching peasants die this way. He needed to sleep and get back to Cuenca. He left them to each other.

She said. "He was a good doctor, but he would have tried to keep them alive." They sat on a bench. Hoffner's hat was lying on it.

He said, "You need to eat something." She said nothing, and he added, "Some of the men remembered Georg. 'The man with the camera' they called him. They said he was here for a few hours. The day before the house burned. They don't remember anyone else."

She stared across the courtyard. She nodded distantly.

He said, "I didn't mention any names."

Again she nodded. Finally she said, "The name from the contact list, here in Tarancón." Hoffner had shown her everything from Captain Doval and Major Sanz. She had memorized the names as well. "He was called Gutiérrez," she said. "What was the first name?"

He knew she knew it, but he answered anyway. "Ramón," said Hoffner. "Why?"

It took her another moment to answer. "Because he was in the room with me the entire time. Because the woman was his wife, and the girl was his daughter."

Hoffner had trouble looking at the man, not because Gutiérrez hadn't bathed or shaved in five days, or that his face was bloated from the crying, or even that his left arm to the shoulder was an oozing scar of blisters and flaked skin beneath a thin wrapping of gauze. It was because he sat there, unaware that he damned Georg with every breath he took.

Hoffner imagined the crates, the guns, the fire set to destroy them all. Had Georg really been capable of this? Had he been so callous, so cowardly, as to slink off in the night knowing that this was to come? Hoffner wore his son's shame as if it were his own.

Gutiérrez continued to stare across at the sheeted bodies, his good elbow on his knee, his body leaning forward, hand pressed against his brow. Hoffner had no idea if the man was even aware they had stepped inside the room.

Mila knelt down next to Gutiérrez. She ran her hand across his back and spoke softly. Slowly, Gutiérrez began to nod. He looked at her. His eyes moved to Hoffner, then the sheets. With her hand still on his back, Mila helped him past the curtain and down the hall. She led him to a chair by the door to the courtyard, and Gutiérrez said, "I want the air. We'll go outside."

"No," she said. "Outside isn't good until they dress your burns again. You should sit here."

Gutiérrez seemed aware of his arm only now. He looked at it as if someone had just handed it to him, a thing to be studied: an arm had been burned, flesh, but whose was it and how? Gutiérrez sat and asked for water.

There was a table across from him with a pitcher and two glasses. Mila filled one and handed it to him. Gutiérrez held it but did not drink.

Hoffner was a few paces down the hall, breathing air heavy with the smell of rotting limes and soap. So this was the scent of burned flesh, he thought. He stepped over and filled the other glass. He drank.

Hoffner said, "You should drink as well."

Gutiérrez's gaze was fixed on the wall, mindlessly searching for something. "Should I?"

Hoffner was glad to hear the anger. It colored Gutiérrez's despair and gave it purpose. The man would find his way back.

Hoffner said, "I'm sorry for your loss."

Gutiérrez barely moved.

"There was a man with a camera," Hoffner said. "A German. A few days ago."

Gutiérrez showed nothing.

Hoffner repeated, "There was a man with a camera—"

"Why are you asking me this?"

"You know why I ask."

Gutiérrez continued to stare at the wall. Finally he said, "Yes." He was unrepentant. "I know why."

"He came about the crates, about Hisma."

"Yes."

Hoffner waited and then said, "Did he set the fire?"

The question came so effortlessly—questions like these always did—even if every moment beyond them lay in their grasp.

Gutiérrez's stare hardened. "You mean did he murder my wife and daughter?"

And there it was. Why not call it what it was. A low humming began to fill Hoffner's ears, but he refused to look at Mila. "Yes."

Gutiérrez said, "You ask only about the one with the camera. Why not the other?"

"The other is not my concern."

"No? He also wanted the one with the camera."

There was a pounding now in Hoffner's chest, the urge to grab Gutiérrez by the arm, scream in his face—Was this Georg? Was this what my son has become?—but instead he asked again, "Did he set the fire?"

Gutiérrez waited, his cruelty unintended.

"No," he finally said. "That is my misfortune. Are you here to rid me of my burden?"

Hoffner felt his breath again. He said, "Then the fire was an accident?"

"There are no such things."

"And the guns?"

"Guns," Gutiérrez said, with quiet disbelief. "What guns? We have no guns. There will be no guns." Self-damning made such easy work of the truth. He refused to look at Hoffner. "You need something more from me, you tell Sanz to come and get it himself. He does me a favor. Otherwise no more messengers, no more visitors, no more questions from this German, that German, talk of those crates"—his voice trailed off—"make room for those fucking crates."

Gutiérrez shut his eyes, trying not to see it.

"A can of oil"—it was little more than a whisper, the creases of his eyes wet from the memory—"a tiny can of oil and all that heat." The tears ran and he forced his eyes open. He looked at Hoffner. "God has sent His message, and I damn Him for it." Gutiérrez looked upward. *"Viva la República,"* he said. *"Viva la Libertad.* Do you hear?" He looked again at Hoffner. "My cause is no longer yours. No longer Sanz's. No longer His. Either shoot me or get out of my town."

Gutiérrez stood. He moved past Hoffner to the curtain. He was about to step through when Hoffner said, "The other German. When was he here?"

Again Gutiérrez's gaze hardened. He peered into the room. This time, though, he hadn't the strength for it. He was suddenly aware of the tears, and he wiped them. "I don't know," he said. "Two days ago, three."

"He came to ask about the one with the camera?"

"Yes."

"In this place?"

Gutiérrez nodded.

There was no point; the man had nothing more to give.

Hoffner nodded and turned to Mila, and Gutiérrez said, "He was strange, that German." Hoffner looked back and saw Gutiérrez staring at him. "Not like the others," said Gutiérrez. "Not like the one with the camera. He had death in the eyes."

"There are Germans like that now."

"No." Gutiérrez shook his head. "Not SS. Not soldiers. Something else with this one." It was as if he were seeing the man in front of him. He stared a moment longer and then pushed through the curtain, and Hoffner watched as the cloth puckered and grew still.

That night they stayed in Tarancón.

The days were slipping by, but Hoffner let them go. He might have convinced himself it was to keep them safe: they had been lucky last night; driving after dark seemed beyond even a Spaniard's arrogance. Or he might have said it was for the time he could take with Mila, hours to sit or walk or stare up from a rusted bed and wait for the breeze to find its way into a room so small that the ledge of the window served as table for both pitcher and glass.

But the truth was easier than that. Hoffner simply believed Georg was alive. He had no idea why he believed this, or why he knew Georg would still be alive when he found him, but time was no longer a concern. There was nothing he could point to in the last days to make this sudden certainty real, and yet here it was.

Hoffner had felt it only once before, this kind of ease, in the same heat, the same silence, the same taste of soured milk in the air. It sat deep in his past and yet lay quietly by his side, and Hoffner chose not to ask why.

He sat up and took a sip of the water, brown with silt. He stared out through the window and saw the hills under the moon.

Mila said, "He's out there."

He had thought her asleep. He nodded and lit a cigarette.

She said, "You thought he'd set that fire."

Hoffner felt the heat of the room on his face. He let the smoke spear through his nose. He said nothing.

She said, "And what if he had?"

Hoffner took another pull as he stared out. "But he didn't."

"No—he didn't. So you don't have to save him from himself."

He looked at her. "What does that mean?"

"The way you do with the other boy. Sascha. That's the one you think you need to save. Georg didn't set the fire, so it wasn't your fault."

He continued to stare at her. "That's a stupid thing to say."

"Is it?"

"You don't understand."

"You're right, I don't." She reached out and took his cigarette. "So I'm left to bring out the trite and the obvious." She took a pull. "I'm thirsty."

Hoffner handed her the glass and watched as she drank.

He said, "I made him what he is."

"No one makes anyone else into anything."

"He was sixteen. A boy. I had a girl on the side."

"A boy with a cheating father. What a remarkable story."

"I threw it in his face."

"I don't believe that."

"Then you'd be wrong."

She held the glass up to him and he took it. He turned and set it on the ledge. And he stared out and knew that somewhere people were sleeping.

"It was at a railway station," he said. "This girl. Sascha was there. He saw us together. There were words. I didn't see him for eight years after that. It's been another nine since."

"Because he saw you with a girl?"

"You don't see it. It sounds . . . different now. Small. It wasn't. It's what I was. It's what he knew I was."

"And what you were makes him what he is now? That must be so much easier to believe than anything else." She reached across him and tapped her ash out the window. Her hair played against his chest, and she lay back.

He said, "So you want me to be blameless?"

"No. You'll never have that. I loved my husband, even when he had a woman in Moscow. He stopped it, and we went on."

It took Hoffner a moment to answer. "It's different."

"Why? Because you think a woman needs to forgive? Because your wife forgave you every time she knew you had another one?"

"He was a boy."

"My husband wrote me at the end. He said he deserved to be dying. Freezing to death, and he needed to tell me it was because of what he had done to me. How much he regretted it. Can you think of anything more stupid than that?"

Hoffner hadn't the strength for this. "No. I suppose not."

She sat straight up and forced him to look at her. "Don't do that. Don't ask to be forgiven because you can't forgive yourself. You're here for Georg. You risk everything for Georg. But it doesn't make you a better man that you do. You do it, and it's enough."

Hoffner stared at her. "And it's enough for you?"

She looked at him. Hoffner thought to hold her but she lay down. He lay beside her and brought her back into his chest.

"Yes," she said. "It is."

And he slept.

VIVA ESPAÑA

"He let him die."

The man behind the bar set the glasses down in front of Hoffner and began to pour. "His own son," he said, a tinge of respect to mask the shock. "That's who sits up in the Alcázar now."

It was eleven in the morning, and the hundred kilometers to Toledo had been dry. They required a drink, something with a bit more bite than wine. This was brandy from the south, Jerez, the last bottles Toledo would be seeing for quite some time. It felt good to have this kind of burning at the back of the throat. Hoffner told the man to refill his glass. He then joined Mila outside. She was on a bench, staring up through the tiled roofs along the narrow street. She took her glass and drank, and Hoffner peered up.

There was no escaping the gaze of the massive fortress on the hill, stone and towers and windows in perfect line. The Alcázar had watched over Toledo for nearly five hundred years. Now it was Toledo that stared up and wondered how soon the stones would fall.

The talk in the bar had been of the fascist rebels inside. There were a thousand of them: cadets, Guardia, their wives and children, and all those fat ones who had scampered up to the gate, pounded on the doors, and begged to be let in the moment it had all turned sour for them. The Republican forces had taken the city, and the fascists were now holed up with no hope of surviving. The Alcázar had become a little city unto itself, with thick walls and iron gates to keep the fascists safe inside, while outside the Republican militias plotted and tossed grenades and waited for the end.

And how had this all come to pass? Because the man keeping the fascists calm inside was a colonel by the name of José Moscardó. Moscardó hadn't been part of the July 18 conspiracy; he hadn't known of Franco and Mola and Queipo de Llano. But he did know which Spain was his. And so, seizing the moment, he dispatched the entire contents of the Toledo arms factory up the hill and into the fortress before the Republican militias could stop him. It was an unexpected coup.

Save for one small point. While Moscardó might have shown remarkable savvy in ferreting away men and soldiers and guns and children, he was less astute at protecting his own. Somehow, in all the mayhem, he forgot his sixteen-year-old son Luis outside the fortress walls. Within hours, the boy was taken hostage by the militias, who promised to shoot him if his father refused to surrender. It was a brief conversation on the telephone, at which point Moscardó asked to speak to his son.

"They have me, Father," said Luis. "What shall I do?"

Moscardó thought a moment. "If this is true, commend your soul to God, shout '¡Viva España!' and die like a hero."

"That," said the boy, "I can do."

It was an act of uncommon bravery. Word of it had spread to the south and the far north, where Moscardó and the Alcázar were already things of legend for the rebel fascist soldiers: the new Abraham, they called him, although this time God had failed to reach out to save his Isaac. This time, faith had truly been tested.

The fascist soldiers chanted their names, and the great fortress became the bastion of all that was good and true in Spain.

Hoffner said, "The barman said we'd do best with a group headquartered near the cathedral." He tossed back the last of his drink. "Republican army. Slightly more organized than the Communists."

"That's no great surprise," said Mila.

"The man said 'slightly.' I don't think this is going to be files in triplicate."

"Is he sending someone to take us?"

"Why?"

"Because it's Toledo. He could draw us a map and we'd never find it." She finished her glass and stood. "And I'm all out of bread crumbs."

Mila was right. It would have been impossible to maneuver through the city without a guide. The boy was no more than ten years old, his canvas rope-soled shoes worn through with a few toes sticking out, but he moved them along at a nice clip. The streets were narrow and dark and slipped from one to the next, turning, then rising up a hill, before seeming to double back on themselves. Hoffner expected the bar to reappear each time they turned a corner—a sheepish look from the boy, a recalculation—but the streets poured on in endless variation: smooth stone against jagged rock, box windows of iron or wood. And always the balconies—barely enough room for a man to stand, rails only tall enough to a keep a child from falling.

The trio arrived at a large building on one of the more sunlit squares—crucifixes and shields emblazoned in the stone—and the boy motioned to the door. He offered a quick nod, shouted the requisite "¡Viva la Libertad!" and raced back to the bar. Three weeks ago he would have been beaten or paid for his services, depending on the client. This seemed better all around. Hoffner led Mila in.

There was a strange similarity to Zaragoza in the look of the large receiving hall and stairs along the walls to the upper floors, but the smells and sounds here were completely different. Barked conversations, along with the crackle of a radio, swirled above, while men sat in half-back wooden chairs, leaning against whitewashed walls and playing at games of cards or pennies. Some were in uniform, most not. Hoffner could almost taste the oregano in the air and something sweet, like the oil of pressed almonds. Odder still was the sound of laughter in the distance, husky laughs with tobacco and age grinding on the throat. Things were getting done. What that might be, though, was anyone's guess.

A uniformed soldier walked over. He wore the brown-on-brown of the Republican army, with a thick black belt and buckle at the waist, both in need of repair. The belt holstered a pistol and a small leather satchel behind. He was at most thirty, and his hair hung loose to the brow.

"*Salud*, friends," he said. "What is it you need here?"

Before Hoffner could reach for the papers, Mila said, "We have a car filled with explosives. We bring them from Buenaventura Durruti. *Viva la República.*"

Bombs were more persuasive than papers. They gave any and all questions about Georg the army's full attention. The car was brought around, lieutenants sent off to uncover the whereabouts of a German and his movie camera, and Hoffner and Mila were invited to eat. The stories of Captain Doval and Major Sanz made for lively conversation.

"Christ, I like hearing that."

A large captain sat at the end of an oak table and laughed through a mouthful of stew. It was potatoes and leeks and something with the taste of cinnamon, although there was too much heat on the tongue for that. Hoffner watched as the large captain dipped a fat wedge of seeded bread into the broth, waited for the crust to turn a nice oily orange, and then shoved it in. The man laughed again, and a chunk of venison popped from his mouth and back into his bowl. He apologized even as he continued to laugh.

"Gentlemen soldiers," he said. "All idiots. You say he put gasoline in the car?" Hoffner chewed and nodded, and the large captain laughed again. "And with the explosives right under his nose? That's marvelous."

Four others sat with them—younger, trimmer—but it was clear they deferred to the large one. He had the thickest mustache, the fattest cheeks, and a jaw that reached out beyond the ears before turning in for the chin. It was a massive face, with warm, thoughtful eyes. He shoveled another spoonful of meat and carrots into his mouth.

One of the others, quiet to this point, said, "And you do all this just to find your son?"

Hoffner took a taste of the wine and again nodded.

The large captain said, "Just to find?" His face was more serious despite the chewing. "Is there anything more heroic? This is what a father does if he's a man." He scooped up another spoonful.

The other said, "And Moscardó? He makes half the country call him a hero."

"Moscardó is a traitor," said the captain, "and a coward. He hides himself away and lets his son pay for his cowardice. A true caballero would have offered his own life."

"And we would have taken it?"

"For a boy of sixteen? Of course." The large captain looked at Hoffner. "The son is alive, by the way. Unlike Moscardó, we don't kill a boy for his father's failings. But of course we can't say it, otherwise Franco or Queipo de Llano would think we're weak. They'd want to see if they can come and try and finish us. Or they might come to avenge the boy anyway, so however it goes, this business with Moscardó is bad for us. Nothing we can do about it now, though."

Franco, as it turned out, had proved to be a fine swimmer. He was already moving up to Seville, according to the large captain, although the reports were still a bit vague. Meanwhile, Toledo's fate was being tossed around like so many mouthfuls of venison boiled too long in a pot. Maybe Barcelona's arrogance did extend this far. Maybe it had to.

The younger one was not done with Hoffner. "And Durruti," he said. "He gave you these explosives so you could find your son? Why would he do that?"

Arrogance and mistrust—the only way to win a war. Hoffner said, "He wanted me to use them in Zaragoza."

"But you didn't."

"No."

"And if you had, you'd be dead."

"More than likely, yes."

"So he expected you to die." This was where the young one had been leading them.

Hoffner said, "I imagine he did."

"And the señora?"

"I imagine her, as well."

Which left only one logical answer: "So the explosives weren't really to help you find your son, were they?"

Hoffner said evenly, "Durruti told me my son was dead. I knew he was wrong. I chose to make fools of the *requetés* instead."

The young one refused to back down. "Fools can still shoot rifles and drive tanks. Maybe better to have used the explosives." He finished his glass and stood. "Good luck finding your German son who takes pictures. I'm sure it will be a tender reunion." He pushed his chair back, nodded once to Mila, and headed off.

Watching him go, the large captain said, "He has a brother and two sisters in the Alcázar. Our hero Moscardó keeps hostages of his own. It makes it difficult. My lieutenant doesn't have the same choices you have in how he tries to save his family."

Hoffner refused to feel the guilt. "I didn't know."

"Of course not. But you bring explosives, so maybe we give Moscardó something to think about."

By early afternoon there was still no word on Georg, although two of the soldiers had yet to report in. Talk of the explosives and the Alcázar continued. What better way to spend the time? With a few more glasses of wine, the large captain suggested it was time to drive up to the fortress and make good on the deposit.

"No, no, no—don't worry," he said. "It's completely safe. They only shoot when they're shot at. They need to save their ammunition."

Naturally, Mila and Hoffner were given no choice but to join him. Nonetheless, the large captain decided they would all three ride up in an old Bilbao armored car just behind the Mercedes, its 7mm gun aimed backward. Why provoke anything?

Inside, the grind of the engine was deafening and the seats smelled of piss.

The large captain shouted, "We make a pass three times a day in this. They'll look a little funny at the Mercedes, but they won't do anything."

Hoffner peered out through the slits and saw the mounting destruction as they climbed. Entire walls lay in rubble, while gnarled iron railings stretched across the stone and looked like claws trying to work their way through. Sandbag barricades remained planted in the middle of the streets, with bullet holes strafing across them and stray caps and canteens lying at odd angles. Evidently the retreat to the Alcázar had not been a quiet one.

Where the cobblestone had given way, the driver slowed and weaved his way around the newly formed ditches and mounds. All this had been on view in Barcelona, except total victory there had made the wreckage distant, an artifact of daring and pride, easy enough for a boy to stand atop and declare his absolute mastery. Here desolation and death still lived in the rock and waited on a final reckoning. It forced Hoffner to pull back even as the streets passed in empty silence.

The car lurched and heaved and finally pulled to a stop. The engine cut out, and the large captain, reaching for the handle, said, "You come too if you want. They won't be able to see us down here."

He pushed open the door and the sun streamed in, along with a spray of air that was breathable. Mila and Hoffner followed him.

They were perhaps thirty meters from the wall, safely behind the bombed remains of a house, an outpost of sorts, with enough of a view to see the spire of one of the fortress towers high above. Part of the fortress roof had been torn away—a few well-tossed grenades from an aeroplane—but for the time being, the Alcázar remained sufficiently intact. A man sat with a machine gun, while the driver of the Mercedes stood a few meters higher up the incline, pulling the explosives from the car and laying them on the grass. Another two remained behind the car, their rifles aimed up at the wall, the barrels moving slowly back and forth along the line of windows and ledges. For men who were convinced the rebels would be taking no notice, they were showing remarkable caution.

The man finished unloading the explosives and began to dart up to the base of the tower, keeping low, a brick in each hand. Five trips in, a man at the car shouted for him to stop. Something had caught his eye. Hoffner inched out and tried to see where he was looking.

Twenty meters above, a group of four women were being forced out onto a ledge, terror in their faces as they clutched at the stone. The barrel of a rifle appeared among them, followed by the shout of a man's high-pitched voice: "These are your socialist whores! Move off or they join you down there!"

One of the women screamed and the large captain barked to his man to pull back to the car. The pile of explosives remained by the wall. The women pressed themselves into the siding and tried vainly to keep their dresses from billowing up in the wind.

The large captain said quietly to the man at the machine gun, "They've done this before?"

The man shook his head. "I didn't think they knew we were here."

"Then you were wrong." The large captain stepped closer to the edge of the house and peered out. He shouted up to the wall, "My man is back."

The voice shouted, "Don't be smart. The explosives as well."

The large captain shouted, "This is what you do, hide behind women? You'll be dead in a week. Ask your God if this is what you want on your gravestones."

"It won't be me who'll be rotting," the voice shouted. "Take the bombs or you'll be taking four more dead ones back with you."

The large captain waited. He looked back at his men, then up to the ledge. "Is it easy to be such a coward?" he shouted.

"If these were women and not whores, I could tell you."

It kept on like this, and Hoffner had no idea what the point was in staying. The explosives were barely enough to put a dent in the wall. It was empty posturing on both sides, until the crack of a bullet rang out and a single body fell from the ledge.

The silence was pure and instantaneous. Screams followed. The large captain yelled to his men not to fire, then shouts and threats echoed back and forth. It was unclear whether this had been intended or a mistake. Mila had suddenly begun moving to the edge of the house, to the dead woman, eyes blank, when Hoffner grabbed her and held her close. Mila's body was rigid, her breathing short; it was all he could do to keep her with him.

Two more rifles appeared in the window, more threats, more screams, when a voice by the Mercedes shouted, "I will remove the explosives!" Everything fell silent.

Hoffner looked out and saw a soldier standing upright, his arms raised high. He held his rifle in the air and tossed it to the ground in front of him. He was staring up at the window.

"I will remove them," he shouted again. "Take the women inside."

A low wind moved across the grass. The soldier stood firm, his legs like thick stalks planted on the rise.

Slowly the rifles pulled back, and the voice said, "Get the explosives."

The soldier made his way up. He raised the first of the bricks above his head and moved back to the car. He turned and repeated, "Take the women inside."

This time the women were permitted to climb through. The soldier placed the explosive in the car and began to make his way up again.

Twenty minutes later, Hoffner sat with Mila and the large captain and the smell of piss as the cars made their way down the hill. No one had said a word. Her eyes remained empty, her face unmoving. Her breathing was quieter, but it was a stillness without calm. Hoffner had taken her hand— she had let him—but there was nothing in her grip.

A ditch in the road jolted them high off their seats, and Mila said, "You have a traitor in Toledo." The sound of her voice jarred, even as her eyes remained empty. "A man who hides guns for the fascists. In crates. Thick crates." The captain started to speak, and she said, "His name is Rivas. I have the address. You must find him and shoot him."

They found Rivas. They found the wires from Bernhardt and the papers from Hisma. And they shot Rivas and his wife and his son, all three against a wall outside the house. There was no talk of the women at the Alcázar, nothing of explosives, only silence, as the large captain beat Rivas with such savagery that he was forced to prop the man beside his wife before stepping back and shooting them. There was blood on the captain's trousers when he returned.

Mila and Hoffner saw the blood. They said nothing.

Georg was no longer in the city. A guard at one of the barricades had remembered the large camera and the German papers. He remembered because Georg had put him on film. It was two days ago. Georg was heading west.

The large captain told them that the Mercedes would stay in Toledo. The town of Coria lay within Nationalist Spain; there was no point in taking the car. Not with CNT-FAI scrawled across its doors. They found an old Ford for them, two seats, with a cracked windscreen and no paint on the side.

It was nine hours to the first of the Nationalist outposts. The large captain wished them good fortune and went to clean his trousers.

Hoffner drove, dirt and rock and distance ahead of them, and somewhere the darkness to come. It was hours of unbroken silence.

Finally Mila spoke. "I killed him." She was staring out, her voice brittle like sand. Hoffner felt it on his cheek.

"No," he said. "You didn't."

"The wife and the son."

"No."

"The girl fell and I—"

Hoffner brought the car to a sudden stop. The dust rose up, but she refused to look at him.

He had repeated the words a thousand times in his head, but still they caught in his throat: I brought her to this. I alone. She is guiltless; she will always be guiltless.

"There is nothing," he said, "no moment you can point to and say, This is why a man is dead. Not now. Not in this Spain. This wasn't for you."

"No." She continued to stare out. "You don't understand." At last she turned, her eyes clear and focused. "I saw the girl fall and I chose for Rivas to die. I would choose it again. The wife. The son. This isn't guilt, Nikolai.

I feel no sadness or despair. This is what it is to be in Spain; I know this now." She stared across at him. "What I don't know is if you can see it and choose to stay with me."

Hoffner stared into the eyes, dry and spent. And he saw hope. Hope for himself. He had never imagined it.

"There is no choice," he said. "I love you."

He took her in his arms, and her face came up to his own. He knew he had given himself to her, and nothing as fleeting as doubt would ever enter his mind again. So he waited and let the unbearable sentiment of it take him. He kissed her. He felt the slenderness of her waist, the need in her hands as they pressed deep into him. And he found his breath and pulled back.

"I love you," he said again.

She waited. "I'm glad of it."

Hoffner clasped the wheel and took the car back onto the road.

There was a village inn for the night, and they slept, and in the morning they crossed just this side of Plasencia. It was a small platoon, papers glanced through, passage permitted. One of the soldiers asked where Hoffner had gotten the car. Stolen, he said, from a peasant using it for chickens. The men laughed and watched them drive through.

In Coria, he told her it would be better if he went to the headquarters alone: no need to explain a woman or the second Safe Conduct. It would be a German looking for Germans. She agreed, but they both knew he was doing it for her. She would sit in a church and wait.

At the headquarters Hoffner met little resistance. He was shown to a sergeant, who escorted him to a lieutenant, who finally took him to see a captain. The man was on the top floor, and when he turned from the window, he struck Hoffner across the face with such force that Hoffner went careening into the arms of the waiting lieutenant.

The captain—recently arrived from Zaragoza, and with a red mark below the eye that he wore like shame—smoothed back his hair and waited for Hoffner to regain his feet. He struck him again.

"Where is the woman?" Captain Doval said.

Hoffner straightened himself up. His mouth was full with blood. He turned and spat and said, "What woman?"

Doval struck him a third time. "Not so clever now." He turned to the lieutenant. "Get this filth out of here and start looking for the woman."

NINE YEARS

His cell smelled of mint. It made no sense. The walls were more mildew than stone, and the bars along the window peeled up in petals of iron and rust. There was a pot in the corner for his shit, and a cot with two chains holding it to the wall. For twenty minutes a day, a strip of sunlight crept up along the iron door, settled on the bolt, and then vanished, leaving behind a mist of heat and decay. At night there were screams, muffled cries of *"¡Madre!"* and *"¡Socorro!"* and always the sounds of a single shot and laughter.

Save for the pain from his beatings, Hoffner felt remarkably at peace. It was time now to sit and wait and die, and while Doval might have thought this a kind of torture, Hoffner lay with his back against the wall and understood that here, at the end, there was nothing to regret. He might have come up short in finding Georg, but the boy was alive.

Doval was proof of that. Hoffner had no doubt that Doval had made the second call to Berlin. He now knew what a fool he had been. If Georg were dead, Doval would have paraded the boy out, just to see Hoffner's face. Georg was alive. As was Mila. These were pleasures Doval would never have denied himself.

Isolation, then, and the sometime wailing of a distant voice were all the solace that Hoffner needed. He was having trouble closing his left eye, and his hands were swollen, but such was the price for a quiet mind.

To be fair, it had taken him a day or so to get to this point. The first night had been a struggle not to lose himself. They had marched him out three times to a wall, set him against the wet bricks, and placed a blindfold over his eyes. Someone had fired a shot. Standing there, Hoffner had waited for the pain. Surely there was pain, he thought, and yet, could it be this quick, this deliberate? A guard had laughed and said, "You're not dead, not yet," and a hand had gripped his arm and taken him back to his cell. There, two others had spent a good hour battering his face.

"Now you're ready," one of them had said, and out to the wall again, the blindfold but no shot. Hoffner had waited for hours, his legs buckling, his eyes wet with tears, and he had heard the guards laugh, and again the rough grip on his arm as he was pulled back to his cell so they could work on the hands.

The third time, with the sun just coming up, there had been no blind-fold, no guards. They had placed him across from the entrance gate, opened it, and left him there alone, twenty meters from the outside. Staring through, Hoffner had seen two women move across the square, a cart rolled into place. A man had filled a bucket with water. And Hoffner had looked up to see the figure of Doval in a window, staring down. Hoffner had kept himself perfectly still. When his legs finally gave out, the guards returned and dragged him back to his cell.

It was only on the third or fourth day that Hoffner realized they never asked any questions. The beatings were silent but no less vicious for it. There was nothing they hoped to learn from him, save perhaps for the time it took a man to sit and wait to be cracked across the face before begging to be killed. Hoffner decided to leave that choice in their hands. He respected the silence, everything beyond his own groans and the sound of his vomiting.

He thought of Mila—of course—and Georg, and little Mendy with his picture of the badge and the scrawl. These were obvious thoughts. Hoffner expected others to follow, the ones where a man sets his life in order before he knows he will die, but such things never came. Instead, it was brief images of Martha and Sascha, the water of Wannsee in the late summer, and the bludgeoned face of a man he had caught in the act of raping a woman nearly thirty years ago. There was nothing to them, no coherence. Hoffner wondered if perhaps this was the way a life settles itself, not with meaning or purpose but with memories recalled despite themselves. A beckoning to God might have brought some sense to it, but Hoffner knew there was noth-ing for him there.

Instead, he kept his mind on Mila. She had come at the end. She had been better than anything he had ever known. There had to be something in that. He pictured her back in Barcelona, and it was enough.

The bolt to his cell released, and the hinges creaked as the door opened. Hoffner sat patiently waiting for the order to stand. He had gotten up on his own two days ago and had received a fist to the groin. Better to wait.

The man barked, and Hoffner stood. Hoffner then stepped out into the hall and fell in behind the second guard.

Hoffner was now familiar with the curve of the wall, the number of paces between each cell, and the sounds of weeping and prayers behind each door. He thought, Shouldn't the praying make it all right, not for the soul but for the soldiers passing by: the echo of a prayer, confirmation of a good Catholic waiting inside? Wasn't that enough for a fascist to set a man free?

They came to the steps that led down to the large courtyard, where the wall awaited him. A light shone from a wire high above, and another was fixed to the wall. Hoffner placed it at somewhere between three and four in the morning. There had been rain and no moon, and the lights spread out in two wide ovals across the mud and tufts of wild grass. The air still smelled of rain and brought a welcome moistness to his lips.

The guards placed him by the wall and stepped to their positions across from him, rifles held at their chests. They waited. Minutes passed before a door in the distance opened and a man emerged. It was difficult to see him through the glare, but Hoffner knew it was Doval.

Doval stepped across to the main gate, opened it, and began to make his way back. He was in full uniform, his boots high to the knee. Hoffner hadn't seen him this close since that first afternoon. Doval moved past the soldiers and up to Hoffner. He had been drinking.

"You're dismissed," Doval said to the two soldiers, as he stared at Hoffner.

The men turned at once and headed for the door. Doval waited for the sound of the latch before stepping closer.

"No one to stop you from going," Doval said, his words loose. "Look around. No one."

Hoffner stared ahead and said nothing.

Doval stepped back and pulled his pistol from his belt. He waved it toward the gate.

"Go," he said. Hoffner continued to stare ahead, and Doval shouted, "Go!"

Hoffner began to walk, and thought, So this was how it was to be. A bullet to the head, quick and painless. Doval was too good a shot not to have the first find its mark. Hoffner kept his eyes on the gate. He felt his legs move. He tasted the rain on his lips, but he heard no sound. It was an odd sensation, the gate closer and closer, and all he wanted was to hear something—anything. Even his feet seemed to drag along the ground in perfect silence. His legs began to pitch, the anticipation of death like the ache of first love, but still he moved. It would come at the gate. This he knew. He needed only to make it to the gate.

He drew closer, and the square beyond widened in front of him. Hoffner saw a fountain off to the side. The back of his neck lifted, and the hairs rose as if they knew it was time. He thought to close his eyes, but why not take it all in?

Beyond him, out in the square, he saw a figure move from the shadows. Hoffner felt a moment's hitch in his step. He heard the trickle of the fountain. The certainty of only moments ago slipped away, and Hoffner forced his mind to focus. The figure remained obscured, and still Hoffner drew closer.

He was at the gate. He was through it and into the square, and the figure was now in front of him. There was a glare on the face, a man, tall and narrow.

"Hallo, Inspector," said the voice.

Hoffner stared. He saw the pale blue eyes of Anthony Wilson. Wilson was wearing short pants and climbing boots, and Hoffner felt his legs drop out from under him.

It was English whiskey.

They had patched his eye, and there was liniment on his knuckles and wrists. The right hand was wrapped, but it had been a quick job, the gauze already peeling up from his palm.

"Rough go of it, I imagine," said Wilson.

Wilson was standing over Hoffner, holding the glass. The room was small, a bed and a desk and a few oil lamps keeping the shadows low.

Hoffner was on the bed. He could feel the springs through the mattress. Wilson leaned in, and Hoffner took another sip.

He heard a rag being wrung out and looked beyond Wilson. Mila stood at a basin by the window. She stepped over and brought the rag to his head. She had a welt under her eye, and her lower lip was cracked. Hoffner reached up to touch it, and Wilson said, "An overeager guard yesterday. Just before we got here. I think the doctor is fine."

Mila continued to press the rag against Hoffner's head, and he ran his thumb along her cheek.

"Yes," she said, "the doctor is fine."

Hoffner kept his hand on her skin. She was warm and alive, and there was nothing that could have moved his fingers from her.

Wilson said, "Doval's a nice piece of work."

Hoffner continued to stare at her. She was concentrating on the cuts and bruises, and a large bump that had come courtesy of a pistol to the side of his head. He winced and she looked at him. She leaned in and kissed his mouth. It was only a moment, but it brought him upright, and Mila went back to the basin. Wilson had stepped over to the table, and Hoffner said, "What are you doing here, Wilson?"

Wilson poured another whiskey. "I don't think they would have shot you."

"What are you doing here?"

Wilson stepped over and handed Hoffner the glass. He retreated to the desk and poured one for himself. "I hear it was quite a performance in Zaragoza. Obviously you still have a few tricks left."

Mila was back at his head with the rag, and Hoffner gently pushed her hand away. She tossed the rag onto the table and sat next to him. He took her hand and said, "Any chance I might find out why you're here?"

Wilson took a sip. "Saving your life, I think."

"I thought they weren't going to shoot me."

"Then saving the doctor's." Wilson took the bottle and pulled over a chair. He sat. "They found her yesterday morning, in a church of all places. Hell of a time convincing them to let her go. God it's hot." He drank.

Hoffner wanted to ask her, but not with Wilson in the room. He felt her thumb across his hand, and he drank.

Hoffner set the glass down. "I didn't know the English and the fascists were on such good terms."

"The Admiralty's on good terms with everyone." Wilson tossed back his glass. "We're even quite chummy with the anarchists in Barcelona, although the Communists are proving a bit much. I imagine they always do."

Wilson refilled the glasses, and Hoffner said, "And Captain Doval was happy to hand me over to you?"

The sweat on Wilson's head had beaded at the brow. A single drop began to make its way down to the cheek. "Did he look happy?"

"No. He looked drunk."

"Good. He might have shot you a few days ago. We had to get General Mola himself to put in a call to save you. God, I would have loved to have seen Doval's face during that conversation." Wilson drank again and smiled.

"And why would General Mola have cared one way or the other about me?"

"Because we told him to."

"And the fascists are inclined to take orders from the English these days?"

"If they want us to keep quiet about what's going on here, yes."

Hoffner didn't follow. "I thought you wanted to expose the Nazis."

Wilson lapped at the last drops in his glass. "Then you thought wrong."

Before Hoffner could answer, there was a knock at the door. Wilson put up his hand and turned to listen. The knock repeated. It came a third time, and Wilson stood. He moved to the door and opened it. Karl Vollman stepped into the room.

Vollman was dressed in peasant clothes, loose pants and a shirt smeared in oil and grit. He smelled of pine oil and manure. He had gotten some sun in the last week, making the white hair seem whiter still.

Wilson closed the door, and Vollman set a package on the desk. Vollman then turned to Hoffner.

"Hello, Inspector. Shithole attics and used-up men. Quite a life, isn't it?"

• • •

Vollman, as it turned out, had been the first German to reach Teruel after Georg. That was over a week ago. He had met with Alfassi. He had seen Major Sanz. He had bypassed Tarancón and Toledo. Why, he said, was unimportant. What was clear was that he and Wilson were on very friendly terms.

Hoffner said, "Nice to see the English and Russian intelligence services working so closely with each other."

"Soviet Intelligence," Vollman corrected.

Hoffner's hand was stiff from holding the glass. He felt it begin to slip, and Mila took it from him. She then took his hand.

Hoffner said, "It still doesn't explain why General Mola would have been happy to keep an old German cop alive. Any chance you can answer that one, Vollman? Wilson here seems less than willing."

Wilson's bald knees had grown pinker in the heat. They stared up at Hoffner even as the man himself remained perfectly still. Finally Wilson said, "A great deal can change in twelve days."

"A straight answer," Hoffner said. "I think you owe me that."

Wilson continued to stare. He glanced at Vollman before saying, "Georg was meant to get the information about the weapons and then come home. Where they were being shipped. How the Germans were planning it. He wasn't meant to go after them."

"You mean he wasn't meant to stop them," said Hoffner.

"No, he wasn't."

"And yet he decided to do that."

"Nobility's a dangerous thing in naïve hands."

"So you're keen to let the Nazis destroy Spain."

"If that's what they want, yes."

Hoffner felt Mila's grip tighten, and he said, "I'm not sure I like it that you're on my side. Either of you."

"Actually, you do," said Wilson. "You just don't understand why. Twelve days ago Georg was missing, Franco was losing precious time in Morocco, and the anarchists were on the verge of beating back the rebellion. The rest of us were agreeing not to get involved."

"I'm aware of all that."

"Good. Then you'll know it wasn't true. The Germans were looking to find a way to get their guns and tanks in. The Americans at Texaco were working out how they could supply oil for the fascists and make their money. The Russians were shipping over what they could to keep the Reds afloat. And the French were doing what they always do—slipping into their turtle shell and hoping no one noticed that they lie directly on the road between Berlin and Madrid."

"So much for a straight answer," said Hoffner. "You've left out your English, by the way."

"Yes," said Wilson, "I have. There has to be someone who steps back and sees what's really happening."

"And that is?"

Wilson blinked several times. The sweat had caught in his eyelashes. He wiped it away, and said, "Can't you see it, Inspector? We're simply not ready to call the Nazis' bluff. We're not all that eager to see if they'll pull back. It's not Franco and Mola we have to worry about. If they destroy Spain—unsavory a choice as that might be—so be it. We can debate ethics another time. But if we start exposing gun routes and secret companies and drop-off points, we humiliate our German friends and everyone starts posturing. Then it's Europe that hangs in the balance."

Hoffner was tasting the bile in his throat. "And it's only in the last twelve days that you've realized you have this ethical dilemma?"

Wilson's jaw momentarily tightened. "I wouldn't play that card, Inspector. You're the ones who elected these people three years ago. I think we're well beyond questions of ethics. You want me to admit it, fine. Our fighter bombers aren't up to par just yet. We haven't the stomach to dive back into full-on war quite so soon. So it's the practical dilemmas we worry about. Twelve days ago the word came down from the Admiralty to step back. Do nothing to embarrass our German friends. The Admiralty knew Georg was in. They knew he'd taken a camera, and they were very insistent that nothing on that film find the light of day. So they needed someone to bring him back."

This last bit seemed laughable. "And I just happened to walk into your office?"

For the first time Wilson showed confusion. Just as quickly his expression turned to muted amusement.

"You?" he said. "You think we would have crossed our fingers and hoped you knew what you were doing? I think Herr Vollman here was a slightly better candidate, don't you?"

It took Hoffner a moment to let this sink in. He looked at Vollman. The man was crushing his cigarette against the leg of the table. He dropped it and brushed off his hands.

Hoffner said, "You really are working nicely together, aren't you?"

Vollman said, "Our aeroplanes and tanks aren't quite up to standard yet, either. The anarchists are going to find that out very soon."

Hoffner tried to forget that Mila was hearing every word of this.

Wilson said, "We knew the Russians had sent Vollman in. We knew he was looking for the same things we had sent Georg to find—German guns. And we knew the two of them had made contact in Barcelona. So we approached the Russians and told them it would be best if their man found Georg and pulled him out. And while we were waiting for their response, you walked into my office."

Hoffner would have liked to have had some booze in his glass. "And yet you sent me in after him anyway."

"Yes," said Wilson. "I did."

Hoffner knew there was only one reason for it. He turned to Vollman and motioned for a cigarette. Vollman handed him one and lit it. Hoffner felt the smoke at the back of his throat.

"I was the decoy," Hoffner said.

Wilson had the bottle and was pouring out another two glasses. "Yes. You were."

"You send me in. If anyone is interested in Georg, they start following me, leaving Vollman here free to do what he wants."

There was no need to answer. Wilson handed the glasses to Mila and Hoffner.

Hoffner said, "And what if I hadn't figured it out in your office—you and the Admiralty?"

Wilson finished pouring for himself, then Vollman. "You really think that was going to happen? I'm surprised it took you so long to come to me in the first place." He handed Vollman his whiskey. "To tell the truth, I never imagined you'd be as good at this as you were. Spanish and Catalan. *And* links to Gardenyes and his crew. Who knew? And then finding the Hisma outposts." He raised his glass. "Well done." Wilson drank.

Hoffner hated Wilson for his glibness. "So you knew about Hisma—knew that it was a company—even before I left Berlin."

"We had an inkling. We found it through Langenheim." He lit a cigarette.

Langenheim, thought Hoffner. The one name in Georg's wire Hoffner had never figured out.

As if reading his thoughts, Wilson said, "Langenheim heads the Ausland Organization in Morocco. Consul general of sorts in those parts. He eats well and promotes the Reich. Always hardest to track down an obscure bureaucrat. That's a piece I don't think you had."

It was time for Wilson to show how clever he was. Hoffner hadn't the strength to stop him. "The Ausland reports to the SS," Hoffner said.

"Yes."

"So Bernhardt is SS?"

Wilson shook his head. "Bernhardt's a businessman. He's just after the money. About ten days ago he and Langenheim flew from Morocco to Bayreuth to meet with Deputy Führer Rudolf Hess. It's where they presented the bare bones of their idea for the dummy corporation to ship in the guns. We knew that Bernhardt had been a personal acquaintance of Franco's for some time. He's also chummy with several of the other Spanish generals. Obviously, Hess was impressed. He took Bernhardt and Langenheim to see Hitler himself—between curtains of the *Meistersinger*, I hear—and they signed the agreement. Hitler gets to send his guns to Franco without ruffling any international feathers. The Spaniards sign over most of their raw materials to Hitler as thanks for the guns. And Bernhardt and Langenheim make a great deal of money. It's all rather ingenious."

"And the nephew?"

"Little Bernhardt?" Wilson gave a mocking smile as he took a long pull on the cigarette. "Not so ingenious choosing a heroin addict and his Chinese friends to ship in guns and ammunition. I imagine two weeks ago that made sense. Apparently your Nazis are learning as they go." He took a last pull and let the cigarette fall to the floor. "The nephew's dead. The SS took care of that themselves. I don't imagine Bernhardt Senior was too terribly put out by it. But what *you* managed to do by compromising those outposts"—again Wilson raised his glass in genuine admiration—"that was a little tougher for them to swallow." He drank.

Hoffner drank as well. Things were coming clearer by the minute. "So the Hisma outposts in Cuenca and Tarancón—"

"And the one in Toledo?" Wilson nodded. "Bit difficult to ship in guns when there's no one there to receive them. Amazing how you managed that. I hear Franco was rather upset. We, of course, were delighted." He noticed the cigarette still lit on the floor and crushed it out under his boot. "You've slowed them down. Franco is actually going to have to earn this, which will keep our Nazi friends occupied for a bit longer and give us some time to work on our own aeroplanes and tanks."

Hoffner couldn't help a momentary bitterness. "How very nice for you."

"Not to worry. Franco's resilient. It's all going to come through Morocco now, or Portugal in the next day or so. He'll get his guns and tanks, and someone to fly in his men. He's a pragmatist. Franco will make do."

Hoffner sat with this for a few moments, and tried to piece it together backward in his head—Toledo, Teruel, Zaragoza. He had been right in Barcelona. It was a boy's playground game. And he had been elected the class fool.

"Georg's wire," Hoffner said, "with the names and the contacts. He never sent it, did he? That was a little invention of your own."

Wilson finished his glass. He took his time setting it on the floor. "We had to give you something to go on. Couldn't have you wandering about without something real to draw their attention. I decided to give you the names. It seemed the best choice."

"So where is Georg?" It was the most obvious question, and the one Hoffner had taken too long to ask. He stared across at both men.

Wilson stared back. He was about to answer when Vollman said, "You know, it's less than three hours in a plane from Aragón to Morocco. If you can find someone stupid enough to make the flight."

Hoffner took a moment before turning to Vollman. Vollman was almost through his second cigarette. He took a pull and waited while the smoke speared through his nose. He stared down at the plume.

"It's not the landing or the takeoff that's the difficulty," Vollman said. "There are plenty of places you can do that. The real problem is holding on to the plane once you leave it on the ground. Best not to be around if and when the Legionnaires find it. Not that a single-propeller four-seater is going to bring the Army of Africa over to Spain, but that's not really the point. So you have to hide the plane well, and that takes time and money—for some reason, the Republican loyalists in Morocco like their money—and you have to hope that the plane will be there when you get back. Luckily mine was."

Vollman finished the cigarette and pulled out his next. His tone was more pointed when he spoke again.

"You see, by the time I flew down, your Germans were already doing most of the work, and a little four-seater was hardly worth their time. They had all those Junker 52s and Heinkel fighter-bombers sitting in Tetuán. And there was a fellow named von Scheele, nice enough, who came with a group of German tourists from Hamburg the week before. Except this von Scheele was a major in the Wehrmacht, and his tourists were the men sent to fly the planes." He lit up. "So you can see how a boy with a camera and his devoted father might not have been our primary concern at that point."

Hoffner watched as Vollman reached for the nearest glass. There was still a bit of whiskey in it, and Vollman tossed it back. He poured himself another and drank. Wilson was oddly quiet.

"So where is he?" said Hoffner. Wilson remained silent. "Did I manage to distract the SS well enough for you?"

Vollman said, "The SS wasn't following this."

"Really?" Hoffner needed one of them to look at him. "I saw two of them dead in the back of a truck in Barcelona."

"Then they were the only ones," said Vollman, still focused on his cigarette. "I would have seen them."

"You're wrong," said Hoffner. His chest began to pound. "Alfassi mentioned a second German three days after you left Teruel. The man in Tarancón mentioned the same German. You must have missed him during all your flights back and forth to Morocco."

"It wasn't SS," Vollman said. "The SS don't kill a man the way Georg was killed."

It was said with so little care, so little effort. It was said because it had been in the room all along.

Vollman took another pull and flicked his ash and his humanity to the ground.

Hoffner sat unmoving.

The taste of vinegar filled his mouth as images of the boy ran through his mind, stares of joy and disappointment and distrust. They vanished as quickly as they had come, leaving only a burning at the base of his throat. Hoffner followed the beads of sweat sliding down Wilson's brow. He felt his own lips purse, his eyes grow heavy, but there was no hope of finding a breath. His chest suddenly collapsed on itself, and Hoffner gasped for air. He held it, waiting, until the breath slowly pressed its way through and out. There were tears, not his own, and he heard himself say, "You know this for certain."

He felt Mila's arms on him, her head against his chest, but there was no weight to her.

Wilson finally met Hoffner's gaze. "Yes."

Hoffner felt the blood drain from him. "You have the body?"

"Yes."

"I need to see him."

It was a room filled with ice, boarded-up windows, boxes and shelves. Wilson had said something about a church, the smell, this the only place to keep him. Hoffner had listened and walked and heard nothing. It was a room with breath in the air, and a boy laid out on a bier of planks and crates.

Hoffner stood over his son and looked at the chalk-white face. He placed a hand on Georg's shirt and felt the scrape of frozen cloth, rigid and sharp. There was a single deep hole at the temple, the knuckles ripped and raw, the neck swollen and red. The blood on the face and shirt had gone black, with little ridges and mounds where it had caked from the freezing.

Hoffner leaned closer in, let his hand glide across the cheek—the skin was so cold and soft—and stared at the untouched face. Hoffner tried to hear words, recall the sound of his son's voice, but it was already gone. How cruel, he thought. How cruel to stand so perfectly alone without even the comfort of memory. He imagined this was God's great purpose, to hold off the solitude at moments like these. Perhaps Georg had died with that? Hoffner heard nothing.

His legs tightened, and his knees ached from the pain, but still he stared and knew there would never be anything beyond this room.

He saw a piece of grit at Georg's ear and gently swept it away. He pressed his hand to the cheek again, held it, and then brought the cloth up and covered him.

Upstairs, Wilson and Vollman were standing and smoking in what passed for a kitchen. Mila sat at the table and drank from a chipped cup. It was coffee, and the sun was just coming up.

Hoffner took the last of the steps and moved through the doorway. All three looked over.

He pulled back a chair from the table and sat.

"I'll take a cigarette," he said.

Mila held his hand, and Vollman shook one from the pack. Hoffner reached for it and waited for a light. He barely tasted the smoke in his throat.

"When?" he said.

Wilson was leaning against a wooden counter. He finished his cigarette and dropped it to the floor. "Two days ago," he said, crushing it under his boot. "He was left on the church steps."

Hoffner stared.

Two days, he thought. Georg had been alive two days ago. The idea of it—sitting in his cell, the stupidity of having let himself get tossed away while the boy had been here—Hoffner had to push that torture from his mind. It was another few moments before he realized the strangeness of what Wilson had said.

"The church steps?"

"Yes."

"Why?"

"Why what?" said Wilson.

"Why would the Spaniards have put him there?"

Vollman said, "It wasn't the fascists." He took a pull.

Hoffner turned to him. "What do you mean, it wasn't the fascists?"

"He means," said Wilson, "they would have told us."

Hoffner hadn't the strength for this. "And you would have believed them?"

"Yes," said Wilson, "I would." He was trying his best at compassion. "They knew we were pulling him out. They knew we were playing along. What could they possibly have to gain by lying to us? We had more reason to kill him than they did."

The carelessness of Wilson's cruelty might have been impressive if not for the short pants and the knees. Hoffner tried to keep his focus. "And did you?" he said.

Wilson's tone was cold when he spoke. "No. We're the ones trying to preserve the body so you can bury him." Wilson pushed himself up and began to open cabinets, peer inside, close them. It was restlessness, nothing more. "We thought at first it might have been someone from the fire in Tarancón, someone who had followed him, but Georg wasn't the one who set it, so that didn't make much sense." He moved to the drawers, and his frustration spilled out. "We have absolutely no idea why Georg has a bullet in his skull."

"Not that the bullet killed him," Vollman said. He was dropping a cigarette to the ground. He crushed it out under his foot. "He was strangled," he added, no less casually. "Then shot. That's not the way the SS does it."

Hoffner sat one floor above his dead son and knew there had never been any hope of saving him. That was agony itself, but to hear he would never know why the boy had died—that was even more unbearable.

Wilson tried sympathy. "I can't imagine how this must be for you, but you have to understand it's no less maddening for us."

Hoffner stared at the table. He tried to find his voice. "So you have nothing."

"We have the camera," Wilson said, "and we have the film. There's nothing in either of them."

Hoffner continued to stare. The table was chipped wood, and there were burn marks across it. He set his thumb on one. It was strangely smooth.

"You're sure of that?" he said.

Wilson watched as Hoffner rubbed deep into the wood. "I am," he said. "But you're welcome to take a look."

Ten minutes later Hoffner sat with three film canisters in front of him. Wilson had set the first of the reels on a device with a crank that ran the film past a lens and a light. It was crude but effective.

"This is the only one with anything on it," Wilson said, as he stepped back.

Hoffner had watched aimlessly—the wires for the battery, the threading of the film, anything to keep his mind distracted.

The first sequences came quickly, images of Barcelona, the games, the little street where Han Shen stood. There were workers with guns down by the docks, militiamen in marching lines of disarray, trucks filled with anarchists shouting their way out of the city. Hoffner saw fields, a single aeroplane along the horizon, and the long drive up into the hills of Teruel—the same priest, the same glasses, the same fountain.

There were other towns, other priests, and in Toledo Hoffner recognized the soldier who had stood sentry at the gate. The man marched with great seriousness, back and forth, back and forth, before he broke into sudden laughter and aimed his rifle up into the trees. He did a strange, wild dance, laughed again, and then walked quickly to the camera and disappeared.

The next pictures were from a different hand, and Hoffner slowed the reel. The motion of the film jerked, and Hoffner then saw Georg standing at the gate. The boy was wearing the soldier's hat. He held the rifle on his shoulder. He marched and turned, marched and turned, before glancing over and smiling for the camera.

Hoffner stopped. He stared at the ragged clothes, the misheld rifle, and the quiet smile of a boy he would never know again. The picture began to lose focus, and Hoffner rubbed his eyes. His hand was wet when he took hold of the crank.

More trucks passed, more soldiers, until Hoffner recognized the town of Coria. This time it was the church, the shops, a few houses, and finally the prison fortress. The camera continued to pan across the square until it came to a sudden stop on an image. Hoffner's hand tightened on the crank. It was by the well. Hoffner couldn't be sure he had seen it correctly, and he began to move the crank slowly as the camera drew closer. He was almost to it when the film went black. Hoffner reversed and saw the image again.

Standing by the well and staring at the camera was Sascha.

His son. Sascha.

Nine years since Hoffner had seen him, yet he couldn't deny it. The hair was all but gone, and the body too thin, but it was the same face, the same look of empty defiance. Sascha gave an awkward wave and the film cut out.

Hoffner closed his eyes, even as the boy remained in front of him.

My God, he thought. The two of them together.

The throbbing returned to his head, and Hoffner felt his head lighten and his body go limp.

6

SASCHA

In the winter of 1919, at the age of sixteen, Sascha Hoffner took his mother's maiden name and left Berlin as the newly minted Alexander Kurtzman. It was an act of unrepentant hatred and was meant to make certain that he would never have to see his father again.

Four years later, Kurtzman beat a man to death.

The killing was of no real consequence, except to the man himself, who had arrived in Munich the day before from somewhere in the Congo. The man was on his way back to Stockholm, and while he had already been traveling for several weeks, he decided to take a few days to wait for a more direct train heading north. November in Munich had always held a certain charm for him, and the man—a radical, and a great believer in the Congolese and their future—was not averse to conveying his political and social views to anyone willing to listen. Not of Africa himself, he nonetheless claimed to understand the soul of the black man. Sadly, he was not quite so savvy when it came to the men of Munich's streets and her beer halls. The great putsch erupted on November 8, and the man—like any good radical—found himself incapable of stepping to the side. The man's words were his weapons and, while the young Kurtzman was by no means an imposing figure, he had been fighting in the streets with the Freikorps for two years and knew well enough how to crack a skull against a brick wall. Hitler ranted from a table, General Ludendorff—war hero, and Hitler's great supporter—turned a pale green, and Kurtzman took the man into a back alley and finished him. It was Kurtzman's good fortune to come out relatively unscathed, so much so that he was able to make it back inside by the time Ludendorff stepped up to speak. A day later, Kurtzman watched with unimagined anguish as his heroes were sent off to prison.

Those were hard days indeed, the party disbanded, the best of them locked away. For a time Kurtzman followed his commander, the elusive and homosexual Ernst Röhm, to Bolivia—a useless place for useless men—but by then such men, such beautiful men, had become a way of life for Kurtzman. Even so, things tended to end badly on that front, and by 1926 he was back in Munich, eager to make up for lost time. He rejoined the party, redoubled his efforts with the Freikorps, and made the lucky acquaintance of a young writer and journalist. When, a few months later, the journalist was asked to take the party's message to Berlin, Kurtzman found himself invited along as the man's chief assistant. Overwhelmed and overjoyed, Kurtzman agreed at once and followed his new mentor, Joseph Goebbels, north to the promised land.

It was a period of unparalleled happiness and, save for one very brief episode in the winter of 1927, Kurtzman learned to love Berlin again. He lived his poverty with pride, and when the tide began to turn, he found himself a girl—on Goebbels's insistence—and even managed to get her pregnant. He married her first, of course, and while he showed the face of a devastated husband when both she and the baby died during childbirth, Kurtzman knew that Berlin had stepped in to save him. He had accommodated respectability. He was now free.

Goebbels moved up, and Kurtzman moved with him. When Hitler finally took the chancellorship in 1933, Kurtzman celebrated with the rest, watched the Reichstag burn, and accepted his post at the Ministry with a sense of quiet destiny.

It was all as it was meant to be, until the day he was told that the whole thing had come crashing down. He was no longer a member of the party. He could never be a member of the party. He was filth: a Jew. A dirty Jew. They had discovered his secret. In a matter of hours, the once untouchable

Alexander Kurtzman was forced to resume his role as the reviled and pathetic Sascha Hoffner. His life, as he had made it, was no longer his. The humiliation and despair might have killed a weaker man. Not so with Sascha. His own death was only of minor concern.

An image of that sixteen-year-old boy—before Goebbels, before the Freikorps—sat with Nikolai Hoffner as he cradled an empty glass in his hands.

Mila was next to him. Wilson leaned against the counter. Vollman stood by the door. They had finished the bottle of whiskey. They had let him drink in silence.

Hoffner set his glass down. He looked over and saw the canisters of film and the viewing machine in a crate by the door. He couldn't recall when any of that had happened.

Mila was drinking water. She pushed her glass toward him, and Hoffner took it. He drank. It tasted of rust and sand, and he saw a few pieces of grit swirling at the bottom. They were the same color as the one he had brushed from Georg's ear. Why that? he wondered.

Wilson said, "You saw something?"

The sound of the voice startled Mila. She looked up, and Hoffner set the glass on the table. He tapped at it, sending it across in little bursts of movement. He might have sent it over the edge had Mila not grabbed it and pulled it back.

Hoffner's head remained unnervingly light as he stared at the table. "I saw what you saw," he said. "Spain, guns—a well."

"And that last image?" Wilson missed nothing.

"It went by quickly."

"Not too quickly."

"No," said Hoffner, "not too quickly." Wilson waited. Finally Hoffner turned to him. "It was my son," he said. "My older son. Sascha. I hadn't seen him in a long time." Hoffner felt Mila's eyes bore through him.

Wilson said, "You're telling me that was Kurtzman?"

The word jarred. "How do you know his name?"

"We're not likely to take a man on and not know everything about his family." Wilson reached for the jug of water and poured himself a glass. He drank. "Kurtzman is in the Propaganda Ministry. Why would he be in Spain?"

The numbing at the back of Hoffner's head returned; he welcomed it. "You saw his face," he said, "the way he was dressed." His eyes drifted back to the table. "You think this has anything to do with the Ministry?"

Wilson needed a moment. "So he's here for the guns?"

Hoffner felt the first taste of acid in his throat. He took hold of Mila's glass and held it. "No," he said. "He's not here for the guns."

"How do you know that?"

Hoffner drank. He felt the water course through his chest.

"He's no longer in the party," he said. "He's no longer a Nazi. They found his Jewish blood—from his grandmother—three weeks ago. And they threw him out." Hoffner set the glass down but continued to hold it. His mind was emptying. "He's not here for the guns or the Ministry."

Wilson wasn't convinced. "I thought you hadn't seen him in quite some time."

"I wouldn't need to see him to know such things."

Wilson looked as if he might press it. Instead he said, "Then why is he here?"

Hoffner heard the voices from Teruel, from Tarancón, from a part of himself he refused to listen to—*An unusual German . . . he had death in the eyes*—and said, "You say it's not the way the SS kills a man." There was nothing in his voice. "Perhaps you're right."

Wilson's uncertainty turned to quiet disbelief. "What?"

Hoffner said nothing, and Wilson continued, "You can't believe that." He waited for an answer. When none came, he said, "You understand what you're saying?"

Hoffner stared at the glass. He had nothing else. "You're asking if I understand how my son could have killed his brother. Tell me. How could I possibly understand that?"

Wilson refused to hear it. "Even if it's remotely true, he could have killed him in Berlin. Why follow him here?"

Hoffner had no answer, nothing but the face of Sascha staring back at him through the lens of a camera. "My son is dead. My other one is here."

He felt his throat constrict, his eyes grow heavy. "If only the world were made of such coincidence . . ."

Wilson looked across at Vollman. He saw his own disbelief staring back. He looked again at Hoffner. "You're talking about your own son."

Hoffner felt his own rage and despair like wet rope coiling around his throat. "Yes," he said quietly, "my own son," and the glass shattered in his hand.

It was nearly half a minute before he realized he was bleeding.

Mila was already pressing down on his wrist, pulling pieces of glass from his skin, as Hoffner stared down at the hand and saw one long cut. A single thick shard rocked easily on the table, while tiny grains of glass shimmered across his palm. Mila picked and brushed, and Hoffner felt nothing. It was a hand, not his own, until she finally took a cloth from Vollman and pressed it into the flesh. Instantly, Hoffner felt the pain shoot up through his arm like the twisting of raw muscle. He heard himself groan, and realized it was the burning of alcohol coursing into his skin. His throat constricted and he coughed.

"Bring over that bucket," Mila said, and Hoffner angled his head as she continued to work on him. Only once did he come close to vomiting, but the acid stayed in his throat, and his hand began to throb with its own isolated pain.

Hoffner's head cleared. He swallowed and looked over to see his hand encased in thick gauze. Wilson had produced a second bottle. He filled a glass with whiskey and held it out to Hoffner.

"He's had enough," Mila said.

Hoffner took the glass and drank. Wilson set the bottle on the table and retreated to the counter. Vollman was back by the door as Mila sat silently.

Finally Wilson said, "You're saying this has nothing to do with the guns or Franco?"

Hoffner kept his eyes on the glass. He flexed his fingers. He could still move them. "Not everything shatters the world as a whole, Herr Wilson. This one shatters just mine."

Wilson started to answer, and Hoffner said, "He left the film. He wanted it found. He wanted me to know."

Wilson was still struggling. "But why?"

Hoffner heard the question in his own voice. "Because I'm his father."

It answered nothing and brought a silence to the room.

Finally Wilson said, "I could help you."

"No," said Hoffner. "You couldn't." He felt the need to stand. He pushed back his chair and steadied himself against the table. "Thank you, Herr Wilson. Thank you for Doval, the doctor"—the word caught in his throat—"Georg. I imagine you'll be leaving Spain now."

Wilson showed a genuine sympathy even if he understood nothing. He nodded slowly.

Hoffner extended his good hand. Wilson hesitated, then took it. Vollman followed suit. It was a bizarre moment of protocol, until Vollman said, "You're going to try and find him."

Hoffner said nothing.

Vollman added, "I have a plane—for another two days. It has room for four."

Mila stood, and Wilson said, "He'd be heading west. Portugal would be my guess."

"He'll be in Badajoz," Hoffner said, his voice empty, his eyes distant: it was as if he were speaking to himself. "He found enough about Hisma to track Georg. He'll know Badajoz is where the last of the guns are going. And he'll think it's where he can find his way back."

Wilson hesitated. "His way back?"

Hoffner looked directly at him. It seemed as if he might answer. Instead, he took Mila's arm and moved them to the door.

They buried Georg in the first light, in a field just beyond the last of the houses. Wilson had offered to take the boy to Berlin—he, too, had a plane—but Hoffner said no. He thought of Mendy and Lotte, standing through the taunts—those roving packs of boys who waited outside the cemetery gates, jeering while a Jew was laid in the ground. Why put them through that? It was quiet here, and simple. Whichever way things went in Spain, it would be better than in Germany.

The priest stood off to the side while Hoffner mouthed ancient words whose meaning he had never learned. He had no idea if this was the place or the time for them, but they were all he knew. His mother had insisted he say them for her. He said them now for his son.

When he finished, Hoffner took a clump of earth and tossed it onto the sheeted body. Mila did the same, then Wilson and Vollman. She held his arm.

The sun had climbed to the horizon as they stood and waited for Wilson in the square. He had gone to see Doval. Mila hadn't let go of his arm. Vollman smoked through the silence.

Wilson appeared from the prison gate, and Hoffner said to Mila, "He'll fly you to Barcelona. It's the least he can do."

Mila said nothing, and Wilson drew up.

"I told him it's a direct request from the Admiralty," Wilson said. His shirt was damp through at the back. "He's promised no interference. You have two days. After that—"

"After that," said Hoffner, "Doval gets to finish what he started."

Wilson said nothing, and Vollman tossed his cigarette to the ground. "I can wait. I can fly on the fifteenth. That gives you enough time."

There was no reason to answer.

Wilson said, "We'll go get the car, then. Vollman and I." It was a moment of unexpected chivalry: he was giving Hoffner a last few moments with Mila. It took Vollman another few seconds to catch on.

"Right. Yes." Vollman gave an awkward nod, and followed Wilson off. Mila and Hoffner watched them go.

"They hid you in the church?" Hoffner said. It was first time he could ask.

"I'm not going to Barcelona."

"There are good priests everywhere. All this must make them shudder. It'll be the same in Germany one day—"

"I'm not going." She waited until he was looking directly at her. "You don't have to do this, Nikolai. If he was capable of killing Georg, what is there possibly to gain?"

Hoffner saw the vulnerability in her eyes. "And what if he wasn't capable?"

"You don't believe that."

Hoffner waited. "No. I don't."

"So you go for—what? To let him finish this, to let him free you from whatever you think you deserve?"

"He killed his brother."

"It makes you a coward."

He hadn't thought her capable of causing this kind of pain. Or maybe it was only now that he let himself feel it.

His voice remained low and calm. "He doesn't get to walk away. If that makes me a coward, so be it."

"No," she said. "You're a coward because you go alone." It was an anger he had never imagined, raw and bitter, and doing nothing to hide its fear. "You're going to stop thinking there's something noble to be done, or that you could possibly know what it would look like. You don't. All you do is hurt me with this and show how weak you are. I know how weak you are, and I know what terrifies you. Your boy is dead, but not because of you. And your Sascha—" She stopped. The words were tight in her throat. "You don't get to throw yourself away because you want to believe that. There's more to it now. You don't get to do this alone."

"I do it to protect you."

"You do it to protect yourself."

She stared across at him, her strength like shattered glass. It hung from them both and fell aimlessly to the ground. Hoffner's hands ached, and still he gathered up the shards. He knew what it was he deserved, knew with every breath he took. It was the weight of this love—brutal and free and untethered from a lifetime of self-damning—and yet meaningless if he chose to run from his past now.

"Then you come," he said.

The little Ford from Toledo appeared from a side street. Hoffner and Mila waited while Wilson and Vollman drove up.

The two men got out. There were a few awkward exchanges, a moment of surprise. Someone might have mentioned luck.

• • •

The car had been stripped down and searched, the rear cushioning all knife tears and disgorged stuffing. The front bench was much the same. Mila laid a blanket across it so they could sit. Even so, they felt the springs in every jolt and bump. Hoffner let Mila drive. He slept. And he dreamed.

He was sitting in a cool meadow, with the sound of flapping wings overhead. He saw a baby lying in the grass, its tiny feet kicking at the sky. Hoffner tried to stand but his legs were too heavy. He pulled at his thighs, and his hands were filled with a thick, wet tar, the smell of it like camphor oil, and he was suddenly holding flames in his hands. Mila pulled him back from the fire, and Hoffner saw her against the night sky. She was older and her body had been burned, her arms peeling in thin flakes of flesh. He reached for her, but she stepped back. He reached for her again and his eyes opened.

They were at an outpost. Twenty Republican soldiers stood off in the distance, each with a rifle and a cap. Mila was talking with a man who was holding their papers. Hoffner heard the sound of mortar fire somewhere in the distance, and he watched as each of the men ducked his head. The sound was too far off to pose any danger, but these were men not yet tested by battle. They flinched and gripped their rifles.

Hoffner pushed himself up and opened the door. His hand had stiffened, and his eye felt as if it had been squeezed shut. He could barely swallow. He forced his legs out, and he stood.

Mila and the soldier looked over while a second barrage erupted. Hoffner made his way to them, his stride unsteady, with the booze in his stomach and a scorching sun to contend with.

He drew up and thought to say something, but his mouth was too dry. He spat, and the man offered him his canteen. Hoffner drank.

"The prison in Coria," the man said. "You're lucky to be alive."

Hoffner nodded and finished the canteen.

"You don't want to go south," the man said. "I've been trying to explain it to the señora."

"The doctor," Hoffner corrected, and spat again. "The señora is a doctor."

"Yes. The doctor. Yagüe has half of Africa marching up from Seville. They're already pressing in from Mérida. It's not going to be good in Badajoz. It won't be good here in a day or so, but we're not going to think about that."

If Hoffner had any inkling who Yagüe was or where Mérida might be, he might have known enough to show some concern. Instead, he told himself not to vomit in front of the soldiers.

Another explosion rattled behind them, and Hoffner nodded his thanks.

"We'll take our chances."

He took Mila by the arm and walked with her back to the car.

An untamed terror now lived in the towns and hillsides surrounding Badajoz. Hoffner had felt tremors of it in Teruel, isolated echoes in the screams behind Coria's prison gates, but it was only here that it penetrated the smallest of gestures: a backward glance from a woman on a cart, the sudden silence from a flock of birds perched penitently in the trees, the grinding of tires on a ground too slick and too beaten down by hooves and trucks and rain to be passable. The men who walked along the roads strode with more purpose than was warranted. It was the surest sign that they meant to meet death on their own terms. Fear makes a man cower. Terror gives him strength.

Like a pouch bag, everything was getting pulled in, barricades and guns and horses to ring the approach from the south and the east. Yagüe was well beyond Mérida. It would come tomorrow or the next day. That was what they were saying. No one was permitted to pass after sunset.

"I have to get through."

Hoffner tried to show his papers again, but the man with the thick beard and the rifle shook his head. It was a gentle shake, one reserved for overeager children.

"If there's still a road to be taken," the man said, "you can take it in the morning. No one moves after dark."

They were in a village called Villar del Rey, thirty kilometers from Badajoz. The man motioned to one of the houses along the square. It was two or three rooms, one bare bulb, the rest lit by candles, with a whitewashed courtyard in front. The sky had streaked into strips of pink and deep blue, and there was a boy of thirteen or fourteen leaning against its front wall. He was long and pale, and he held his rifle in arms taut with new muscle.

The thick beard shouted over. "Julio. Your mother needs to make a bed for these two tonight. The woman is a doctor."

The boy pushed himself up and nodded, and Hoffner followed Mila across the mud.

Inside, the house was old stone, the ceilings too low for a tall man to stand upright. Pots and pans hung from hooks and shelves, and a drinking trough of wood stretched along the back wall. Two young girls sat at a round table, with a few photographs in frames hanging behind them. One showed a man with a mule and a rifle.

The man was seated across the room on a low stool. He was rubbing a cloth along the rifle's barrel. He looked up when the son called for his mother.

There was silence, and then the sound of an aeroplane from somewhere above. The man set his rifle against the wall and crossed to the doorway. He stepped outside, stared up for several seconds, and then looked out across the fields to the men in their caps and their uniforms—each of them staring up—before he returned. He took the rifle, sat on the stool, and began to rub it again with the cloth.

The mother appeared from the back room in an apron skirt and green blouse of coarse cotton. She was slender, and her hair fell from its ties in thin wisps of brown and gray. In any other place, she and Mila might have been sisters.

She spoke to the boy in a kind of Spanish Portuguese, only a few words making themselves known to Hoffner. The voice was deep and quiet, and she turned to Mila and continued to speak. Hoffner heard the word "*frango*" several times and thought she might be referring to the general, until Mila said, "She wants to know if we'll eat chicken. I told her yes."

Hoffner nodded, and the woman motioned to the two girls. They followed her out into the courtyard, and the boy sat where they had been. He found a cloth and began to rub his rifle in the way his father rubbed.

Hoffner said to Mila, "Tell him the boy is too young to have a gun."

She knew why he said it; and she knew there was no point in repeating it.

The father, still focused on his rifle, said, "Will they make such distinctions in who they kill?"

Hoffner watched as the man continued to clean. "No," said Hoffner. "They won't."

"It was a German plane," the father said, "or Italian. Hard to tell in the dark. He was lost. Tomorrow or the next day he'll drop his bombs here. For now he saves them for the city."

"Then you should send your family east."

"You have a car. You're more than welcome to take them east if you like."

"And you'd let me?"

"No." The father looked over. "If you want to make it to Badajoz, you need to go tonight."

Hoffner was struck by the sudden candor. "The captain outside thinks otherwise."

"The captain wants to herd us into trucks and send us back to where you came from, or into Portugal. He'll take my wife and daughters tomorrow. He'll get them somewhere safe."

"But not the boy."

"If Badajoz falls, a boy with a rifle sitting here won't make any difference. Neither will his father. So we go to Badajoz with you."

"You'll have to talk to the captain about getting me my car."

"Your car is already halfway to the city," the man said. "It's loaded with rifles and ammunition and food. The captain probably drives it himself. He's very brave. He'll make three trips tonight, and he'll hope the fascists choose to sleep before they make their full assault. At dawn he'll tell you your car was needed, and that you can't go south, impossible now with Yagüe only twenty kilometers from the city. He might ask the doctor if she can stomach the war, but you—he'll tell an old man not to think beyond himself. Do you want to get to Badajoz?"

"Yes."

"With a boy too young for a rifle?"

"Yes."

"Then we eat and sleep, and I come for you later."

At just after 1 a.m. the man shook Hoffner awake. They had laid a straw mattress by the trough, and the smell of garlic and chicken fat was still thick in the air. A dog or goat lay sleeping under the table, and Hoffner looked up to see the man and his son already with their rifles slung across their backs. The man waited until Hoffner was sitting. He then held out a small pistol to him.

"I have my own," Hoffner said. His hand was throbbing.

"I'll take it," said Mila. She was standing somewhere behind the man.

Hoffner looked over. He hadn't heard her get up. They had slept. There had been no questions last night. She had given him that.

She was in trousers and had borrowed a shoulder wrap from the mother.

The man led them to the back room. His wife was sitting on the bed with the two girls, each in a long nightshirt. The mother's hair was down across her chest, and she looked much younger. She held out her arms and the father nodded the boy to her, but the boy shook his head. The father reached over, took the boy by the shirt, and pushed him to his mother. There were no tears as she held him, and the boy finally wrapped his arms around her. He then kissed his sisters and stepped back. Hoffner looked away as the boy ran his sleeve across his eyes. The father leaned in and kissed his daughters and his wife. The wife said something too low to be heard, and the father kissed her again and then stepped over to the window. He peered out and climbed through.

He led them across a field and into a gathering of trees. Hoffner smelled the horses before he saw them, two deep brown colts tied to a tree and gnawing at the grass. Each had a blanket where a saddle should have been, but at least they had bits and reins. Mila ran her hand along the nose of the first and then quickly pulled herself up. Hoffner found a stump and brought himself up behind her. He wrapped his arms around her waist, pressed himself into the shallow of her back as she took the horse deeper into the trees.

The moon followed them through the branches, and Hoffner let himself find sleep.

They were on an incline of high grass and boulders when first light came. The horses had proved more than worthy, a steady canter for much of the night. No one had said a word. Now it was little more than a walk, the horses' nostrils heavy with breath and their hides moist and glistening.

The trees had thinned just beyond Villar del Rey, leaving an open sky and white moon to light the fields and scrubland along the way. Hoffner had lost feeling in his right foot an hour ago, but it was better than the shooting pain that now circled his thighs and backside. Either would have been enough to keep his mind distracted, and for that he was grateful.

Badajoz appeared across a valley as they crested the hill. Red tile roofs climbed haphazardly from the banks of a river and settled at the top of a hill, where a wide wood stretched up, then down another slope. Two stone towers, the color of wet sand, edged themselves beyond the tree line, no match for cannons or grenades. An ancient gate—Roman or Moorish, it was impossible to say which—stood along the bank and waited imperiously at the end of a solitary bridge.

The aeroplanes had already done their damage. Sections of the outer wall lay in rubble, with hastily positioned sandbags and trucks at the breaches. Roofs throughout had been torn away, while streams of smoke spooled up into the air. The father pointed to a larger cloud rising from a distant hill. It was from the east.

"Lobón or Guadajira," he said. Hoffner imagined these were towns on the other side of the river. "They're leaving nothing behind." The man looked down into the valley. "It's quiet. No aeroplanes. It means they'll be here this morning. From the south. We need to cross."

He led them down the path and spurred the horses to give what little they had left. The grass gave way to low shrubs, and the horses snorted as the ground grew more uneven. The smell of burned wood and gunpowder filled the air. At the bridge, not a single soldier was standing guard.

"There's no reason," the father said, as if reading Hoffner's thoughts.

"Yagüe and his Africans will be coming from the other side. If they take the city, we'll need to defend this."

They were on the bridge when the sound of a solitary motor stopped them. Instantly, the father brought them back down and pressed them close to the first of the stone stanchions.

They all peered up, waiting to see the aeroplanes. Instead, the echo grew louder off the water, and they turned to see the little Ford from Toledo driving through the gate. The car bounced its way across the bridge, until the thick-bearded captain at the wheel saw them and pulled to a stop. The father led the horses back onto the bridge, and the captain cut the engine.

"*Salud*," the captain said.

"*Salud*."

"I was wondering where those horses had gotten to." It was the same easy voice from last night.

"My friend here was wondering the same about his car."

It was a good answer. The captain nodded. "Two thousand from Madrid have come down to defend the city. Militia and Guardia. They're setting up barricades."

"It's quiet."

"The last of the aeroplanes came an hour ago." The captain opened the door and stepped out. He turned toward the city and waved his hands above his head. A mirror glinted from somewhere on the wall, and the captain brought his hands down. "They'll let you in the gate."

"They would have let us in anyway."

"Yes," said the captain, getting back in the car, "but now you won't waste so much time shouting up from the bridge." He closed the door. "You choose to go in, it's no coming out until it's done. You know that."

"So there's a chance we'll be coming out?"

The captain waited and then looked at the boy. "Your rifle is clean?"

The boy nodded.

"Good."

The father said, "And they've brought guns from Madrid?"

"They have the high ground. It should be enough." The captain looked at Hoffner. "You know how this might go, friend, and still you feel the need to get through."

Hoffner said nothing.

"I've heard the stories of Coria," the captain said. "The prison fortress. Terrible things."

"Yes," said Hoffner.

"Badajoz isn't a place to find revenge for what they did."

"I'm not looking for it."

"Maybe revenge isn't such a bad thing to be looking for." The captain turned to Mila. He seemed to want to say something. Instead, he started the engine. "I'll see you inside the walls." He put the car in gear and headed off.

There was no escaping the silence. The streets stood empty, save for the occasional grind of a truck or a voice rising from somewhere behind the stones and brick. The horses moved slowly. Twice Hoffner saw young children—tears running down their cheeks—pulled along by mothers, whisked through doorways, and locked safely away. This was how war finally came, he thought, not in the open back of a truck with songs and rifles raised or on a road where men could trade stories and cigarettes. Even the crack of a sniper's rifle signaled nothing. It came in the silence and the waiting, and the grim certainty that, one day, the dying here would all but be forgotten.

Hoffner heard muffled laughter and peered down an alleyway. Two men, old and unshaven, sat on stools in the shadows, a wooden crate between them. They were drunk. Their heads rested back against the stone of the building. One was humming something low. The other looked over. For some reason he nodded. The man coughed and laughed again. Hoffner nodded back.

"This isn't their fight," said the father. "They've had theirs. At least they know it."

The father led them through the streets and into a wide plaza at the foot of the southern gate. There was a strange symmetry to it all, trucks and cars lining the wall, with blue-shirted men and women and uniformed soldiers nestled above in whatever cracks and openings they had found for cover. The two largest trucks stood in front of the gate, while a group of soldiers directed boxes of ammunition to different points along the line. It was already hot, and the dust and grit beneath their feet swirled in tiny clouds of gray smoke.

The father took the horses close enough to hear voices—orders shouted, the relay of information from men with field glasses standing at the topmost reaches of the wall. This was where they would make their stand.

The father and the boy dismounted, and the father handed Mila the reins.

"You take them where you're going. No reason to have them here." He nodded to one of the streets off the plaza. "You take that one around, six or seven streets. It's to the left. You can follow the numbers."

Hoffner had shown the father the address for the last of the names on Captain Doval's list—the Hisma liaison in Badajoz, the man hoarding those too-thick crates. There had been no reason to tell the father why.

"Thank you."

The father nodded and looked at Mila. "You'll be needed here. A doctor."

"Yes," she said, "I know."

Hoffner waited for her to say more. Instead, he watched as she dismounted and held the reins up to him. He stared at her, disbelieving, and saw the same eyes from the hospital, the same eyes from Durruti's camp. She was needed here.

She squinted through the sun as she continued to look at him. "You find what you need and come back."

Hoffner barely moved.

"Take them," she said, and she placed the reins in his hand. "I'm needed here."

"I thought you'd be with me."

"Not for this."

"I thought you'd be with me," he repeated.

"I am. But I'm needed here."

Hoffner hesitated. "And if you're not here?"

She stared up at him. "Then you'll find me."

She drew closer. She waited for him to lean down and brought her hand to the back of his neck. She kissed him, and he felt her fingers press deep into his skin. She released him and whispered, "You'll come and find me." And she pulled away.

Hoffner watched as she walked off. He thought to turn and go but called out, "Mila." She continued to walk. Again he called.

She stopped. The father and the boy moved on, and Hoffner dismounted and brought the horses behind him.

She looked almost pained as he drew up. "You need to go," she said.

"I know."

"Then why don't you?"

He watched her face grow darker, and he pulled her in. His arm drew tight around her as he felt her cheek press deep into his neck.

"There is no going anymore."

Her hands clasped at his back. Her lips pressed gently into his neck and she pulled back and he kissed her. She then turned away, and this time he let her go.

THE GERMAN

The house was like the rest, three crumbling floors of iron and stone, the wood at the bottom of the door split in wide gaps. Hoffner tied the horses to a post and knocked with the side of his fist. He listened. He knocked again, then spoke the name, loudly enough to be heard in the next house. There was movement, and the door slowly pulled open.

A man, small with gray hair, stood in a shirt, trousers, and suspenders. His left arm and hand were shriveled by disease. The fingers reached only to his waist, and the rest hung limp at his side. He leaned his head out the doorway and peered down the street, as if he was expecting to see others. He stepped back and looked up at Hoffner. He spoke with caution. "The fighting has started?"

"No," said Hoffner. "Where is the German?"

The man continued to stare. "You have the wrong house."

"No." Hoffner spoke in German. "I have the right house. I don't care about the guns. I want only the German."

The man waited and then said, "I don't understand this language."

"I can find a few militiamen at the gate to translate for you. Shall I go get them?"

It was clear why the men of Hisma had picked this Spaniard. He remained unflappable. He waited another few moments and then pulled the door fully open and motioned Hoffner in.

The hall was narrow and dimly lit, with stairs at the side leading up into the shadows. The man led Hoffner beyond them, into a room at the back. It held a few wooden chairs, a low table, and something that had once been a rug. The place had the smell of wet towels left too many days moldering in a corner.

Hoffner looked over and saw the man holding a small pistol in his good hand. It was aimed at Hoffner's chest.

Hoffner said, "Is the German here?" The man remained absolutely still. Hoffner said, "I've told you I don't care about the guns."

"Take your pistol out and place it on the table."

Hoffner removed his pistol and set it down. "The German—is he here?"

"I don't know about any guns."

Hoffner stared back. What else was the man going to say?

"He's told you he comes from Berlin," said Hoffner. "That he's part of Hisma, Hispano-Marroquí. He isn't. He lied."

The man continued to stare, and Hoffner looked around for a chair. He found the least uncomfortable one and sat.

They waited like this for perhaps a minute before Hoffner said, "I'm not sure what the sound of a bullet would do right now, but I'm thinking you're not that eager to find out."

He located the source of the smell. It was a rope mop propped against the wall, standing in a pool of oily water.

Hoffner said, "Yagüe will be here in the next few hours. He'll take the city. He'll thank you for the guns, and you'll march around with him and point to the people who've done you and your little arm the most cruelty. Then you'll watch him shoot them, all for your Spain. I don't care one way or the other. I want the German. I want my son."

The man's eyes widened for just a moment as gunfire erupted in the distance. It was pistols and rifles. The man turned his head and listened intently. The fighting continued to build as mortars began to explode. He looked at Hoffner. "The sound of one bullet wouldn't make much of a difference now, would it?"

Hoffner tried not to think of Mila. He shook his head easily.

"You say he's your son." Hoffner said nothing, and the man continued. "He told me he was forced to burn his papers. It was too dangerous to keep them in the Republican zone."

"He never had any papers. You should clean that mop."

"He knew important names."

"Sanz in Teruel, Doval in Zaragoza."

The man hesitated.

Hoffner said, "Obviously I know them as well. He isn't here to help you. You need to believe me. When does he come back to the house?"

The man kept the gun raised.

Hoffner said, "Does he know where the crates with the guns are hidden?"

This seemed to snap some life into the face. The man waited and then shook his head.

"Good," said Hoffner. "Then he'll need to come back. You shouldn't be here when he does."

It was clear the man was running through the last few minutes, making sure he hadn't missed anything. Yagüe might be at the gates, but he wasn't inside them just yet. Slowly the man brought the pistol down and slid it into his belt.

"If you try and follow me," he said, "I'll shoot you. If you try and leave, I have someone who watches the house who will also shoot you. You understand?"

"Which room?" Hoffner said.

The man showed a last moment of indecision before saying, "Top floor. The attic room."

Hoffner stood. He picked up his pistol and moved to the door.

It was hours of waiting under a row of slanted beams. There was room enough for a bed, a bureau, and an open window that peered out to the south and brought the sounds of killing up through the streets.

Hoffner had found a little alcove behind one of the beams. Mercifully it was out of the sunlight. He sat in a chair with a glass of water—two or three days old—but the heat was too intense not to drink. There was no door, just the stairs, climbing up through a breach in the floorboards. Two pictures hung in simple frames behind the bed, the Madonna gazing out and a saint pensive at his desk. There had been no attempt to hide them. Such was the faith in Yagüe and his troops.

Hoffner listened from his perch. The sound of gunfire crackled like oil in a hot pan. Had he been able to block out the screams and the shouts, he might have imagined himself on a summer night in Wannsee, the sky wild with lights and a warm explosion of fireworks from above. But the screams and the shouts continued. It was a time without feeling, without memory. All Hoffner had was the image of Sascha standing by that well. It waited with him.

He heard him first on the floor below, then on the stairs. Hoffner sat very still and turned his head. He remained obscured behind the beam as he stared across the room.

Sascha emerged through the opening. He had shaved, and what hair there was lay slick across his scalp in stray lines of black and gray. He was bone thin in a peasant shirt and pants, and his face was red with blotches from the heat. He carried a bag. He set it down before walking toward the window. He leaned out and peered across the city.

Hoffner found it oddly peaceful watching his son. He tried to see something he knew of the boy, in the posture or the gaze, but there was nothing. Hoffner set down his glass and said, "Hello, Sascha."

Sascha turned, a quick movement though not sharp, and his eyes settled on his father. Whatever surprise he felt he kept to himself. He continued to stare.

Hoffner said, "You look well."

Sascha said nothing.

"Did you kill him?"

Sascha's eyes narrowed. It was the only hint of recognition. He saw the pistol on his father's lap. "Are you intending to use that?"

Hoffner waited. He shook his head.

"I didn't kill him."

"You're lying."

There was something so broken-down in the way Sascha stared. It was as if all his strength lived in the tightness of his jaw, his narrow shoulders taut and high against the neck. Were he to release, he might have collapsed or wept, although Hoffner couldn't recall even a moment's tears from the boy.

Hoffner said, "You left the film. In Coria."

"Yes."

"So I would see it."

"When it went back to Berlin. Not here."

"What a stunning act of kindness."

"And yet you're here."

Hoffner tried not to see the hatred in the eyes. "Do you ever ask yourself what you've become, Sascha?"

Hoffner expected anger or accusation, but Sascha showed neither. Instead, he turned slowly to the window and stared out.

Sascha said easily, "They'll be breaching the wall soon. You can hear the grenades. They're actually close enough to be throwing grenades. They'll have to climb over their own dead to get to it, but they'll take the wall." He stared and listened and said, "You think I killed my brother."

"I know you did."

Sascha breathed out as he stared. He shook his head. "How could I kill him when he'd already killed me?" He continued to gaze out. "You still think you won't be using that pistol?"

Hoffner felt suddenly rooted to his chair. It was all he could do to say, "Killed you?"

"This"—Sascha turned and glanced around the attic—"this is what I'm forced to be because of Georg. He took my life. I took his."

Hoffner heard the words but refused to admit what they meant. His head began to compress.

"How?" he said.

"'How?'" Sascha repeated lazily. "And that makes a difference to you?"

"Yes."

"With my hands around his throat, and his around mine." The voice conveyed nothing.

Hoffner heard himself say, "And the bullet?"

Sascha's stare was equally empty. Something registered for a moment and then was gone. "I don't know why that. Maybe it just seemed right." He turned back to the window.

There was a long silence, and Sascha said, "Not enough for him to be the Jew. Not enough for me to tell him it was a mistake, too dangerous."

Hoffner hadn't been listening. "You killed him—"

"Because he was a Jew?" The bitterness poured out. "Don't be so stupid. You think that meant anything to me? You think that could mean *anything* to me? He made his choice. It was his to live with. He knew it had nothing to do with me."

Hoffner heard the unintended anguish in Sascha's voice, the eyes searching through the memories. It was a mind now tearing itself apart. Hoffner felt no less undone. "And for that he's dead?"

Sascha regained his focus. He looked again at Hoffner, the loathing directed at both himself and his father.

"No," he said. "Not for that."

Sascha reached into his pocket and pulled out a piece of paper. It looked as if it had been balled up, then flattened and folded into a neat square. The wrinkles across the front showed dirt and fingerprints. Hoffner stared at it and felt the blood drain from his face.

"This is what he did," Sascha said. He held the paper out to his father. Somehow Hoffner found the paper in his hand. "This is what he was too much of a coward to admit."

Hoffner felt the creases on his fingers, the moistness of the paper. He forced himself to open it and, in an instant more unbearable than any he had ever known, Hoffner saw the words he knew would be there:

```
To the Ministry Secretary in the Matter of Alexander
Kurtzman:
```

Hoffner closed his eyes, and the air drew out of him. There was no reason to read any further. No reason when he knew the letter by heart.

"At least he led me to the guns," Sascha said, now staring out. "At least here they'll show me some respect."

Hoffner heard the desperate certainty in the boy's voice, the invented logic of a mind no longer in control. Sascha had convinced himself the Spaniards would take him for a Hisma envoy, a man sent from Berlin. He had convinced himself he could be Alexander Kurtzman again.

Sascha said, "They'll probably have to be taught how to use them. Still—"

Hoffner felt his hand begin to shake, his throat tighten. It was barely a whisper when he spoke.

"Georg didn't write this."

Hoffner saw the paper scrolling through the typewriter, the keys planting themselves on each line, and the words:

```
Alexander Kurtzman, born Alexander Hoffner, is the son
of Nikolai Hoffner, the son of Rokel Hoffner, a Jew. By
the Nuremberg Statutes of 1935, Kurtzman is a Jew. He
must be expelled from the party.
```

Hoffner had left his signature off the page when he had sent it—a month ago, maybe more—and here it was in his hands again. Such letters always came with anonymity. It gave them substance. Even the fool at the Ministry—Steiner or Stiegman or Steckler—had said it.

Hoffner opened his eyes and saw Sascha staring at him.

Hoffner said, "I was the one to tell them you're a Jew."

Sascha's stare became almost hypnotic.

Hoffner continued. "It didn't matter what happened to me. But you— you had to be given a way out."

Sascha's brow lowered and his face began to contort. "A way out?"

"I wrote it to save you, Sascha. To get you away from these people, once and for all." Hoffner struggled to find the words. "I did it to save you, and you killed him."

Sascha began to shake his head, slowly at first, then more forcefully. He turned to the window and tried to stifle his breath, but each came with greater force.

"You're lying," he said. It was as if he were pleading with himself. "You were in the letter. You were mentioned in the letter. He wanted to destroy us both. Don't you see that?"

Hoffner felt the weight of Georg's death like a vise pressing down on his head. There was no escaping it now. He had killed his son, just as if he had wrapped his fingers around the boy's throat himself.

"No," Hoffner said, his voice hollow. "Georg would never have done anything to you. He loved you."

Sascha's hands clenched at the sill.

"I did it to save you," Hoffner said. His eyes filled. "I did it because—"

Sascha turned. There was no seeing beyond the hatred in the eyes now. He came at Hoffner, hands stretching out. He grabbed his father's chest and pulled him from the chair. The force brought them into the beam, and Hoffner felt the wood slap across his face. A moment later, Sascha was throwing him against the wall; Hoffner tripped back, down onto his knees. He tried to bring himself forward, but Sascha began to kick his feet into Hoffner's gut, the face pure madness. It was a face beyond redemption.

"You stupid, selfish man!"

Hoffner reached for Sascha's legs. He pulled them out from under the boy, and Sascha toppled back, his head smacking against a beam. Sascha began to stumble toward the floor, and Hoffner pulled himself up. He began to speak, but Sascha's foot caught him across the cheek as the boy fell. Hoffner felt the room begin to spin, and he saw Sascha on his back. Hoffner lunged.

The body was so thin, the chest and arms little more than bones and flesh; Hoffner felt his own weight clamp down onto the boy. Sascha's fingers dug into Hoffner's chest, but Hoffner leaned his arm farther into the throat. He heard him choke—he heard his son gasping for breath—and he stared into Sascha's face, the cheeks red, the lips full with blood.

"You killed him." Hoffner heard his own voice, small and desperate. "You killed your brother." Sascha struggled, and Hoffner brought his other hand to the neck. "You let me kill my own son."

Sascha broke his arm free. Hoffner braced for the nails against his cheek, but he saw Sascha's fingers begin to claw against the floor. The pistol lay just out of reach. Hoffner watched as Sascha's hand drew closer to it. He saw the fingers on the barrel, the sound of the pistol scraping against the wood, and he felt his own weight press down, his own hand tighten around the throat. There was no voice, no pleading, no miracle to save this boy from himself.

Hoffner stared at the pistol. He heard Sascha cough for breath and felt his own life drain out of him.

I did it to save you, he thought.

Hoffner saw the gun in the boy's grip, and he closed his eyes.

A silence came, filling Hoffner whole. He lay there, pressing down on the boy's throat and begging to feel the metal of the pistol against his own skin. If this was prayer, it was the only one he had ever spoken. He heard the snap and he called out, but it was his own chest, his own gasping for air that he felt. The stillness was suffocating, and Hoffner opened his eyes.

"Oh God."

He stared down and saw Sascha perfectly still, eyes frozen on the gun, arm outstretched. The boy's neck had broken.

Hoffner staggered back. He pushed himself up and sat with his head against the bed. There was no thought. There was nothing but to stare at this lifeless boy. Hoffner cried out to a God he had never known and damned Him for His silence.

Outside, the guns breached the wall, the dying began, and Hoffner grabbed for Sascha's chest. He pulled him in and wept—for the boy who had been his and who now lay in his arms.

Hoffner cradled his son to his chest and wept for the life he had never known.

It was nearing sunset when he heard the grenade. Hoffner opened his eyes. He was still sitting, his back to the bed. The gunfire had drawn closer. Sascha's body was heavier, his face paler. A second grenade exploded, and Hoffner turned toward it. His neck was stiff. He wondered if he had slept.

Hoffner's hand was still under the boy's head. He moved it to the shoulder and tried to lift. Down in the street a man talked about the smell of pigs. Hoffner heard laughter. He got to his knees and hoisted the body up. He stood and brought the boy up onto the bed.

Hoffner looked at the face, the way the hair had matted against the ear. He smoothed it back. There was no texture, no heat in his hand.

He turned from the boy and saw the pistol on the floor. He leaned over and picked it up. He held it in his hand and heard more of the shouting, a single shot from a rifle, laughter. He felt the weight of the gun and slid it slowly into his belt.

Hoffner turned to the bureau. Inside, he found a brush and a razor, worn-through clothing, and a collection of pins. They were small, each with the swastika or SS insignia. Hoffner closed the drawers. He looked around the room and saw the bag Sascha had brought. He stepped over and placed it on the bed.

It was a tunic and pants, and when Hoffner laid them out, he recognized the uniform of a Waffen-SS Oberleutnant. The shoulder boards held one gold pip each, the collar the usual dark blue-green felt, with sewn-in boards of its own. They were a deep Bordeaux red, and the white braiding was frayed at the edges. The breast eagle showed bleach on the left wing. Hoffner smelled the lye and realized the wool had recently been washed. There were signs of repair in the lower pockets and on the French cuffs, and the third button down was a slightly darker gray than the rest.

Hoffner began to undress the boy.

It was rough bringing him down the steps. Hoffner held Sascha over one shoulder, the boy now in full uniform. He leaned him against the wall when they reached the bottom floor, and then carried him to the door. Hoffner listened. The gunfire was more sporadic now, and deeper into the heart of the city. Yagüe's men were going street to street, house to house. Hoffner waited and pulled open the door.

At once the smell of gunpowder and blood filled his nose. There was a smoky residue in the air, and the windows along the street were smashed in jagged lines of glass. By some miracle, the horses were still tethered to the post. One of them was on its side, dead, its eye shot through. The other was bucking from exhaustion, pulling at its reins. Hoffner placed his hand on the animal's nose and waited until it began to calm. He then hoisted Sascha onto its back, took the reins, and began to walk.

Bodies lay in pools of blood in the doorways and along the street. There were screams and shouts and the sound of glass shattering in the distance behind him. Hoffner continued to walk toward the plaza and the southern gate. He kept his pistol in his belt. If this was how he was to die, so be it.

He saw a pair of legs, stretched out and moving in a doorway. They were sliding back and forth. He heard a woman's stifled moan and a man's laughter and drew closer.

The man was on top of the woman, her legs pulled high, her face bloodied. The man continued to drive himself into her. Hoffner kicked at the man's feet, and the man turned. Hoffner pulled out his pistol and shot the man in the face. He then pulled the body off the woman, turned away, and continued to lead the horse.

If there were other such moments, Hoffner never remembered them. All he knew was that he found himself at the southern plaza, where the wall had been blown to rubble, and where bodies lay stretched across the stone and earth like packed rolls of soiled newspaper. The sun had gone, and there were long poles with white lights perched at the top of them. There was no gunfire here. Yagüe had taken the square.

Hoffner saw a group of uniforms standing by a door. He moved toward them.

One of the soldiers turned, and Hoffner said in German, "I have the body of a lieutenant. Waffen-SS. He was protecting the guns sent in from Morocco. He's dead. I was sent by Captain Doval from Coria."

The man stared at Hoffner. Hoffner repeated what he had said, this time in Spanish, and the man continued to stare. The man called another soldier over. Hoffner spoke the same words a third time, and the new man said, "You're the German."

Hoffner said nothing.

"We have orders not to touch you. We have your woman."

Hoffner handed the reins to the first man. "Leave the body as it is," he said. "He's not to be moved." Hoffner looked at the other. "Take me to the woman."

The man led him across the plaza to a building where the doors had been blown off. The front wall was pockmarked from machine-gun fire, the windows above all but gone.

The man took him inside. "You wish to meet General Yagüe?"

Hoffner felt the darkness of the place; he smelled the stench of cigars. "No," he said. "I don't wish to meet him."

The man looked momentarily confused and led Hoffner down the hall.

Mila was sitting on a stool in a small room lit by a lamp. There was an alleyway through the window. She was leaning against the wall, staring out, her hands limp in her lap.

The soldier left them, and Hoffner heard heavy footsteps on the floor above, the sound of men's voices. Mila continued to stare out.

She said, "They had use for a doctor." It was a false strength that masked her pain. "They had use, until the wall fell."

Hoffner watched as she stared out. She began to rub her thumb across her open palm.

She said, "They knew who I was. They shot the rest." He saw her thumb dig deeper in. "Did you find him?"

It took Hoffner a moment to answer. "Yes."

"Is he dead?"

Again Hoffner waited. "Yes."

She nodded quietly. She released her hand and turned her head to him. There were black streaks of gunpowder residue across her cheeks and neck, and her eyes were red from the crying. She showed no feeling behind them.

Whatever comfort they had hoped to find in each other was no longer possible here. Hoffner waited and stepped over. She seemed incapable of helping herself, and he cupped his hand under her elbow. He brought her up. He started to move them to the door and she stopped.

"I don't want to see any of them," she said. "I don't want to see their uniforms, their faces."

Hoffner looked into her eyes. He thought he saw the unimaginable.

"No," she said. "It wasn't me they touched." There was no relief even in that.

He brought his arm around her. She laid her cheek against his chest and closed her eyes, and he took her out into the square.

The sound of gunfire echoed from somewhere up on a hill, and Hoffner moved them across to the men. Sascha was still on the horse. A small car was waiting with them.

One of the men said, "The road to Coria is secure. The guard posts have been informed."

The man nodded to two of the others, and they stepped over to Sascha.

"Don't touch him!" Hoffner shouted.

The men stopped and stared. Hoffner stared back, filled with rage at his own helplessness. His throat was suddenly raw. He moved Mila to the car and placed her inside. He opened the rumble seat and went to Sascha. As he pulled him down and onto his shoulder, he stumbled momentarily. One of the men moved to help him, and again Hoffner shouted, "Don't you touch him!" The man stepped back, and Hoffner carried Sascha to the car and placed him in the seat.

The man from behind him said, "Follow the truck out." There was an open-back truck with bodies laid across it. "It goes as far as the river."

Hoffner nodded without turning. He got in behind the wheel, fixed his eyes on the tires in front of him, and drove.

Beyond the river the road climbed through scrubland and brush, the sounds of Badajoz faded, and the moon kept itself hidden behind the clouds.

The night's darkness brought pockets of scampering figures, men and women with frantic stares, darting in front of the headlights and vanishing into the blackness. Trucks appeared from every direction, their lights blinding, with the stench of men still fresh from battle. Echoes of gunfire drew closer, then drifted. Hoffner stopped again and again at makeshift barricades, showed his papers, and drove on.

All the while, Sascha sat perfectly straight in his seat. A guard at one of the posts asked him for a light, then saw he was dead and stepped away.

Mila woke just before daybreak. She said nothing and took Hoffner's hand. It was resting on the seat, and she laid it on her lap and unwound the gauze that had grown tight around his palm. He felt the air across the wound, as she dabbed at it with his handkerchief. She stared along the lines of the cut. It seemed a very long time before she rewrapped it, set it on the seat, and placed her hand on his.

Hoffner said, "It's not so far from here."

She nodded as she stared out.

He said, "It feels better."

"Good."

They found the priest in Coria, and a man with a spade. He brought his brother, and they dug a good grave by the side of Georg's. Hoffner watched as the spades moved through the dirt. He saw the pile rise higher and the men grow wet under the first light of the sun. He let them take Sascha from the car and watched as they lowered him on a white sheet and then pulled the sheet up and rolled it into a ball. The priest read and spoke. It was simple and without time, and when the priest had finished, he walked away, and Hoffner and Mila watched as the men covered Sascha with earth. Hoffner gave them money and they nodded their thanks before moving off.

Hoffner let Mila take his hand. He stared at his sons' graves.

"I cried for the wrong one," he said. There was nothing in his voice. "He was so small, so thin. How does a man become like that?"

He felt her draw his hand up. She kissed it. It was strange to feel so much life standing here.

The door to a house at the edge of the field opened, and a woman stepped out. She didn't notice them. She continued around to the other side and was gone.

Hoffner looked back at the graves. "I brought them to this." He felt almost nothing, saying it. "I brought my sons to this, and there's no coming back from it, is there?"

Mila waited. "It depends on what you come back to." She let go of his hand and started to walk. "You come when you want." She continued toward the houses.

Hoffner closed his eyes and let the sun settle on his face. He crouched down and placed a hand on the earth. If there were words he was meant to say, he didn't know them. Instead, he clutched at the earth and felt it squeeze through his fingers. He had no rage, no despair, no need to ask forgiveness. It was an emptiness without end. He turned and saw Mila moving slowly past the houses.

Hoffner opened his hand and let the earth fall away. He then stood and followed behind her.

Vollman had waited. The aeroplane was fitted with enough gasoline to get them to Barcelona. He would refuel, then go on to Berlin.

They slept for the three hours of the flight, and when Vollman brought the plane low they both woke and looked out to see Barcelona as they had left it. The stories of Badajoz had yet to reach this far east; news that the armies of the north and the south had joined hands would wait another few hours. For now, the city stretched out contentedly under the sun.

Mila and Hoffner stood in the short grass of the runway and watched from a distance as Vollman tipped canister after canister of gasoline into the fuel tank. A car would come for her. They had telephoned her father.

"The wife and the little boy," she said. Her arms were across her chest as she stared out at the plane. "You have to go. To Berlin. You have to tell them, make arrangements. I understand."

Hoffner nodded. He hadn't asked her to come. He knew she wouldn't. Anywhere else, he would have given himself over to this kind of will. He would have acquiesced or backed away or fallen silent in her presence. But that's not what this was.

"And what is it you understand?" he said, as he turned to her. He forced her to look at him. "You think there's something for me to find in Berlin? What Berlin? There *is* no Berlin, at least nothing in it I know. So I go for the wife and the boy. I go to destroy what life they have left. What is there to understand in that?"

"You go because you love them," she said. "You go because nothing else matters. Why is it so hard for you to see that?"

Hoffner tried to answer, and she said, "You go for the same reason you'll come back to Spain."

Hoffner saw his own need in her eyes. He saw a way beyond a life lived in the shadow of those two graves, beyond the dampness of the earth still on his hands and in his nails.

She said quietly, "I'm not asking you to stay."

"I know that."

"I'm not asking you to come back. I'm telling you what's here. What more is there?"

The buzz from the propeller cut through, and they both turned to see Vollman walking to the ladder. She waited for Hoffner to speak. Finally she said, "You have to go."

Hoffner stared across at the plane. He watched as Vollman slipped on his goggles.

Hoffner turned to her. He took her in his arms and he kissed her, her body pressed against him. She pulled back and brought her lips to his ear. She whispered, "Then love them, Nikolai. Love them and know it's enough."

He held her. Her body shook, and he knew it would never be enough.

Hoffner let go and started toward the plane. He let the sound of the propeller draw him. He reached the ladder, climbed up, and stepped into the seat. The plane began to move, and he felt the air against his face. He waited for the speed, and the plane lifted.

Somewhere below, the sea crashed against the rocks and the sun played havoc on the surf, but Hoffner kept his eyes on the blue of the sky. To look back, even for a moment, would have made living beyond this an impossibility.

7

FOREVER FROM HIS GRASP

The city lay beneath clouds, and Vollman banked the plane low to cut his way through. The rain was colder here and fell across Hoffner's face with the sour taste of wild turnips. It was familiar enough, and he breathed in and tried to remember Berlin in August.

The plane touched down easily. A gray dusk covered the fields and runways. Vollman cut the engine, and the two got out and walked toward the hangar.

"I have a car," Vollman said. "I can take you into town."

The drive passed in silence. Dusk slipped into evening, and the oncoming headlights flashed across the windscreen like the sudden flares of a match. Hoffner kept his window down and let the rain slap at his face. The chill and the quiet seemed foreign. Cars raced by, the streets grew brighter with lights and people, and Hoffner wondered if there was anything to recognize in these lives lived so carelessly.

Vollman pulled up in front of an old repair garage. There were two large rooms above, furniture, a telephone. The lights were on.

Vollman said, "This is it?"

Hoffner continued to stare up at the rooms. He nodded.

"You'll be all right?"

It was a pointless question. Hoffner turned to Vollman. There was nothing more to this; still, he asked, "You'll fly back to Spain now? Or Moscow?" Vollman said nothing. "We won't be seeing each other again, I imagine."

Hoffner waited. Vollman stared through the windscreen and Hoffner opened the door. He stepped out.

Upstairs, the last of the Berlin he knew trundled along as it always had. A table stood at the far end of the room, large Rolf behind it, with a line of men winding its way back to the door. Rolf was writing out slips of paper and handing them to Franz, who entered them in a ledger. The men were a ragtag bunch—pickpockets, swindlers, thieves—each with a little something to show for a day's work. Most carried a battered cigar box, the tools of the trade smelling of old Dutch tobacco. Hoffner recognized the son of a man he had sent to the gallows fifteen years earlier. There had never been any hard feelings. The father had beaten the boy's mother to death. The boy had been happy to see him hang.

Radek was in the second room, lounging on a long sofa and reading through one of his papers, when Hoffner stepped through the line.

"Pimm always did this at daybreak," Hoffner said. "Kept them on their toes."

Radek looked up. He tossed the paper to the side and nearly sprang up. He did nothing to hide his delight. "About time." He pulled Hoffner in for a hug. Hoffner tried to return it. A few men looked over. The rest knew not to take notice.

Radek pulled back and smiled. "You found a plane." He was already moving to a small cabinet where glasses and bottles stood in disarray. He uncorked one. "I had to bring Mueller back," he said as he poured. "Couldn't be helped, but I gather it all worked out."

"Yes."

"He said you met Gardenyes. Lunatic, even by my standards. You weren't around when he got shot, were you?" He handed Hoffner a glass.

"No," Hoffner said.

"Good." He raised his glass. "*Salud.*"

Hoffner watched as Radek drank. He watched as the eyes peered across at him. And he watched as the glass slowly came down.

Radek stared for several moments. Finally he said, "Georg didn't make it, did he?"

"No."

"Christ. I'm sorry. How?"

Hoffner waited, shook his head. "The usual way. What you'd imagine." He handed back the glass. It was untouched. He glanced into the other room. "Business seems good."

Radek set the glasses down. "Have you told the wife?"

Hoffner watched the men. He followed the slow movement of the line, the great care Rolf was taking with his penmanship. Hoffner shook his head.

Radek said, "She has the mother and the father in Berlin. And the boy. That should make it easier."

A man was sitting at the far end in a chair by himself. He had bruising around his eye and cheek. He had been crying. Hoffner had no idea why. He turned to Radek. "It's all gone, isn't it?"

"What?"

"This. The city."

Radek knew to tread carefully. "You should have that drink."

"She won't be finding her way back, will she?"

Radek recorked the bottle. There was no point in fighting it. "And what would you have her go back to, Nikolai? Berlin wouldn't know herself, even if she went looking." Radek stared down at Hoffner's glass of whiskey. He picked it up and tossed it back.

There was nothing real to this, thought Hoffner, nothing he could touch. "Sascha's dead," he said.

Radek brought the glass down. He waited before saying, "Is he?" He lapped at what was left and set the glass on the cabinet. "I'm sorry for that." He refused to look at Hoffner. "We'll go out. Rücker's, the White Mouse. Last night of the games. Everyone wants to have a drink the last night of the games."

Hoffner saw Radek's face grow tighter, and Hoffner said, "You enjoy the drinks, Zenlo." He turned toward the door.

Radek said, "They weren't yours to save, Nikolai."

Hoffner might have heard him say something else, but he chose to ignore it.

•   •   •

The house was dark, all but Lotte's bedroom window. Hoffner stared up at it. He had been standing like this for the better part of an hour. The street was quiet. A car drove by, and Hoffner saw a figure peer through the curtains. He stepped out under the streetlamp, and the curtains fell back. Hoffner walked to the front steps.

The door opened before he could knock, and Lotte stood in the vestibule, her face pale, her hair fighting against the pins. Hoffner saw her father and mother—Edelbaum and his wife—standing by the stairs. There was nothing to hide the age and the fear in their faces.

Lotte looked at Hoffner. She saw the swelling around his eye, the gauze on his hands. Her breath grew short and she stepped back. Hoffner reached for her, but she was already sliding to the floor, her back against the wall, her legs tangling in her apron and skirt. She sat there and began to weep, and Hoffner crouched down. He heard her mother crying.

Arms limp at her sides, Lotte began to slap the back of her hands onto the tile, one after the other. Her weeping became moans, and Hoffner took hold of her and brought her close into him. He lifted her and carried her inside. He set her on the couch, and her mother quickly moved to her. Hoffner stepped back. He stood by the father.

"How?" said Edelbaum.

They both stared across at Lotte. She had nothing but memory now, stripped of hope and more desperate by the minute. How easy to shatter a life, thought Hoffner, drain the strength from it, and make courage something only vaguely remembered.

"Wilson never came?" he said.

It took Edelbaum a moment to answer. He watched his daughter and said absently, "Who?"

"The man from Pathé Gazette. He never came by?"

Edelbaum tried to think. It was too much. He shook his head, and Hoffner wondered if this had been kindness or cowardice on Wilson's part.

Edelbaum said, "Two SS came, or Sipo, I don't know which. I had to sedate my wife after."

Hoffner heard the fear, and Lotte became quieter. Her head was in her mother's lap, and she stared out across the carpet. Hoffner said, "How soon could you go?"

Edelbaum turned to him. There was genuine hurt in his eyes. "Go? This is my daughter."

"Out of Germany," Hoffner explained. "All of you. How soon?"

Edelbaum struggled to understand.

Hoffner said, "You need to get out. You know it. You need to take Lotte and the boy and get out."

Edelbaum began to shake his head, and Hoffner said, "This is what it will be every day from now on. This fear. And it will get worse. I have friends. They can do this for you. You get your affairs in order, and you go. You understand what I'm saying?"

Edelbaum stared at Hoffner. He waited before saying, "Leave Berlin?"

Hoffner realized it was a broken man who now gazed up at him.

"I'm giving you my grandson," Hoffner said. "I need to know you understand that."

Hoffner saw Lotte raise her head from her mother's lap. She was staring across at him, her eyes no longer lost. She began to push herself up.

Hoffner said, "She needs to sleep."

Edelbaum turned and saw Lotte. He began to nod. "Yes, of course." He spoke to his wife, "Keep her still. I'll get my bag."

Edelbaum moved toward the hall, and Hoffner followed. He then walked to the stairs and headed up. The boy was known to sleep through anything. Hoffner pushed open the door and saw the small lamp at the edge of the room, its glow making it just to the skirt of the bed.

Mendy was on his back, one arm tossed above his head and resting on the pillow. His knees were splayed and high, and his body lay absolutely still. He never moved in sleep. Hoffner had spent hours watching him, staring at the little shape in all its contortions. He leaned over and picked up the books that were strewn across the sheets. He stacked them and laid them against the wall. Mendy was known to sense when a book had gone missing from his bed, an eye quickly opening, then closing. Hoffner set them within arm's reach and pulled the blanket up over the waist.

This was a perfect boy, he thought, quiet and still, and untouched by anything beyond that doorway. Hoffner wondered how such things were possible. He imagined they had always been possible—even with his own—but why try to understand that now? It was never enough to want to protect, or to recognize the frailty. It was only in the doing, and that had always been just out of reach. He stared down at this living boy and knew there was no way to remedy that. Hoffner placed a hand on the boy's cheek. He felt the warmth and the smoothness of it, and he let himself believe he could hear the tiny voice. Here, he had no need for anything else.

He pulled his hand back and saw paper and pen on the small table. He sat on Mendy's stool, took a sheet, and wrote in the dim light.

The note was folded, with Lotte's name written across it, when Hoffner heard her behind him. He turned and saw her in the doorway. How long she had been there was impossible to say.

She said, "You can tell me what it says now, if you want."

Hoffner looked up at her. He shook his head. "Better to read it."

"We're going. It's been decided. My father says you'll come with us."

Hoffner waited. "I've tried the going, Lotte. It doesn't much work for me."

"Mendy won't understand."

"No, he probably won't. You'll help him with that."

"Did he die in peace?" She spoke with no trace of empathy.

"Yes," he said. "I think he did."

There was no reason to tell her how much Georg had loved her, or how the boy had been his life. She knew. She would find that comfort. What she could never know was the unimagined horror and emptiness of his death.

Hoffner stood and moved across to her. He held out the note.

"It's nothing too important," he said. "The names of people who can help you, where there's a bit of money. Something for Mendy. You'll read it after I go."

She stared up at him. She had always been able to see so quickly through to the heart of things. "And where is it you're going, Nikolai?"

He tried a quiet shrug. "Just out. Find a drink."

He saw the first break in her otherwise flawless stare. "Is that it?"

Hoffner had spent a lifetime showing nothing. It came so easily. "There are plenty of places to find a drink tonight. I'll make my way."

He needed her to believe the lie. He needed her to give him this, here at the end. But her own sadness was too much to leave any kindness for others.

She said, "I would never forgive you for that, Nikolai. Neither would Mendy."

Hoffner looked into her face. So much pain, he thought, and so much more to wait for. He tried a weak smile. If nothing else, he had to save them from that.

"Mendy needs to be safe. You need to be safe. Safe no longer exists here."

"And you couldn't find that safety with us?"

Again Hoffner waited. "He won't always be a boy."

She stared up at him, and he brought his arms around her. Her eyes were wet when she let go. She wiped them with her handkerchief.

Hoffner took a last glance at Mendy and headed for the stairs.

The deep of night came more quickly than Hoffner expected. This far west the trees were more sparse, the sky a churning of clouds and stars.

The sound of water against stone beat out a quiet rhythm. He stared down into the canal and saw the strength of the current. He remembered how quickly it had taken little Rosa Luxemburg, a minute or two, a sudden swirling, and then gone.

Hoffner had imagined he would feel more at this moment, a chance to regret or despair. Instead, he stared with a kind of childlike wonder at the coal black of the water, and thought, It isn't much of anything to stop a life. It isn't much to know what has come before, and to know how it must weigh on what is to come. And it is only then, in that absolute silence, that a man can say, This is enough. No matter what longing or hope live on and elsewhere, that silence cannot tell him to step back. It can only weigh on him all the more deeply. Hoffner stepped closer to the embankment. He looked out into the darkness. He imagined the water would be cold.

There was a popping overhead, and he looked up to see the sky filling with lights. They were sending the games off with fireworks. How easy to imagine Berlin covered in light. How easy to watch the lights fade and convince himself to embrace the chill of his own cowardice and fade away with them.

But not tonight, he thought. Not when he knew which life it was that had come to an end. There was nothing here. Nothing. And there was no reason to mourn it.

Hoffner stepped back. Out by the trees, a second set of lights flashed. Car lights. Hoffner stared out across the water for a moment longer and moved toward the car.

Inside, Radek was smoking.

"We need to go," Radek said. "He'll fly with or without you."

Hoffner got in, and Radek put the car in gear. He said, "You saw what you needed?"

"You have the papers?"

There was a tinge of frustration in the answer. "Yes, Nikolai. I have the papers. They're still in my pocket."

Radek would get them out—Mendy, Lotte, her parents. Radek would do this for him.

"You know I could set you up as well," Radek said. "Paris. London. You're sure about this?"

The car emerged from the trees, and Hoffner stared out as the city flickered and pitched above him. He closed his eyes and let Berlin slip forever from his grasp.

A lifetime later a dying sun lingered across the water as the old Hispano-Suiza ground its way along the coast road. Mueller slept, Hoffner drove, and the first glimpse of Barcelona's Montjuïc appeared on the horizon.

Hoffner felt the heat. He felt the damp from the sea. And he felt a rush of life that, if not entirely his, lay just beyond that horizon in the waiting arms of the only faith he had ever known.

ACKNOWLEDGMENTS

The earliest idea for this book came during a trip to the Semana Negra festival in Gijón, Spain, and my first encounter with Paco Ignacio Taibo II. PIT II is a force of nature, unique and untamable in his commitment to writing. He was instrumental in sending me in the right direction when it came to preliminary research, and even more important as the story began to come together. If he shares a passing resemblance to any of the characters in this book, it is out of deepest admiration, nothing more.

Chris Ealham at Saint Louis University in Madrid was perhaps the most forgiving of my sources—fielding queries at all hours of the night—and by far the most essential. His understanding of Spain at the outbreak of the civil war is nothing less than encyclopedic. He is a remarkable scholar, although why he should have at his fingertips the best anarchist truck route out of Barcelona on August 3, 1936, remains a thing both of awe and mystery to me.

James Amelang at the Universidad Autónoma de Madrid was the first to bring the story of the protest games to my attention. He was also an absolute mine of information when it came to primary texts on the early days of the war. For all his digging I am eternally grateful.

Sarah Crichton, an editor of unerring intelligence and artistry, knows Nikolai Hoffner perhaps as well as I do. She posed just the right questions to make sure there was always a clarity and a humanity to him as he made his way across Spain. I wouldn't have made the trip without her.

All such trips begin and end with Mort Janklow, my agent. Without him there would not have been a second, let alone third, book in this trilogy. I thank him for his wise and honest counsel, his passion, and his unflappable faith in this book.

As ever, Peter Spiegler was there at every stage of the manuscript, with sympathetic encouragement and a seasoned eye, and I thank him for his abiding friendship.

My parents remain great readers, but I owe a special gratitude to my father, a brilliant writer who long ago taught me the craft of writing, perhaps even despite myself.

And finally, my wife, Andra, and my children, Benjamin and Emilia— there is nothing without them and everything with them.

Jonathan Rabb is the author of *Shadow and Light*, *Rosa*, *The Book of Q*, and *The Overseer*. He lives in Savannah, Georgia, with his wife, Andra, and their two children, Emilia and Benjamin. He is a professor of writing at the Savannah College of Art and Design.